THE BOAT HOUSE

By the same author

CHIMERA
FOLLOWER
VALLEY OF LIGHTS
OKTOBER
DOWN RIVER
RAIN

STEPHEN GALLAGHER

THE BOAT HOUSE

NEW ENGLISH LIBRARY

British Library Cataloguing in Publication Data

Gallagher, Steve
  The boat house.
  I. Title
  823.914[F]

  ISBN 0-450-52228-8

Published by New English Library,
an hardcover imprint of Hodder and Stoughton,
a division of Hodder and Stoughton Ltd,
Mill Road, Dunton Green, Sevenoaks, Kent TN13 2YA.
Editorial Office: 47 Bedford Square, London WC1B 3DP.

Photoset by Rowland Phototypesetting Ltd,
Bury St Edmunds, Suffolk

Printed in Great Britain by Mackays of Chatham plc,
Chatham, Kent

PROLOGUE:
AFTER THE DROWNING (I)

Old and young, we are all on our last cruise
Robert Louis Stevenson

He hadn't been out to McCarthy's old place on the Step in almost a year. It held too many memories for him, and not only recent ones; the bad and the good were all thrown in together, and sometimes it seemed as if the good could be almost as painful. He'd think of childhood summers, spent in that same shaky wooden cottage with his sister and her family after their parents had died, and of the three years with Nerys when they'd just been married, both of them too poor to afford anywhere better as they saved for a stake in the boatyard. Now the boatyard was all his, had been since before Wayne had learned to walk, but Nerys was long gone.

Those had been hard times, but happy ones. He only wished that he could have realised it then.

"Shape up, Ted," he told himself. "Don't get morbid." And he tried not to crash the van's worn second gear as he made the turn onto the leaf-strewn headland track.

If only.

If only that last, terrible summer could be wiped away. Not just burned out of his mind with a controlled dose of lightning, but actually wiped away as if it was a poem on a blackboard that had somehow turned wrong, and the rhythm picked up again as if nothing bad had ever happened. What would he give? The answer to that one was anything, right down to his soul. Anything, just to have it all back the way it had been. The memories, he'd keep. As memories alone they wouldn't be able to hurt him then but, by God, how they'd make him appreciate what he'd had.

So much for not getting morbid.

The track was fairly rough, and had begun to get overgrown. The van bounced where old ruts had dried-in, and in some places low branches slashed at the windshield. As a child, he'd always loved the Step best of anywhere in the valley. It was a high, wooded headland jutting out into the lake, a steep climb to its summit from the shore and a tortuous drive from the road; easier access would have made it less private and less privacy might have taken away some of the magic, and the magic was what had made it so special.

He'd played here, he'd grown here; and the last time he'd been here, he'd sat on the high rocks overlooking the water and he'd wept in solitude and without shame.

He didn't need to wonder what the view from the top would be like today. It would be of the valley and, whether the sun shone or the clouds cast a shadow across it or the rain came down, it was the homeland that would never let him go.

The track was coming to an end. The old place – lately McCarthy's place, although Pete McCarthy had moved out almost a year ago – lay just ahead.

Springtime was pleasant enough, although most of the valley people seemed to think that the autumn was the best time of year around these parts. Then the sunsets were like red gold in the mountains, and the woodland stood as dark and shady as anything out of a fairytale. Strangers had been known to spend an hour or more out on the terrace behind the Venetz sisters' restaurant, watching the evening mists rise from the lake with tears in their eyes.

The valley people, meanwhile, were probably all indoors with their Casio calculators, checking the high season's rakeoff from the visitors and wondering if this was going to be the year that they could afford a new Volvo or even a winter cruise. They'd worked flat-out through the summer, sometimes so hard that they'd forget to raise their heads and remind themselves of the real reason for living here. It wasn't the money, or the uncertain pleasure of servicing the tourist trade; it was just the valley, a subtle presence which seemed to get into people and which never let them go.

Ted Hammond knew that he could never leave. It was too late to stop the dance; the valley had held him close for too long. Friends might come and go, but he'd always be the one to stay behind.

He pulled in before the old house, onto the strip of rough ground before the covered wooden porch. A few yards ahead, the overgrown track petered out and became an even more overgrown footpath. The house stood in the silence of desertion. Neither the track nor the path had any destination other than this.

It had been given a name, once, Rosedale, but the board had weathered away and the name had been mostly forgotten. It was a one-storey frame building, too run-down to sell or even to rent; the walls and the roof were sound, but it would need a lot of paint and timberwork as well as some new windows before it could charm the holiday crowd.

That was his sister's plan, anyway, and she was still the owner even though she let Ted look after the key and the box with all the paperwork. And it was the only reason for his coming up here today, because she'd asked him to sweep out the gutters and fix the blocked stove and generally check the place over before she advertised it. Ted's feeling was that he'd rather see it left to fade away. It already had the air of some forgotten corner in a churchyard, with the roses long-dead and the side-garden turned to moss and the trees crowding in too close. A gingerbread house, gone stale and old. Better to let the valley take it back.

Or else, the thought made its presence known in the back of his mind, *keep it as it is until McCarthy returns*.

He stepped out of the van, and looked across the porch to the locked front door. He could almost see it standing open, Pete McCarthy coming down the unlit hallway and into the light, carrying an old Heinz Soup box that was crammed with his shirts and had a radio balanced on top. Not the best mechanic that Ted had ever employed, but easily the best to work with. He always forgot the punchlines to jokes and his whistling was a public embarrassment, but Ted had known even then that he was going to miss him.

And he had. He'd missed the two of them, a lot.

That had been the reason why he'd come out here last; to say goodbye. Their car had already been loaded and the boy sat playing behind the wheel as the three of them stood out on the porch and talked around everything other than what really needed to be said. They were putting off the moment, and they knew it; much better if they all just shook hands, and then they got into their car and went.

Oh, Ted, Diane had said simply, and she'd stepped up to him and hugged him hard. Ted had put his arms around her, and it had come to him in a sudden realisation that Diane was about the same age that Nerys had been when she died, the age that she'd be in his memory for ever. There hadn't been a week of his life since that he hadn't wished for her back at least once; and now, for a moment that had already passed as the realisation had emerged, it seemed that wishes could come true.

He'd hugged her back, and she'd become Diane again; a different scent, a different presence, a different life ahead of her. No less dear, but not the young woman who had quietly slipped away from him on that November night. There had been tears in Diane's eyes as she'd finally let go and taken a step back.

Then Pete had stretched out his hand. *Goodbye, Ted*, he'd said seriously. *I'm sorry for what I brought you.*

It wasn't your fault, Ted had told him. *You couldn't know.*

But Pete, being Pete, was probably blaming himself still.

As he unlocked the main door, Ted was wondering where they

were, how they were doing. He'd had a couple of postcards in the early months, but nothing since. They'd checked out the south coast where Pete had been offered boatyard work but they couldn't find anywhere cheap enough to rent, and then they'd headed over to the east somewhere. Opening the door, he found himself overtaken by a certainty that, in spite of everything that had happened here, they *would* come back; the worst of the memories finally buried, perhaps, and that under-the-skin presence of the valley drawing them home.

Let his sister think that he was getting the house ready for rent. He'd get it ready, all right, but he'd tell her that the roof needed work, that some of the boards were too rotten to be safe. He'd say that he'd fix it when he could, maybe have it ready in time for next year.

And in the meantime, if Pete and Diane should return, the old place would be waiting.

A cool, musty smell hit him as he stepped inside. There was a stillness in the air that made any sound seem hollow and intrusive; the atmosphere was as empty as at four o'clock in the morning, here in the middle of this spring afternoon. He felt as if he were standing in a doll's house. Doorways along the hall before him; a couple of bedrooms and a sitting room, a bathroom with an old cast-iron tub, the big kitchen at the back with the wood-burning stove that didn't work and the electric ring that did. All of the doors leading off the hallway had been left open, except for one.

The door that had led to Alina's room.

He might as well start there, since he couldn't skip it; putting it off would only give his imagination the chance to get to work in a department that already had too much going on inside. Even so, he felt a strange kind of anticipation as he started to turn the doorknob. Would Pete and Diane have cleared everything out before they left? They must have. Surely one of them would have said something if they hadn't.

He opened the door, and stepped through.

With some relief, he saw that the room was bare. The bed had been stripped to the mattress and there was nothing on the walls, nothing on the dresser. He checked the drawers and they were empty, too. It was as if she'd never been here.

Which left another question, occurring to him as he gave a couple of tugs at the sash of the window which looked out onto the overgrown side-garden. What had they done with Alina's stuff? He couldn't imagine either of them wanting to take it away.

He found the answer a short time later, when he came to work on the wood-burning stove in the kitchen.

It was dimmer in here than in any other room in the cottage, because the trees around the back had been left to get so wild that their branches scratched against the windows in anything more than the mildest breeze. Some other time, he'd bring along a chainsaw and trim them back. Right now, the job was to clear out the stove.

But when he opened everything up to take a look, he found that it had already been done.

The flue had apparently been unblocked some time ago, and the stove had then been used. Pete had said nothing about it but there was the evidence, there in the cold ashes. Ted unhooked the iron poker from its nail on the wall alongside and gave them a stir around.

Whatever had been burned, it hadn't burned completely. He turned up hairpins, part of a melted comb. A piece of fabric with some of the pattern still discernible. And paper ash, lots of it. In amongst the ash there was the corner of a postcard or a photo. He tilted it to the light with the tip of the poker, but it showed no recognisable detail.

He raked the cold embers together in a mound and then, using deadwood that he found within a few yards of the house, he relit the stove and clamped everything down tight. This way it would burn hot, and it would burn until only the ashes of ashes remained. For Ted Hammond, even one surviving scrap of Alina Peterson would be one scrap too many.

He waited until he was sure. Then he turned to go.

Leaving the cottage and locking the door behind him, Ted found himself thinking of something that Diane had once said. That of those who'd known the truth, they were the only ones who had made it through. She hadn't exactly put it like that, but it was what she'd meant; that they were a survivors' club, whether they liked the idea or not.

He went down the porch steps to the van, climbed in, and started the engine. And then he sat for a few moments, letting it idle as he found himself looking at the faint line of the path that picked up from the track only a few yards ahead. It led on up through the woodland to the high rocks where he'd gone to look down on the flat expanse of the lake after the goodbyes.

It was a path that Alina had walked before him, many times.

Diane was wrong. The three of them weren't alone. Others knew what had happened, and how.

But they'd never speak out again.

I: Beginnings

*We are familiar merely with the everyday,
apparent and current, and this only
insofar as it appears to us, whereas the
ends and the beginnings still constitute
to man a realm of the fantastic.*

  Fyodor Dostoevsky, *Diary of a Writer*

*Everything must have a beginning . . .
and that beginning
must be linked to something that went before.*

Mary Shelley,
Introduction to *Frankenstein*

ONE

But there's no clear point at which one could say, *here it began.*

Instead, there are many. Like the day that Pete McCarthy turned up at Ted Hammond's auto-marine with nothing more than a cardboard suitcase and the hope of a season's maintenance work (a season that ran on into a year, and then into the next, and seemed set to run on indefinitely should nothing ever happen to break up their growing friendship); or perhaps the one some years before when a seven-year-old Russian girl named Alina Petrovna led a teenaged boy out into the marshlands near her village and came back alone. Or the day that Alina, now grown, gathered whatever possessions she could carry and made her first, unsuccessful attempt to cross the border out of her Karelian homeland.

Or perhaps, getting closer to it, the night that Pete McCarthy set out from the valley to attend his mother's funeral, while Alina Petrovna, hardened if not chastened by her punishment, got most of those same possessions together and tried it again. As beginnings go, this one's probably better than most.

McCarthy first.

As the woman who was to change his life was boarding the train that would, indirectly, bring her to him, Pete McCarthy was doing his best to kick some life into his shabby old heap of a car.

But the shabby old heap simply didn't want to know; it sat under the workshop lights, mean and dark and unco-operative, its chromed grin shining dully and a spirit of mischief showing deep in its sixty-watt eyes. It was a black Zodiac, close to twenty years old and easily the ugliest car to be seen on the roads around Three Oaks Bay, and even if its colour was appropriate for a funeral it was going to be of no damn use at all to Pete if it didn't get him there.

This was all that he needed. This, after three hours of tweaking and tuning and a once-over with the Turtle Wax to make it look halfway presentable. He'd given it loving care, he'd given it attention. What more did it expect of him?

There was nothing else for it.

He took off his suit jacket, rolled up the sleeves of the shirt that he'd changed into in the back washroom less than ten minutes before, and reached for the bonnet release.

He was still working at it when Ted Hammond called by after a late session in the auto-marine's office. "Having problems, Pete?" he said, and Pete made two fists, growled, and kicked the nearest wheel. The Zodiac's hubcap fell off and rolled into the grease pit. The two of them had the carburettor in pieces by the time that Wayne, Ted's sixteen-year-old boy, put in an appearance; Wayne spent no more than a few seconds contemplating the engine before saying that he knew exactly what was needed.

"I've got to have some money," he said, and then he went off in the breakdown wagon (which, in only seven months, he'd be able to drive legally), and returned fifteen minutes later with a party-sized can of beer.

It was almost midnight when Ted found the fault.

The fault was in the new set of contact breakers that Pete had fitted as part of the routine service. If he'd left everything alone, he'd have had no trouble. Nobody, fortunately, was unkind enough to say so out loud, or they'd have received a look that a laser would have been hard-pressed to match.

They put everything back together, and Pete tidied himself up again. Because there were no chairs around the workshop, they opened up the Zodiac and all three of them sat inside as they finished what remained of the party can. Or rather, Ted and Wayne took care of it, seated in the back of the car; Pete turned around the rearview mirror in the front and tried, without much success, to make a decent job of knotting his borrowed black tie.

Ted said, "Wayne can take the van up to the cottage every now and again, check on it for you while you're away." And Wayne raised his styrene cup, and burped loudly in assent.

"Don't worry about it," Pete said. "If anybody's desperate enough to steal my stuff, they're welcome to it." He gave the knot a final check in the mirror before half-turning himself to face the two in the back. They were sitting there patiently like a bleary-eyed jury, Ted looking like a Toby Jug in a frayed old sweater and Wayne slumped into the corner with the skull on his Judge Death T-shirt grinning out of the shadows.

Pete said, "How do I look?"

"You want the truth?" Ted asked.

"Not necessarily."

"You look fine."

"You look like they just let you out of prison," Wayne added helpfully.

"Oh, thanks," Pete said. "Just what I need." And then, to signal that the brief and sober goodbye party was over, he got out of the car and went around the back to close the open boot lid on his suitcase. The drive ahead would take most of what was left of the night. His brother had promised to fix him up with a borrowed flat for the stopover, but now he'd have to skip it and catch up on his sleep sometime later. Big brother Michael – the respectable one in the family, who'd taken it upon himself to make all the funeral arrangements – probably wouldn't be pleased at the change in schedule, but that would cause Pete no extra grief at all. Mike was so uptight, he probably couldn't even fart without the aid of a shoehorn.

Ted Hammond and Wayne climbed out and then Pete walked all around the Zodiac, slamming and checking the doors. Wayne followed him, looking doubtful. No denying it, the car was a rustbucket; in the past Pete had welded so many pieces onto the underside that he could have driven over a landmine without personally suffering a scratch.

"Think you'll make it?" Wayne said.

"Are you kidding? She's running like a dream."

Wayne stepped back, so that he could take the whole car in at once; the pitted grille, the yellowing headlamps, the small chip-crack in the windshield that had never quite become bad enough to star, the wrapping of black tape that held the radio aerial into the bodywork.

"Yeah," he said, finally and with distaste. "I had a dream like that, once." And then he moved to open the workshop's big double doors as Pete got in behind the wheel.

Ted bent to speak to Pete through the car's half-open window. "Anyway," he said quietly and seriously, "I'm sorry about your mother."

"Yeah," Pete said. "We could see it coming, but . . ." And he shrugged; it was a thought that he'd been unable to complete in any satisfactory way since the news had first come through, in a phonecall from Michael three days before.

Ted took a step back; Wayne now had the doors open to the darkness, standing just inside the workshop and trying not to shiver in the March night's chill. Pete nodded to Ted and smiled briefly, and then he reached for the key to start the engine.

* * *

5

The Zodiac eased out into the lake-misted night, smoothly and in silence.

It moved in silence because Ted and Wayne were pushing it; Pete's earlier attempts had run the battery down, and the jump-starter was way over on the marina side of the yard. Grunting and wheezing, they got him across the dusty forecourt and onto the stony track that went on to the main road, and after a few yards the engine kicked and turned over and coughed into a ragged kind of life. On came the lights, making sudden and bizarre shapes out of the boat hulls, trailers, and half-dismantled cruisers that were crowded in along the trackside verge, and then the car was out from under their hands and pulling away as the two of them stopped to catch their breath.

They watched his tail-lights all the way down the track, until they started to flicker as he made the turn around behind the trees. A few moments after he'd gone from sight, there came a faint singsong vibration of tyres on metal as the Zodiac crossed the iron bridge that was their link to Three Oaks Bay, the lakeside resort which brought the yard most of its business. The sound lasted less than a second, and left silence behind.

Ted put his hand on Wayne's shoulder as they turned to go back inside.

And then he winced as, somewhere far off, there was a loud backfire. The high valley sides caught and echoed it, like a gunshot deep in some vast, empty building.

"Don't worry," Wayne said. "Think of it as advertising."

"In what way?"

"If he can keep that old heap on the road, he can probably fix anything on wheels."

Wayne closed the big workshop doors, and turned the handle to lock them from the inside. Ted stood by the smaller back exit, his hand ready on the lightswitch. He was thinking that things were going to seem strange around here for a while, with Pete away. He had another mechanic, a quiet, intensely private man named Frank Lowry, but their relationship wasn't the same; in the four years since he'd joined them Pete had become more like another son to him, and almost like an older brother to Wayne. Maybe it wasn't your standard family unit, but in a world where it seemed that just about everyone was damaged goods in one way or another, they'd made themselves a fairly happy corner of the junkheap.

It wouldn't last forever, of course, because nothing did. Wayne was starting to spread his wings a little, swapping *Custom Bike* for *Playboy* and getting into a relationship with a girl named Sandy which seemed to consist mostly of baiting each other and trading insults and playing music somewhere around the pain threshold. And Pete; Pete, eventually, was going to hook up with someone who really appreciated him, and then it would be goodbye to those evenings of beer and popcorn and frozen pizza and rented videos, and all those other little touches that made up a uniquely masculine view of the Good Life. Both of them would leave him, and then he'd be alone.

But maybe not this year, was his consoling thought as they moved out into the main part of the yard and he closed and locked the door behind them. It wasn't much of a lock, but then it didn't need to be; Chuck and Bob, Ted's two German shepherd dogs, were let to run free in the yard on all but the coldest of nights. *Survivors will be prosecuted*, Wayne had once chalked on the main gate, but then Ted had made him clean it off.

Wayne Hammond was a likeable boy, much as his father had been at the same age. He wasn't academically bright, but he was sharp in all the ways that counted. He was taller than his father, with a lithe swimmer's body and an averagely pleasant face that wouldn't break any hearts – but then it wouldn't stop any clocks, either. Ted would look at him sometimes and, just for a moment, he'd see the boy's mother again.

As the two of them crossed the yard to their unlit house – Wayne going along to raid the fridge before returning to his two-roomed teenager's den above the workshop – the woman who would bring disaster to their lives and to the valley was making a crossing of a different kind, more than two thousand miles away.

Nikolai had done little more than to sit watching her for the first couple of hours, until he'd realised that he was making her nervous. That was when he'd moved from the fold-down seat to lie full-length on the compartment's upper berth, leaving Alina below to gaze out of the window at the passing landscape. This was continuous and unvarying, birch and pine forests standing dark in the moonlight; occasionally the trees thinned out for settlements of low wooden houses with small-paned windows and snow-laden roofs, but for the most part it was just a rolling backdrop for their dreams and fears.

He adored her. One dream, at least, seemed to be coming true for him.

He was nervous about their situation, but nothing more. This wasn't like the dark old days, where people were let out grudgingly if at all and then only with the certainty of family ties to draw them back; Nikolai knew that, had he chosen to travel alone, he'd almost certainly have faced no difficulty in getting permission. Border

7

controls were easing, the Berlin Wall had fallen, there was a different kind of outlook all around. The problem lay with Alina; she'd some kind of a criminal record and she'd told him that there were charges still outstanding that she'd have to answer if ever they caught up with her. He'd never asked her what the charges were. He trusted her.

But he knew that she'd spent time in a prison psychiatric hospital, and that she'd slipped out on a technicality and they wanted her back, and that before he'd met her she'd already lived without a permanent address or identity for at least two years. He couldn't imagine himself surviving in that way, but he could see what it had been doing to her. There was no question about it, she had to get away; and after he'd known her for only a short time, there had been no question but that he'd have to go with her.

A sharp rap on the wall by the door brought him slithering down from the berth. Alina was already standing as the guard came in, a boy soldier in an iron-grey uniform and with a deep cheek-scar like a cattlebrand. He was carrying a short stepladder in one hand, their passports in the other; after setting the ladder down he read out the names on their papers, mispronouncing them, and then turned to the photographs. They were French passports, guaranteed stolen but not yet reported, and the flimsy visa forms inside were simple forgeries.

There wasn't much room. Alina was standing close beside Nikolai, her head only just level with his shoulder, and she was looking at the floor. Nikolai felt a small flame of apprehension coming to life inside him at this, and the flame became a steady heat as the guard – barely out of school but already as tough and as ugly as a board – looked up from her picture to find her avoiding his eyes.

Nikolai began to feel scared.

It wasn't as if he needed to be here. He'd *chosen* to be here, gone out of his way to take the risk, elected to travel on forged documents instead of legitimately under his own name because it meant that Alina would be less conspicuous than if she made the journey alone; but if her nerve folded now, if she gave them away, it would all be for nothing.

Alina lifted her head, and returned the guard's level stare.

Everything fell back into place. Her self-possession was as cold and as hard as the light of a star. She was around twenty-eight, perhaps a little more; it was hard to tell because she was small and slim with a dancer's compact grace and a clear north-country skin, a feature that still caused her to be mistaken for a teenager almost everywhere that she went. Her hair, not quite shoulder-length, had been tied back. It had been longer, once, but in one of those rare moments where she'd unwound a little and told him something about herself he'd learned that they'd cut it short during her time in the hospital. He tried to imagine her like that, gaunt and defeated, but he couldn't.

The worst was over. The boy soldier handed back their passports and then hopped up onto his ladder to check the luggage rack and the vent seals. He then unhooked a flashlight from his belt and shone it into the space under the lower bunk; this ritual completed, he stepped out into the corridor and closed the door on them.

There was no baggage check.

The train rolled on slowly.

Alina lay back in the shadowed corner of the lower berth, and this time Nikolai sat beside her. The scene outside grew more and more empty, the forests cleared back from the trackside in a sure sign that the border was approaching. He saw the ruined remains of old concrete bunkers, many of them roofless and all of them half-buried in the snow; the train glided on in near silence past the tracks of earlier ski patrols and the occasional bulldozed vehicle road, the snow thrown up at its sides like dirty concrete.

There was daylight in the darkness as they came under the first of the searchlight gantries. These straddled the track every fifty metres or so, and the effect was of a slow pulsing as the thousand-watt arrays passed over. There were other lines here with other trains, all of them freightcars and none of them moving; it was like a forgotten railyard, the place where all the ghost-trains ended their runs, the only sign of life a small fire that had been lit under one of the diesel engines to free its iced-up brakes. The fire's attendant was a silhouette that stepped out to watch them go by, an eyeless, faceless shadow of a man.

Alina hitched herself up, and moved closer to the window.

The train was slowing in its river of light. At this moment they were being watched from a two-man tower out across the tracks, a dark shape sketched in darkness that stood taller than the pines. Alina stared out at the tower; even in this harsh gantry light she was a wide-eyed madonna, and Nikolai felt his heart turn over. He couldn't understand her power over him, and had no urge to; if he was a lost soul, then he was grateful to be damned.

They stopped briefly in a wooded clearing so that the border control people could disembark. The train was already rolling again as the officials trudged off in ranking order, the two junior soldiers last in line; they were filing down a snow-cut path toward a green-painted building about a hundred metres away, and then the trees closed in again and they were gone.

Alina was now staring into the reflected eyes of her own, ghost-glass image.

"Don't celebrate too soon," she said; perhaps to Nikolai, perhaps more to herself. "I've been this far before."

He wasn't aware of having fallen asleep. But when he woke the train had stopped, and Alina was already up and buttoning herself into her mid-length overcoat. He looked out. By now the darkness had given way to that strange northern twilight that took a little of the colour out of everything but which sharpened up edges and outlines and presented them in a range of greys that shone like opal. It wasn't daylight – it wasn't even full dawn – but daylight couldn't be so far away.

"What's happening?" he said, but she didn't give him a direct answer.

"Get the bag," she told him.

The pre-dawn chill began to seep into them from the moment that they took the long step down from the carriage. Nikolai paused to look around, his breath misting in the grey air as he tugged his gloves on a little further and zippered his overjacket a little tighter. At first glance they seemed to be at an anonymous spot in the middle of nowhere, endless woodland crowding right up to the trackside and cutting off any chance of seeing what lay beyond. Further along the track, a crowd was gathering by the engine. Alina was already heading to join it.

He hurried to catch up.

He was walking on snow-covered gravel that had been stained brown with the throw-off of the passing trains. There were faces at most of the windows above him, and people were hanging out of the open doorways at the carriage-ends as they craned to see what was going on. Everybody seemed dazed, rumpled, slightly shocked to find themselves active and awake at such an hour.

He and Alina joined the crowd, stepping over the collapsed wire of the woodland's boundary fence so that they could circle around and get a better view. Two Finnish policemen in fur caps and cold-weather gear were doing their best not to argue with five of the railway's people, all of whom were looking around anxiously when not taking a turn at protesting. Glancing around, Nikolai could now see that they weren't in the middle of nowhere after all but on the outskirts of a small township of wooden buildings, a few brick sheds, and a grey metal radio tower; the *Poliisi* van had been moved in to block the train on the township's solitary level crossing.

Keeping his voice low, Nikolai said, uncertainly, "They're not searching."

But Alina was looking past hope, to harder possibilities. "No," she said. "But they're waiting for someone who will."

It was hard to know what to do. Some passengers were drifting back to their compartments as the cold worked its way into them, and others were taking their places. Two or three men were tramping off into the woods to relieve themselves out of sight of the train, but everyone could see them go.

The sounds of cars, being driven hard.

They came around the bend, three of them with their lights full on, and at the sight of the van they had to stop suddenly with a squeal of snow tyres and a cloud of road grit. They didn't look like police cars, just ordinary saloons. There were four men in each. They started to get out.

Nikolai could hardly believe what he was seeing. They were Russians, not military or border patrol but just the ordinary militia, on the wrong side of the frontier in cars with Soviet registrations. Some were still in police uniform, and had thrown on anonymous-looking topcoats as if in an attempt at disguise; they looked around nervously as they stepped out by the rail tracks, aware that they were off home territory and in what was potentially a diplomatic minefield.

Their leader was an older man in plain clothes, overdressed even for this kind of weather: a raincoat over a heavy topcoat, which in turn was over a jacket and at least two baggy sweaters. Everything was unbuttoned, his scarf hung loose, and still he appeared to be steaming. His old-fashioned spectacles had one milky, sandblasted lens as if he'd lost an eye or, at least, the use of it. He approached the Finns and started to talk. The Finns didn't look happy. Cross-border co-operation, it seemed, was being pushed to the limits and beyond, here.

Nikolai said, "None of them knows us."

"Yes, they do," Alina said. "Pavel's with them."

She was looking at the last of the three cars. Nikolai followed her gaze and saw a young Russian policeman of the lowest rank, the last to climb out; he was scanning the windows of the train and in his eyes was a certain desperation, as if his presence here was the result of a drive beyond that of uniform and duty.

If he should happen to lower his gaze to the trackside crowd, he'd see them in moments. The Finns and their cross-border counterparts were almost arguing now and those from the cars were gathering around, but the young policeman was ignoring them – eyes still scanning the train, his lips moving slightly as if keeping a tally or reciting a prayer.

And with a quick glance around to judge the moment, Alina took a few steps backward and then turned and headed for the trees.

Realising almost too late that she'd begun to move, Nikolai followed her. A few heads turned, but the crowd mostly screened them from the police and nobody called out.

He caught up with her. The immediate cover was sparse, mostly leafless silver birch; Nikolai was expecting a shout at any moment, and he ran hunched as if he anticipated it coming as an actual physical blow between the shoulders. When he stumbled and slowed, he felt Alina's steadying hand on his arm. She was surprisingly strong, and she hustled him forward a little faster than he felt able to run.

They climbed. The tracks seemed a long way behind them now. One moment when Nikolai lost his footing, he almost brought Alina down with him. When finally they came to a stop they were both breathing hard, the cold air feeling like broken glass in Nikolai's lungs, but he forced himself to keep it under control so that he could look back down the trail and listen. The early-morning air was still, a silence broken only by the occasional rustling of tree branches shedding their snow.

But then, after a few moments, they were rewarded by the sound that they most wanted to hear.

The train was leaving. Without them.

Nikolai said, "Why do I get the feeling there's something you haven't been telling me?"

"There's a lot I haven't been telling you," Alina said. "Mostly for your own protection."

"So, who's Pavel?"

She looked at him, her breath feathering in the cold air. Her face was a hard, perfect mask; the face of a stranger, her grey eyes like chips of slate in the light of dawn.

"He's the one I've been living with," she said.

For Nikolai, it was as if the ground had dropped away beneath him. But then before either of them could say anything more, they were stopped by the sound of a distant whistle as it cut through the air.

Just the cry of a bird, Nikolai wanted to say, but he couldn't bring himself to believe it. Alina took the lead and said, "They guessed. They left someone."

12

Another whistle answered, from some way further down the ridge. This one was more distant, less expert.

It was definitely no bird.

Alina faced him again.

"Listen, Nikolai," she said. "I'd have abandoned you anyway, once we got to England. You could never be happy with me, and I'd hurt you in the end. I've used you, and I'm sorry. But I can't let them take me back. I'll die before that happens."

"We can still make it," he insisted.

"Perhaps *you* can," she said. "Be happy, Nikolai."

And she gave him a hard shove, much harder than he would have expected, sending him on his way and nearly pushing him off his balance on the slippery path.

By the time that he'd recovered enough to protest again, she'd gone.

II: THE KINDNESS OF STRANGERS

Two

By nightfall, Pete had made it as far as a window seat in a motorway services cafeteria overlooking three lanes of northbound traffic. He could feel that he needed a shave, and his dark suit now looked and felt as if a family of dogs had been using it for a bed. Wayne had told him the previous night that he'd had the appearance of someone who'd just emerged from prison, but Pete now reckoned that he looked more like somebody who was heading for one. The worst of the day was behind him; before him on the formica tabletop were a cup, the remains of a sandwich, and the key that Mike had given to him.

He'd an address to go with it, for some place that he knew nothing about. Mike was in the property business – buying, leasing, renting, renovating – and for Pete it was simply a case of getting whatever happened to be going through the books at the time. Pete didn't know exactly what his brother's business entailed, but it enabled him to run three cars and to spend two months of the year in an apartment in the Canary Islands. Needless to say, that was one key that Pete was unlikely to be offered. Their mother had always said that Mike was the worker, Pete the dreamer; but Mike's true knack was in finding the free ride on the back of someone else's labour, while Pete's dreams had more or less burned themselves out in an adolescence of fast second-hand cars and Marvel Comics. The cars had given him a few saleable skills, the comic books he'd sold off to a market trader a long time ago. The old girl had been proud of Mike, but she'd worried for Pete; he'd been irritated by it then, but he realised now that it was something else and he missed the feeling already. Even though they'd been miles apart, just knowing about it had somehow been enough. He wondered if there would ever be anyone who'd worry for him again.

Family funerals. The only bright thing about them was that, unlike at weddings, the family didn't tend to end up fighting.

Pete glanced around. The cafeteria was quiet at this time of the evening, the empty tables around him uncleared and one whole section across the way roped-off and unlit. There were a few people down the far end, but not many. Airport traffic, at a guess; the airport was only ten miles on and they had the look of late arrivals heading for homes with empty refrigerators. Some had ski tans, others were in loud shirts from some tropical beach. Beyond them, a young woman in a mid-length coat stood reading the menu.

He lowered his eyes, and looked at the key.

It wasn't as if he had a guarantee of a four-star hotel, or anything. For all that he knew, Mike was probably expecting him to camp out amongst dust sheets and bags of plaster. *It's costing you nothing*, the logic would go, *you ought to be grateful*. Pete's brother could make a personal favour seem like a tip to the bellboy. He was tempted simply to press on, see if he could make it back to the valley by morning; the Zodiac was still giving him problems, and this way he wouldn't have to cope with a cold engine after a night in the open.

Turning the key around on the tabletop had made a faint pattern in spilled sugar. Strange, how he felt more attached to the valley as home than he did to the area where he'd been raised. But then, the old town and its suburbs were barely recognisable now. New roads, new buildings, a shopping centre that was down-at-heel less than five years after it had opened. He dusted off the key, and pocketed it. Then he glanced out at the endless river of lights that he was soon to rejoin.

A wraith stood at his shoulder.

It was a trick of reflection, of course, but still it startled him. He turned to face the woman who stood by his table, and the shell of darkness became filled-out and real.

"Excuse me," she said. "Do you have a car?"

At a distance she'd hardly appeared to be more than a girl, but now he could see that she was probably closer to his own age. Her face was clear and hardly lined, but her grey eyes had a depth that could only have been earned. And she had a trace of an accent – not one that he could immediately identify, but enough to transform a simple question into something strange and unexpected.

"Yes," Pete said, guardedly; given the location, he could hardly say anything else.

"And you're alone?"

"I suppose I am." He was looking her over as he said it, half-aware of what was coming. His usual response to roadside hitch-hikers was the same as that of ninety-nine per cent of the population, which was to zip on by, feel bad for a while, and then forget all about it. But this kind of approach was different. For one thing, it was personal. And Pete, when it came down to it, knew that he was your basic and average Nice Guy; couldn't help it, that was the way he'd always been.

What the hell, she seemed okay. Sane, clean, and probably decent company. Maybe she could even help him to stay awake.

"Can I have a ride?" she said.

"You don't even know where I'm going."

"It doesn't matter."

And then she smiled; and Pete's momentary suspicion faded, like a drowned sailor returning to the deep.

They walked out through the big glass doors and into the night. The parking area was well-lit and, like the cafeteria, almost empty; there were a couple of dozen vehicles in the bays before them, but beyond these lay an acreage of line-marked space running all the way out to the landscaped boundary hill and the trees. Motorway noise was a continuous background drone, the sodium-glow buzz of the airport just over the horizon. Pete led the way across the paved area and onto the asphalt.

The Zodiac stood alone. It was as if the cars on either side had waited until nobody was looking and then quietly rolled away.

"This is it," he said when they were close enough for it to be obvious which one he was talking about. "Want to change your mind?"

She didn't even take time to think it over. "No," she said, and she took in its battered old lines as if it was as good as anything she'd become used to. "Is it American?"

"No," he said, unlocking the door, "this is one of ours. It's the kind of car they're usually talking about when they say how they don't make 'em like that anymore. This is just before they cross themselves and say, Thank God. Any luggage?"

"Just this," she said, showing the yellow carrier bag that she'd brought out with her. "Where are we going?"

"You really don't care?"

"I'm kind of touring around. I haven't decided where I'm going to settle, yet."

Well, it was probably none of his business, but it struck him as a dangerous kind of thing to be doing. There could be some pretty weird people around, and at this time of night they came into their own. But what was it to him? She was over twenty-one, and at least with him she'd fallen on her feet and would be safe for the next couple of hours. He checked all the doors, and then he got in beside her. She was all ready to go, hands folded in her lap.

The Zodiac played for sympathy a little, but started anyway.

Without looking at the woman, Pete said, "Where are you from?"

"You wouldn't believe me if I told you," she said.

"Try me."

There was no reply for a moment, and when Pete glanced up from switching on the headlights he saw that she was looking across at him with an expression that he couldn't make out in the half-shadows of the car. It might have been mischief, but it looked like something more.

"I'm a Russian," she said. "I came here tonight on a stolen passport. I think they may have caught the boy I was with, but I carried on."

She watched him for a few seconds longer, until he was the one who turned away.

"Sure," Pete said as they rolled forward and he swung the car around toward the motorway sliproad.

After all, he could take a hint as well as anyone.

THREE

About an hour later, he was saying, "You were telling me the truth, weren't you?"

They hadn't covered much in the way of mileage, mainly due to Pete's mistaken choice of motorway exit that had taken them way out on the wrong side of town before he'd been able to find a place where he could get off the road and turn around. So much for his ability to make it home without a map; even on roads that he was supposed to know, he was no better than a stranger. Motorway lighting was giving the entire night journey a sense of unreality; he wasn't even accustomed to that, any more. He and his passenger had talked about a number of things along the way, but the topic of her background wasn't one of them.

Perhaps that was it; the way that she'd said it and then said nothing more, while everything else about her seemed to indicate the kind of deep streak of honesty that resists analysis, but calls up certainty like a half-awake bear from its cave.

I'm a Russian. I came here tonight on a stolen passport.

Could such things happen?

They could, and they did; sometimes in full colour on the six o'clock news, but never in a way that seemed to intersect with Pete's life in any meaningful sense. She wasn't particularly remarkable. Different, but not remarkable. She wasn't bad-looking, but you could lose her in a crowd without too much problem.

I think they caught the boy I was with, but I carried on.

Belief had been simmering in him for some time now, and it seemed that this was the moment that it had chosen to boil over.

They were off the motorway network and it was starting to get late, but Pete had a kind of instinct for seeking out the low-life places that traded outside normal hours. The café was one of a row of old shops, and the parking area behind the row was a half-acre demolition site that had been bulldozed flat and which now served as rough and unlit standing for heavy lorries. The two of them had picked their way carefully over bricks and glass and half-buried timbers. Some of the original street layout of the site was still visible,

21

but only just. The extractor fans over the back yard of the café were working full-time, pumping out a steam that carried with it the scents of hot fat and bacon.

In the doorway, they stopped. And in response to his question she said, "You think these things don't happen?"

"Not to people I know."

And then she smiled faintly, as if it really didn't matter whether he believed her or not, because his belief or the lack of it could do nothing to alter the facts.

And she said, "Well, here's your first," and then they went on inside.

She was the only woman in the place, but no one seemed to worry. Few of the tables matched each other, and none of the chairs did; the floor was bare and the tablecloths were checkered plastic, and some driver with a deep reverence for Willie Nelson had spent all of his spare change at the jukebox. There were three pinball machines, and as Pete went over to place an order at the service counter she went over to take a look at them. The most garishly lit of the three was a game called *Sun Runner*, and when Pete joined her she was studying it. He put down some change, and showed her how to play. The pinball table was old, its glass split and some of its bulbs dead, probably edged out of some arcade by newer and flashier video games. He tried to see this ordinary, common place and this broken-down machine through her eyes. But he didn't know how.

He said, "What are you going to do?"

She shrugged, her eyes on the silver ball as it made its rounds of the table and ran up almost a thousand points in a frenzied dalliance with the bonus section. The lights flashed and the bells rang, and the silver ball made a quick exit down the left-hand side of the layout where the flippers couldn't reach.

"Do you know anyone?" he persisted. "Have you got anywhere to go?"

Again, she didn't answer. She didn't have to.

"Any money?"

"More than seventy pounds."

"It won't last."

"I know. But I'm feeling lucky."

Her last ball shot around the table and dropped out of sight with a zero score.

Their order came up, and they moved across to a table in the window. A red neon sign hung against the glass, and its backglow was like the rays of a sunset. He hadn't had much of a chance to study her, not in the comparatively short time that they'd been on the road, but he'd started to catch up during the game and he carried on with it now. Even in the soft red light she seemed tired, a mechanism of some elegance and delicacy that was being pushed too far.

For a moment, he wondered what they'd make of her in the valley. But then he let it go.

"You should go to the police," he told her.

Her reply was quick and emphatic. "No."

"They're the people to handle something like this."

"No police," she said.

She seemed genuinely scared of the very idea, and so he didn't press it. It was the first time that she'd shown even a hint of strong feeling, and it was like a powerful heat that made him back away. Whatever her experiences in that direction might have been, they clearly hadn't been good.

There was an awkward silence for a while, and Pete wondered if there was any way to repair the mood that he'd managed almost to destroy. He'd grown to like her company and, although he knew that he'd be losing it before the night was over, he didn't want to see it go with bad feeling. She rubbed at her eyes, and Pete could see how close to the edge she'd been driven. Something was holding her together, but he couldn't have said what.

Then he had an idea.

"A suggestion," he said.

FOUR

After hearing him out, she'd reached across the table as if to take his hand. But she'd touched his sleeve instead, a stand-in gesture for two people who didn't know each other well enough for the real thing; and then, five minutes later, they'd been walking back to the car. It had come home to Pete how awesomely alone she must be; and after the day that he'd had, he could feel himself sliding into perfect harmony with her outlook.

An outsider, and an outcast. They made a neat kind of set.

This time, he dug out his old road atlas from under one of the seats and took no chances with his navigation. It should take no more than a half-hour to get to where they needed to go. After leaving her, and by driving through most of what was left of the night, he could still get back to the valley by dawn.

They did a slow drive-past before they pulled in. Pete flicked on the Zodiac's interior light to check the address on the paper that Mike had given to him, and it was right. The Russian woman was looking out of the window. Just back from the road, standing in their own grounds, were a series of linked low-rise apartment blocks. Probably a mid-seventies development; service flats with the most perfunctory of services.

She said, "Why would you do this?"

There was only one answer he could think of.

He said, "Why did you ask me for a ride?"

There was a big suburban hospital just across the way and, judging by some of the nameplates against the entranceway buzzers, the flats were occupied mostly by single medical staff. The key loaned by Mike opened the main door. The apartment was three floors up. There was no lift.

They climbed to the topmost landing, and found the number they wanted. The hallway lights cut out on a timer just as Pete was getting the door open, but by then they were as good as inside.

With a glance back at him to be sure that she was doing right, she went in ahead.

So, this was the accommodation that his brother had lined up for him. Actually, it wasn't too bad. A short passageway led to a pint-sized sitting room with some plain contract furniture. It had the look of a reasonably-sized room in a cheap hotel with the back wall cut into an arch and the sleeping area divided off by a folding screen partition. There was no phone.

He went around switching on all the lights, and checking the kitchen taps for water; she moved to the window where the curtains stood half-open, and looked out.

Pete said, "You should be okay for a few days, but after that I don't know what will happen. It ought to be better than just being on the road. You can work out what you want to do from here."

"You don't know what this means to me," she said quietly, without turning around.

"I know," Pete said, moving up to take a look out from beside her. "I'm a saint."

They were at the back of the building. Three floors below were sloping gardens of borders and bushes, and a lit zigzag path that led down to a parking lot with a few cinderblock garages. Some of these appeared to have been rented by residents, but most seemed to leave their cars in the open. The Zodiac was down there amongst them.

All seemed as calm and unthreatening as it was possible for a night to be.

"I don't even know your name," she said.

"Pete. Peter McCarthy."

"Alina Petrovna."

He didn't know exactly how it happened. It was as sudden and unexpected as a rockfall. One moment they were standing side by side, the next she was hugging him so hard that he could barely draw breath. He didn't know what to do. He held her awkwardly, like a teenager with his first-ever dance partner. And he patted her shoulder, as if to say, *There, there, everything's going to be fine.*

Trying to make light of it, he said, "We shouldn't be doing this. I hardly know you."

The pressure lessened. She looked up into his eyes.

Her own, he saw, were sad and remote.

"Believe me," she said. "You wouldn't want to."

An hour later, he was still with her. She was on the hard sofa and he reckoned that she was asleep, but he couldn't be sure. There was a duvet cover in the bedroom – no linen, just the white cotton shell of the duvet itself – and she didn't stir when he brought this through

25

and laid it over her. He'd already turned off most of the lights.

He knew that he ought to slip out quietly. Leave her, walk away. He'd already done more than most people ever would.

But he kept turning the strange syllables of her name over and over in his mind.

And, for the second time and without any prompting, he found himself wondering what they'd make of her in the valley.

He couldn't even think of taking her back with him, that much was certain. Imagine the complications. Everyone would jump to the wrong conclusion, even Ted Hammond; *especially* Ted Hammond, who worried over Pete like a mother hen. He kept hinting at how Pete, though hormonally sound, wasn't getting any younger, while the supply of eligible women in the valley was meagre at its best. There was the passing-through traffic of summer, but Pete didn't find that he was much tempted by the seductive signals of bored rich women – or rather, bored women with rich husbands – of a certain age. The men came to play with their big boats, their wives cast an eye along the dock and saw Pete. Maybe it was the way that he had to clamber aboard and ram in the pump nozzle when they called by for fuel, started them thinking and gave them all kinds of ideas. He didn't exactly have to beat them off with a stick, but some of them were so upfront it could be embarrassing. They tended to have tight, well-kept figures, expensive bleach jobs, and the skin tone of a crocodile handbag after a lifetime's forced tanning. Thanks, but no thanks.

Somebody like Diane Jackson, though . . . that was a different proposition entirely. She was a Mrs, but as far as he'd been able to ascertain her husband had long ago been booted out into the street with his hat thrown after him. She'd arrived in the valley only a few months before, to work on the Liston estate at the head of the lake. She lived in the big house, she sometimes came down to the yard on estate business. They'd kind of eyed each other and although nothing had exactly happened yet there was something in the air that said that it might. Something like the highly-charged sense of impending lightning.

Or maybe he was kidding himself.

Maybe, for all that he'd been thinking, he really wasn't anything more than a walk-on in the drama of her life. A couple of lines to say, not even a name to be remembered. Whatever the case, he could be sure of one thing; come home with a good-looking stranger in tow, and his chances with said Mrs Jackson or anybody else would nosedive within hours of the gossip mill getting to work.

Ah, well. Then it would be back to his daydreams of Debbie

Harry and a baby-oil massage, and wait until some other prospect might open up in his life.

Alina's hand was out from under the cover and turned slightly, so that the inside of her arm caught the faint electric light from the almost-closed bathroom door. The edge of her sleeve had fallen back to show a line of tiny, puckered scars down the soft part of her forearm. He frowned. There was always the possibility that she was actually an addict, and that the rest of it had been a lie; but these scars were white and long-healed, more likely a permanent record of an abuse that had once been inflicted upon her.

So it probably *was* all true. He didn't doubt it now, and hadn't really needed this evidence to persuade him.

"I only wish I could do something more," he whispered, mostly to himself.

And she heard him.

"You don't know what you're saying," she said from the darkness. She spoke softly, but she sounded as if she was fully awake. "But it doesn't matter. After tonight, you won't see me again."

"What do you mean?"

She raised herself onto one elbow, and the duvet slid from her shoulder. "I mean that I'd hurt you. I'm a *rusalka*."

"A what?"

"You'd say, a heartbreaker. I have it on the best authority."

He moved around the sofa, and crouched down before her. As once before, her face was in shadow with only the slight, bright flicker of her eyes to betray her attentiveness.

He said, "Listen, don't worry about me. I can look after myself."

"That makes no difference. I'm not just an ordinary runaway, it's not that kind of a situation at all. I could be the worst thing that could ever happen to you. I use people, and then I betray them. It's not a choice that I make. But it happens, again and again."

He shook his head, half-smiling. "I don't understand you," he said.

"That's right," she said. "You don't."

At which point, there was a sharp knock at the apartment's door.

Alina shot upright, any hint of drowsiness gone, as tense as a hunted cat getting a scent of the pack. "It's probably nothing," Pete said, rising, but as he turned to go to the door he could sense her wary, watchful presence behind him. The fact of it was, he was a little uneasy himself. When it came down to it, he'd no right to be here other than on Mike's say-so, and that could prove to be an authority of little substance. And then when the shit that he'd handed you hit

27

the fan, Mike was the kind of person who'd shrug and then offer to sell you a washcloth.

A woman stood outside.

She seemed surprised to see Pete. She was around forty, trim and well-preserved, anxious-looking and in a dressing-gown. She said, "I'm sorry. I saw the light and I thought . . . I thought Doctor Singer had come back."

"I'm a close friend of his," Pete improvised quickly.

"Oh." She hesitated. "I'm sorry to ask, but . . ."

"Is something wrong?"

She picked her words carefully, uncertain of being misunderstood by someone she didn't know. "Well . . . there's a strange character hanging around outside. I'm not sure, but he seems to be looking in all the windows."

Pete felt himself unwind a little. A peeper? Here was something that he could handle, much better than being put on the spot as a squatter. He said, "Just give me a minute," and he stepped back inside. Alina had switched on the table lamp next to the sofa; she looked rumpled but alert, and presumably she'd heard what had been said.

"I have to go out for a few minutes," Pete told her. "Will you be all right?"

"Of course," she said, and she glanced at the woman in the doorway.

"I'm sorry," the woman said. "I won't keep him long."

Alina nodded briefly, as if to show that she didn't mind. Pete told Alina to lock the door behind him, just in case; and as they went out into the stairwell, Pete couldn't help reflecting on the woman's attitude. She'd been deferring to Alina.

Borrowing her man.

They went down to the next floor.

FIVE

Her name was Janis, and she was a nurse; a senior staff nurse, and she'd known the occupant of the upstairs apartment well. Pete decided to say nothing on the subject, or risk betraying some fundamental ignorance. Her flat was larger than the one they'd left, with two bedrooms and a decent length of lounge. It was in the semi-chaos of redecoration with the furniture all sheeted, the walls stripped down to the plaster, and the smell of drying paint in the air.

"Sorry about the mess," Janis said. "I'm doing it all myself."

"No worries," Pete said, stepping over books which had been stacked in the middle of the room and protected by old Sunday colour supplements spread out over the heap. "Does this happen a lot?"

"Two or three times a year," she said. "You get a lot of single women in the flats. It's a bit of a magnet for peculiar types."

He stood at the window. They were on the opposite side of the block now, facing across the street to where the grounds and towers of the hospital complex stood. With the curtains open and the lights behind him, Pete's silhouette would be easily visible to anyone who might be prowling around out there.

He said, "Where did you see him?"

"By the road. He was just . . . watching. Looking at all the windows. Then he disappeared for a while, then he came back."

"I don't suppose he could have been looking for someone he knows."

"For nearly an hour?"

Pete looked all over the grounds immediately below. These were the same open-plan gardens as around the back, dotted here and there with windblown litter. Concrete-set lights illuminated a paved walkway which led up to the street, casting deep shadows from the bushes on either side.

"Well," Pete said, "he doesn't seem to be there now."

"So now you'll think I imagined him."

29

"Hey, come on. He could be circling the block, looking in some of the other windows. Don't you usually call the police?"

"Only as a last resort. You don't like to cry wolf too often. Hospital security used to send a man over once or twice a night, just to keep all the nurses happy." And then, after a moment in which she realised what she'd just said, she started to colour up red. "I didn't mean that the way it sounds."

"I get the idea," Pete said quickly.

"But they don't do that any more. Money's tight, and this is a private block. It's really nothing to do with the hospital. A lot of us live here, that's all."

Pete said, "Switch the lights off, for a minute."

"Can you see something?"

"I'm not sure."

The glare of the unshaded light in the room wasn't doing much to help Pete's night vision; most of what he could see was his own reflection. The room went dark, and Janis came to join him as he scanned the bushes where he thought he'd seen a movement.

There was an almost immediate response. One of the shadows moved, stepping out into the low-level light of the path.

A young man, fit-looking, with short, fairish hair; pale-skinned and unfashionably dressed, he was staring straight up at their window.

"Is that him?" Pete said.

"He's the one." Janis's voice had the kind of tone that she'd probably use to point out a particularly unappealing patch of slime.

"Well, he's seen me."

The prowler was still staring. There was no doubt about it, their window was the one that interested him above all the others; and far from being scared off by Pete's appearance, he'd actually moved out to become visible himself.

Janis said, "It doesn't seem to have discouraged him much, does it?"

"No." Pete took a step back, and drew her with him. "Have you got a big flashlight, something really bright?"

"There's one I use with the car. But I don't want you doing anything stupid."

"Me? No chance of it. I'm just going to ask him what he thinks he's at. It's the only way to deal with those people." *Either that*, he was thinking, *or slug 'em with the flashlight*. The bigger and heavier, the better.

Janis was dubious. She didn't like what she'd started, but she was a single woman living alone and she'd been around enough to know that she'd be fooling herself if she didn't get nervous at something like this.

She brought the flashlight from her kitchen. It was of a square, free-standing type with a carrying handle on the top. Pete did his best to meet her concern with confidence.

"Don't worry," he said. "I'll bring it right back."

Pete didn't switch on the stairwell light for his descent. He slipped out into the grounds unseen.

Once in the cool night air, he stopped for a moment and told himself that he was going to have to slow down; otherwise, he might be heading for a nasty surprise. He didn't have to impress anybody – and even if, for understandable reasons, he felt that he did, he wasn't going to do it by taking on more than he could handle.

He doubted that the prowler was going to be much of a problem. Adequate people didn't get their kicks from watching bedroom windows – or at least, that was the theory.

He moved out into the shadows beside the path, and at first he didn't switch on the flashlight. He saw no one. So then he cautiously checked the dark spaces in the undergrowth with the beam, but again with no result. The peeper had guessed that someone was coming and had run, that was the only explanation that Pete could see.

He was about to go back, when he heard voices from the direction of the street.

So, moving quietly, he went to take a look.

It was a big and anonymous-looking saloon, pulled in close to the kerbside and just far enough along to be screened from the apartments. Two men sat inside. A third stood on the pavement with the nearside door open, talking to them.

The third man was the prowler, as seen from the second-floor window.

A sense of wrongness, hard to explain and impossible to ignore, began to take root somewhere deep inside Pete McCarthy. Since when did perverts hunt in threes? The two in the car, shown up by the interior light, seemed to be taking more interest in their trays of carry-out food than in what was being said to them. The one on the pavement, in contrast, seemed to be taking the whole thing more seriously. The man in the passenger seat – leather jacket, bearded, a face you could see and then forget – was nodding over his fried rice in a way that said, *Yeah, sure, you carry on and let us know when it's all over*. The man on the pavement straightened, and Pete took a step back into deeper shadow.

The young man turned. Under the yellow streetlights his face was a deathmask, a short-lived effect that faded as he walked back to the pathway. Pete, still in the bushes and now feeling like a prowler himself, held his breath as the man passed him no more than a few feet away. A dozen yards further on the man stopped, raised his head, and lasered-in on the same second-floor window as before. Janis had kept her lounge in darkness, but there was enough spill from one of the inner rooms to make out her moving shadow with surprising clarity.

Pete moved onto the concrete path in silence, out of the sight of the car again. The blatancy of this really pissed him off. His outdoor job kept him reasonably fit and even gave him a certain physical grace developed on narrow ladders and slippery decks, and he knew that he could look mean as long as he didn't smile. He didn't think there was much danger of him smiling now.

He reached out with the flashlight, and pushed the man on the shoulder.

"Seen anything you like?" he said.

The man spun around, startled, but Pete was well back and out of reach. He held the flashlight ready, a weapon for if he needed it.

"So," he went on. "What's the idea? This isn't some free show."

They faced each other.

The man was struggling for words. Shock made the struggle almost physical, like that of a beached fish for air. There was something strange about him, something off-key.

And then he spoke.

His accent was like Alina's. Only more so.

"I need to see her," he said. "She has to talk to me."

Suddenly Pete didn't need to ask who. How long had they been following, the three of them in the car? He felt blind, he felt stupid. He felt like a man who'd picked up an exhausted hare and then turned to see the dogs bearing down on him. He swallowed, hard, and wondered what the hell he was going to do now.

"Listen," the man said, with a glance towards the road; he was holding up his hands as if to fend Pete away, or to show that he wasn't going to attack. "Those two men in the car, they're British policemen. Once I've identified her, they'll come for her. I don't want that to happen until I've at least had the chance to talk to her. Will you tell her that? Tell her you saw Pavel and he wants to talk. Please."

The man was circling, heading back for the car and keeping safely out of range. Pete glanced up at the window again, long enough to see that Janis was there and staying well back in the room. She was a shade, a silhouette; at this distance, she could have been anybody.

"Please," the man said again, still backing off, and with a note that was like desperation in his voice.

A moment later, he was gone.

Pete watched the space where he'd been; a light breeze shook the bushes, and a car horn sounded somewhere far-off. Then he turned, and briefly switched on the flashlight to signal to the block that everything was okay.

One thing was clear to him. The prowler – Pavel, or whatever his name was – had been looking at Janis's outline and thinking that he was seeing Alina. As long as this mistake went uncorrected, they had time.

Back indoors, Pete spent a couple of minutes in exploration before he knocked on the door of the third-floor flat.

Alina opened it.

"You found your burglar?" she said as Pete came in and made sure that the door was closed behind him; he then set the flashlight on the teak-effect sideboard, and turned to face her.

"Does the name Pavel mean anything to you?" he said.

Her reaction was instantaneous. Astonishment. Fear.

She said, "I don't understand."

"He's the one, the man outside. He knows you're here."

"But how?"

"I don't know. Could anyone have told them where your flight would be taking you?"

"Nikolai," she said bleakly.

"Well, it looks as if somebody near the airport must have seen me picking you up. They'll have put out a call on the make of the car. They'll think we're around here somewhere, but they won't know exactly where. You know what that means?"

"No," she said uncomprehendingly, and she sat heavily on the sofa. She put a hand to her forehead. "No," she repeated; but Pete was already on the move, grabbing her few possessions together.

"We're still one ahead," he said. "They're watching the wrong window on the wrong side of the building. We can sneak out and be away before they know it."

"Away to where?"

He stopped by the window, and checked on the view.

Nothing moved.

He said, "I'm taking you home with me."

He looked at her then, and found that her gaze was already on him; but what he saw in it was nothing like what he might have expected. It wasn't relief, it wasn't even apprehension; it was something cool and remote and yet strangely compelling, as if there could only ever have been one outcome to the night and both of them had somehow known it all along.

Rusalka.

Heartbreaker.

Wasn't that how they said it?

III: OUT OF DARKNESS

Six

Daybreak tended to steal up gently on the valley, re-inventing a fresh landscape out of the leftover mists of the night; lake breezes would then strip away the shrouds one by one to uncover the forests and the shores and the mountains behind. Three Oaks Bay was a small resort town on the lake's eastern side, busy in the season and almost dead outside of it. The Bay had a square, two pubs, a promenade walk overlooked by three medium-sized Victorian hotels, and a restaurant with a terrace that stood out over the water. It rated one resident policeman and a mention in the *Shell Guide*. People came in the summer to walk and to sail and, if development plans succeeded and the roads could be kept clear, they'd soon be coming in the winter to ski.

Pete had seen a fair number of valley mornings, although not so many had been as early as this. He shivered a little, and turned up the collar of his suit jacket.

It didn't make much of a difference. He was standing on the exposed rocks at the highest point of the headland; the ground fell away steeply from here, mostly bare rock and scrub, with just a narrow shelf of land that was almost a beach down at the water's edge. He could see the upturned hulls of a few boats drawn up onto the shore, mostly of fibreglass but some of varnished timber, all of them de-rigged and tied down against the weather. Out across the water, the end of the lake had not yet emerged from the mist, and the mountains above it were no more than a delicate shadow of grey against a deep grey sky.

Alina was still in the car. Still, as far as Pete could tell, asleep. He'd covered her over with a coat and taken her few possessions inside, and she'd slept on; she'd been the same way for the last couple of hours of the journey, ever since they'd made their final stop at a twenty-four hour garage so that he could fill the Zodiac's tank and buy some tape for a running repair to the headlamp that he'd broken when, lights doused to escape notice, he'd clipped the corner of the garage block on their way out of the parking area. The repair didn't look much, but it would keep the rain out.

A sound came from behind him. He didn't turn.

Alina scrambled up alongside, and found herself a rock just a couple of feet lower than his own. She'd brought his coat from the car, and she wore it around her shoulders against the cold.

They stood in silence for a minute or more.

And then she said, "This is where you live?"

He looked at her then. "You like it?"

"It's . . ." She searched for the words. "I *do* like it. I like it a lot."

"Actually, the house is a dump, but the boss lets me have it cheap. It belongs to his sister's family."

"I think it's fine," Alina said, and Pete watched her for a moment longer, almost as if he was checking her score on a test.

"Yes," he said finally. "It's fine." And he turned again to the view. The mist over the northern end of the lake had now begun to clear, uncovering a part of the Liston estate. A piece of land that had held no particular interest for him at all until the arrival of its new estate manager.

"This isn't going to work," Alina said despondently. The silver dawn was turning into plain old daylight now, its magic fading and taking her momentary confidence with it.

"Why shouldn't it?"

"Because I'll mess up your life. I poison everyone I touch. Look what I already did to your car."

"Forget the car."

"I can't even pay you rent."

"I don't want anything from you. You think that's using me, forget it. You're a guest." Pete stepped down. "Come on," he said, offering his hand. "We'll put your stuff in your room."

Alina accepted, and he helped her along. "I get a room?" she said.

"You even get a bed, until you decide exactly what it is you want to do from here. There's more space than I can use. I'll clear it with Ted, but nobody's going to mind."

They descended to the gingerbread house; Rosedale, the cabin in the high woodland, paint flaking, boards weathered silver, the place that Pete called home.

She didn't look like someone who could poison what she touched, whatever she might think. Nobody could blame her for taking life as seriously as she'd had to, but the way to some kind of peace and personal balance would surely lie in the opportunity to stop running and relax a little. She could lose herself in a place like this; if not in the valley itself, then in some other part of the region. Tourists passed through here in their thousands, and the face of a stranger would be nothing to remark upon in the approaching season. Even her accent wouldn't give her away; all kinds of nationalities came to take up casual work in the restaurants and hotels. Endless human variety, but on a manageable scale. It would probably be just what she needed in order to find herself again.

And she certainly needed to unwind, at least a little. He couldn't help thinking of something that she'd said in all seriousness when they'd left the apartment building behind and a lack of any interest from a passing night patrol on the motorway had told him that no, the police didn't seem to be keeping an active watch for his car; she'd looked at him and she'd said, *Promise me, Peter. Don't ever try to get too close to me. Don't even think of it. And I promise that I'll try never to hurt you. Is that a deal?* And Pete, who hadn't been entirely unaware of some of the paths that such a newly-founded relationship might follow, suddenly found himself shifting into back-off mode. Helping her was one thing. But even to consider getting involved with someone who could talk in such a way . . . well, that would be to enter dangerous waters indeed.

The room that he'd given her was smaller than his own, but she got a bigger wardrobe. Not that she had much to put in it . . . the only other pieces of furniture were the bed and an old dressing-table with a cracked mirror. Her window looked out of the back of the house, onto what had once been a small garden.

She sat on the bed, next to her bags. Pete stood in the doorway and watched as she bounced a little and made the mattress creak. When she looked up at him and smiled, he could see that the dangerous edge of last night's exhaustion had been blunted.

He said, "I only wish I could help you more. But I wouldn't know how."

"You *are* helping me."

"That's not what I mean."

"I know what you mean," she said. "Please don't worry."

"There's tinned stuff in the kitchen if you wake up and I'm not around. If I'm not here, I'll probably be down at the boatyard. When I get the chance, I'll show you the sights."

"I'll manage," she assured him.

And so he made a gesture as if to say, *It's all yours.* And then he withdrew, closing the door after him, and went to his own room to stretch out for a while.

Alina stayed where she was, her eyes closed, almost as if she was listening to the silence. Pete must have dropped onto his bed without undressing, he made so little sound. Then she turned to the much-travelled carrier bag on the bed beside her.

From it she took a book, which she carried over to the dressing-table. It was a cheap scrapbook, coarse paper between cardboard covers, so well-used that some of the pages were starting to fall out. She laid it flat and opened it up.

The book was filled with photographs. A few of them would have been a serious giveaway in any frontier search, but these she'd covered over with postcard views bought from the Europiskaya Hotel.

She began to take out the postcards, revealing the snapshots underneath. When she reached a particular one, she stopped.

It was a group view, slightly blurred, a dozen friends on a day in the country. They were in rows like a football team, the people in the front row all kneeling on the ground.

Old times, sad times, a million miles away. For a while Alina sat looking at her younger, unmarked self. She was in the back row, lifted higher than anybody by the boys on either side of her.

That was how she'd been, back then. Open, smiling, everything before her.

Lifted on the arm of a boy named Pavel.

SEVEN

Pavel's was a city dawn, seen from the rear seat of the unmarked car as they circled back in on the motorway network toward their base near the airport. The night had not been a success. He knew that he'd been close, but then somehow it had all slipped away from him; when Alina hadn't come out and the three of them had finally gone into the building, it was to find incomprehension from the woman who lived alone and an empty flat where she said she'd gone for help. Pavel had no names, no numbers. He could go no further.

And his two escorts had shrugged and sympathised, and called it bad luck.

A couple of years ago, he'd never even have been able to get this far. The notion of such international co-operation would have been unthinkable even at senior investigator level; but here the arrangements had been made and he'd been on a plane within a matter of hours. He had no official status and no powers of arrest, but once he'd identified Alina then the two officers along with him would have been able to detain her on immigration charges. Since she'd entered the country on stolen papers, she could then be deported back to Russia and the knotty question of extradition would never have arisen. An appeal for political asylum would have been likely to get her nowhere; Alina wasn't political, and never really had been. By most people's definition, she was a common criminal and nothing more.

For most people, but not in the eyes of Pavel. To Pavel, and probably to many of the others who'd fallen under her influence, she was the most uncommon criminal ever.

The Finns had found the boy within half an hour. He'd been hiding in a woodland graveyard, only half-heartedly concealed behind one of the leaning roofed crosses. He'd known almost nothing. Nothing of her true nature, not even – and here Pavel had been holding his breath at the back of the Border Control's interrogation room – where she'd been living for the past two years. The boy's eyes had met his own, and for a moment Pavel had been afraid; but the

41

boy hadn't said anything, and after a moment he'd looked away.

An example of her power: scared as he was, the boy Nikolai had managed to hold out against telling them of her destination until it was too late for them to prevent her from reaching it. She'd used him and then abandoned him, and yet still he'd continued to protect her.

It was an impulse that Pavel could understand only too well. And compared to some in her past, the boy had been lucky.

The car rolled into the police yard, a hurricane-fenced compound within sight of the main runway and with a constant background of big jet engines racing up to power. There were a few marked vans here, but most of the cars were officers' private vehicles. As Pavel stepped out onto the asphalt, he could see the takeoff of a Cathay Pacific 747 through the chainlink and across a few hundred feet of grass; it seemed shockingly, dangerously close, and he turned his face away to look toward the main building. This was in four storeys and in a no-frills, prefabricated style that could have been anything – a tax office, a really dull hotel, a leaking hospital doomed never to come fully into service. Only the crest over the entrance door gave it away and that didn't entertain the eye much, either.

"I'll tell you what," one of the two men said. His name was Roger, and he'd made a few stabs at conversation in the course of the night. Pavel knew that he'd not been the best company but then, they hadn't been treating this job as anything particularly special. Some novelty value because he was the first Russian they'd ever had in the car, but that was all. Roger went on, "Why don't we put you in the canteen for a while, and I'll go and look for my boss. He's the one who's going to have to decide what to do with you now."

And Pavel said, "What's a canteen?"

They grinned as if he'd made a joke, and they walked him inside.

Pavel sat alone at a table in the corner of the police cafeteria. He bought nothing, because he'd no English money. Only half of the counter had opened up at this early hour and there were no more than half a dozen people in the place, most of them in uniform. He idly pushed around the salt and pepper to avoid meeting anyone's eyes, and then he took out a sachet from the sugar bowl and looked at it with curiosity. The label read *Sweet'n'Low* but the sachet appeared to be empty. He tore it open and found that it wasn't empty, just that the fine powder inside took up so little space. He tasted it, and then he put a few of the sachets in his pocket.

A policewoman came to get him. Her uniform shirt was crisp and her red hair had been tied back and she had a hint of an overbite. She said, "Are you the Russian officer? I'm sorry, I don't know how to pronounce your name," and Pavel said, "Please don't worry about it," and got to his feet to follow her.

They smiled at each other politely in the lift, but nothing passed between them. Pavel was feeling as loose and unconnected as a bag of spanners, and with about as much energy. He looked at the floor. He'd closed his eyes once in the last forty hours, and that had only been a restless doze in the back of the car on the way to the border. He hadn't been able to sleep on the plane at all. He'd been wound-up and anxious ever since he'd come home from his shift and discovered her missing, an empty space under the bed where her bags had been and her photograph album – probably the most precious single item that she owned – gone. His first reaction had been one of panic. But Pavel was level-headed, and he knew that he had a certain inner strength; nobody could have kept her and cared for her in secret and for so long without it. After he'd found the half-burned counterfoil slips from the railway tickets stuffed down the back of the apartment's disused fireplace, his next move had been to return to his Militia post and report that an anonymous source had given him some information on the whereabouts of Alina Petrovna, escapee from the prison hospital and probable murderer of the psychiatrist Belov.

What else could he have done? It was this, or lose her completely with certainty and forever – a prospect that he couldn't even begin to face. He loved her too much even to be able to imagine such a thing; Pavel's was the love of Judas, a devotion so great that it encompassed even betrayal.

The chief superintendent had a corner office with a view down onto the place where tenders took on loads of aviation fuel from huge land-based tanks. The chief superintendent was a man in his forties, with thinning hair and pale blue eyes that didn't seem to blink. Pavel sat gazing out at the loading area as the man looked through a small number of memos and facsimile messages. All pipelines and white stones, it had the look of an alien landscape. The chief superintendent looked from one sheet to another and then back again, as if there were certain connections that he was looking for and was unable to find.

Pavel was calm. He was here, and the hardest part was over; he was on the soil where Alina walked, he breathed the same air again. There was no doubt in his mind that he'd find her. A few hours' sleep, and he'd come up fresh and begin to learn the system around here. They'd no internal passports in this tiny country, but from what he'd seen of this building they had computers the like of which the Leningrad Militia could only dream about. He knew her, he knew her ways, he could guess how she'd operate.

With luck, he might even get to her before somebody else died.

"Look," the superintendent said, "I only just came on and I can't make head nor tail of this. I don't understand why they sent *you*."

"I'm the only one who knows what she looks like," Pavel said.

"Couldn't they just have sent us a photograph?"

"There are none." There were none because, after volunteering to bring Alina's file from the records department up to the chief investigator's desk, Pavel had quietly removed them in the corridor. "I know her because I'm the one who first arrested her."

He'd been sent to escort her back after that first long-ago attempt to cross the border; and with that, it had begun. Belov had studied her and contrived her release . . . and for him it had ended with his body face-down in the icy waters of the Neva.

"The best chance would have been to grab her on the way in," the man said. "But it was too late for that. All this business last night was an obvious waste of time; it probably wasn't even her and if it was, she could have had five different rides before daylight. The way I see it now, it's best treated as a problem for Immigration. You say she's got no friends or contacts here so she can't get work, and she can't get money – sooner or later, she's going to surface."

Pavel was nodding.

"So when she does, we'll get in touch. I understand there's a return flight booked for you this afternoon."

For Pavel, it was as if his thoughts had skipped a beat.

"A what?"

"There'll be a ticket waiting at the check-in desk. You've to pick it up and then make yourself known to the check-in supervisor. He'll walk you through the formalities and then he'll sit you somewhere and tell you when it's time to board."

Pavel stared, saying nothing.

The superintendent said, "I think that's all. Why don't you go and get some breakfast? You look as if you need it."

Pavel couldn't get any breakfast, because he still didn't have any English money. He had ten roubles and some change. Other than that, he had the clothes he was wearing.

And they were sending him home without her.

A couple of people got into the lift as he was riding down. They glanced at him curiously. Both of them got out on the restaurant floor, but Pavel carried on down to the entrance lobby.

There was a Dan-Air flight coming in as he crossed the asphalt lot, dropping like a gull with its undercarriage outstretched. He was close enough to hear the skid of rubber on tarmac, and then it was past the building and away out of sight. The grass waved in the morning breeze, the yellow frames of landing lights rising from it at intervals like isolated rigs in a weed-choked sea.

He glanced back. One of the bigger vans made an effective screen at the end of a line of the unmarked pool cars, meaning that he could look them over without being seen from the main building. Two of them were locked, including the vehicle in which he'd spent most of the night cruising. The third was locked as well, but the keys were in the tailpipe.

He sat in the driver's seat to get the feel for a few moments before he started it up. A hell of a car. Armrests, and everything. When he switched on the ignition, he saw that the tank was more than three-quarters full. After resetting the rearview mirror, he turned and looked through the back window toward the entrance to the compound. There was a security booth at the gate and a drop-down barrier, but when he'd arrived the booth had been empty and the barrier had been up. That situation hadn't changed in the past hour.

His first move would be to find the airport's long-stay car park and to switch the plates on his vehicle for those on one of the more recent arrivals. That would give him a week's grace at least, and then he'd do the same thing again in some other place to stay untraceable. He wasn't familiar with the model but he was sure that the car itself would be pretty unremarkable; police vehicles always were.

He reversed out of the parking space, and braked too hard. He was used to heavier controls than this, but an hour's practice would make all the difference. When he'd switched the plates he'd have to give some thought to ways of raising a little cash to live on. He wouldn't need much – he could sleep in the car – but he'd still have to eat and buy fuel. There was no knowing how long this was going to take.

He drove out through the unattended gateway, and joined the morning traffic on the airport perimeter road. He switched on the radio. It was some music he'd never heard before, but he turned it up loud anyway and took a deep breath and settled back into his seat.

THE BOAT HOUSE

She could be anywhere now. Alone, in company, under another name.

But he'd find her.

He was certain of it.

EIGHT

Down at the one-time pavilion that was now the Venetz sisters' lakeside restaurant, Angelica Venetz had decided that it was time for the big old mallard's appointment in duck heaven.

She'd watched him at his breakfast out by the terrace, and he could barely feed himself. She'd wondered briefly about trying to pass the job along to Adele, but knew right away that it wouldn't work out; she was supposed to be the unsentimental one, after all, the hard business-head and the scourge of the tradesmen. The two sisters were both in their fifties, both ex-nurses, neither ever married; they'd taken on the restaurant as a late-life decision when their father had died and left them a shared inheritance. They'd hesitated for almost a year before they'd made the move, finally spurred along by the fact that they'd grown sick of talking about it. The first two years had been the hardest – there was hardly a piece of equipment in the kitchen that didn't have a *hospital property* stamp on it somewhere – but things had grown steadily better since.

You'll be doing him a favour, she'd thought, and so as he wandered past the kitchen on a mid-afternoon stroll she crept up behind him and grabbed him by the neck.

His name was Donald. He squawked and he struggled, but she was stronger. The road accident that had left him lame had also worn him down. He fought and he flapped and made little gurgling noises, but Angelica hung on.

And realised that she wasn't quite sure what she was supposed to do next.

She was hurting Donald, but he wasn't actually *dying* . . . there was some knack to this, and she didn't have it. So much for mercy killing. Her grip began to slacken and he kicked a little harder, perhaps sensing a reprieve, and he managed to turn his head around so that he could look at her. *Why?* his small beady eyes seemed to be saying, *What did I do?*

"You're holding it wrong," a younger woman's voice said.

Angelica looked up, feeling faintly ridiculous. She hadn't planned for a witness, but it seemed that she had one; the woman was over on the iron steps, watching her across the restaurant deck. Donald flapped and fought and struggled, damaged but not done for, and Angelica – not unaware of the absurdity of trying to maintain some kind of formality under such circumstances, said, "Can I help you?"

"Perhaps I can help *you*," the young woman said, and she stepped forward onto the terrace planking. "You're holding it wrong."

"Have you done this kind of thing before?"

The woman gave a brief smile to show that it was no big deal.

"I was raised on a farm," she said, and she took the duck from Angelica and efficiently flipped it upside down and twisted its neck. The bird's flapping became as frantic as a wind-up toy's for a few seconds, but this quickly petered out and its body became limp.

She held it out to Angelica, and said, "For the kitchen?"

"For the dustbin," Angelica corrected. The lake birds appeared to be healthy enough, but they were always scrounging food from the tourists and picking over the debris that washed up on the lake shore. A menu featuring *Canard aux Parasites* wouldn't be much of a crowd-puller for the coming season. The woman handed her what was left of Donald, and Angelica said, "People feed them and they wander into the road . . . it's not surprising they get hurt. I know it has to be done, but it seems I'm no good at it. Would you care for a coffee?"

"I brought no money with me," the woman said.

"Restaurant's closed anyway. This is on the house."

The woman shrugged, smiled, inclined her head – a gesture of polite acceptance in the continental manner, none of the foot-shuffling embarrassment of the local stock at all. Angelica loved the valley people – some of them, anyway – but at times she could find them . . . well, *basic* more or less summarised the idea. Had it not been for seasonal visitors, the list of locally popular dishes would have been depressingly brief; burned steaks, fried fish, and barbe-cued chicken. Preferred background music; anything classical that could be recognised from TV. Major fashion influence; the Kays catalogue.

This woman was clearly different.

Compared to some, she was almost a china doll. She seemed dressed for colder weather, in several layers of woollens and a heavy shawl; dull colours, nothing gaudy, and her hair was pulled back and had been pinned in a clasp. She followed as Angelica led the way toward the kitchen, careful not to hold the dead duck too close. The main part of the building faced the lake, and the half-glassed partition of the western wall could be rolled back in decent weather to allow a dozen or more tables to be set in the open air, right out over the water.

As they were stepping inside, the visitor said, "This is a lovely place."

Angelica, trying to place her accent but not managing it, said, "You should see it when the season gets going, it's madness. Let me take a guess. You're not on holiday."

"No. I live here."

"Since when? I'd better warn you, they've a bush telegraph around here that works faster than the speed of light."

"I haven't been here for very long. I only just arrived."

"That would explain it," Angelica said, pushing open the service door that led through into the kitchen. "So, what do you think of the valley?"

The visitor smiled.

"I plan to stay," she said.

They were hit by the scents of baking and spices, the results of the afternoon's work put in by Adele Venetz. Adele, the younger of the two sisters although some privately reckoned that she looked a little drawn-in and slightly older than Angelica, was wiping down the flour from the big kitchen table as they came through the door.

She fixed a baleful eye on Angelica, and said, "If ever they bring back hanging, I wouldn't advise you to apply for the job."

"You were watching?"

"I was listening. Couldn't help it, the racket you were making. Thank God you got some expert help or we'd have been hearing duck screams in our nightmares forever."

"Just get a move on," Angelica said, "so we can use the table. And say hello to one of our neighbours." She pulled out the kitchen trash hopper, a laundry-basket kind of affair on squeaky castors, and set Donald on his journey to duck heaven by dropping him into the grey plastic liner. "I'm Angelica, this is my sister Adele. All this is our place."

"Ours, and the bank's," Adele put in.

"My name's Alina Peterson," the young woman said.

Angelica switched on the Cona machine and Adele brought an extra chair. They sat around one end of the work table, which now seemed vast and empty, and Alina Peterson explained how she'd walked down to the village to look around and, where it seemed appropriate, to introduce herself. Angelica said that such a gesture would certainly catch the local people off-guard; a new policeman

had been appointed to the area about two years before, and everybody still referred to him as 'that newcomer'.

"You don't think it's such a good idea?" Alina said.

"Well," Angelica said, "I wouldn't want to discourage you. But
I wouldn't say it was necessary, either."

The oven timer buzzed, and Adele moved over to attend to it;
Alina dug around inside her layers and brought out what looked like
a colour postcard. "Well, what do you think of this?" she said, and
slid it across for Angelica to see. "Is that a good idea, or is that not
how they do things, either?"

Angelica took the card and looked at it. The picture side featured
some green-and-white palace, all columns and arched windows and
with a couple of tourist buses parked off to the side. She turned it
over, and read the *situation wanted* ad that Alina had drafted on the
back.

"I didn't make it up," Alina said. "I copied it out, mostly. I know
they show cards like this in one of the stores, I saw it on the way
over here."

Angelica briefly held the card up so that her sister could see it.
She didn't have to say anything more. Adele looked back over her
shoulder, read it through, and then gave a brief shrug as if to say *no
objection*.

Angelica laid the card down, and looked at their visitor.

She said, "Where are you living right now?"

"On the headland to the north, the place I think they call the
Step. I've a temporary room in a house there."

"Anywhere near Pete McCarthy's place?"

"Not too far from him," Alina said.

"I'm not trying to pry, I'm only wondering how far you'd have to
travel," Angelica explained. "You see, we usually take on a couple
of girls locally for when the season picks up. I don't think we've
anything fixed yet. Have you ever done restaurant work?"

"You mean like a cook, or like a waitress?"

"Waiting on, mostly, although you can get all sorts thrown at you.
Of course, it's not the kind of thing that everyone would want to get
involved in . . ."

"Try me for a week," Alina said. "Two weeks, I'll take no money.
You'll see how fast I can learn."

"You want to be careful what you say," Angelica warned her.
"You don't know how much we can throw."

Alina stayed for about twenty minutes longer. They talked mostly
about Three Oaks Bay, its people, its peculiarities. Angelica
reckoned that she was a reasonable judge of people – one could

hardly be a nurse for twenty years without picking up one hell of a lot of insight – and it hadn't taken her long to decide that Alina Peterson was either dead straight or very plausible. Given that she'd nothing in particular to gain, the chances seemed to favour the first of these options. She was bright and she was presentable, which meant that she already scored on two counts over the help that they'd hired last year. Her clothes were neat enough but her shoes were a giveaway, so old and worn under their polish that they almost telegraphed her need; there was a story to be told here, Angelica thought, and Angelica was a sucker for an interesting story.

But Alina hardly talked about herself at all, not at this first meeting. They talked about hours to be worked, they quickly fixed a rate. She said that she was waiting for some of her belongings to be sent on, but she'd supply all her tax and National Insurance details as soon as they came. She said that she could start whenever they needed her; tomorrow, if they wanted.

When they'd covered more or less everything and it was time for her to go, Angelica walked with her to the main door. The empty restaurant lay in linen-and-silver silence behind them as she undid the bolts and opened up to the daylight.

Alina said, "What time should I be here?"

"Say eleven. It doesn't much matter what you wear during the day, but we'll find you something for the evenings."

"You mean a uniform?"

"No, just something plain."

As they moved out onto the entrance steps, they saw a breakdown wagon thundering by and raising up dust in the square. Without warning, it suddenly let out a blast of the first line of *Dixie* on a five-tone airhorn, so loud and so unexpected that it made Alina take a startled step back.

"Ten to one that's young Wayne Hammond," Angelica said. "You'll probably get to meet him. He's a regular."

Alina looked out to where the wagon was already disappearing from sight; and she nodded, barely perceptibly.

"I'll get to know them all," she said.

NINE

Even though he was still only sixteen, Wayne had been driving the yard's vehicles around the quiet back roads in the off-season for the past two years. There was nothing unique in this; it wasn't uncommon in the lanes to find oneself stuck behind a slow-moving tractor with a twelve-year-old in the cab, using public highways to get from one piece of a farm to another. Ross Aldridge, the 'newcomer' policeman, must have been pretty well-briefed by his predecessor, because he restricted himself to friendly off-the-record warnings when the practice occasionally became too obvious. He couldn't really complain too much; not after the time that he'd run his patrol car into a ditch only three weeks into his new appointment, and the Middlemass girl (14) had turned up with a chain and towed him out.

Wayne was driving now as they left the last of the houses behind, following the lake shore for a while until the wooded hillside of the Step rose up and screened it from their sight. Liston Hall was about a mile and a half further on, reached by its own private drive. The gates to this were kept permanently locked but there was a less conspicuous entrance, hardly more than a mud road, amongst the trees a hundred yards along.

They pulled in onto a white gravel forecourt. The place wasn't huge by country house standards – two storeys, twenty-something rooms – but its main entrance was a covered carriage porch with stone pillars and broad steps leading up to the doors. The house wasn't run-down, either, but there were touches here and there betraying the fact that it hadn't been lived in for a couple of years; the windows that weren't shuttered weren't clean, and there were weeds pushing up through the gravel.

"Wayne," Pete said as he opened the wagon's door to get out. "You're already driving without a licence. Don't you think that the Dixie horn's pushing it a bit?"

"I know," Wayne said sadly. "The devil makes me do it."

Pete walked over to the steps. Seen from close-to, the columns were peeling; they were also heavily stained with pigeon crap. It was hard to think of a place like this as somebody's home. It looked more like a public building or a sanatorium. This was mostly a matter of scale; Pete's feeling was that you couldn't own such a place, you could only be owned by it. You could die or go bankrupt and the house would stay basically unchanged, still mouldering slowly and running up a ransom of a heating bill . . . unless you were so fabulously rich that you could afford not to give a shit, in which case all arguments foundered. The latter category could hardly include Dizzy Liston; otherwise, why would he consent to selling off his toys to cover his expenses?

Pete found the bellpush, and pressed.

Nothing seemed to happen, so he pressed again.

Still no response. He glanced over at Wayne, and Wayne pointed helpfully to the Dixie horn.

"Do you want me to . . .?" he said, leaving the offer hanging.

"No," Pete said quickly. "No, thanks. Wait here, I'll check around the back."

There was a brick path down the side of the house, and he followed it. There had to be *somebody* around, although from the state of the path he wouldn't have laid any bets on it being a gardener. The path brought him out into the rest of the grounds.

This was obviously the side of the house that was meant to be considered as the frontage, with its six-foot windows and its first-floor parapet and views over formal gardens. It was, however, as lifeless as the forecourt area.

Well, at least the place had atmosphere. It had something of the look of a decaying Italian *palazzo*, stone urns and all.

"Anybody home?" Pete called out, and then two things happened very close together.

Firstly, a couple of birds were scared up out of a nearby bush by his call; and secondly, there was a detonation so loud that he almost felt it as a physical shockwave. The birds squawked and flapped, and the very top of the bush seemed to be flicked by an invisible hand which knocked a few shreds of leaf out into the air. Pete didn't know whether to duck or run, and the choice was fairly academic anyway, as for the moment his body seemed to be about as responsive as a sack of rocks.

A woman with a shotgun stepped out onto the path some way ahead.

Diane Jackson, the woman he'd come to see.

"Sorry about the bang," she called, much as someone might apologise for slamming a car door too loudly, and she started to walk towards him. "It's the bloody pigeons. They've been driving me mad ever since I moved in, but as soon as I come out with a gun they all disappear. See up there?" She pointed. "Pigeon shit," she went on, without waiting for Pete to reply. "The roof's covered in it. I was going to blast a couple and then string them up to scare the others. Do you think that would work?"

"It would with me," Pete said.

He was pretty sure that she hadn't recognised him.

Well, what could he expect . . .? He'd been no more than another face around the yard on the two or three occasions that she'd been by, no reason that he should have made any lasting impression on her at all. She'd been polite, and he'd been too quick to imagine that it might signify something more. No big deal, it had happened in his life before; but suddenly he was intensely, *intensely* relieved that Wayne had stayed in the van and couldn't see this. And better he should get the hard lesson now, than later.

She breezed on by, presumably expecting him to follow; she was heading for a side-entrance to the house that was reached through an overgrown kitchen garden. At the second attempt, he got himself moving. His ears were still ringing from the gunshot. On the evidence of her marksmanship so far, the safest place to shelter would probably be squarely before the target.

"I tried the bell at the front," Pete said as they went in through a whitewashed scullery. This led into a Victorian-style kitchen with a tiled floor and copper skillets hanging in the middle of the room.

"It doesn't work," Diane Jackson said. "Like most of the estate staff who were supposed to have been keeping the place straight. I seem to be doing nothing but making lists of things that need fixing."

She kicked something in the gloom, and stopped briefly to pick it up. It was a *Speak & Spell*.

"Jed's," she explained. "He's going to be a litterbug when he grows up."

There was more evidence of Jed's presence on the pin-up notice-board alongside the kitchen door. It was covered in paintings and crayon drawings, obviously by a child of pre-school age. The largest and most colourful of them showed a woman with a shotgun, blasting away at Red Indians.

Stopping to look was a mistake. By the time that he'd stepped out of the kitchen and into the main hall, he'd lost her.

The hallway was of a fair size, high-ceilinged and with an oak stairway that led up to a gallery-style balcony. The floor was of black and white marble tile, some of them cracked and none of them even. The few pieces of furniture looked old, solid, and unprepossessing, the kind of stuff that Pete would have expected to see at the bargain end of a market-town auction. The light, as soft and grey as evening snow, came from an ornate wrought-iron skylight at the ceiling's centre.

Her voice led him to her. "I'm not a great shot," she was saying, "but I'm getting better. There's an old clay range up in the woods, and I've been practising on that. I'll turn myself into a countrywoman yet."

She'd gone on into a book-lined room which appeared to be in use as an office, and she was placing the shotgun along with two others in a locking steel cabinet. From the doorway, Pete watched her turn the key on it with a certain relief.

"Now," she said, turning to him. "Shall we go upstairs and get this out of the way?"

"Upstairs?" Pete said.

Diane Jackson was already on her way past him, and heading for the wide stairway.

"I am *desperate*," she admitted. "It's getting so I can't even think, let alone sleep. I've told Dizzy that I want the whole works, and I don't care what it costs him."

"What exactly were you expecting me to do?" Pete said uncertainly.

She stopped on the third step, and looked back at Pete. She looked good in the soft light, he was thinking, but then she had the kind of face that you didn't need to flatter. She looked good in country clothes as well; in fact she looked pretty damned good all round, and right now it was the world's greatest pisser that he was no more than a rough-at-the-edges motor mechanic whose chances with her had to rate at somewhere close to zero.

There was a growing puzzlement in her expression. She said, as if she was seeing the possibility of doubt for the very first time, "You *are* the man from the pest control?"

"No," he said, "I'm the man from the auto-marine. I'm here to do an inventory on your cruiser."

If she'd stung him before then he got his revenge now, and in spades. Her mouth fell open, and she clapped a hand over it. She went pale, and then coloured up red.

And when she could speak again, she said, "I thought you'd come about the pigeons! Oh, God, what must you be thinking?"

He was tempted to tell her.

But he didn't.

Wayne's antennae went onto visible alert when he saw the two of them emerging from the Hall. The ice not so much broken as dynamited and blown out of the water, they were both giggling like kids out of school. Pete went over to the wagon, and as he was taking out the inventory clipboard he explained that they'd be going down to the boat house in Diane's pickup truck.

"Big treat, Wayne," he added. "You get to ride in the back."

"Wow," Wayne said, obviously wishing that he could stay in the front and eavesdrop.

Her Toyota was a big red Hi-Lux with four-wheel drive, much easier for her to manage than the estate's lumbering ex-army Land Rover. As they bumped down the narrow track from the house to the lake shore, Pete asked her exactly what her job entailed.

"Basically it covers just the house and the immediate grounds," she said. "All the woodland's leased to the forestry people. I want to get sorted and ticking by the time that Dizzy and his pals arrive. Sometimes I feel as if I haven't even started."

"What's he like to work for?"

She looked at him, and half-smiled. "You want the truth, or the reputation?"

"I already know the reputation."

"You, and everyone else around here." She returned her attention to the track, just as a couple of low branches took a swipe at the cab roof. "He's fine. A bit self-centred, but nothing like most people seem to think. It was my ex who got me fixed up with the job; Dizzy owed him, and he owed me maintenance for Jed, and I wanted to get away from town and get involved in something where I could start to respect myself again . . . everything kind of fitted into place. Balancing the books has been the toughest part. The Estate income's pretty regular, but it can't handle big bills that all come in at once. So if the furnace needs an overhaul and Dizzy wants to throw a party for the locals to improve his image, then Dizzy's Princess might just have to go."

"The party idea's for real, then?"

"So he tells me."

Most people in Three Oaks Bay were awaiting Dizzy Liston's return with mixed feelings; mainly apprehension, mixed with trepidation. Rumours of a social evening at the Hall with the entire village being invited hadn't exactly dispelled all worry, since it was his summer parties that had made him so unpopular around the area in the first place. Free booze for the locals was all very well, but what would happen when the famous charmer got too well-oiled and started to proposition all the schoolgirls?

But when Pete mentioned this – in rather more diplomatic terms – Diane said, "That's the point, he can't. He can't drink for six whole months, that's why he has to get himself away from town and temptation and live out in the country. Otherwise he's been told that he won't even be able to sell his liver for cat food. It's perfect."

And with that thought in mind, they reached the boat house.

TEN

The boat house resembled a small chapel built into the sloping land that led down to the water's edge, except that it was windowless and the bell in the tower no longer rang. No lights came on when they tried the switch just inside the heavy oak door, but a minute's search with a flashlight found the main fusebox further in along the wall. Throwing the contact-breaker caused the overhead lights to flare briefly, and a well-aimed thump on the side of the box made them come back up. This time, they stayed on.

"High tech," said Pete.

"Another job for the list," Diane said gloomily.

They were standing on rough wooden boards. These extended like a hayloft about one-third of the way into the building. Beyond the rail, reached by a stairway so steep that it was almost a ladder, was the main lower level.

"There it is," Diane said as they moved to the rail. "Just don't ask me anything technical about it, that's all."

The lighting was from downward-angled spotlights on the roof grid that gave the place an odd, studio-like atmosphere. Pete and Wayne looked down, and saw a sleeping princess.

It was actually a Princess 414, more than forty feet of white GRP hull with blue flashes and waterline markings. It had been run nose-first into the boat house where it lay like a huge, sleek beast in an undersized pen, the deep V of the forward end tucked under the gallery on which the three of them were standing.

Pete held out the clipboard. "Do your stuff, Wayne," he said.

After a moment's blankness Wayne took the board, and the hint that came with it. He slid down the stairway in one easy jump and hopped from the quay to the cruiser's deck, and within a minute he'd located the power switches and was down below, checking through the fittings.

Pete and Diane stayed at the rail.

Diane said, "What will happen after this?"

"Well, we'll get a list of everything on board plus the age of the

58

boat, condition, everything like that. Then Ted can work out a market price and phone it through to you in a day or so. If you like what you hear, we'll put it in the yard and advertise it and take a commission on the sale. If you don't, there are other good yards you can try. But Ted's okay. He's dead straight."

"I know," she said, "I've met him. In fact, that's where I first saw you."

"You remember? I was pretty sure you didn't."

"Mind on other things. You'll have to forgive me."

"I'll think about it," he said.

Diane glanced at the cruiser, and lowered her voice in case Wayne should be able to hear. "Is that Ted Hammond's boy?" she said.

"His name's Wayne. There's another one, an older boy called Shaun. I never met him, he works abroad somewhere. I don't think they ever got along. Wayne's as good as you'll get, though."

"Didn't Ted's wife die young?"

"You heard about that?"

"Talk about gossip around here . . . you couldn't get the news faster with a satellite dish. I heard stuff about you, too."

"Really?" Pete said, suddenly getting extremely interested. "Like what?"

"I'm not telling you," Diane said.

And then Wayne climbed out onto the cruiser's deck, and they let the subject drop, and Wayne was left standing there glancing from one to the other, damned sure that something was going on here, and equally damned if he could tell what it was.

Pete gave another look over the Princess, and wondered what Ted would have thought of the berthing arrangements had he been here to see them. It had been such a tight squeeze to get the Princess into the boat house at all, that someone had come up with the bright idea of removing the edge boards from the quay platforms on either side. This had given a couple of extra feet of clearance, but it had also left the steel ends of the support joists exposed. They'd been muffled with rags and pieces of tyre, but it was still a lash-up. The Princess deserved better; a high-performance seagoing cruiser, it would be wasted on such a sedate stretch of inland water as the lake beyond the boat house doors. But what could anyone expect? Dizzy Liston had won the cruiser on a bet, or so the story went. It was hardly going to be any great wrench to part with something that had been picked up so casually.

"All okay?" Pete called, and Wayne signalled that it was. So Pete and Diane left the rail and stepped out of the boat house into the mild spring air to wait for him.

"What are they saying about me?" he said, but she stayed tight-lipped and shook her head. Probably nothing, he was thinking, she's only winding me up, and the thought that she was gave him a pleasurable kick.

Wayne handed the clipboard to Pete, and then locked the boat house doors behind him.

Pete said, "Any problems?"

"No, massah," Wayne said, and then he turned to Diane. "Will you want us to hang onto the keys?"

"You may as well. No one else ever comes here, and you'll need them before I will."

"Okay," Wayne said, and he stuck the bunch into his jeans pocket.

The beeper alarm on Diane's watch sounded as they were driving back, the signal that it was time for her to go and collect the litterbug Jed from his minder. This meant a quick goodbye at the Hall, and an instant disappearance from Diane. Pete stood with the clipboard under his arm and his hands in his pockets, watching the dust behind her Toyota as she sped off down the service road.

There was no longer any sign of her when, with Wayne once more behind the wheel, the breakdown wagon re-emerged into the outside world in Diane's wake. Pete had arranged himself in the passenger seat so that he could get his feet up on the dashboard. Wayne said nothing for a while, and Pete allowed his attention to wander down the inventory list; his eyebrows raised at the mention of a waterbed, a hi-fi system and a video hookup in the after stateroom. None of these was Marine Projects standard, and he couldn't help wondering what kind of water sports the original owner might have gone in for.

Just before they got to the village, Wayne cracked his silence. Pete had known that it was coming – the only question had been, when?

"She actually fancies you," Wayne said, almost unable to believe it.

"Of course she does," Pete said. "I'm a wonderful specimen of a man."

Wayne glanced at him, less than one hundred per cent certain that he wasn't being sent up.

He said, "She's all right, as well."

No response to this from Pete.

"A bit old, though," Wayne ventured again, and Pete slowly turned to give him a stony look.

"Just drive," he said.

ELEVEN

It was dusk when Pete finally made it back up the track to the old wooden cottage. He switched on the Zodiac's headlights, for the shadows. The damaged one was still working, although it was a little way out of alignment. The rest of the afternoon had been more or less normal for the time of year except that Ted had been following Pete around for most of it, trying to pump him for details of what had happened between him and Diane Jackson. He'd been exactly the same once before when he'd found out that Pete had seen *Last Tango in Paris* ("Yeah, but what did they actually *do*?") and now, as then, Pete had taken care to fine-tune Ted's frustration to the point of obsession.

Finally, as Pete had been opening out the canvas deck cover on a relaunched Fairline Fury while Ted paced the dock alongside, he'd looked up at his employer and said, "You really want to know?"

"I really want to know."

So then Pete had told him, truthfully, word-for-word and without any embellishment; about the shotgun, and the pigeons, and the misunderstanding on the stairs. And when he'd finished, Ted had stared at him for a moment in open disbelief.

"Oh, piss off," he'd said finally, which was exactly the reaction that Pete had been expecting.

Now it was getting late.

He pulled in onto the rough ground before the house, switched off the engine, and got out. Sometimes he remembered to lock the car behind him, sometimes he didn't, and sometimes he remembered but couldn't be bothered. In all the time that he'd been living out on the Step Pete had seen only one stranger go by, and that was a hiker who'd stopped to ask the way because he'd been lost. The Zodiac was no big attraction to a thief, anyway. Most of the time he'd nothing more serious to worry about than squirrel shit on the seats if ever he left the windows open.

When he stepped up onto his porch, he saw that the front door was ajar. The windows to either side had been thrown wide as well, and the ends of the tattered old curtains had blown out to hang over the sills. It looked as if somebody had been giving the place a pretty thorough airing, and it wasn't too hard to guess who. He went inside and the kitchen scents hit him then, laying down a trail that drew him across the creaking boards and down the hall.

He paused for long enough to throw his jacket onto one of the hallway hooks, and called out, "It's me."

"Through here," Alina called from the back of the house.

He went through.

The first thing that he noticed was that the lights were out and that she'd set up candles from his emergency supply in one of the kitchen cupboards. They were on the dusty painted dresser, on the shelves, and on a tin tray before a freckled old mirror that had been hanging in the bathroom. The big pine table in the middle of the floor had been set for dinner, and on it stood a bottle of cheap wine from the village store. Pete picked it up, looked at the label, and then set it down again; and as he was doing this, Alina appeared in the doorway.

Her eyes shone in the warm tallow light.

Pete felt a stirring of apprehension then, rising like a deepwater fish to the sunlight; and although he tried not to let it show, Alina seemed to perceive it.

"Wait," she said, moving into the room. "Wait, I know what you're thinking."

"I'm not thinking anything."

She stood before him, looking up into his eyes. "Yes, you are," she said. "Look, I'm not about to invade your life. But I like this place, Peter, I like this valley. Today I got a job."

"What kind of a job?"

"A waitress job." She gestured at the table. "So, don't get the wrong idea about all this . . . tonight I get to practise on you, so tomorrow I don't look so stupid."

"A *waitress* job?" Pete said. Was this girl a fast operator, or what? She saw his expression, and grinned.

"I know," she said, "I'm shameless. You wouldn't believe what I had to do to get an introduction to the sisters. But now I'll meet more people, I'll begin to feel at home. And then as soon as I can find somewhere else, I'll move out and leave you alone. I'm nobody's charity case, and I won't be a burden to you. You've been good to me, Peter, I wouldn't want to see you hurt by having me around."

"Really, it's all right," Pete protested.

But there was a sadness in Alina's eyes now, unlike anything that he'd seen there before; a sadness not for what had been, but for what could never be.

"No," she said. "It isn't all right."

And then she turned away, and went over to check on the stove.

She was, almost without exception, the worst cook that Pete had ever come across. Worse even than Ted Hammond, who'd once closed the yard for three days with the after-effects of a home-made chili. This meal was a haphazard trawl of the village store's shelves, an unappealing source of supply at the best of times; Pete realised with a sinking feeling that he'd no choice other than to put his head down and plough on through like a pig at the trough. Alina seemed to think that everything was fine.

The alphabet pasta, that floated in a sauce of over-thickened packet soup.

The frozen peas, that she'd fried.

The . . .

Oh, God, he didn't even want to think about it.

Fortunately, the conversation was better. There seemed to be a sense of ease in their company that hadn't existed the night before, and she opened up a little on her background. She'd been a school-teacher once, she told him. She'd lived in Leningrad for ten years but she'd had no work for the last two of them. Her father was dead but her mother was still alive, and had managed to hang onto the old apartment where she now used the extra space to accommodate short-stay workers who needed a bed in the city. As soon as she could, Alina planned to write to her.

He asked her about the place so much like the valley, the place where she'd been born. She said, "They moved everyone. Nobody lives there now."

It was weird. They could speak the same language, but there was almost nothing else in their past that they'd shared. She'd read Shakespeare, Pete hadn't; not unless you counted *Julius Caesar* at school, which he'd managed to get through with a lot of patience and a set of Coles' Notes. Alina, on the other hand, had never even *heard* of James Herbert.

One thing that he noticed; every now and again she'd glance at the uncurtained window, as if she was checking the progress of the oncoming darkness. Perhaps she was edgy about something, Pete wondered; but if she was, she kept it well-concealed.

Finally, the conversation came back around to the subject of Alina's new job.

She told him that as soon as she had some money she wanted to buy some decent clothes, the kind that she could wear to her work in the evenings. Pete, thinking of the Venetz sisters' reputation for efficiency and attention to detail, asked her if she'd hit any problems over having no social security records or documentation; she currently had the status of an illegal immigrant, after all, and had even dumped her hot French passport as she'd walked out of the air terminal. Alina said, no, no problems . . . and then amended this to well, not yet. Pete suggested that in a few days' time he could take her out to the nearest big town on the coast, and there she could look for clothes in the department stores and check out the library for the addresses of any useful organisations or people to contact. The sooner she made a move to get some kind of official recognition, the better. She said that this sounded fine. But he wondered if he'd convinced her.

"That *is* what you want?" he said.

"Of course."

Pete was now beginning to wonder if she was feeling ill; it was almost as if, for the latter part of the evening, she'd only been keeping up a show of enjoying herself and now the strain of the charade was getting through to her.

Or maybe it was the food. That wouldn't have surprised him at all.

He asked her if she was all right and she said, "I'm fine," but it was with a weak smile and her eyes barely focusing on him. "I think I'm just tired." And then she glanced at the window; the darkness outside was complete.

"You go on," Pete said. "I'll clear away."

But Alina got to her feet, causing the candles immediately around her to dip as if in sudden fear. Some of them had burned low, and didn't recover.

"No," she said. "I think I'll take a walk."

"But it's late."

"I know. But I like to walk at night. It helps me to think. Don't worry, I lived in the country before, I know what I'm doing."

"At least take a torch."

"There's a moon. That's all I'll need. Don't wait for me."

The moon was hardly more than a pale sliver, and surely not enough to see by. Pete stood on the porch and tried to make Alina out as she climbed the path toward the highest part of the headland. From there she'd be able to go down to the lakeside if she chose, or else pick up one of the shore paths that would take her further into the valley.

It bothered him to let her go like this, but she'd insisted; for a while he couldn't see her at all, until she reached the skyline and stopped for a moment.

65

The silence of the valley was like the stillness that sometimes follows a hard rain. Somewhere far off a dog barked, one small sound in a vast and empty theatre.

Alina kicked off her shoes and then went on, descending from sight.

TWELVE

Sometimes it was hard for Gazzer to believe how stupid some people could be.

Take this one, for example; walking along the canal towpath at this late hour of the night, as if it was the park on a pleasant Sunday afternoon and life held no dangers for him at all. The canal route was dark and it was deep and it was a secret vein that ran through the heart of the city, and only the scum dropped down here after hours and expected to survive. Up at street level, on the other side of a high wall, the town centre traffic moved and the neon club lights flickered and police vans stood on street corners waiting for trouble to start. But even the police didn't come down here. Only tramps and serious drunks, and occasionally Toms seeking out shadows in which to do business when the client didn't have a car, and people like Gazzer who didn't give a shit. Gazzer was twenty-two years old and had been compared in looks to a pit bull, entirely to the dog's advantage. He wore a T-shirt regardless of the season of the year and kept his hair cropped short enough to reveal the half-dozen tiny scars on his head where the stubble wouldn't grow. Gazzer had been seriously disappointed in love on this night. His mates had all scored and he inexplicably hadn't, in spite of the money he'd blown on all those lime-green cocktails for the bleached slag in the dress with all the red spangles. It was clear that she'd been taking him for a ride, in that there was no ride in it for him at the end of the process. When the evening had ended she'd disappeared into the pub toilet and from there she'd disappeared, full stop.

Gazzer was not only pissed off, he was seriously out of pocket. He didn't mind spending the money if it brought a result, but something like this put the whole world out of balance. Never one to wallow in self-pity, he'd started by mugging a couple of Indian kids in bright shirts behind the bus station and then he'd followed a Yuppie type from his bank's Cashcard machine to the stairway of a multi-storey car park, where they'd had some dealings involving a Rolex and all the wad in the Yuppie's wallet. After that he'd come down and hopped through a hole in the fence where the canal ran alongside some waste ground, and now he was staying off the streets as he made his way across town and toward home ground. The Indian kids wouldn't matter, but the Yuppie type might get half an hour in the back of a police car checking the pavements and the pub car parks for some sign of his attacker.

Now this. A bonus. An innocent who'd somehow wandered down into the rat run, just asking to get bitten. Gazzer only had to stand in the middle of the towpath and wait as the man approached him. There was nowhere else for the man to go other than back, or into the canal itself.

There were yellow sodium lights down here, but most of them had been broken by kids throwing stones. Odd survivors burned like overhead beacons; there was one under the bridge just ahead, and another one about a hundred yards beyond. They showed the narrow dirt towpath, the black water, the broken windows of empty warehouses . . .

And the silhouette of the stranger, still walking toward him.

Gazzer flexed his fingers. They cracked like static.

The stranger stopped.

"I'd like to pass, please," he said, and Gazzer's heart soared. A foreigner. He need have no trace of conscience at all.

"Only when I get your money and your watch, fuckface," he said.

"I need money myself," the stranger said pleasantly. "May I see your knife?"

"I don't need a knife," Gazzer said, and he took a step forward to close the gap between them.

Something went wrong.

Gazzer aimed his headbutt, and the stranger moved; he tilted his own head and Gazzer's brains exploded.

That was what it felt like, anyway. Gazzer's legs went and he sat down heavily in the dirt, his nose smashed and his eyes full of tears. The stranger stood over him. He was rubbing the top of his skull just at the hairline, but seemed otherwise unaffected.

Gazzer started to rise. But the stranger reached down and took hold of his nose.

"I wouldn't," he said, as he twisted the broken cartilage and Gazzer's brains went nuclear. His arms flapped in panic, and he screamed. The scream echoed in the depths of the brick canyon.

"The bone can work its way in, you see," the stranger explained as he knelt and checked Gazzer's pockets with his free hand. Gazzer felt the roll of notes being removed from his jeans, but only as some distant background sensation. He reached for the stranger, but the stranger gave his nose another warning tug.

He screamed again.

"I've been down here half the night, waiting for someone like you," the stranger said. "You can keep your watch, I already have one of my own. But I really do need the money."

Gazzer blinked away the tears, and looked into the stranger's face. He was fair, he was young, he was nothing special; but with rare insight, Gazzer saw beyond all of that.

He knew that this was no accidental encounter. He knew that he'd fallen for bait like a fool. And he knew with certainty that the stranger would be capable of doing anything that he threatened.

Anything.

The man released his nose, and straightened.

"Thank you," he said pleasantly.

Gazzer coughed, and spat blood in a terrifying wad.

But the stranger had already turned and walked off into the night, back along the towpath in the direction from which he'd come.

THIRTEEN

Angelica Venetz stands at the rail of the restaurant's terrace. She's watching Walter Hardy – seventy years old, and still the Bay's most reliable handyman – as he moves out with waders and a boathook to take a look under the terrace's decking. Walter is small, thickset, and white-whiskered; he does everything with patient slowness and, once started, he's impossible to stop.

"Is there a problem?" a voice from behind Angelica says, and she turns in surprise. She hasn't heard Alina walking across the terrace, and hasn't even been expecting her for another half-hour. Alina stands there, her hands in her overcoat pockets, hair tied back and ready for business. She's been with them now for just over a month, and Angelica has never known a worker like her.

"You can bet there's a problem," she says. "Something's stuck under the terrace, and it's drawing the flies."

"What is it?"

"That's what we're going to find out."

Walter, down below them and with the waters getting perilously close to the tops of his waders, says, "Something's rotten under here. You been burying the people you've poisoned?"

"Go on, Walter," Angelica says. "You know perfectly well we put them in the curry."

"Buryin' 'em at sea," Walter persists, and he lifts the boathook and starts to stir around in the darkness beyond the terrace's supporting pillars. The boathook is usually kept on the wall behind the bar. It's a relic from the building's yacht pavilion days, and was originally used for hauling drunks out of the water. Now it catches on something, and Walter's round face tightens with the effort of pulling it free.

"Something there," he says, and he plunges the hook in again, this time with the intention of getting a secure hold so that he can heave out whatever it is into sight. If he can't, Angelica's thinking, it's probably going to mean the expense of having a part of the terrace decking taken up and relaid.

Alina leans on the rail beside Angelica, both of them looking down at Walter as he makes another thrust into the darkness beneath them. Angelica's thinking that a bag of garbage has probably been carried along on the night swell and has become caught up amongst the pillars and the metal cross-ties; there will always be somebody who'll think that a couple of heavy stones and a drop out over the deepest part of the lake are an adequate way of disposing of all their empty cans and peelings and plate-scrapings.

Now the gulls are starting to circle, taking a big interest. Definitely a bag of garbage, Angelica is thinking.

Walter's managed to get the hold that he needs, but now he's tugging and nothing's happening. He calmly changes his grip, and tries again.

"Come on, Walter," Angelica says. "Put me back in business."

She wouldn't have believed that he could move so fast as, with a rushing like that of fluid from a punctured sac, the rotten body comes slithering out in a wave of its own juices. The boathook is planted deep in its belly, a grotesque fifth limb that rears up into the air as it turns over.

Not a bag of garbage, then. Not unless you're really prepared to stretch the definition.

Finding it difficult to believe how controlled she's being, Angelica says, "Alina, the police constable's car is just across the square. Can you go and get him for me?"

But there's no reply.

Alina is no longer on the terrace.

FOURTEEN

The dead dog under the restaurant deck was to be a talking-point for a couple of days, and then interest would shift elsewhere. Walter Hardy used the boathook to push it into the shallows, and then went off to borrow a small motor cruiser so that he'd be able to tow the carcase out to one of the marshy islands further down the lake. Here it could be wedged among the reeds, and would eventually be picked clean. For now the dog lay there, skinless like a rabbit and bloated with decay, awaiting his return. Angelica tried to avoid looking at it, but like the village children who gathered on the bank she found herself almost fascinated. Apart from some of its bones showing, it could have been some alien kind of embryo.

"It was probably hit on the road and then somebody threw it into the lake," Ross Aldridge, the young constable, told her. He was fair and quite softly-spoken and actually a little shy-looking, and he'd made a point of taking off his uniform cap when he talked to her. "Or else it just died of old age and the owners dumped it. I'll mark it down as a stray."

"So," Angelica said, "nobody's lost a dog around here?"

"If they have, they didn't report it. Without a collar, that's as far as we can go."

Needless to say, the boathook didn't go back to its place on the restaurant's wall. The planking was washed down with Jeyes fluid, and the deck was reopened to take advantage of the increasingly fine weather.

And towards the end of that week, Pete walked over from the yard to see for himself how Alina was doing.

Alina was serving morning coffee on the terrace. She was wearing what appeared to be a borrowed jacket in place of her own heavy overcoat and shawl, something light enough to allow her to carry on even though the sun might go behind a cloud every now and again. Down at the far end of the valley, there was still snow on the upper slopes of the mountains; they looked as if they'd been sugar-dusted, with stone walls showing like fine, black veins above the treeline.

Against this backdrop, the small Russian girl stood out on her open-air stage and put all of her concentration into learning the role of a waitress.

Right now, she was clearing an empty table. From where she was standing, she wouldn't see him. She was backlit by the late morning sun, the diamond greys and blues of the lake and mountains behind her. She was beautiful, serene, a vision by a Dutch master – and, by the terms of their agreement, completely out of his reach.

The thought disturbed him.

He'd nothing to say to her; he didn't even plan to tell her that he'd been to see her. So why, exactly, he now found himself wondering, had he come out to look at her like this?

Nothing came.

He had no ready answer.

And so, feeling faintly and inexplicably troubled, he turned to head back to the yard.

FIFTEEN

"So where does she go every night?" Wayne said as the two of them sat in the empty hull of a partly-restored cruiser on the Saturday morning, but Pete could only shrug.

Wayne knew about Alina. Pete's guess was that everybody in the valley knew something about her by now, and nearly all of them would know that she was staying in his house. Nobody apart from Wayne had mentioned it to him, though, which probably meant that while their mouths were shut their minds would be running in overdrive. Well, they'd had a few weeks of mystery, of secrets kept and of wrong conclusions avoided. His hope had been that she might have moved on before the word got around, no chance for gossip and so no awkwardness, but his sense of firm control in that area seemed to have slipped away from him. It wasn't that he minded her presence; and he didn't mind her company, on those occasions when he actually spent time with her.

He simply wished that he didn't have to contend with the unspoken supposition that the two of them were hiding up there on the Step and banging away like a couple of baboons, which he saw in the eyes of more than one person who wished him good morning when he went into town to pick up his mail.

The truth of it was that he was even less certain of her now than he'd been at the beginning; how she thought, the way she might react as the world around her changed. It seemed to be something beyond language, beyond culture; it was a more profound sense of the alien, of their lives as separate rivers with uncrossable ground in between. He could hardly begin to imagine what it must be like for her – everything severed, no turning back, the entire texture of her life abandoned for the deep terror of the new. Little wonder that her scrapbook of photographs appeared to be her dearest possession, or that she prowled the landscape at night like an unquiet spirit. Two evenings back Pete had found his front door open to the darkness, and the porch light on; rain had been falling outside in a continuous silver curtain and in the sheltered area at the top of the steps, Alina's shoes had lain discarded. If there had been a moon that night, the clouds had been keeping it hidden.

"I don't know for sure where she goes," he admitted to Wayne. "I don't even know when she sleeps."

"And she's going to the big party on Saturday?"

"So she says. You bringing Sandy?"

"If it works out." Wayne made his "desolate-and-misunderstood" face. "Her mother's having another Wayne-hating week." And then he glanced at Pete. "Nothing compared to your problems, though, is it?"

"What do you mean?"

"Well, two women on a string, and at your age."

"I haven't got anybody on a string. Alina's just a guest in the house, she's not a personal masseuse."

And Diane Jackson? Well, Pete decided to say nothing on that subject. Back at the village post office he'd sorted out the usual junk mail which never made it past the door of the shop and found that he was left with one real, honest-to-God letter. He'd opened the envelope and a piece of white card had slid out.

It was a formal invitation for the big party at the Hall; not a specially-printed card, but the kind sold over the stationery counter with spaces for the date and the names to be handwritten in. This one was a joint invitation; alongside Pete's name was that of Alina Peterson, the Russian girl's newly-adopted identity.

The handwriting, he could only assume, was that of Diane Jackson.

Damn, he'd thought.

Diane always tried to keep her weekends for spending with Jed, but because of the rain they had to spend the early part of the day in their own below-stairs lounge, watching the Saturday morning cartoons on television. She'd hoped to be able to take him out, perhaps for a longish walk through the forest where they could hope for a glimpse of a deer, but at its heaviest the downpour would have called for wetsuits rather than waterproofs. And he seemed happy enough.

Jed was coming up to five years old, very bright but also very quiet . . . so quiet that she worried sometimes, wondering if there were things wrong that he wasn't telling her. He was small for his age, dark, large-eyed – in fact he seemed to be all Diane and almost nothing of his father. About twice a day, she'd ask herself whether this move had been right for him. Jed had watched his parents' marriage break up and had never said a word; he was hardly likely to start making his feelings known now.

So she watched him closely, and she tried to read the signs, and when he seemed to be wanting something special she did her best to see that he got it. Jed's idea of doing something special was to be allowed to help her out on the estate, almost as if he was afraid that he'd find himself abandoned if he didn't make himself useful. Diane told herself that this was just a kind of paranoia on her part, an over-apprehension that came from reading too many doctor articles in women's magazines, but it didn't make her any less uneasy.

But what could she expect? She'd taken him from the town and the friends that he knew and she'd brought him to this great, dusty mausoleum of a place where he didn't even like to run around because the echo of his footsteps sounded too much like someone faceless who was following too close. He spent two-thirds of his day at a school ten miles away, and the rest of the afternoon looking through the older children's comics at Mrs Neary's until Diane picked him up at five. Aimless and with no company, what kind of a life was that?

Too much like her own, she was beginning to suspect.

By negotiation when the rain had stopped, the proposed deer-spotting walk became a combined walk and trap shoot. Jed liked to pull the lever which fired the clays into the air while Diane would blast away and try to improve her shooting. It took him both hands and all his weight, but at least it was exercise. They loaded the launcher and a box of black clays into the back of the Toyota, and drove up an old gated track to the little-used range.

The range was a clearing in the forest with some open sky beyond, along with a couple of huts and an open frame for the would-be marksman to stand. They brought out the launcher and fastened it to its base, and Diane spread out some plastic sheet for Jed and weighted it with the box of clays. She'd wrapped him up so well against the weather that he could hardly be seen in the middle of all his clothing. Around them was the silence of the dense conifer wood, a moment of stillness held forever in time while the rest of the world moved on outside.

Jed did everything by the book, sounding the warning horn before every pull and staying well clear of Diane and the gun. The launched clays zipped across the window of sky, and Diane followed each with a two-foot lead before squeezing the trigger.

And then, if everything ran true to form, the undamaged clays would sail down to a landing somewhere out of sight.

Diane scored five hits out of twenty, which was the limit that she'd set herself because of the cost of the cartridges. Afterwards they went scouting for clays that could be re-used; some cracked on landing, but others had come down whole. Diane carried the box, and Jed filled it. The trees around them stood tall and straight, like a phantom army. The ground sloped, strewn with fine moss and bark so soft and spongy that their footprints took minutes to disappear. The earth had been churned up black where forestry vehicles had passed through during the week, and there were cut and trimmed logs waiting for collection alongside the track.

"It's raining again," Jed said, looking up at the sky.

"Must be coming our way," Diane said. "We'd better hurry."

The rain put an end to their chances of a walk – not that they'd have been likely to spot a deer anyway, after the noise made by the horn and the gun. They drove back to the Hall, and Diane grilled a beefburger for Jed and put it on a bun. He insisted on tackling it with a knife and fork. Diane sat on the opposite side of the refectory table, watching him, chin in hand, as someone with nothing better to do might watch somebody mending a clock.

"You might as well pick it up," Diane said at last. "You're getting it everywhere."

"No," Jed said, with some determination as he attacked the bun from the other side.

"It's allowed, picking a beefburger up."

"No."

There was silence for a while as Jed ploughed on. And then Diane said, "So how's the school?"

"All right."

"Only all right?"

"The games are all strange. Everybody keeps *touching* everybody." He made a yuck-face, and then carried on.

Diane gave a slight, wry smile, and looked at the rain on the window.

It was still raining steadily when she'd put him to bed, after a last half-hour of television and a couple of chapters of *Stig of the Dump*. She stood at the beaded glass and looked out into the gathering darkness.

And, without really meaning to, she found herself wondering what Pete McCarthy might be doing.

Probably having big fun with that Russian waitress.

Damn, she thought.

SIXTEEN

He was in the bathroom that night when he heard her go. He was waiting for a couple of soluble aspirin to break up in a glass of water as he stood before the opened mirror-cabinet. He looked up sharply at the sound of the door – *Again?* he thought disbelievingly, and he winced as the movement aggravated the mild headache that he'd brought home with him.

He listened for a while, and the silence of the house told him yes, again. Still carrying the glass, he went out into the hallway.

This time she'd closed the door behind her. He opened it, and looked out. She'd gone. Tonight there was a moon, starlight even, and he knew that after a few minutes away from the house it would be possible for her to see with surprising clarity; but moon or no moon, it seemed to make little difference to her and she'd been spending hours abroad at even the deepest, darkest point in the cycle.

This was the part that troubled him, that he found difficult to understand. He could remember how, after moving out here and having been a city-dweller all of his life, he'd come to realise that he'd never known what true darkness was; even away from houses and street lighting there had always been a faint, reflected amber cast to the sky, but here there was nothing. He could remember the first time that he'd stepped outside into country darkness and closed the door behind him; it was as if he'd been struck blind with the click of the latch, and he'd begun to panic at his inability even to tell which way was up.

Alina said she'd been raised in the country. Maybe that was it, you grew up with a knack that you otherwise couldn't acquire, like the owls and the bats and the creatures of the lake. She had it, he didn't. Could it be that what he was feeling was a kind of envy, in the sense that he'd brought her here, to a place that he felt he'd made his own, and in a matter of weeks she'd already grown closer to it than he could ever hope to be?

No, he tried to tell himself, that wasn't it; nothing so mean, nothing so unreasonable. Even though he was looking forward to the day when she moved on, he was already beginning to sense that her leaving would be something of a wrench. As they'd agreed, there was nothing between them . . . but he knew that he'd miss her.

Without even realising that he'd moved, he found himself standing by the door to her room.

He put his hand on the handle.

Hesitated a while longer.

Took a sip of the aspirin.

And then, with a guilty look over his shoulder, he opened her door and stepped inside.

She kept the room neat, her bed made and her work-clothes carefully preserved on a hanger on the front of the wardrobe. Her party dress was alongside, bagged in polythene to protect it from dust. Over on the dressing-table, one of her notebooks lay alongside the photograph album. He went across to it, still thinking that it wasn't too late to back out and close the door behind him and pretend that he'd never even been in here.

But instead, he opened the book of photographs.

The pictures were strange. Not all of them, but some. A number were of the same place, some old village with nobody in it, the first a shot down a dusty road and the rest of individual buildings or, in some cases, of open fields enclosed by split-rail fencing. The houses were all of dilapidated wood, with the tallest building a spired church right in the middle of everything. Fir trees grew in amongst the roofs, and weeds and flowers grew everywhere else. The village stood next to a lake.

A fast flick through some of the other pages showed images of a more easily recognisable kind – strange faces, old friends, scenes from a life. He closed the album carefully, making sure that none of the loosened pages could fall out and give him away.

Then, quietly, he left the room.

SEVENTEEN

It was midway through a Friday afternoon, and Adele Venetz had
taken the restaurant's van to the cash-and-carry for all the last-minute
supplies they'd be needing for Saturday's party catering job, leaving
her sister and Alina to manage the business alone. It was quite a
drive and quite a list for when she got there, so she was unlikely to
be back before the early evening; but this was no great problem,
because they'd soon be closing the doors so that they could make a
start on the next day's preparations. It had been a quiet afternoon
so far, and it showed no signs of picking up. A few day-trippers and
walkers had stopped by, but almost no locals at all.

When the outside deck stood empty and all the tables had been
cleared and reset and there still wasn't a prospect of any trade in
sight, Angelica said to Alina, "Come on, let's take a break," and
they headed into the kitchen.

Alina mostly took her breaks alone; she'd sit in a corner with a
magazine, usually one of Adele's old wildlife partworks, and be
about as obtrusive as a church mouse until her time was over. At
which point she'd stand, lay the magazine aside, and get straight
back to business. When they did converse, she said little and mostly
listened; it had only recently struck Angelica that she knew almost
nothing more about Alina now than she had at the end of that first
day.

And, as for the reason *why* it had struck her . . .

"I had to make a guess this morning," she told Alina, glancing
back over her shoulder from the Cona machine as she waited
for the water to run down through the filter. "I hope I guessed
right."

"What do you mean?" Alina said, warily. She'd moved over by
the window and had been reaching for a chair, but now she stopped.
She wasn't sure where Angelica was leading, and so Angelica went
straight to it.

"Whenever we employ somebody, there are formalities we have
to go through. Tax. National Insurance. It can get complicated."

"I'm sure it can."

80

"Especially," Angelica said, "when you're trying to make out a form for somebody whom you know won't appear anywhere in the records."

She glanced over her shoulder again.

Slowly, Alina closed her eyes. Her face was as blank as a porcelain mask. She lowered her head, as if to look at the floor.

Angelica went on, "I'm right, aren't I?"

Alina nodded.

"Want to tell me about it?"

"Sing for my supper," Alina said with a kind of bitter weariness that ran completely against Angelica's perception of her character. It stung her to a sharp reply.

"Nothing of the kind," she said, the coffee forgotten as she turned to face her. "It's just possible that I may be able to help you."

Still guarded, as if the real centre of her personality stood behind glass and in silence, Alina said, "What do you want to know?"

"You might start by trusting me. I think I've earned it. Begin at the beginning."

Alina looked at her for a while. It was as if she was deciding. And then she shrugged. What had she got to lose, she seemed to be saying, now that it had come to this?

She folded her arms, and leaned back to rest against the work surface behind her. "I was never a waitress before I came here," she said. Her gaze was level, a challenge to disbelief. "I've told you that already."

"I know, you've learned fast. What were you before?"

"I was a schoolteacher. This was at the language school in Leningrad, with all the lessons in English. It was a good job, a *very* good job, but I lost it."

"How?"

"I never knew. It was one of those mad things where you don't know if you've done something wrong and no one will ever tell you. What happened was, one of my students wrote something in an examination essay and it got me fired. I never found out what. I never got a chance to defend myself and I wouldn't have known the right thing to say if I had. I couldn't get another job. After a while I started to get official letters threatening to send me to prison if I didn't find work. I lost my flat, and I had to move in with friends. I was living off my car savings for a while, but then they ran out. For a while I was sleeping on a floor . . . I'd never had to live like that before. I finally got one job offer, but when I turned up to work I found that it had been a mistake. I'm pretty sure that someone had called them."

This was worse than anything Angelica had expected. She said, "Is that why you decided to get out?"

"That, and other reasons." Alina looked down. "I'd had some old trouble. They were threatening to bring that up, too. I couldn't face it. So I decided to leave. But the first try was a shambles, and I was caught."

"They took you back?"

"Worse. I was examined by three doctors and declared insane. They did that kind of thing, back then. They put me in the prison hospital. I was there for nearly six months and by the end of the first week, I wanted to die. Sometimes I thought I was going to; sometimes I was even more scared at the thought that I wouldn't. They interfered with me there. I don't even like to think about it."

Angelica now knew why Alina had disappeared from the terrace so promptly on the day that Walter Hardy had hooked out the dead dog. It wasn't the sight of the dog itself that had driven her indoors, but the certainty that the police would soon be arriving. Seeing that Alina was upset by the memory, she said, "You don't have to go on," but now Alina was determined to be heard.

"Now you know I've no right to be here," she said, "I want you to know what's waiting for me if ever I get taken back. I only got out of the hospital because of an old unclosed file, and a doctor from the outside who took an interest in my case. They didn't officially let me out – I escaped. Otherwise, I'd still be there. And that's the reason why they want to get me back."

"And how did you reach England?"

"By using somebody," she said, and her voice sounded hollow with guilt.

Angelica, the coffee now standing cold and forgotten in the jug beside her, said, "Go to the authorities, Alina. They wouldn't send you home, not with a story like that."

"You can guarantee it?" If Alina was looking cynical, Angelica could only suppose that it was because she'd earned the right to be. "I don't think that you can. According to the record, I'm a criminal and wherever I am, I'm there illegally. If the authorities get hold of me, it won't matter what I say – I'll be returned, and then I'll be lost."

"But you can't just hide forever."

"I have plans. Please don't worry about me. I don't intend to leave this valley."

There was a determination in her eyes now that was almost frightening; how little Angelica had understood, she now realised, reading only the surface and never suspecting that any of this lay beneath.

Alina added by way of explanation, "Everyone needs to belong somewhere. And this is the place that I've chosen."

"Well," Angelica said, "I want you to remember that you've got friends here. If you should need any help . . ."

"When the day comes, I'll ask," Alina said. And then she glanced out of the main kitchen window, the one that had a partial view of the terrace; Angelica looked as well, and saw that they had a few customers arriving and looking around uncertainly at the unstaffed deck.

Alina said, "Do I still have a job?"

"Of course you do."

Angelica had already decided that her money could be taken out of the petty cash and then lost in the books somewhere . . . and if ever they should be caught doing it, she didn't feel that it was a crime she'd be ashamed of.

Alina smiled, with some confidence but also a lot of apprehension still, and she moved around the table toward the door. She took her notepad from the pocket of her apron as she went, and at the doorway she stopped for a moment as if to gather herself.

She took a breath and, in the space of a couple of seconds, seemed to re-invent the waitress from the refugee. It was a faintly unsettling transformation for Angelica to witness, an unasked-for revelation of a totally private process. One shell was discarded and a new one immediately hardened into its place, but for the brief instant in between there was a glimpse . . . of what?

Angelica couldn't have said. She reckoned that she could only take on board a limited number of surprises in any given period, and her quota for the year had just been reached. She already had plenty to think about.

Alina, meanwhile, went on out into the daylight.

EIGHTEEN

Midway through Friday afternoon, the early-shift newsreader watched the red transmission light die on her last bulletin of the day and sat back from the microphone with a sigh of relief. That was it until handover on Monday, which she hoped would be enough time to shake off the cold that had been dogging her for the last couple of days.

Her name was Isobel Terry, and she was twenty-two years old. She'd been in commercial radio for eleven months following nearly three years on a regional newspaper; she reckoned to stick around this particular station for another two years at the most. After that she reckoned that if she hadn't moved on to somewhere bigger, she'd probably be stuck here forever reading out the latest sheep prices at six o'clock every morning. Isobel was ambitious, and had her sights set on the national news media; unfortunately, so did every other young news-hustler in every backwater station in the country, and few of them were having to contend with sinuses that felt as if they'd been stuffed with pillows. God only knew what she sounded like on the air. Inside her cans, she sounded like Elmer Fudd.

"There's someone to see you," the technical operator called through over the talkback system as she pushed her chair back to stand, gathering together her yellow bulletin flimsies with their handwritten amendments. The TO was only about three strides and two sheets of glass away from her, but the talkback gave his voice the quality of a long-distance call.

"Who?" she said, and she saw him shrug. Beyond him she could see the afternoon DJ in his studio, a couple more strides and another set of double-glazing further on, hunched over his microphone like a harassed co-pilot.

The TO said, "He talked to you on the phone and you told him to come in. That's what he says, anyway. Amanda put him in the newsroom."

Isobel stepped out into the corridor, quiet except for the ever-present low murmur of the station's output as it played over unobtrusive speakers. Dave, the afternoon DJ, was talking over the intro of a record that he was saying had been a big hit in Europe. Dave talked right on and over the start of the lyric, and then made it worse by trying to pretend that his mistake was intentional.

Isobel winced. Here on Sheep-shagger Radio, Dave was about as polished as they got.

She passed the sales office and made the turn toward the newsroom. There was no one in the office, the entire sales team having discovered important appointments that gave them excuses to sneak off home and start the weekend early. There was only one person in the newsroom, and he quickly got to his feet as she entered.

"I'm sorry," she said. "I know we already spoke, but what was your name?"

"Please, call me Pavel," he said.

Pavel.

She remembered the call, now; remembered it as soon as she heard his accent. Something about an emergency appeal to a missing person. The fact of it was, Amanda should never have brought him in here at all; she should have kept him in Reception, as per company policy. The man had all the markings of a weirdo. His clothes, dated and drab, appeared to have been slept in. He'd had a bad shave and his hair looked as if it was growing back after having been cut too short. And there were dark rings under his eyes, which burned as if with a fever.

But he'd sounded sincere enough. And he seemed sincere enough now, his piece of paper held ready in his hands, and so with the safety of the newsdesk between them she reached across and took it.

She read it through. She tried not to smile at the wording, and then she handed it back.

"The name's all we'd need," she said. "We can handle the other part ourselves."

"You do this kind of message?"

"Sometimes, when we can fit it in. But we usually work it into the show format somewhere, rather than make it a part of the news. Did you try the BBC? They do emergencies on Radio Four, and it's national."

He nodded. "Nothing came back," he said. "But this is more for young people. I may have more luck."

"If she's in the area," Isobel said.

And Pavel inclined his head, conceding the point.

"So, who is it that's ill? Someone in the family?"

"No. It's her."

Isobel's eyes widened. Her antennae quivered. "Something contagious?"

Pavel smiled, weary but still polite. "No," he said. "This is for her own safety, as much as anything else. But please don't say so on the air."

"Of course," Isobel said, and scribbled a quick memo on the back of some out-of-date wire agency material while the name was still fresh in her mind. A schoolteacher from Eastern Europe, believed to be touring in the area. From what Pavel had said earlier he was working his way around the country, from station to station, leaving exactly the same message at each.

"If anything turns up," she said, "I'll arrange for word to be left on the front desk. That's really all I can do."

"Thank you," he said. "I'll call once every morning."

He probably would, too. He probably had a list of numbers that he called every day, adding to it as he moved around. She wondered if he slept rough, or in his car; he looked as if he might.

At the one-way door that led back into the station's tiny foyer and reception area, she stepped aside for him and said, "I hope you find her."

He smiled weakly.

"So do I," he said.

And after he'd gone, and Isobel had returned to the newsroom to file all the dead stories and check the agency printers for the next hour's updates ready to hand over to Jim, the late-shift newsreader, it briefly crossed her mind that maybe, just *maybe*, a rising star of journalism with her eye on the national media might have asked a couple of more searching questions. Might have dug a little for the human interest; might even have probed around to see if there was any backstory worth the follow-up.

But the thought didn't stay with her for long.

Instead, she was wondering what kind of remedy Kate Adie used whenever *she* got a head-blocker, and whether she'd ever had to read over livestock prices to what was probably a total early-morning audience of three men and a dog.

Their brief talk slipped painlessly from her mind.

While Pavel set out for the next town on his list.

NINETEEN

Diane's employer and his immediate circle arrived on the Friday evening.

The circle consisted of Bob Ivie and Tony Marinello – the Old Indispensables, as Dizzy Liston called them – and four examples of the species that Diane had quickly come to recognise as Dizzy's Women. These were well-bred, impeccably turned-out, and as dim and empty-headed as pumpkin lanterns. After one drink, their voices could be heard over half a mile away. Fortunately, Jed was going to be sleeping at Mrs Neary's that night; they couldn't have made more noise exploring the Hall if they'd found it to be haunted.

The preparations for the party were set to move into top gear on the Saturday morning; Diane would have little more to do than to stand aside and watch the professionals at work. The lights had already arrived that afternoon, the disco would be set up from ten o'clock tomorrow, and a small group of hostesses and security people would be due to arrive some time around three.

The best place for Jed during all of this, she'd decided, would be with his minder; she'd worked out a special weekend rate with Mrs Neary some time ago and had been working on her conscience ever since. It felt too much as if she was shunting him off for her own convenience, even though she knew that it was the only sane and sensible thing to do. She'd explained that he'd be staying away for the two nights, which he'd never done before; she only hoped she'd explained it well enough. Just before seven she left Jed to pick out some toys and books to be taking with him – and it's got to be a portable amount, she warned – and went to check that she wouldn't be needed for a while.

Liston and company were out on the lawn behind the house, where an old-fashioned wrought-iron table and some matching chairs had been set for them in the evening sunlight. There were the long shadows of wine bottles and glasses across the table, some of the bottles already empty.

"Mineral water for the invalid," she heard someone say as they handed Dizzy a glass, and she saw Dizzy give a wry smile.

"I suppose that's me," he said.

He was in his late thirties, and he had the look of a well-worn schoolboy. His face was young, but the mileage showing on it was high. Nevertheless, for all that he'd been around there was definitely something that was attractive and appealing about him; only his eyes gave him away, because they could turn cold and introspective while those around him were whooping it up. Dizzy knew the exact value of the people he kept, which was why he'd given the estate management job to Diane and not to one of his regular hangers-on.

"Your lawn's a bit overgrown, Dizzy," one of Dizzy's Women said, looking critically at the grass around her feet.

"You can cut it for me after the party," he told her, which everybody took to be a big joke.

Summer in the country, was the toast echoing in Diane's ears as she went back inside; and she shuddered, and wondered if she could think up something really cutting to say the first time one of them tried to treat her like a servant.

Jed had made his selection; three toys stood out on their own in the middle of the floor, these being the ones that he reckoned he could do without.

Diane settled down, and started patiently to negotiate.

In the end she got him down to his Micronauts, his plastic airport, and a bag of Dinky cars. For books he had two by Maurice Sendak, the Skeleton one, and a well-worn *Pinocchio* using pictures from the film. She put everything into a carrier and took this out to the car with his overnight case, and then she came back to get him into his shoes and his coat. And then, because she didn't want to be saying goodbye to him any sooner than she had to, she took him for a wander through the main part of the Hall to see how the preparations were going.

The lights had been rigged but not yet tested, and cabling still lay everywhere. Signs for the cloakrooms and toilets were already in place, and two posts and a rope had been set at the top of the stairs to keep visitors out of the private apartments.

It all seemed kind of strange to Diane. The way she'd always known it, when you decided to throw a party, you threw a *party*; you pushed back the furniture, you got all the food together yourself, you invited close friends who knew each other and for a while you let them invade your most private and personal space. And then when it was all over, you threw open the windows and you vacuumed, and as likely as not while you were doing this you'd find someone left asleep behind the sofa. Not like this, people hired-in to do everything. Dizzy might be well-off, but Diane knew from the estate accounts that he wasn't rolling-in-it rich. The estate and the house might both be high-value assets, but the conditions of his inheritance forced him to keep both intact and he got little currency out of them beyond the woodland leases and the shooting rights.

No, the fact of it was, Diane and her employer might easily have been two different species for the way that they looked at the world. This wasn't going to be a party. It was to be a local public relations exercise, bought and paid for – nothing more.

In the middle of the hall Diane said, "Well, Jed, what do you think?" And Jed took another look around and made a face that suggested mild indifference lying over mild disapproval.

Diane knew exactly what he meant.

"Yeah," she said. "I'll be glad when it's all over, too."

And then together they walked out to the Toyota.

TWENTY

That night, after Alina had gone out, Pete decided to find out exactly where she went.

She couldn't have gone too far. She'd been out ten minutes, fifteen at the most. And wherever she might wander, she always set out in the same direction.

The path down to the lake shore was steep and difficult, and several times he almost fell. Roots tripped him and rocks made him slip, and in places the path was so soft-edged that it simply dropped away from under him in the darkness. And yet this was a descent that she made barefoot. Pete could only guess that she must move with the grace of a gazelle.

A breeze was coming in from the water, stirring the branches overhead and sending a low, unearthly moan through the woodland.

And as Pete emerged by the rocky edge of the water, he saw her.

She was fairly easy to make out against the glitter on the lake. She looked almost as if she was standing on the surface itself, although Pete knew that there were rocks and shallows and that the effect was no more than illusion. Her head was bowed, she was leaning forward.

And, as he could now hear, she was singing softly to the water.

It was strange music, full of strange sounds that he knew he couldn't hope to understand. She was keeping her voice low, much as one might while singing a lullaby to the one wakeful soul in a house full of sleeping children. He felt his skin tingle, he felt the fine hair all along his spine react as if a low current had been run through him.

She reached down and, for a moment, Pete was half-expecting some response; a stag, perhaps, breaking the surface of the lake and climbing out to her, water streaming from its flanks as it came to her hand. She stood there like a dark messiah with some unseen flock before her, and Pete couldn't help but begin to assemble shapes out of the grainy darkness and to give them solidity and movement.

But nothing moved, and nothing save the breeze disturbed the calm of the water. And then she straightened, and the illusion faded.

She spoke.

"Don't ever follow me again, Peter," she said, totally unexpectedly; she hadn't even looked his way, and he felt as if he'd been caught in a searchlight's beam in the middle of some guilty act. Everything that he'd had in mind to say to her was suddenly gone from his head, his mind as blank as a new wall and his belly full of sudden, inexplicable dread.

She turned to him now. She was a silhouette against the moonlight that sparkled on the lake.

"It's not an easy path," she said. "You could fall."

There were a hundred things that he knew he ought to say.

But he simply said, "I know."

"Go back, now, Peter. Please."

He wanted to ask her what she thought she was doing.

But instead he turned, and slowly started to make his way back up toward the house.

IV: THE REVELS

Let us eat and drink; for tomorrow we shall die
Isaiah 22:13

Twenty-One

Ted was having trouble picking out a shirt; his sister had given him a couple of new ones last Christmas, but this was the first time that he'd really had to study them with regard to presentability. The one with the fine stripes looked slightly flashier, but he'd made a better ironing job of the plain one. In the end he decided on the stripes – after half an hour of wear, the ironing job wasn't going to matter anyway. Now he'd have to pick out a tie. He had two of those, as well . . . Ted reckoned that, like Pete McCarthy, he simply wasn't one of nature's tie-wearers. He certainly hadn't done anything like this in ages. He'd once thought of asking one of the Venetz sisters out, but they were pretty well inseparable; a turndown didn't worry him so much as the prospect of being accepted by one and so giving offence to the other. And where would he have taken her? You could hardly take a woman to her own restaurant, but because of his limited social life he knew of nowhere better. And somehow, he couldn't imagine either of them coming around to the house for some beers and a pizza and a John Wayne movie on the video.

A problem.

So he'd let it go.

Besides, there was still the shadow of Nerys. He knew that it was a stupid notion and that she, of all people, wouldn't have wanted him to think this way, but he couldn't help it. Even though she'd been dead for so long it could sometimes seem that she was still with him, a presence in the next room, someone on the other side of a door who waited and listened but who never stepped through, except when he dreamed. He'd known her since they were both thirteen years old. All right, so he'd never feel that he was betraying her memory. But sometimes, her memory could be all that he needed.

He could hear the van outside. Wayne was home, and the two dogs were barking and scrambling to greet him. Ted stood there waiting with the shirt over his arm, waiting to hear the inevitable sequence completed before he went on; slam the van door, up the outside stairs to the flat over the workshop, another door to slam, and then LOUD MUSIC. Ted still couldn't work out how Wayne

95

was able to cover the distance from the door to the CD player so fast. The glass in the windows was shaking even before the dust on the stairs had begun to settle.

Wayne wasn't Ted's only son. He had another, older boy, Shaun; but Shaun had taken himself to Australia at the age of eighteen and hadn't been home since. Ted got occasional letters, written in a rush and saying almost nothing. He had one photograph, from Shaun's wedding, and the photograph's arrival had been the first that he'd known about any of it. Shaun's last years at school had been difficult – he'd even taken a swing at a teacher at one point – and he'd earned a reputation for the motherless Hammond boys that Wayne had found himself sharing even though he'd done nothing to earn it.

Perhaps he'd come back, one day, at least for a visit. But he was making a life out there, and probably felt that there was no place here for him any more. Ted would sometimes wonder if he hadn't made Pete into a kind of surrogate son to fill the hole that Shaun had left . . . it was impossible to say for sure, and nothing to be ashamed of anyway.

He hung his chosen shirt on the front of the wardrobe, and slid back the mirror-door behind it to put the other away. He was planning on a shave and a slow, hot bath; he might even throw in some of that stuff that Wayne had bought him for his birthday, that came in a dubious-looking novelty bottle shaped like a tiger's head. It was nearly two hours yet to the start of the party, he'd have plenty of time.

He had his son, he had his dogs, he had his friends. He had his memories.

He could hardly call himself lonely, could he?

Wayne had his own hot water supply, direct from the gas-fired geyser that also supplied the workshop below. When it was running, the geyser roared so loudly that the place felt like a rocket in the middle of a takeoff. He turned the music up a little louder, to cover it.

Barely more than half an hour before, he'd driven into the village on an errand for the Venetz sisters and although he saw almost no one along the way, he'd been able to sense a tension in the air; it was a faint background buzz like that of power lines in the rain. Even at this hour, bedroom curtains were drawn and lights were burning inside. Party night was big news, and people were starting early.

He didn't mind responding to a panic call at such a late hour, especially not when it meant transporting three microwave ovens up to the Hall and so getting an advance peek at the preparations. Adele Venetz, the sister that Wayne always thought of as the quiet one, had been sitting at the big rolling-out table as he'd entered the restaurant kitchen. He'd rapped on the open door as he'd passed it, and said, "Who called for International Rescue?"

And then he'd faltered.

Adele had looked up at him, not quickly but as quickly as she'd been able. She appeared to have been holding a makeshift icepack to the side of her head and a couple of the cubes had skidded out of reach and begun to melt, almost as if she'd been in too much of a hurry to stretch over for them. From what Wayne had been able to see of her left eye, it had looked as if it had a couple of drops of blood in it.

"Thanks, Wayne," she'd said, only a little unsteadily, and Wayne had been able to see that questions or even concerned enquiries were definitely not being encouraged. "I hope this won't hold you up too much."

"Don't worry about me," he'd said, but then he couldn't just leave it at that and so he'd added, "Will you be all right?"

She'd nodded, barely. "I just need to lie down for a while. Wayne, I'll be grateful if you don't mention this to anybody."

"Don't worry, total silence," Wayne had assured her and then he'd loaded the ovens into the van and left her to make her way upstairs, touching the wall as she went. And then, restraining himself from a farewell blast on the Dixie horn, he'd set out for Liston Hall.

With the first of the ovens he'd gone the long way through to the Hall's kitchens, taking in the sights as he went. It seemed that the hallway itself was going to be the disco area, with a glitterball and nets of balloons overhead and several of those special-effects lights that would make the walls appear to be dripping with coloured slime. The doors through into two of the biggest reception rooms had been folded back, and a false wall between them opened to reveal what had once been the ballroom and which now, for one night, was a ballroom again. The whole setup had been quiet, almost deserted; there had been music playing, but that had been somewhere far-off in the house. Probably Dizzy's gang, keeping out of the way in case the sight of others working made them feel weak.

The scene in the kitchens had been considerably more lively; as he'd shouldered his way through he'd come upon a spectacle of controlled panic with Angelica presiding. Mixers had been mixing, blenders had been blending, and Angelica had been pushing cloves into the biggest baked ham that Wayne had ever seen. The three

97

local women that she'd brought in as help for the evening had been buzzing around behind her, greasing dishes and setting up trays and napkin-wrapping cutlery.

"Oh, Wayne," Angelica had said. "You're an angel. Did you speak to Adele?"

A moment's hesitation told her that he had, and that he'd seen. But all that he'd said was, "She'll be along in about an hour. Just a few things she has to do."

"You're a good boy, Wayne," Angelica had said, and they'd both known that she was meaning for more than just the errand.

"I'll even shake paws for a biscuit," Wayne had said.

Now, as he was waiting, he took a dispirited look around. As much as he could be aware of someone else's problems, his own were the ones that preoccupied him most. All right, so he had a flat, but it wasn't exactly the kind of place that Warren Beatty would have wanted to call home. Behind him in the bathroom stood a chipped old tub slowly filling with water that was the colour of weak tea; the bathroom walls had been replastered and roughened for tiling, but they didn't have any tiles. He'd tried posters, but they curled in the steam.

Straight ahead were his sleeping quarters, the lounge, the dining area, and kitchen. All of this sounded pretty impressive until you understood that they were combined in the one room. He'd folded his bed back into the sofa, but somehow the sheets always managed to peep out around the edges. The carpet was in two pieces that didn't match and the cooker was a tabletop model, non-functional except for the hotplate, rescued by Ted from an old Dolphin 20 on its way to being broken up. Wayne's going-out stuff, all hung over the back of his one upright chair, had the definite air of being from another world altogether.

As a seduction suite it had its shortcomings, he reflected as he unzipped his jeans, stepped out of them, and slung them onto the sofa with the rest of the day's rubbish. He was working at a distinct operational disadvantage, but he reckoned that this could be changed.

Odds could be altered. He was already making his plans.

In the constabulary house on the south side of Three Oaks Bay, Ross Aldridge was putting a new message onto the outgoing tape in his telephone answering machine. Loren was upstairs, engaged in that long getting-ready process that he'd never quite been able to fathom. He could hear her hairdryer, almost as hard on his nerves as a dentist's drill; it had ruined three attempts to get the message down already, but he didn't want to ask her to lay off for a while in case the uneasy peace was threatened yet again.

Silence.

He gave it another try.

When the message was finished and checked, he went upstairs. Neither he nor Loren liked the house, much; it had been built not too long after the war, and with its small windows and pebbledash it had none of the atmosphere of the "place in the country" that they'd been hoping for – if anything, it looked more like the married quarters for lower RAF ranks to be found around old and run-down airfields. He'd had ideas about them buying somewhere of their own, but so far they'd had to stay as ideas.

Loren was sitting in a slip before the dressing-table mirror. Her hair was pinned back, and she was shaking a blob of some kind of cream onto a ball of cotton wool.

She said, "I only hope they can leave you alone for one night."

"They'll all be there," he said. "Nearly everyone got invited."

"Not everyone." She started to work the cream into the skin around her eyes, staring straight ahead at her reflection as she did it. "Some of them around here wouldn't think twice about dragging you away for no reason."

"Well, if anything turns up, you can stay."

"Oh, thanks a lot," she said drily.

Aldridge made no sign or sound as he went through to the airing cupboard to get himself a fresh towel. These were old grounds, and he didn't want to go over them yet again. He was wondering if there would be many at the party likely to recognise him out of uniform. As he moved back down the short landing toward the bathroom, Loren's raised voice came to him again.

She said, "I'm going to enjoy myself tonight, Ross. I'm not going to let anything spoil it."

He stopped in the bedroom doorway. "Yeah. Rub shoulders with the local laird."

"He'll probably just show his face and then disappear."

But he could read her too well, and he could see that she was hoping for something more. She was looking for something memorable, probably for the first time in two years, and he didn't want to deny her that.

He said, "Whichever way, it should be a good party. And it's not a night for trouble."

There were no sounds of any kind coming from Alina's bedroom, and hadn't been for more than an hour. Pete listened in the hallway for a few seconds, and then he knocked on her door. After a moment he knocked again, harder, and he heard her say *Come in*.

He opened the door, but he didn't step all the way through. Alina was over on the far side of the room, sitting at her table with the lamp angled to spill across the pages of the scrapbook that lay open in front of her. The rest of the room was in near-darkness. She didn't seem to be looking at the album, at least not any more; she didn't seem to have made a start at getting ready, either.

Pete said, "You can go ahead and use the shower as soon as you like."

She looked up at him, and smiled thinly. "You first."

"There's only enough for one. You know what the heater's like."

"But what will you do?"

"I've got every pan in the place filled up and on the cooker. I'll manage. You wearing your new dress?"

"Yes," she said. Again, that smile . . . as if she was barely managing to conceal some kind of pain.

Pete said, "Is everything all right?"

She looked at the book first, and then at him. Her eyes were bleak, reflections of a landscape where nobody walked. "I don't think I'm winning, Peter," she admitted.

"Winning what?"

"My own little battle. The fight to stay."

She was serious. Pete crossed the room and crouched beside her chair. "You're doing fine," he insisted. "You've found a place you like, you've found people you like . . . you're working and you're not even paying any tax. That's some people's idea of paradise."

"It's not what I mean."

"Do you mean the official part?" Pete said. "What have you heard?"

"Not that, either," she said, and she tapped the side of her head with a forefinger. "I mean, in here. This is where I'm losing it. It's like there's two of me – one who knows what she wants, and the other who tells her what she can have. And *she's* a lot stronger than I ever thought she could be."

Alina was looking totally lost; Pete yielded to an impulse for once, and put his arm around her shoulders. She felt small, and as frail as a bird. Wearily, she let herself rest against him.

He said, "I didn't realise you felt this low. I thought you were really happy at the way things were working out."

"One of me is," she said.

He gave her shoulders a squeeze. "Hey, come on," he said.

"Brighten up. Get yourself ready, and we'll see how they enjoy themselves in the Big House."

It wasn't much, but it seemed to work; or at least, it was a start.

"Do my best, chief," she said with a smile. And as Pete was standing, she reached over and closed the scrapbook.

TWENTY-TWO

The party started at nine, and was raging by ten.

Diane could hardly believe how well it was going, and Dizzy hadn't even put in an appearance yet. Bob Ivie and Tony Marinello were running the bar, having a great time, and making themselves easily popular; they were ignoring Dizzy's Women in favour of the locals, leaving the Sloanes to stand around looking remote and faintly embarrassed in a way that displeased Diane not at all. Bob Ivie's speciality was his Hawaiian Punch, made to a secret Hawaiian recipe which became less secret every time he mixed up another batch before an audience, and which changed in its details anyway. Tony Marinello's speciality was to escape from behind the bar whilst Ivie was holding forth, and to ask any unescorted woman for a dance regardless of her age or her inclination.

The agency girls were doing an excellent backup job. They were zeroing in on the wallflowers, splitting up couples and effortlessly getting them to mix. There was almost nothing for Diane to do but move around saying hello, accept a couple of dances, and nod amiably to people that she hardly knew. She saw Ross Aldridge, whom she knew slightly from when he'd processed her shotgun licence application, and wondered for a moment if the rumour was true about how he and his wife had moved to the area a few months after their baby had died.

And then she checked her watch. Dizzy would be appearing soon. If everything continued to go like this, there was a fair chance that he'd have the village back on his side for the rest of the summer. He didn't have to change, he simply had to present himself as more of a lovable reprobate than as a spirit of corruption; PR was everything, as long as it didn't cross the thin line over into patronisation. After a quick wave to Ted Hammond across the crowded floor, she managed to catch the arm of one of the hostesses.

"Everything all right?" she said. She could see for herself that it probably was, but she was starting to feel a little useless here.

"Everything's going fine," the girl said, not quite so much of a girl when Diane looked at her close-to. She was blonde and doll-

102

faced, but her blue eyes gave the impression that she'd just about seen everything, and rather more than was healthy for so short a life. "I never worked a crowd as happy as this one with their clothes still on."

"Anybody been spiking the drinks?"

"Not from our end. Yours?"

Diane shook her head. "Not that I know of. Maybe it's just anticipation."

"Well, they're all high on *something*. Tonight's not a night they'll forget in a hurry."

Out in the big hall, the DJ made a smooth change between tracks. He was running what was mostly a sixties disco with a sprinkling of classic rock and only a few recent standards. He had big banks of lights and speakers on either side of his console with some lower-level relays here in the ballroom; he'd been running some smoke and dry ice earlier, and some of it still hung in the air and gave the lighted area beyond the doorways the effect of some offworld film set.

She could also see that Pete McCarthy and his waitress had just arrived.

They'd stopped on their way across the marble floor, both of them blue-white in the lights and the fog. She was saying something to him, and he was glancing around and nodding. Alina was wearing a plain white dress that left her back and shoulders bare. She wore no jewellery, and her hair had been simply gathered and tied. Even though she'd told herself that she wasn't going to have any thoughts or feelings on the subject at all, the sight of Alina looking so good made Diane feel just a little bit sick. Maybe there was some envy in it, she could be honest about that. But mostly it was directed towards herself, and whatever it was in her that seemed to respond to some call given out by the least suitable of men; despite what she'd been through in the past couple of years she appeared to have learned precisely nothing. Either she'd imagined McCarthy's interest when there was really nothing there, which on its own would be humiliating enough, or else McCarthy was a no-good dissembling two-faced piece of garbage, which was slightly better for her self-respect but still got her nowhere.

But she could at least go over and say hello.

She'd almost started out, but she was stopped by a touch on her arm. Turning around, she found herself facing the dark, handsome-looking woman who'd arrived with Ross Aldridge and whom Diane assumed to be his wife.

"I just wanted to say something," Loren Aldridge told her, leaning close and raising her voice to be heard over the music.

Diane tried not to wince. The music wasn't *that* loud. Loren seemed to have desperation in her eyes, and the good time that she was having was a fierce one. Diane said, "Feel free."

"I'm having a wonderful evening. This is the best time I've had since I came here. I just wanted you to know."

"That's good," Diane told her. "Did you dance with Tony yet?"

"Yes. He's a wonderful dancer, isn't he?"

"So they say." Diane was starting to wonder if Bob wasn't being a little too liberal with the strong stuff in his Hawaiian knockout juice. She'd have to mention it to him – and pretty soon, if Loren's slightly wild-eyed look was any kind of an omen.

Loren said, "I want you to tell Mister Liston how much I appreciate this. The invitation, and . . ." She gestured around, lost for a description. "Everything."

"You can tell him yourself. He'll be down in a couple of minutes."

"Really?" Loren said. "But I won't know what to say."

"You could always ask him to dance," Diane suggested. "Someone has to."

Dizzy's late and short-lived appearance hadn't been planned entirely for effect; the truth was that he was still fairly weak after his illness. He couldn't be expected to manage much more than an hour on his feet, after which he'd be living up to his name, although not – Diane hoped – to his reputation.

She looked again for Pete, but Pete was no longer there; and now she could hear a scattering of spontaneous applause – *applause!* – and a few cheers and whistles which told her that the host had finally arrived on the scene. People were squeezing by her in the general drift to get a look at him, and she let herself go with the crowd a little in order to see how he was doing.

He was doing fine.

He was, she supposed, a minor celebrity in his own right after all, extensively written-up in the *News of the World* and a regular in the Grovel columns of *Private Eye*. Now he was looking rumpled and approachable, thin and still a little yellow-tinged after the hepatitis. Diane couldn't deny his charm, even though she knew more about him than most; he came over as something like a wind-up toy that was apt to go bashing itself into the nearest wall without guidance and protection.

The agency girls were taking expert care of him. Veterans mostly of conferences and corporate operations where the good time masked a definite hidden agenda, they were steering him through the introductions deftly and with an impressive display of memory. They were

supporting him, they were making him look good, and the overall
strategy seemed to be working.

Diane felt a sense of relief. If Dizzy the prodigal was to be received
back onto his family's old stamping-ground without too much in the
way of resentment, her own job would be a lot easier to carry off.
The pity of it was that she hadn't made a bigger part for herself
in the night's scenario; she was getting polite nods and hellos
from people that she already knew slightly, and curious glances
from most of the others. It was as if the estate and the valley
people were opposing armies under truce, mixing freely but still
in uniform.

She spotted Wayne, over on the fringe of the crowd with his girl.
He'd introduced her to Diane about half an hour before. Her name
was Sandra, Sandy for short. She wasn't tall and she was slightly
heavy, but she had a pleasing face with soft eyes; perhaps she'd
never be a beauty, but age would never make her ugly either. She
was craning to see over the shoulders of the people in front, and
pushing Wayne's hands away as he playfully offered to lift her.

The music changed to slow numbers. Diane was just thinking that
she'd go around to the back and see how the Venetz sisters were
getting along with the buffet, when somebody moved in and stood
beside her; Pete McCarthy, wearing a more-or-less new jacket and
a pleasant smile, his tie already undone. He was alone.

He said, "Happy with the way it's going?"

"I reckon so," she replied.

"Alina got curious. She's gone over for a closer look."

"And what about you?"

"I can live without it. Dance with me?"

"Sure."

The marble-floored hall was almost deserted now, just two couples
moving slowly under the glitterball light. There were chairs around
the sidelines with one or two pairs of beady eyes watching from the
gloom. It was the kind of music where you had to dance close.
Perhaps that was why he'd waited.

They took hold of each other with an awkward kind of formality,
and he said, "I was looking for you earlier."

"I've been around," she said as they moved out onto the floor. It
was hopeless. Maybe one day, she was thinking, her head and her
hormones might agree over something; and on that day the sun
would rise and shine all morning, and fish would leap in the river,
and all of her bills would turn out to be rebates.

"Listen," Pete said, and she sensed a deliberate change of track.
"I'm not sure how to say this, but I want to ask you something. I've

been working on it for most of the week, so don't make me mess it up. Okay?"

"Go ahead."

"Would you go out with me?"

She waited.

And then she said, "That's it?"

"That's it."

"And you're being serious?"

"Now, wait. There's been a big misunderstanding and I want to clear it up before it gets any worse. You get to hear that I'm sharing my house with a five-foot bombshell who can make a grown man go weak at a single glance, and you leap to the obvious conclusion. Right?"

"Who wouldn't?"

"Well, you're wrong. Dead wrong, and that's what I have to explain. I like you, Mrs Jackson, and I think I could get you to like me. And life's too short to miss out on the chance of it for the wrong kinds of reasons."

"You can keep talking, Mr McCarthy. But you'd better bear in mind, I've been worked-over and walked over by experts. If you're going to tell me that she's your sister, I'd say you'll have to try harder."

He shook his head.

"I barely know her. The more I see of her, the more I realise how much of a stranger she is to me. She came over to me one night and she asked me for a lift. She had nowhere to aim for and she was just about destitute, and there was trouble following her as well. She asked me for nothing more, she didn't want to cause me problems, but I couldn't just walk away from her. So I brought her to the valley. I didn't expect her to stay so long, but I made the offer and I have to stick with it. We've got separate rooms, we lead separate lives, most days we don't even meet up. We're only together tonight because you put us both on the same invitation. I don't know what else I can tell you, Diane, but that's the way it is. What do you say?"

He seemed serious. She said, "Why are you so keen to convince me?"

"Say you're convinced, and you'll find out. Well?"

He was watching her. Either he was dead straight, or else he was the sharpest operator – bar none, including the guy she'd met on a singles' holiday who'd almost managed to convince her that he was on his final fling with only ninety days left to live – that she had ever encountered.

He was still watching her.

"I'm thinking about it," she said.

With their curiosity satisfied and the music too slow to be interesting, Wayne and Sandy had taken themselves out into the gardens to cool off. It was dark out there and it was relatively private, and Wayne had managed to spirit out an entire punchbowl, still half-full. They sat against the wall of the house, just under the stone parapet of the first-floor terrace. Wayne was hoping that nobody else would get any ideas about joining them.

He said, "So that's the Lord of the Manor. What did you think of him?"

"He's okay," Sandy said, in the same kind of tone that she'd probably use to describe an indifferent sandwich. "A bit too smooth, though."

"He didn't look it," Wayne said. His own feeling had been that Dizzy Liston looked like some amiable, well-heeled scarecrow.

Sandy said, "They're the dangerous ones," and then she looked into her glass even though it was really too dark to see anything of it. "What's in this stuff?"

"Fruit juice, mostly," Wayne said airily. "Maybe a bit of wine."

"How strong is it?"

"Not very. They water it down, that's how come there's so much of it knocking around."

Tentatively, he put his arm around her. She leaned against him comfortably, and he began to wonder about the possibilities in aiming for the wide sleeve of her dress.

"I expect my mum would like him," Sandy said. "She likes them well-worn but lovable. Comes from listening to a lot of Country and Western music."

"What would it take to make her like me?"

"Well, you could stop picking me up in that van. And you could inherit a couple of million and go to Oxford. And maybe win a medal for rescuing Prince William from a fire."

"You think that would do it?"

"You'd be about halfway there."

Sandy turned herself slightly, and Wayne suddenly discovered that he was sitting there with his sleeve strategy in tatters and most of her right breast in his hand. She wasn't wearing a bra. He didn't know what to do next. Sandy, leaning with her head on his shoulder, carried on as if nothing was untoward.

"She doesn't actually say anything against you," she explained. "She'd just be happier if you were a drip with glasses and lots of qualifications, that's all. I mean, I'd like to make her happy, but there are limits."

"Yeah," Wayne said, still feeling somewhat stunned and very lightheaded. "Yeah, I suppose there are."

She looked down at his hand, which was tense and unmoving.

She said, "Are we doing anything here, or what?"

Inside and on the dance floor, Pete and Diane suddenly found that people were drifting back and the music was getting loud again. It was a sure sign that Dizzy's fraternisation period was over. Conversation had now become difficult, and Diane still hadn't given Pete a definite answer to his question.

Nor did she feel quite ready to; and now she leaned close to his ear, and raised her voice.

"Give me some time," she said. "I'd better go and see how it went."

Pete nodded and moved off to look for some more of Bob Ivie's jungle juice, and Diane eased her way through into the ballroom. She was already starting to feel battered by the increased level of the sound, and it was a relief to get out into the lower buzz and the cooler lights. The buffet tables were now open, and most people in here were either crowded around them or else standing in line with plates; she could see the two Venetz sisters and their fill-in staff working the tables, carving, serving, and fetching. They seemed to be doing a good job. Diane started to scan for one of the agency girls, but then one of the agency girls found her.

It was the blue-eyed blonde, the one that she'd spoken to earlier. Diane said, "Are we a success, or what?"

"The men all like him, and the women all love him. But there could be a problem."

"How do you mean?"

"Mister Liston's gone back upstairs, and he's taken a lady with him. The lady didn't come alone, and I'm not sure whether we ought to be doing anything about it."

Diane felt her heart beginning to sink. Of a number of possibilities, one shone out more bright and unpleasant than any of the others.

"Oh, hell," she said. "Not the policeman's wife. He was going to *behave* himself tonight!"

"No, not her. It's the foreign woman with an accent I couldn't place. She's with the man I just saw you talking to."

"Really?" This was something else . . . and whilst it might not exactly be welcome, the results would certainly be interesting. "Well," Diane said, "in theory, we're in the clear."

"Oh?"

"They came together, but they're not a couple."

"Is that what he was telling you?" There was a certain cynicism in the agency girl's eyes, but Diane wasn't somebody who'd just climbed down off the backwoods bus.

She said, "That's what he was telling me. Now we'll find out how much truth there is in it. Don't worry about it."

The agency girl moved on. Most of her work would be over by now; Dizzy was out of the way, and the party was running under its own momentum. It would probably carry on like this for at least another hour, and then the first of the departures would begin; the ones with an early start in the morning, the ones with teenaged babysitters, the ones who rarely went out anyway . . . an hour after that they'd be down to the hard core, and an hour after *that* it would just be a case of guiding out those last drunks who were too far-gone to find the door.

She wondered what Dizzy and Alina Peterson were doing, right now. Others besides the agency girl must have seen them leaving together; she wondered how long it would take for the news to reach Pete.

And what, she couldn't help wondering, would happen then?

TWENTY-THREE

The reason for Dizzy's locking of the door behind them became apparent within a minute, when Alina heard a hesitant tap on the other side followed by a young woman's voice calling Dizzy's name. Dizzy shook his head and put a finger to his lips, calling to her for silence; so Alina waited, and after a while the young woman gave up and went away. Alina relaxed a little. Dizzy hadn't even been tense.

He took her through to show her the four-roomed suite that was his private living space within Liston Hall. The lounge was as big and as bare as a dance studio, with three evenly-spaced sets of french windows on one side that could be opened out onto the unlit stone terrace; the floor was of deeply polished boards with no carpet, the furniture was mostly plain white leather, and at the focus stood a hi-fi system which looked like a stolen chunk of a space shuttle.

Alina turned to Liston. He was leaning on the wall with his arms folded, waiting. His little-boy mask had slipped by a fraction, a sure sign of the energies that had been taken from him in the past hour, and someone else was looking out – someone much harder, more calculating.

She said, "If it's what you want to hear, I'm impressed."

"I'm glad something impresses you."

"What do you mean?"

"Nothing." He seemed to rouse himself, and as he stepped away from the wall his mask was back in place. "You're just not what I'm used to. How do you think I did?"

"How do I think you did what?"

"My public relations act. I'm under threat of death from Bob and Tony if I don't carry it off." He led the way across the room to one of the white sofas, and dropped onto it gratefully without waiting for her.

She said, "I saw them earlier. Do they work for you?"

"Kind of. They're friends from way back, they look after me. It's generally agreed that I need looking after. I always seem to get into

110

trouble on my own. My mother always reckoned I'd end up either in prison or in parliament."

Alina perched herself on the far end of the three-seater.

"You don't look like a troublemaker to me," she said.

"I don't *make* trouble, it just follows me around like some dog in the street." He gave her a sideways, half-serious look. "This is a warning, you realise."

"And is there anything else I ought to know about you?"

"Oh, I'm feckless, shiftless, untrustworthy . . . I'm also very, very devious."

"So I can see. Why did you ask me up here?"

"Why did you come?"

There was silence for a moment as they held each other's eyes, broken only by the faint sound of dance music from down below.

Finally, Alina said, "You made me curious."

Liston smiled, as a Grand Master might at an adept chess move from a lesser-rated opponent. "That'll do as a beginning," he said. "Look, I'm supposed to go down and do another five minutes of charm and chat with the ladies in the kitchen now they've done their stuff. Will you stay around?"

"Why?"

"Because I'm asking you to."

"What if I'm with somebody?"

"Are you?"

He waited, but Alina didn't reply. She kept her gaze even.

"It's your choice," he went on. "I honestly won't be long. You can pick out some music and crack open a decent bottle. Can't join you in that, I'm afraid, but don't trust the stuff downstairs."

She seemed to sharpen, and to look at him now with sudden suspicion. "Why not?"

"I know the way Bob works. I wouldn't put it past him to be slipping something into the juice when nobody's looking. Guaranteed way of loosening off everybody's self-control. Problem is, take one too many and you'll start to see hair growing out of the walls. What do you say?"

"I'll think it over," Alina said, and she got to her feet. Something in the atmosphere of the room seemed to have changed in the course of the last few moments, and Liston couldn't say for certain what it was. She said, "Can I get some fresh air?"

"Try the terrace," Liston said. "You can get a good view of the moonlight on the lake, if you go in for that sort of thing. See you later?"

"Perhaps," Alina said.

She was already crossing the room to the nearest of the french windows, moving with an urgency that she didn't seem prepared to explain.

"Your choice," Liston reminded her as she stepped out into the air. Maybe she's a control freak, he was thinking, getting into an unreasonable flap just because she might have taken something that could unclench her a little; but then if he'd kept his mouth shut, she'd never even have known.

A control freak might be interesting to play around with, he was thinking, especially in his weakened condition – get her so far along, and then she'd almost certainly want to do all the work.

But she didn't even look back.

"What was that?" Wayne said; but Sandy, it seemed, hadn't heard anything.

"What was what?"

"I heard a door," he said, glancing up into the darkness in the direction of the stone parapet. Sandy pulled her dress back up over her shoulders, just in case, and the two of them sat as still as they could and listened.

There was no sound other than that of the distance-filtered disco music, but the mood of solitude had been broken. As he zipped Sandy up, Wayne said, "You want to go somewhere else?"

"If you mean that crummy flat of yours, no."

"That's not what I had in mind."

"Not to your dad's house, either."

"No, better than that. And really private."

"Where?"

"It's a surprise. Satisfaction guaranteed."

Sandy considered for a moment. Wayne knew how finicky she could be about place and mood, but this plan was one which had all objections beaten before they could even be raised.

Finally, she said, "How far?"

"A short walk in the woods, a warm summer night," (he was embroidering a little here – the night was warm enough, but it was hardly summer yet) "moonlight on the water, what more could you want?"

Sandy looked critically at her shoes, and hiccupped. "A taxi," she said.

"Well . . . I could run ahead and get the van."

"Oh, great," she said, and she hitched up her dress so that she could get to her feet; there was simply no elegant way of doing it.

112

"Come on, I can probably use a walk anyway. Something in this stuff's starting to mess up my head."

The "stuff" in question was Bob Ivie's Hawaiian special; between them they'd managed almost to empty the bowl that Wayne had sneaked out. Wayne had halfway believed in his own account of the innocence of its contents, but now he wasn't so sure. It didn't taste of anything much, and it didn't hit particularly hard, but then he didn't exactly feel steady on his feet as he came to stand, either.

Sandy was already picking her way through the garden towards the front of the house.

Leaving the punchbowl lying there for the clearup people to find in the morning, Wayne followed her.

Above them on the balcony terrace, Alina Petrovna stood a little way back from the parapet. She looked at the moon, the lake, and the dark forest beyond, but she saw only defeat.

She might have known that all of her efforts would end like this; it was simply a truth that she hadn't been wanting to face. She'd been avoiding it for so long, but she had no choice about facing it now. She moved to the parapet, and paused with her hand on the stonework. Wayne and Sandy were gone. It wasn't too late. She could ignore the call. She could turn around and go back inside, smile, lose herself amongst strangers again.

She closed her eyes for a second and touched the small space of forehead between her brows. But the pressure didn't help, and nor did the night air, nor any of the great machinery of circumstance that had, without her realising it, been combining against her to produce this moment.

Again, she looked at the moon.

And then, with a dancer's grace, she cleared the parapet.

She landed with barely a sound.

TWENTY-FOUR

Pete was beginning to think that the party had taken on an unpleasant edge. The noises had become louder, the lights were brighter and sharper, and the people around him seemed to be turning into over-expansive parodies of their true selves. For Pete it was almost like being a teenager again, going to see *2001* on magic mushrooms. They'd tasted like shit but they'd sure done the stuff; everybody else had been whining about the story while Pete had been lying there with his tongue hanging out. Tonight, only a few minutes earlier, he'd been following handwritten signs down a service passageway to the toilets when, for one brief half-second, he'd seen a local councillor emerging through the doorway with the head of a pig on his shoulders. It was barely more than a flash impression and the man was turning and the light wasn't at all good; and besides, he pretty much resembled a pig anyway, so the effect was probably no more than a moment's mistake. But after that Pete had sworn that he'd touch nothing stronger than tapwater for the rest of the evening, and so far he'd been sticking to it.

He couldn't see Alina anywhere around. He supposed that she had to be somewhere and he reminded himself that they weren't supposed to be together so what did it matter, but still he kept catching himself scanning the crowd for her. Plenty of known faces nodded back at him, but none of them was hers.

He stopped by a book-lined alcove to remove his tie completely and to get some air. The books were behind glass, and the reflection that stared back at him showed the face of a stranger. He'd no reason to be anxious, and no right to it either.

So stop it, he told his reflection.

"Ross Aldridge," Ted Hammond announced breathlessly, triumphantly, as he appeared at Pete's side. He was flushed, happy, and in his shirtsleeves.

Pete said, "Who?"

"Name of the local copper that I couldn't remember. He just left. If it's the host you're looking for, he's long gone, too."

"It's tough at the top."

"Well, it isn't so great here at the bottom, most of the time. Do me a favour?"

"What kind of a favour?"

"Dance with one of the Venetz sisters for me."

"Which one?"

"Doesn't matter, but we have to ask both because you can't split them up, see?"

Pete took his jacket off, and hung it on one of the bookcase doorknobs. There was a cloakroom somewhere, but this would do as well. He said, "Okay. But if either one of them gets frisky, you're on your own."

"Deal," Ted Hammond said, and they set off to see if the sisters had joined the party yet.

Sandy was a few months younger than Wayne, but unlike Wayne she'd stayed on at school. Her mother had ideas about her going to university, but Sandy knew her limitations; she planned on a two-year course at a catering college, and had diplomatically said nothing about it yet. Wayne, in her mother's view, was more than just an ordinary valley kid; he was a walking symbol of everything that she didn't want for her daughter.

It was a big weight for him to be carrying, but there didn't seem to be a lot that he could do about it. He stayed out of the way as much as he could, and Sandy mentioned him as infrequently as possible.

The one thing that she didn't do was to give him up.

He was walking just ahead of her now, checking out the trail in the darkness. It was mostly soft grass and woodchips here, and she'd stepped out of her shoes and was now carrying them, walking barefoot.

Wayne said, "Feeling any better?" He was referring to the slight dizziness she'd experienced when they'd first come into the moon-shadow of the trees.

"Yeah," she said. "A bit. Must have been all those flowers. I'm sensitive to flowers."

"Is that right?"

"And perfume. There's only certain perfumes I can wear."

"Better make me a list for Christmas," Wayne said, and he gave her his hand to help her out onto the lakeside track. She stopped for a moment, and put her shoes back on for walking on the hard tarmac. She was curious as to where they were going, but so far Wayne had refused to say; as far as she knew, this was just one of the Estate roads and it led nowhere.

Sandy said, "We'd better not be heading for your place, even if you've been doing it up. Oil and stuff affect me worse than anything."

"It'd take us an hour to get there. This is really close." His shadow touched her lightly on the nose. "You're not going to believe your eyes."

Their destination, Sandy discovered a few minutes later, was the Liston Hall boat house.

He took out the keys that he'd brought from the office back home, and opened the door. He went in ahead of her and tried the lights; they flickered once, but he seemed to know what to do because he went inside and Sandy heard him thump something, and then all the lights came on. As she stood waiting, she felt again that wave of dizziness that bordered close to nausea, and she put a hand against the rough wall of the boat house to steady herself. As Wayne returned, she quickly took her hand away; she wasn't going to tell him about this, not if she could help it.

He beckoned her in, and took her to the rail to look over. What she saw under the lights was a boat, a big one in too small a space.

"We're handling the brokerage on it," Wayne explained. "Wait until you see inside."

She had to be careful on the stairway down to the quay, because it was steep and the treads were so narrow. Wayne helped her aboard and then darted ahead, switching on all the lights and then dimming some of them to create an impression of instant welcome. When they reached the after stateroom, he left her prodding the waterbed as he fiddled with the stereo to get some low-level background music. He asked her what she thought.

"It's just like something in a film," she said.

He stood behind her and unhooked her dress; a shrug of her shoulders, and it fell easily to the floor. She shivered a little as its touch ran over her. The room seemed to give a lurch, but she ignored it. She stepped out of the dress and then turned and sat on the bed, rather heavily; smiling at Wayne to show that she was okay, she kicked off her shoes one at a time.

Wayne sat beside her, unbuttoning his shirt. "We can run a video if you want," he said. "There's some really strange stuff in there."

"Things are strange enough, thanks," Sandy said.

She got to her feet again, hooked her thumbs into her white cotton briefs, and took them off. That was everything, not counting the thin gold chain around her neck. Wayne seemed frozen in mid-action as she quickly threw back the top sheet of the bed and climbed in; but then he recovered, and started an awkward fight to get his shoes off without actually untying their laces.

Something bumped against the hull, and sent a faint thud all the way through the boat.

"What was that?" she said, half-sitting up and holding the sheet against her.

"I don't know. Driftwood, probably."

"Are we locked in?"

"No," Wayne admitted. He might have lied about it if he'd been able to think more quickly, but the truth was out before he knew it.

"Go on, then, Wayne," she said. "Just to make it safe."

Wayne smiled, and she could see that he was nervous; not of the shadows outside, but of the uncertain country that lay ahead. Once entered, there was no true return. Shirtless and now shoeless, he went out to put the lock on the boat house door.

As soon as he'd gone, Sandy lay back on the waterbed. She heaved a great sigh. She so much wanted this to be exactly right; and perhaps, by the time that Wayne returned, she'd have enough of a grip on herself to ensure that it would be.

A small, sick feeling lay in Wayne like a swallowed stone. It was starting to go wrong, and he couldn't quite work out how or why. The participants were willing and the setting was ideal; they'd been close to it often enough, so what was happening now?

Forget it, he tried to tell himself. Everything's going fine. Everything's going to be great.

He stepped out onto the deck of the Princess, and looked over the side into the water. He checked all the way around the boat – or at least, as far as he could – but he saw no driftwood, nothing. Perhaps it was in the shadows under the overhang, propelled there by the lake swell; but as he was trying to see, the overhead lights blinked once, and then again, and then they went out completely.

The only illumination now was from the dim curtained portholes and the deck light of the boat itself. He called out, "I won't be a minute. Don't fall asleep on me!"

But there was no reply from inside.

Leaving the lit Princess was almost like leaving home, because its glow in the darkness was so warm. He climbed to the upper level, and from the top of the stairs he could see a wide slice of moonlight telling him that he'd not only forgotten to lock the door behind them, in his haste he'd neglected even to close it; he crossed the decking and closed it now, switching the key from the outside to the inside and turning it in the lock. Then he felt his way along the wall to where he knew the faulty junction box to be.

He made a fist and banged on the casing, hard.

There was a loud spat, a brilliant flash of blue that almost burned out his night vision, and a sharp smell of ozone and cinders. Wayne was so taken aback by this that it was a moment before he realised something else; the hand that had touched the box had come away wet.

He couldn't understand it . . . but he knew that he'd narrowly avoided a serious shock, and there was no way in which he'd be prepared to touch the box again. The Princess had spotlights, he'd turn them around this way when it was time to get Sandy to the door and then he'd go back on his own to switch them off. That wouldn't be easy; even now he was beginning to remember what it had been like when he'd been small and afraid of the dark, unable to sleep without a nightlight.

He decided that he couldn't tell her about this. Not until afterwards, anyway.

Slowly, carefully, he felt his way back towards the stairs. The boards were rough and splintery underfoot. There was a noise as he started to descend; but it was just the boat, moving slightly with the swell of the lake and rubbing against one of those padded joists that stuck out too far from the quayside.

Anticipation was building with every descending step. He was almost trembling with it. His grip on the rail was shaky. On the quay, he almost tripped himself as he went to re-board.

Wayne, he heard in a whisper from behind him.

He spun around so fast that he came close to falling over, his heart leaping like a bird in a snare. They weren't alone; and then the next thought was that Sandy must have come up from below and was now standing on the quay, but then that thought died as what he'd taken for her shadow came out from under the stairway.

Relief coursed through him like a shot of heroin.

"Miss Peterson," he managed to say. "What are you doing here?"

But as she came forward he faltered, and his certainty died; it *was* her, but it wasn't, in a way that he couldn't even have begun to explain. What he seemed to see was something else, something that wore her like a shell, and it was walking towards him. Her skin was blue-green and marbled in the reflected lake water, and her eyes were as dull and expressionless as a shark's. He wanted to move, to step back, but nothing seemed to be happening.

This wasn't the choice I wanted to make, Wayne, she said. *Please try to forgive me.*

And then she reached for him.

*   *   *

118

Sandy lay still for a while, hoping to feel better; but being flat on her back didn't help, and closing her eyes only made it worse. Finally, she had to give in.

"Sorry, Wayne," she said, although he wasn't around to hear. "Tonight just ain't the night."

Slowly, almost painfully, she got out of the bed and started to dress. By now she'd definitely come to pin the blame on the stuff they'd had to drink; every time she even thought of it she came close to throwing up. It wasn't drunkenness – she'd been drunk twice, and neither time had been anything like this – but something else altogether. She didn't know what her mother was going to say when Wayne finally got her home; she could only hope that things would improve along the way.

Wayne came down the stairs behind her, walking slowly. She didn't turn, not wanting to see his obvious disappointment on top of everything else.

"Another time, okay, Wayne?" she said, doing her best to sound bright and cheerful and hearing the evidence that she wasn't succeeding. "I don't think I'm such a good sailor. Will you zip me up?"

She'd definitely annoyed him. He zipped her dress in silence, and his touch was cold.

Sandy tried to think of something to say, something that would explain how she felt; but the image that formed in her mind was of a punchbowl brimming with vomit, and she knew instantly that she was about to do likewise. Without even looking at him, she dashed for the companionway and the open deck above.

Which was how she came face-to-face with the phenomenon of the two Waynes.

Wayne number two was sitting – or rather, slumped – in the dining alcove of the deck saloon, and he was leaking all over the expensive-looking upholstery. His head was at a strange angle because of the way that he'd kind of subsided into the corner, and his eyes were slightly open. They didn't seem to be focused on anything in particular. His hair was dark and wet, and plastered down close.

Sandy was so much taken by surprise that her sickness was forgotten. Life had suddenly taken a mis-step, and she was completely thrown. She turned around, looking to Wayne number one for an explanation.

Everything caught up with her then, and everything slammed into its proper place.

Alina surged up the companionway towards her, eyes burning like new stars. Sandy drew breath to scream but she was stopped halfway by Alina's clamped-down hand, which filled her mouth and lungs with the rank taste of stagnant water. Quickly, Alina stepped around her so that she could hold Sandy's head in both of her hands; Sandy made a weak attempt to struggle, but it was like fighting a rock.

Alina gently turned her, so that she was facing Wayne again.

I'll take you to where he is, she said. *He'll be waiting there for you.*

Sandy fought for air. Her vision was starting to blur, with something more than just tears.

Then blackout.

Tom Amis is a carpenter. Seven days a week he works on the new ski lodge in the woodlands overlooking the valley, his private quarters little more than a sleeping-bag in a back room behind the new reception area. The bricklayers were the first to leave, followed by the tarmac gang and the plasterers. Amis is a loner, which is just as well. Because Amis is alone.

The owner has been calling by every few days to check on progress, but now is in Barbados. Amis hopes that it's cloudy, but not so cloudy that the owner should come back and start breathing over his shoulder again. Amis has only three definite things in his life; his skills, his van, and his career plan, and all of them seem to have been taking a beating over the past few weeks. Two of his new windows, big ones, have warped and had to be redone. The van has broken down. And by his career plan he should have been finished and out of here by now, instead of which he's way over time on a fixed-price job and his prospects of retirement at thirty-five are receding now even faster than they were before.

It had once seemed like a reasonable strategy for a loner: live cheap, move around, invest everything and then cut loose while still young and really start to live. But it isn't working out. The money's mostly there, but the spirit in him seems to have been leaking away. He's starting to realise that by the time he's in a position to do anything that he wants, there'll be nothing that he really wants to do. He'll be returning to an empty fairground of deserted stalls, with only the faint remembered echo of the music that he's been ignoring.

He's not just a loner any more. He's lonely. But the habit of solitude is something that has to be kicked, like a drug, and Tom Amis isn't sure that he has the reserves. There's a party at Liston Hall tonight; he could have gone, but instead he's here, same as every night, in this hundred-year-old hunting lodge with its rambling outbuildings and its faulty generator and only a photograph to talk to.

And the radio.

Some nights, he calls up the late show DJ on the request line. He never gives his name, and he always asks for the same dedication. They love that kind of stuff on late-night radio. They call him the mystery man with a record for his mystery girl; people have been writing in wanting to know more, women especially, but Amis doesn't have the will to respond. Six months ago he'd have gone for it, maybe written back to some of them, seen it as a way out of the rut that his life had become . . . but not now. There's no way of explaining the rules of attraction, and Amis is even less expert than most.

He stretches out on his camp bed. The lights flicker to the beat of the generator. He looks at his photograph.

He took it himself, out on the terrace at the lakeside restaurant. Amis doesn't have much in the way of material goods but his camera, like his watch, is one of the best. He ran off almost an entire film that day, mostly on views, but of all the shots this one was the best of them. What does it show?

His waitress.

He stares at the photograph. He knows almost nothing about her.

But he can't get her out of his mind.

He wonders why.

In another town, outside yet another radio station, Pavel Ilyitch returns to his car. It's still in the shadows where he left it, grimy windscreen reflecting the neon tracery of a department-store sign on the next block. Five floors below, somebody is sounding off as the traffic before them makes a slow start at the lights.

Will it be here? Will this be where he finds her?

Pavel levers himself into his car, forcing movement out of a body that longs for sleep more than anything else. The most that he can promise it will be a few snatched hours on the back seat in a quiet place somewhere. This is how almost all of his days have been spent, casting bait, checking behind him, moving on; apart from odd nights in hostels where he can get a bath and about thirteen hours of near-coma to catch up, he's been continuously on the road since the dawn that he stole the car and the cash that has become his fighting fund.

The car is barely recognisable now; so filthy that some kids have finger-written their names in the dirt on the boot. He's had a couple of bumps, as well, one of which has left a long and jagged crease in the body almost from headlight to tail-light; that one wasn't his

121

fault, but he drove away from it fast to avoid the questions that would certainly follow. The inside is a mess, even though he's come to look on it as his only home and so tries to keep it straight.

He switches on the interior light and picks up a bundle from the passenger seat. The main part of the bundle is the Daily Mail Yearbook, *much-creased and stuffed with notes and odd bits of paper. It's held together by an elastic band which has two ballpoint pens clamped under it. He takes the band off and starts to sort through; he ticks off one more name from the* Yearbook's *list of radio stations, and then copies its telephone number across onto his checklist. When he's exhausted the list, he isn't sure what he'll do; he's heard of pirate stations and Citizens' Band clubs, but he'll have to find out more.*

The idea of giving up is no longer a real possibility. For Pavel, as for Alina, there can be no going back.

He yawns and then he rests an elbow on the steering wheel, his head on his hand. Nobody is around. Nobody will mind if he just grabs a few minutes' rest before he moves on – although rest, for Pavel, has become little more than a bothersome physical requirement with no spiritual element in it. Pavel is driven, and the edge has become his home territory.

Someone raps on the window.

Pavel is jerked awake; he sees a uniform.

The man mouths at him through the glass.

"This is the hotel's car park, you know. Not a public doss house."

Pavel nods, embarrassed, and he doesn't meet the parking attendant's eyes as he starts the car.

And as he drives away, he's thinking not about the assertiveness of a petty official, but about the horizon. In the province of Karelia, close to the border with Finland, the horizon beyond the land and the lakes is always flat and far away. This was the landscape in which Alina spent her childhood; he wonders in what kind of landscape she finds herself now, and if her chances of happiness are any greater.

He's doubtful.

Because he knows that no matter how hard you might try to reach it, no horizon ever gets any closer.

V: Rusalka (I)

TWENTY-FIVE

The next time that he saw Diane was at the funeral, some three weeks later. She came alone, as a representative of the Liston estate, and she stood alongside him in Three Oaks Bay's tiny hillside churchyard. Together they watched across the old gravestones as Ted Hammond waited patiently by the lychgate, thanking each of the mourners as they left.

"I don't know what to say to him," she admitted.

"Who does?" Pete said.

Ted was looking dignified, but broken. His clothes didn't fit, his skin was grey, his eyes were dead. His sister had come over with her family from the next valley and was standing just behind him; Shaun had flown home as well, a taller, broader Wayne-that-might-have-been, but he hadn't yet come out of the church.

When Pete finally turned to move away, Diane had gone. Standing in her place was Alina, red-eyed and waiting to be taken home.

They'd found them after five days, with Sandy's parents hammering at Ted every minute of the time. Ted's initial fear was that they'd done something stupid and run away together, but then after a while he'd begun to hope for this and nothing worse. The missing keys to the boat house and to the Princess had been the clue, spotted by Pete and reported to Ross Aldridge in a phonecall when Ted was out of earshot. It all made a horrible kind of sense, and he hoped that he was wrong. But he wasn't. Aldridge had found the lights shorted out, the cruiser's batteries run down, and the two children lying just under the surface of the water inside the big sliding gates. They'd been entwined in an embrace, and Sandy's hair had been spread like a fan; by Aldridge's account it had been a touching, harrowing sight.

The inquest was local, held in the parish hall and presided over by a doctor from the big resort town further down the lake. The locked doors, the circumstances, and the lack of contradictory medical evidence led to a verdict of misadventure within fifteen minutes. One of the tabloids got a couple of columns out of it – *Teen Lovers' Nude Death Riddle on Dizzy's Yacht* – but mostly the papers left it alone. The entire village closed down on the day of the funeral, and the trickle of early-season trippers found themselves looking around bemused at the drawn curtains in the houses and the handwritten notes in the shop windows before shrugging to themselves and passing on through. Two kids drowning in an accident didn't sound like much to the world outside.

Neither Pete nor Alina spoke during the drive home afterwards. Alina had sniffled her way through half a box of Kleenex from the glove compartment, and she seemed even more disinclined toward conversation than Pete. He couldn't help noticing how much she was being affected; it was a sign, he supposed, of how she'd come to consider the valley her home and its people her own. On a day when good feelings were pretty scarce, it didn't seem wrong to spare just one moment to be glad for her.

As always, she went straight to her room when they got home. Pete went to the refrigerator, took out a beer, and then carried it along with a kitchen chair out onto the porch. His inclination was to be down at the yard. But Ted had his real family around him now.

Pete was remembering the night – it seemed like years ago, but it wasn't so long – that the three of them had sat in the Zodiac down in the workshop and Wayne had made some gentle fun of Pete's funeral suit. He was wearing it again today. So much change, in so short a time; Pete felt as if he'd aged more in ten weeks than in the ten years that had gone before. Now he sat out on the porch with his chair tilted back and his feet up on the rail, and he sipped at his beer as he watched the patterns of sunlight on the forest over on the far side of the track.

He remembered what Alina had said to him, way back at that first dawn. Her instincts were right, this was a fine place to be.

It was just that some days could be rather less fine than others.

After an hour he went to see how she was doing, and to see if she needed anything. She smiled weakly, and said not. She was sitting on the bed with her album – that sparsely-peopled record of whatever it was that she'd left behind – and she wasn't leafing through it but hugging it close, as if it was a physical source of comfort to her when times were at their lowest.

She said, "I've been trying to think about Wayne, but instead I've been thinking about myself. Isn't that terrible?"

But Pete said that it wasn't, because for much of the hour he'd been doing the same. It wasn't something that he'd intended, but it wasn't something he could help. All through the valley people would be reflecting on the brevity of life and their own missed chances at happiness, and thinking of their common frailty in the shadow of the dark beast that had passed so close and taken someone so young.

And then he said, "You want to come for a ride in the car? Get out of the valley for a while, see somewhere new?" But again she smiled and she shook her head, saying that she preferred to stay here for a while and . . . just think about things. And Pete was relieved, because he hadn't really felt like going anywhere, either.

He left her in her room, thinking that perhaps he'd climb up to the rocks on the crest of the headland and watch the sunlight on the lake until the mountain shadows took it away.

He left her there, on the bed, with the book held close.

And then, when Pete McCarthy was safely out of the way, she opened the book, and the book spoke to her.

You've been unwell, the book said. *My name is Belov. I'm a doctor.*

Interlude: What the Book Said

He didn't look much like a doctor to Alina. He was crouched in the corner by the big tiled kitchen range, his sleeves rolled up and his shirt and trousers covered in white ash. He'd been cleaning out the fireplace and clearing the flue, neither of which appeared to have been used in years. He was a big, dark, heavy man something in the manner of a friendly black bear, going a little thin on top.

He smiled at her, and started to get to his feet.

Alina said, "Am I still in prison?"

"Technically," he said, "you never were. But no, this isn't a prison."

"It doesn't look like a hospital."

"No."

What it looked like was a long-deserted log farmhouse, with stale rush matting on the floor and at the windows coarse-woven net curtains that had faded almost to nothing. Alina was holding onto the door, because the six steps that she'd taken to reach it had almost been enough to exhaust her; Belov dusted off his hands and came over to her now, and he took her by the shoulders and turned her around and steered her back toward the bed that she'd just left.

His touch was like a doctor's, firm and impersonal. And, of course, she'd seen him before; he'd been the third man on the commission that had interviewed her, the one who'd sat next to the Cheka's doctor and who'd listened to her slurred responses without ever saying anything. Now he was straightening the covers over her as she lay, utterly spent, and he was promising her answers to her unspoken questions in the morning. She could barely turn her head to watch him as he backed out of the room and closed the door; a moment later, the sounds of the fire irons against stone resumed. It was this strange subterranean thumping that had wakened and drawn her in the first place.

She was still wearing the thin cotton dress that she'd worn in the prison hospital, but now there was a shawl around her shoulders as well. She didn't know how she'd come by it, and she'd only the vaguest memories of her journey to this place. Why she was here, she couldn't imagine; but her head was clearer than it had been in a long time, which meant that she must have gone for some hours without any kind of an injection.

There was no denying the fact that there were gaps in her memory because of the drugs. There was no way of being certain how long she'd spent on the ward; it might have been six weeks or six years, but she was guessing at six months because this had been the first commission review that she'd received.

Unless there had been others, and she hadn't remembered.

They'd taken her from the police cells after two days. She'd been half-expecting a trial and then a labour camp but instead, there was an ambulance. Seeing this, she'd known what lay ahead. They took her out, across the wide Neva river to the north-east of the city, to a long street of factories and high concrete walls where tourists and visitors had little reason to go. The prison hospital fitted into its surroundings perfectly, a four-storey warehouse of human cargo. It had small, dark windows in a main building set back from the road behind a staff block and a perimeter wall of newer red brick. *Grim* and *forbidding* were the two well-used words that came to mind as she looked up at the building for the first time; but there were no words that could easily describe the helpless terror that she felt as the side-gate opened before them and the ambulance had driven through.

She'd thought that at least she'd be put with her own kind – border-crossers and minor political dissidents – but it didn't happen. Her "own kind" were in a minority. Instead she was confined for twenty hours a day on a ward for the criminally insane, most of them doped and many of them bruised from the warders' heavy handling. She'd sit in her dressing-gown by the window and try to listen for the electric trams on the distant street, anything to give some kind of shape or structure to her day, but the noise made even this impossible.

And then her programme of treatment started, and the idea seemed to lose its importance to her.

This was better, she thought as she lay on her cot in the farmhouse. *Anything* was better than the ward. At least now she was beginning to get her focus back, even if her strength hadn't yet come with it.

Belov brought her some broth about an hour later, and he helped her up to the bowl. Apparently his efforts with the kitchen range had finally paid off. For a while Alina was afraid that she was going to throw it all up again, but she didn't.

Tomorrow, he promised her whenever she tried to ask him anything. Tomorrow, when she'd be stronger. And then he left her alone, climbing the wooden stairs to what she would later learn were his own makeshift quarters on the floor above. If he locked her in, she didn't hear it.

The next morning, she got to go outside.

It was only a few steps, but now she was leaning on his arm for steadiness rather than support. She felt almost weightless, as if she was made out of eggshells. The daylight brought tears, and not only because of its brightness.

They were in a village of perhaps a dozen houses and a white log church, out on a plain somewhere under a big, big sky; each building stood well apart from its neighbours with just open common land between them, and the grass on that common land was deep and uncut. It rippled in the light breeze like a sea.

Alina said, "I don't see anyone."

"No," Belov agreed. "Nobody lives here now."

"No one at all?"

"The entire community was resettled a long time ago. The place hasn't been used since then."

"But why?"

"Well, you know the military. We're not so far from the border. Maybe there's a radar station over in the woods, or maybe they want everyone to think there is."

They were making a slow circuit of the farmhouse and its barn, a lean-to of roughly dressed timber made dark and smooth with age. The roof was of shingle with planks nailed over.

Alina said, "What if we're found?" But it wasn't something that seemed to worry Belov.

"I've got permission for us to be here," he said. "As long as you stay around the village and the paths I'll show you tomorrow, you shouldn't have any problems."

"You said it wasn't a prison."

"No more so than anywhere else."

So, another tomorrow.

Alina woke to this one feeling sharp and dangerous and – within limits – ready to go. She found that Belov had laid out her own clothes as she slept; she'd lost weight, she noticed as she dressed, and she hadn't really had much to lose.

After a plain breakfast they went out again, still taking it slowly but this time with more of a distance in mind. Belov told her the name of the village. It meant nothing to her.

"I don't suppose it would," Belov said. "It's the kind of place that no one ever hears of, where nothing ever happens. Something happened here, though."

"And that's why you've brought me?"

"Let me tell you the story. Questions later."

They took a winding dirt alley that led through the back of the village between houses and outhouses. By the sides of the outhouses were stacks of trimmed poles and branches and brushwood, all grown-over with moss. Alina had assumed that Belov was taking her to another of the buildings, but it seemed now that he was going to lead her out of the settlement altogether.

He said, "The farmhouse we're staying in, a small girl lived there. She slept in the room where you're sleeping now. She was bright, and she did very well at school. Most families in a village like this expect their children to work on the farm when they get older, but in this case it was different. She was an only child, and her parents wanted more for her. As soon as she was old enough, they were going to send her to stay with relatives in the city so that she could get a better education. They were tied to the land, but their daughter wouldn't be. With me so far?"

"Yes," Alina said, although in truth she was wondering what point he might be trying to make. As far as she could tell, they were completely alone in the village. Back at the farmhouse they had food supplies in a cardboard box, and Belov himself had taken the role of housekeeper as well as doctor. Today he was tousled, and even more in need of a shave; under his suit jacket, he now wore an old pullover.

They were passing the last of the houses now. Ahead lay marshy fields, neatly divided by a raised path consisting of two parallel rails of wood pegged into the ground.

Belov said, "This girl was small, and very fair. They say she looked like an angel." He waved his hand. "Now, see this house. The Markevitch family lived here, very big family, lots of sons. Not enough brains to go around, though, according to the neighbours, and the youngest boy was out of luck. He was born a simpleton. When he was seventeen years old, he was still playing with wooden blocks. But happy. His name was Viktor."

They moved on, out toward the fields, and Belov continued with the story.

"He followed the girl around all the time. He was like a puppy, completely devoted. She was only nine years old and she wasn't much of a size for that, but everybody knew that Viktor was harmless. A lot of the time she just seemed to forget that he was there, and he'd shamble along behind her just happy to stay close."

"How long ago was this?"

"Quite a few years. The girl's still alive, but Viktor was drowned. I'm going to show you where."

They came to a simple fence which was crossed by a stile, and here Alina rested for a couple of minutes before going on. The place that Belov had in mind was just a couple of hundred metres further, he told her. It was reedy marshland here, the grasses awash in several inches of diamond-clear water. The path zigzagged between dry rises in the land. On one of these, Belov stepped down from the wooden rails.

"A lot of this would have been different then," he explained. "The shape of the marsh has changed over the years, but we're somewhere close to the spot. They came out along the track we just followed, the very same one. Only the girl came back, and she was soaked and muddy and she could hardly speak. Two of Viktor's brothers came out, and found him."

"How could he drown?" Alina said. She was looking down at the water, which was only inches deep.

"Nobody knows. It could have been that someone forced him down, and held his face under. But that wouldn't have been easy. He wasn't bright, but he was big and he was very strong. He'd have struggled hard." Belov looked thoughtfully at the ground around them, as if he might still read signs that had long ago disappeared. "They called the doctor in from the nearest town, and the local militia chief questioned the girl. I've seen both of their reports – the file on the case has never been closed, in all this time. They asked her what had happened, and she said that a *rusalka* from the lake had hurt Viktor. You know what the *rusalki* are?"

Alina peered toward the lake, which was hardly more than a sliver on the horizon. She said nothing.

"They're an old superstition, lake spirits in female form. Very beautiful, very dangerous. Men can't resist them. They're supposed to bring a strange kind of ecstatic death by drowning – although it isn't really described as a death at all, more a passage from one world to another. There's something like it in the folklore of just about every culture. And no matter how many times they asked the girl, no matter how many different ways they approached it, her story was always the same."

"So nobody believed her."

"She was a child. She looked even younger than she was. What were they going to do, beat it out of her? Maybe they even tried that. They didn't put it in the records, if they did. But the harder they pressed her, the more confused she would probably have become. Children's fantasies are as real to them as anything else; but not many get thrown up against them so hard."

"What happened?"

"Officially, it became an accident. What else could they say? There was nobody else in the area, and there were no other tracks through the reeds. The girl became so ill that she had to be taken away. She stayed in the city and never came back. And that's all anyone knows . . . except for the girl herself."

Alina looked at him, but his face gave nothing away. He seemed open, empty of guile. She said, "I think you're trying to tell me that I should remember something of this."

"And do you?"

"No."

"Then I'm saying nothing of the kind."

They went back. The subject wasn't raised again.

That evening, Belov set the fire as Alina opened some canned stew. She was feeling as if she'd made a long, exhausting hike instead of just the kilometre or so that she'd actually walked, but it wasn't a bad feeling. Most of the food was of a kind that she'd never seen in the shops; there was no wine or beer, but Belov had a hip-flask of vodka.

There was no electricity, either, but as night fell they lit candles. Belov chatted easily, although his real talent lay in persuading her to talk without her realising that she'd been persuaded. All that she really learned about him was that yes, he was a psychiatrist – "one of the dissertation-writers", as he referred to himself – and that his wife had died after an illness about five years before. Through all of this there was a shadow falling across the conversation, and it was a while before Alina could bring herself to give it a name.

But it had to be faced, and so she finally said, "How long can I stay here?"

It seemed that Belov had only been waiting for her to ask. "What you're really asking, is whether you'll have to go back."

"Will I?"

"In theory, yes." But there was a faint glimmer in his eyes, like those of a favourite uncle hiding something unexpected behind his back. "I may be able to arrange something. It's mostly a matter of timing . . . but I'll do what I can. Please don't get your hopes up."

There was a long pause.

And then Alina said, "Who was the child?"

But now it was Belov's turn to say nothing.

Some time later, she lay in her bed without sleeping. She was

136

wondering if it was true, if he could somehow arrange her release; doctors had ordered her internment, so surely it was possible for another doctor to end it. But did Belov have the power? Borrowing her for dissertation research was one thing – she was sure now that this was the reason behind her removal from the hospital – but a release seemed, frankly, unlikely.

She'd seen no trace of anyone else in the village, and no sign of anyone along the afternoon's walk. There were no locks on the farmhouse doors. Perhaps, when she'd grown stronger, she could slip away into the night and keep on walking . . . after all, what was the worst that could possibly happen to her? The answer to that was, nothing that hadn't happened already. If they caught her, they caught her. And if they shot her instead – well, perhaps that wouldn't be quite so bad. With this thought in her mind and the sound of Belov's restless pacing on the boards up above, she finally drifted away.

When she awoke late in the morning, Belov wasn't there.

She checked his room, but his bed was cold. His small suitcase had been packed, and looked as if it was ready to go. She went straight back downstairs, got her own clothes together, and made a bundle with some of the provisions. Then she let herself out of the farmhouse, and started to walk.

There was nothing to indicate that he was anywhere in the village, and she didn't want to waste time on being any more thorough than this. She struck out across-country, heading away from the marshes and the distant water with its old-time tales of death.

At any moment she expected to hear his voice behind her, calling her back. If it came, she wouldn't respond. There was a woodland of spruce and pine ahead, where the ground began to climb toward a low, sinuous ridge that was the only feature on this otherwise flat horizon; it rose like a shadow from the plain, dense with trees but delicately etched around the edges.

It took her an hour to reach it, and a patrol was waiting.

There were three of them. With the binoculars that they carried, they must have been able to see her from the moment that she set out. Two of them stood with their rifles levelled at her and the third raised his palm and made a short, brusque, fly-swatting kind of gesture. Not a word was spoken, but the meaning was clear; go back, or else.

The "or else" was a possibility that she'd already considered and decided to embrace, if it came.

But she turned around, and began the long, slow walk back to the village.

There was a red car waiting outside the farmhouse when she reached it; the car's wheels had cut deep tracks through the long grass, tracks that were only just beginning to fade as the plains wind breathed across them. Belov was loading up, getting ready to leave, and he seemed to be in a hurry. He showed no surprise at her obviously unsuccessful attempt to run, nor did he even comment on it.

Instead, he said, "In the car, quickly. We have to go back to the city." And then, when she only stared at the car without responding, he added, "I said it was a matter of timing. Trust me."

What else could she do? She trusted him, and climbed in. As they left the village and found the dirt road by which he'd arrived, she could see that he was nervous. The road was crossed by a locked-down barrier about two kilometres further on, but Belov had a key and the barrier hardly slowed them at all.

Somebody was out of town for two days, he explained, somebody who would block any proposal for her release as a matter of course. They'd have to move fast.

Alina said, "Are you taking a risk for me?"

But instead of answering, Belov said, "Is there anyone you can contact? A friend you can stay with? It's better that you shouldn't be too easy to find."

Alina didn't have to think for long. She said, "There's Pavel."

"What does he do?"

"He's just . . . well, he's someone I know. He offered me a place to stay, if ever I should need it."

Her nerve almost failed her when, more than three hours later, they came into the city along Karl Marx Prospekt and made the turn towards Arsenal Street, where number nine waited for her like the transit house to a hundred-year-old hell. Belov warned her that she'd have to go in, but he promised her that she'd be going no further than the administration block on the street. She followed him obediently, out of the daylight. Once inside he left her in a dim, dingy room where she sat with her bundle and the firm belief that the cruel joke would soon be over and she'd be taken back to her ward. It had all been a dream; perhaps she'd never even left it. She signed the forms that he brought her to sign, even though the name on them wasn't always her own, and then Belov slipped them into a file under a stack of others and took them away again.

Half an hour later, he was back. He led her to a door; the door opened out onto the street. "Hurry," he urged, checking behind him for witnesses, but she had one more question.

"Why?" she said.

But even his eyes gave her no answer.

She saw him once more, a couple of months later. Somehow he'd managed to trace the block where Pavel lived, and he stood in the stairwell and called her name. This was all that he could do, because the numbers on the apartment doors had all been defaced by the people who lived behind them.

He was turning to leave, when he heard a door opening somewhere above.

They found her file lying open on the desk in his office. They'd suspected him of rigging her escape, and now their suspicions were confirmed. They found no mention of Pavel in the file, nor any address for Alina.

Nor did they find one on Belov's body, when they pulled it out of the river the next morning.

Rusalka (II)

TWENTY-SIX

Dimly doing her best to remember what they'd taught her at school, Diane believed that she'd managed to work out the map reference by the time that Ross Aldridge arrived at the Hall. She'd left a message for him about an hour before, within minutes of receiving a call from the foresters' agents. Together they climbed into her Toyota and, with Aldridge keeping the map open on his knees, they drove down toward the lake shore.

Instead of taking the boat house turning, they followed the shoreline in the opposite direction. After a few minutes they passed the first of the estate workers' cottages, two-storey, stone-built, and around three hundred years old. After the last of these (which, being the keeper's, now stood empty) the road degenerated into a track, and the track degenerated even more over the next mile until it was only twin ruts with grass between them. Roots had split the ground in places, and the thickest of these jarred the Toyota so hard that Diane had an uneasy vision of the entire truck falling apart as every spot-weld gave at once, leaving her sitting in the driver's seat with the steering wheel in her hands and nothing but open air all around.

Aldridge, hanging on grimly, said, "Does it get any worse?"

"Don't ask me," Diane said. "I never came this way before."

What looked like another fifty yards on the map turned out to be another quarter-mile of cart track. It brought them out into a grassy clearing by the lake, a shallow bay with a fringe of stony beach. Diane pulled in as soon as the ground was level enough.

They got out.

This was one of the older parts of the forest, and its silence was a thousand-year atmosphere so distilled that it was almost physically affecting. There were high dark trees on every side with slanting shafts of late morning sunlight, with the lake beyond flat and faintly glittering like a slow-moving mirror.

"Hardly anyone ever comes out this far," Diane said, walking toward the middle of the clearing where about half a dozen mounds of earth appeared to have been dug over. "We lease the land out to the forestry people, and they've been doing a helicopter survey."

"When did you get the call?"

"This morning. It showed up when they developed Friday's photographs."

Diane stopped by the first of the mounds, not too close, and waited for Aldridge to catch up. She already knew what she was going to see, but the knowledge didn't make it any less unpleasant. The mound was no mound at all, but actually a deer; a very dead deer, and a long way from fresh. Its eyes and part of its face were gone, and its belly had swollen up hard and tight.

"You explain it," Diane said. "I can't."

Aldridge glanced around the clearing at the others. "You'd do better to ask your gamekeeper," he said.

"I would, but he quit just after I got here."

"Why's that?"

"I told him to. He was taking more from local butchers than he was in wages. I've advertised for a replacement, but I haven't filled the job yet. Could this be a revenge thing?"

"I wouldn't have thought so," Aldridge said, walking over to the next one. "Not from a keeper, killing stock."

"Poachers, then, using poison?"

"We'll need a vet's report to be sure. But poisoned meat isn't much use to anybody, is it?"

"Well," Diane said, with an edge of exasperation in her voice that she couldn't fully conceal, "what do *you* reckon?"

Aldridge shook his head. He seemed to be finding it more than puzzling. The bodies all appeared to be at slightly different stages of decomposition; the one before them now looked to be the most recent of them all. It carried flies like a nimbus of stars.

He prodded a limb with the toe of his boot, but it was rigid. He tried harder, and the whole carcase moved a little and water came from the animal's nose and mouth. Weird, Diane was thinking, as he then put a foot on the animal's side and pressed down.

The reaction was immediate. It collapsed like a punctured airbag, except that what came forth was not air but rank, fetid water, vomiting out in a copious stream and bringing with it a stench that sent them both staggering back several paces.

"Christ," Aldridge said. "I only ever had that once before. It's a drowning smell."

Diane knew that she'd gone pale. "How could they drown?" she said. "They're yards from the lake."

"I don't know. Could be a disease with the same kind of effect, some kind of bloat. Look, could you get hold of some petrol and some plastic sheet?"

"I should think so."

"Well, get some of your lads down here before dark." He indicated the most recent-looking of the bodies. "Have them cover that stag with the polythene and then drag the others together and burn them. Tell them to use gloves and then throw the gloves on the fire when they've done, and then make sure they all go back and have a good scrub down."

"You think it's that serious?" Diane said as they walked back towards the pickup.

"I don't think anything. I'm only playing safe. I'll get in touch with the agriculture people and get them to send someone out first thing tomorrow."

Diane nodded, and then sighed. "I could have done without this," she said, and then she got into the truck.

Ross Aldridge looked back at the six deer.

"So could they, I should think," he said.

That evening Ted Hammond emerged from his house, wearing the old dressing-gown in which he seemed to be spending most of his time these days, and carrying a stiff drink. He took one of the outdoor chairs from the stack at the end of the nearest jetty. It was a fine night, no mist on the lake at all. The air was warm, and the stars were sharp and cold. Someone on a boat out there was having a party, people singing and making more noise than the music they were playing. He wished them well. But he didn't wish that he was with them.

He sat, contemplating the few lights that showed at this hour. Some kind of a fire appeared to be burning far away on the opposite shore, a tiny pinhole in the screen of night. Ted was awake and out here because he'd been hearing Wayne speaking to him, and he was worried about his sanity.

It had happened several times in the weeks since the funeral, and it scared him. The voice always seemed to come from the shadows or from somewhere just aside from where he was looking; and usually the words didn't make any sense, and they passed through his mind so quickly that they'd gone before he could reach for them. He resisted any temptation to treat this as some kind of a revelation because Wayne was dead, and talked to nobody.

The plain message to Ted, actual words apart, was that he was cracking up.

He'd spent most of the evening wrestling with the one fragment that he'd managed to retain, picked out of the air behind him as he'd been standing at the cooker watching his soup boil. He couldn't be sure, but it had sounded like, *We're with her, now*. But with who? His best guess was that the reference was to Nerys, that his unconscious mind had been looking for comfort in the prospect that Wayne would at least be with his mother, in which case he decided that there was probably some hope for his mental state after all. In many ways, he would have preferred to have been able to give himself over to the delusion and accept it as truth; but there seemed to be a definite boundary here, and it wasn't his choice whether or not he crossed it. Just before coming out, he'd phoned the health centre and left a message on their answering machine as his first step in getting himself along to a psychiatrist.

It still wasn't too late to back out. But he didn't think that he would.

The blaze across the water flared, and then died down a little. The party boat came to the end of its song, and the party people gave themselves a round of applause. Two small signals in the night, affirmations of existence from two groups of people who knew nothing of Ted or of each other.

We're with her, now.

Ted didn't feel good.

But he felt a little better.

Tom Amis lay on his fold-down bed in a back room of the ski centre, an unread paperback lying open on his chest. He was bored, and he was lonely. The road gang had turned up unexpectedly that afternoon and had laid and rolled more than two hundred yards of hot tarmac from the main building all the way around to the other side of the restaurant block; now the place didn't look quite so much like a building site any more, and winter opening seemed more of a possibility. It had made for a lively few hours but now that they'd gone the place seemed oddly, unnaturally quiet again. He didn't know when they'd be back; all he knew was that his boss had some kind of private deal going with the gang foreman of a motorway sub-contractor, and the boys always appeared without notice, worked at the speed of practised moonlighters, and probably got their money in a plain envelope passed under a pub table somewhere. There were five of them, and whenever they arrived they came up the woodland track on a big spreader wagon with a battered old van bouncing along behind. They were as ugly as sin and they had no conversation, and he missed them already.

Christ, he thought to himself, I *must* be getting desperate.

He could have taken the isolation better if it wasn't for the batteries in his radio dying on him without warning; usually they faded over a couple of nights but this time it was just *zonk*, no signal. He couldn't even run down to the village to get a new set – they had them in the marina shop at the auto-marine – because his van was temporarily off the road. Now, when he tried to read instead, the lights kept flickering and screwing up his concentration. He knew what it was – tank sediment kept getting into the fuel pipe that fed the generator – but short of a total drain and cleanout, he didn't know of any way to cure it. When it got really bad, like when it cut out completely, he'd take a wrench out and tap all the way along the pipe; sometimes that would help, but having to do it could be a real pain.

Especially if it meant he had to go out into the dark.

He'd never had any particular fear of darkness, but over the past few weeks he seemed to have grown more and more nervous at night. He couldn't explain it. But his skin would crawl as if he'd somehow sensed that he was being watched, and he'd switch on every light that he could find, including the big spotlights out over what would one day become the car park. The entire ski centre would then be laid out before him, a brightly-lit, deserted playland with one sole scared occupant looking out towards the woods. And then he'd lock the doors to the reception block, and he'd retire to his back room and make himself as small as a child on his bunk in the corner.

Nothing was hanging together right any more. Everything seemed to be falling apart. You could even sense it in the village, ever since those two kids had been drowned; business was running as usual, but the spirit of the place somehow wasn't quite the same. Most people probably noticed nothing, but Amis, perhaps because he was an outsider, could feel it like a pulse. Sometimes he thought that he'd have liked nothing more than to be like Michael of the tarmac boys, gap-toothed and thick-headed and with no greater concern than that of pissing his money away at a speed roughly equal to that at which he made it, but he had to make do with the hand that he'd been dealt – thin-skinned and solitary, one of nature's observers.

The lights went out on him.

Damn.

Well, it was late – the simplest answer would be to drop the book on the floor, throw off his T-shirt and his jeans, and crawl under the covers and go to sleep. But it wasn't *that* late, and he wasn't particularly tired, and he knew that he'd do little more than lie there on the hard mattress tormenting himself with thoughts of that waitress. It had been fun, for a while, but he was too old to be entirely at ease with such fantasies. They were for teenagers, looking ahead to a life where anything wonderful could happen. At Amis's stage of existence, the options were narrowing fast and he knew that out of all the possibilities, wonderful was hardly the most likely.

He'd spoken to her often enough. For a while, there, he'd as good as haunted the place in the late afternoons . . . but then the van had broken down and getting into town hadn't been so easy, and besides the restaurant had become so damned busy that he'd become just another face in an ever-changing crowd. It didn't seem hopeless. It *was* hopeless, and he knew it.

He tossed the book aside and swung his legs off the bed, reaching underneath for the flashlight that he always kept handy. The generator itself was around the back of the reception block, protected from interference or vandalism by a welded metal walk-in cage inside a lean-to shed. Amis never bothered to close the cage door; he had enough keys to lug around and remember, and didn't want to add to them.

The night was warm. He could see stars. He'd never seen stars like he'd seen them around here, cold and diamond-sharp and so *many*. He walked barefoot around the reception building, on the new tarmac for the first few strides and then onto the beaten earth pathway that would lead to the back, his flashlight beam ranging over the ground as he moved. There was silence, no regular *chug-chug-chug* of the working generator, which meant that it had to have stalled. In the silence he was aware of the woodland, standing just out of reach. Sometimes he could feel as if this were a frontier post, with everything out there just waiting and passing time until the opportunity came to grab the territory back.

Well, it wouldn't happen. Too much money had gone into the place for that, now. Pity that it hadn't extended to something better than this undersized diesel-driven power supply. Mains electricity was supposedly going to be brought in at some stage, but God only knew when that would be.

Once inside the shed, Amis entered the cage and cast around for the big wrench that he'd taken to keeping in here. When he found it, he tapped along the feed pipe at random and then gave a couple of good, square bangs on the connectors before he tried the starter button. The generator caught immediately, coughed once, and then ran on smoothly.

He switched off the flashlight as he came back around the dirt path. The big lights were on again now, and he wouldn't need it.

Someone was waiting for him.

He stopped, and she turned.

It seemed as bright as day out on the newly-laid forecourt and it was as if she'd been caught by the lights, trapped and dazed like a rabbit on a long country road. He tried to speak, and all that he could say was, "Where did you come from?"

And Alina said, "Is that what you call a welcome?"

For a moment, he couldn't move. There was no way of explaining this, no parallel that he could reach for other than to say: that he'd once made a wish, and the wish now appeared to have come true.

And then he took a step toward her, the dead flashlight still in his hand, and he said, "I'm sorry, you gave me a scare. How did you get here?"

"I walked." He must have looked disbelieving, because she went on, "I walk a lot at night, on my own. It's a good time for thinking things over."

"But it's miles."

"Not so many. And at this hour, I have all the time that I need." A sudden realisation seemed to trouble her. "Were you sleeping? Did I come too late?"

"Sleeping? No," Amis reassured her, hurriedly. "Just kind of . . . lazing around."

She nodded, as if this was what she'd been expecting, and then she took what was probably her first real look at her surroundings.

A designer village, was the intended effect; sidelights along the pathways, mauve-tinted floods on the buildings, and a mini-spot on each of the directional signs wherever two paths joined. When the place was up and running, with guests in all the woodland chalets and the cafeteria open until late, it would feel safe at any hour; and now that he was no longer alone here, it seemed that way now.

She said, "So this is where you've been working."

"Yeah," Amis said. "Want to take a look around?"

His head was spinning as he led her into the reception building. What was he going to say to her? And why was she really here? All that he could think of was to show her his work on the counter and the panelling, which was probably as good as anything that he'd ever done. For a moment, when he'd first stepped back from it, he'd experienced the satisfaction of the true craftsman. By comparison, what he'd been doing in the cafeteria block was mere journeyman stuff. He'd show her, and even if she didn't appreciate the work it would perhaps give him a moment to think, to recover his poise.

She said, "Did I *really* scare you?"

"Surprised me, that's all. I don't see many people up here."

She looked out of the big foyer window, which ran from the floor almost to the ceiling, at the empty pathways and the silent buildings outside. She said, "It's quiet. I think I could like it here."

"So did I. The feeling wears off."

She stared out for a moment longer, and then she turned her attention back inside. She gave him a brief smile, and a thrill ran through him like a low current of electricity. She moved over and touched the polished wood of the counter.

She said, "How much of this did you do?"

"All of it," he said. "All of this, and the panelling, and all the carving. Are you really interested?"

"Of course," she said, and then she looked at him. "You always work alone?"

"It's what I prefer."

"And there's no one else here."

"No."

She let her hand fall from the counter, her eyes still on him and seeming to see deeper into him than was immediately comfortable. She said, "And are you happy?"

She'd caught him off-guard again, because this wasn't what he was expecting. It was a serious question. But he couldn't bring himself to give it a serious answer.

"Well," he said. "What's happy, anyway?"

But she wouldn't be put off. "I know what you're feeling," she said earnestly, "that's why I came." She took a step towards him. "I think I can help you."

Oh, wow . . . but now, inexplicably, he felt an urge to back away, to turn and run from her. Still trying vainly to keep it light, he said, "Thanks for the thought."

"I mean it," Alina said, her gaze so searching now that Amis couldn't break contact or look away. "I know what it's like. You sit up here alone and you think of all the friends you made, and lost. You think of women you've known and wish you'd known better, and you wonder what they're doing now. You look at your life, and it's like all the good things you ever wanted are loaded up onto a train that you didn't run quite fast enough to catch. And you know what you miss most of all?"

He tried to crack a grin, and his face felt like breaking plaster.

150

He said, "Why don't you tell me?"

"You miss having someone you can trust enough to tell them about it. You think that you'll die without there being anyone who's ever seen who you really are. Now, tell me if I'm wrong."

"What do you expect me to say?"

But her gaze was beyond words; even if he said nothing at all, she could read him with ease.

"Look," she said, "I can give you what you need."

"Really?" One simple word, and his voice caught on it and gave him away.

"Turn around," she suggested, her hand on his arm as she steered him to face the big window. "Look outside."

The lights out there were flickering again, probably getting themselves ready for their second failure of the night. He'd be alone, in the dark, with Alina.

He said, "I thought about asking you up here, sometime. I thought about it a lot."

"I know," she said. "Hold your breath."

"Why?"

"Don't speak, just listen."

By now, he was ready to do anything that she asked. She stood on tiptoe and reached up to cover the lower part of his face with her hand. To do this, she had to press against him. He was putty, she was the sculptor.

She whispered softly into his ear, "Do you see the lake from here?"

He couldn't speak because of her hand, but he made a negative-sounding grunt. This wasn't exactly comfortable, but he could stand it for a while longer.

"It doesn't matter," she went on. "Try to think about it. And think about this. When I first came here, I was like you. An outsider. We're all outsiders in our way, but for me it was even worse than most. But then I finally stopped resisting and found that there's a life in the land beyond the life of any one person, Thomas; the lives of the people only stand in the way."

He didn't want to push her away, but he was getting close to his limit; his blood was starting to pound in his ears and he was seeing haloes around all of the lights outside.

"Join us," she whispered, and then two things happened; there was a sharp pain, almost as if he'd swallowed broken glass, as she started to take her hand away, and in that same moment the generator missed another beat and caused the lights to drop for barely a fraction of a second. The blip of darkness seemed to sweep around the site like a wave. The glass before them became like a mirror for the briefest time but it was a distorting, ghost-train mirror, more shadow than substance with his mind adding hallucinatory details to the little that he could see. He saw not Alina, but something with eyes of blazing green; her hair a long mane strewn with weeds, her dress a dripping shroud, her teeth sharp, her skin pale and scaly as a snake's.

It was over as soon as it had happened, and as he turned in panic he could see that in reality she was exactly as before . . . except that she was looking at him now in a way that was more detached, stepping back as if to observe whatever he was going to do next.

He took a breath.

But nothing happened.

He tried again, but the air simply wouldn't come. He looked at Alina, wanting to ask her what she'd done; but she was standing just out of his reach, and watching him with something that looked like compassion. He was straining hard now, and still nothing was happening; everything had gone a couple of shades darker, and the roaring in his ears drowned out everything else. He put his hands to his throat, anything to ease the pain and help him to get just a little air . . .

To find that she'd pinched his windpipe shut.

It must have been in that one moment of darkness, as she'd been taking her hand away. He couldn't believe the strength that it must have taken.

But he had to.

Why? Why had she done this to him? His chest, his entire frame, were like a fire-walker's bed of coals. But he wouldn't give in to it. Oh, Christ, just for one *breath*! He turned from Alina, trying to retch but with his clogged windpipe preventing even that; he threw himself towards the doors, trying to get out into air, air that he couldn't quite reach.

He burst out into the open. His tools were all over in the cafeteria, there had to be something that he could use to open himself up. He'd saw his own damned throat open, if he had to, but he *wouldn't let this happen*.

He was lying at the bottom of the steps where he'd fallen, pulling up into a near-foetal curl that he couldn't prevent. He was being drawn into that single point of pain that burned like a hot light. He was only dimly aware of Alina coming down the steps toward him, only dimly aware of her crouching by him to smooth the hair from his forehead. He started to shiver, completely out of control now.

He could see the end coming, and it was just as she'd said; the friends he'd made and lost, and the women that he wished he'd known better.

"There, there," he heard her say. "It'll soon be over."

And it was.

TWENTY-SEVEN

"You're looking tired, Peter," Alina said when Pete came through
to breakfast the next morning. He'd heard her moving around and
had almost panicked, thinking that he was late; but then he'd
checked his old wind-up alarm and realised that he wasn't, and so
then he'd used the spare fifteen minutes to stand under the tepid
shower in an attempt to shock himself awake.

He said, "That's no surprise. The yard's having its busiest season
in ten years, and two of us are handling it all."

This was hardly an overstatement. The yard staff presently consisted of Pete himself and Frank Lowry, with very little practical
help from its owner. Business had started to pick up with a May
heatwave that had brought out the sun umbrellas and the city hordes.
The umbrellas were on the Venetz sisters' restaurant terrace, and
the hordes were under them and everywhere else. They jammed the
roads with their trailers and caravans, they turned up in shorts and
sandals and herded in the village centre looking for postcards and
souvenirs, and they crowded the inshore waters of the lake with
dinghies and windsurf boards and dangerously cheap inflatables.
They sat on blankets on the shore, they dropped ice creams on the
promenade, they tried to fly kites, they argued. They pulled into the
passing places on the narrowest roads and treated them as laybys,
setting up a whole living room's worth of furniture by the open
tailgates of their cars.

And when those cars broke down – which, many of them being
underserviced and badly prepared, they tended to do with an inevita-
bility that amazed only their owners – they demanded instant service
from the staff of an auto-marine yard that was already being run
under the strain of some of the heaviest lake traffic that it had ever
experienced.

He hefted the old tin kettle. It was half-full, and still warm. He
set it on the stove to heat up again.

"How do you do it?" he said, picking up the cereal boxes and
shaking to see which was the least empty.

"Do what?"

154

"You work longer hours than I do, you walk all the way there and back, and you don't even sleep at nights. I'd really like to know what's keeping you going."

She gave a slight shrug. "I don't even think about it," she said. "Why do you mention it now?"

"Forget it," he said, and he gathered up the cereal box and a bowl and everything else and headed out through the house to breakfast alone on the covered terrace.

She appeared after a couple of minutes, and set one of the cabin's old china mugs alongside him.

"I made your tea," she said.

He looked down into the mug.

"You always make it black," he said.

"Only because you took the milk," she said.

He looked at her. He'd never seen her looking better; her eyes were bright and her hair shone and her skin glowed like a small child's. Pete, by contrast, was feeling as if he'd been broken into pieces and badly reassembled.

He looked away.

He hadn't intended to sigh, but he did it anyway.

"What's the matter?" she said, moving around him and half-hitching herself onto the wooden rail so that he couldn't avoid her again; and Pete felt embarrassed, because he knew that he was acting with just a touch of stupidity.

"Nothing," he said. "Really, nothing. I'm sorry. It's just the pressure of the work, I think it's wearing me down."

But he knew that this was only a part of the answer. Late at night, when Alina was out and he was unable to sleep, he'd find himself thinking that maybe – just maybe – he could pick up a phone at this hour and dial the old number, and his mother would answer the same as always. Not at any other time, but only then; that particular hour of the night when the rest of the world seemed to have closed down and the morning stood at a distance almost beyond imagination. But he'd no phone in the house, and to leave the house would be to break the spell; and so he'd lie there, and after a while he'd be further twisted by the certainty that she was waiting somewhere, waiting on the other side for a call that would never come.

That had to be it, didn't it? For what else could have bypassed his defences, what else could have burrowed so far under his skin?

"I know what you need," Alina said.

"Really."

"Yes, really. Listen to me, I'm serious." But she was smiling, so

155

it was *that* kind of serious. Behind her was a backdrop of spring woodland, sunlight and shade moving in a gentle morning breeze.

She said, "You've been on your own for too long. You need someone. I don't mean someone like me, just being around, I mean you really need someone to be close to. People who've lost, they become vulnerable. Believe me, I know."

"What are you leading up to?"

"Mrs Jackson. From the estate. I heard how you danced with her on the night of the party. She'd be perfect for you, Peter."

He could only stare.

She said, "Doing what I do, I hear all kinds of things. About everyone. She had a husband, they say he used to 'knock her around'. If that means what I think it means then she needs someone like you, too. You're one of the kindest people I ever met. I know that probably embarrasses you, but it's true. You ought to give her a chance to see it in you. That's my idea, I can help it to happen if you want me to. What do you think?"

Pete said nothing for a moment.

And then he stood up.

"For Christ's sake," he said, and he stalked back into the house leaving everything behind.

After a few moments, she appeared in the doorway to his room as he rummaged for a spare work shirt.

She said, "People having a conversation usually stay in the same building."

He turned to her.

"You really don't know what you're saying, do you?"

"Tell me."

"Forget your matchmaking. Don't even think about pushing me together with anyone because it isn't going to happen. It isn't going to happen because they look at me and they look at you and they put two and two together and what they come up with tells them, *back off.* You think you get to hear all the gossip down there but, believe me, there's talk going on that you obviously don't even dream about. I'm the kindest person you ever met? Yeah, well, so much for the good that it's done me. I'll tell you what, I'll have them put it on my gravestone. Here lies Mister Nice Guy, but who gives a shit anyway. I mean, look at you. You're out every night like fucking Dracula, or something. And me, I might as well have rabies. If that's where kindness gets you, I'm going to kick pigeons. Even *Hitler* had a fucking girlfriend, and who'd got a good word to say about *him?*"

He was sorry immediately, of course, but too much of the truth had come out for him to want to take any of it back; so he sat heavily on the bed and he looked away from her and he rubbed at his still-tired eyes, anything to avoid meeting her gaze and then having to concede his embarrassment. Now it was as if his anger had blown away into the air, like so much steam.

She sat beside him, and laid a hand on his shoulder.

"Oh, Peter," she said.

She didn't seem to be offended. It was a voice of sadness, almost of pity. He looked at her then and her face seemed to be saying, *I understand*; and then he tried to speak, but the sense of it somehow skipped away from him like a stone across water.

"Listen to me," she said. "I'm sorry it came to this, and I want to set it right. I'm going to leave you. I'm going to leave you soon, but first I want you to understand how much you've done for me."

"I just blew up," Pete said, giving in to it as he'd known that he would. "I'm sorry. This isn't necessary."

"Yes it is, and that's why I'm moving out. I don't mean this minute, probably not even today. But as soon as I can, I will. I won't even tell you, I'll just go. You'll see me around, but after a while I'll just be someone you once knew. I wish I could get out of your life forever, but I don't think that's possible any more. You see, I have to stay in the valley – I've started to make it my home, and every time you leave a home you die, just a little. And there's only so much life in any of us . . . use it all up and we're gone, even though we're still walking around. That could have happened to me already, if it wasn't for you – you brought me here and you set me up and suddenly I was in a place where I felt I could belong again."

She stood up and, walking out of the room, left him there.

Well. This was exactly what he wanted. Wasn't it?

Wasn't it?

He could hear her moving around elsewhere in the house. After a minute, he got up and followed the sounds in her room.

Her door was open.

"I appreciate what you're saying," he said, as she looked up from folding some of her clothes for the drawer. "But something about all this bothers me."

"What do you mean?" she said, leaving the drawer and walking across the room towards him. She'd made almost no changes in here; with its bare walls and near complete lack of oramentation, the room looked virtually as it had on the day she'd moved in.

Pete said, "You once told me you were losing a battle. Inside."

She didn't seem to understand.

"I feel fine," she said, and closed the door on him.

By the time that he'd reached the yard, Frank Lowry was already in and working.

There was a Vauxhall on the hoist and a Land Rover half-inside the workshop with its bonnet already open. Five more cars stood waiting on the strip outside, and others would undoubtedly join them as the day went on. The phone was ringing. Hanging on its regular nail, the clipboard on which the boatyard worksheets were kept was well overloaded and straining at its spring. Pete flicked at the papers as he walked by, and the clipboard rocked like a pendulum. No matter how hard he worked to clear it, the backlog was getting bigger and bigger. The phone was still ringing.

Ted Hammond came around from behind the hoist, and picked it up.

He glanced at Pete as he took the call, something about a brokerage job, and he winked. The differences in him were slight, but immediately noticeable. His shirt was clean, he'd shaved, his hair had been combed. While he wasn't exactly back to normal, he had the bright, clear-eyed look of a lifelong drunk who'd just come to realise that there was something worthwhile in staying sober.

As Ted was hanging up, Pete turned to Frank Lowry. He'd just emerged from the floor in the cab of the Land Rover with a length of broken accelerator cable in his hand.

Pete indicated Ted and said, "Who's this?" And Frank Lowry shrugged.

"His face is familiar," he said. "Didn't he used to work here, once?"

"All right," Ted said with a gesture of pretended weariness, "I've got the message. I'm sorry, lads. What more can I say?"

"Forget it, Ted," Pete told him.

"No," he said. "You two have been working flat-out to keep my business going, and I've just been dicking off around the house. I don't deserve it, but I'm grateful."

"He's getting sentimental," Frank Lowry muttered, glancing around like a cat looking for a way to avoid an impending bath. "I'm off." And he wandered away into the depths of the workshop; under the levity, there had been a trace of real embarrassment. Lowry, a man who didn't show his own feelings, obviously didn't like to be around when others were showing theirs.

But Ted didn't seem to be offended. He'd known Lowry for too long and, besides, there seemed to have been a rebirth of the spirit in him that wasn't going to be choked off so easily.

Pete said, "You're looking better, Ted."

158

But Ted sighed. "I wish I felt it. Life's finally shaping up in the best way you can hope for, and then something else just comes along and wipes the slate clean. Everything, bang. I wish it had been me, instead of Wayne. I could live with being dead, if Wayne was okay."

This made perfect sense to Pete, and the two of them pondered it for a while before Pete said, "What got you going again?"

"I'm a long way from that," Ted said. "What you're looking at now is only skin-deep. But I never before spent one working day on the skive while others got on with the job, and I'm ashamed it ever came to that. I don't know how to thank you."

"Big pay rises," Pete suggested as the phone started to ring again.

"Get out of it," Ted said; "can't you see how far behind we are?" and went off to answer it.

Angelica and Adele were in the restaurant kitchen when Alina arrived, later that morning. Adele was cutting salad, and Angelica was rewriting the evening menu.

Angelica looked up from the corner of the table that she was using, and said, "Good morning, Alina. It's Wednesday."

"I know," Alina said, hanging her shoulder-bag over the back of one of the chairs.

"And you know who always phones at around eleven on a Wednesday," Adele said, before the kitchen was filled with the five-second roar of the blender as it swallowed a pound of carrots and extruded them as a mass of fine strands. Alina glanced at the clock. It was just after eleven-thirty.

When the blender cut out, she said, "I like my admirers to be predictable. It saves me from having to worry about how to keep them interested."

Angelica, in the spirit of the running joke that they'd all been sharing for several weeks now, said, "We told him you'd taken a boat onto the lake and couldn't be reached for the rest of the day. I think perhaps he's starting to get the message. What excuse would you like us to give him next time?"

But the young Russian woman seemed to have other things on her mind.

"He's probably had enough excuses by now," she said. "Next time, I think I'd better speak to him."

TWENTY-EIGHT

Ross Aldridge stood in the empty caravan, feeling like an intruder in a place owned by strangers. In fact it *was* owned by strangers, a family who lived more than two hundred miles away; they used the caravan for about six weeks of the year, on and off, and they rented it out for some of the times in between. The van was an old one, and looked it compared to some of the sleeker units on the other lakeside pitches. The site owner had told him straight, he wouldn't be unhappy to see it go; it lowered the tone of the place, he reckoned, and he knew that he could easily re-let the pitch a hundred times over for something bigger, something newer . . . he handled sales, as well, so he'd make a two-way profit on the deal.

Aldridge had disliked the man on sight. And the way that he talked about lowering tone and maximising profits hadn't made Aldridge like him any better, not when a five-year-old who'd probably last slept in one of these very bunks now slept dreamlessly in a mortuary cabinet.

One of three kids, altogether. Their father a one-time shipyard welder, out of employment for nearly two years now, their mother working half-days as a checkout assistant in a retail cash-and-carry. This had been the family's first holiday in ages; the boy's first holiday ever. Aldridge sighed, and looked around. He knew that he was taking this harder than he ought to, but he couldn't help it. The whole thing was just too personal for him.

The curtains had been drawn against the world outside. They didn't fit too well. In the half-shade he could see that the caravan was spotless, as if it had been scrubbed compulsively by whoever had occupied it last. He checked it over. There was a double bedroom at one end, a kitchen in the middle, and a lounge at the other whose uncomfortable bench sofas made up into equally uncomfortable beds. There was a chemical toilet in an adjoining shed, and for showers there would be the communal block at the other end of the site. He knew the kind of thing. Timer-operated, and as cold and draughty as hell; a hook for your towel, and nowhere dry to put your clothes. It had been years since he'd done anything similar, but

160

he'd been there. There couldn't have been many people who'd need to use the block, not these days; not when most had big vans with names like *Mistral* and *Wayfarer* with their own bathrooms and WCs built-in. This van belonged to another, altogether less well-appointed age. When he moved, the floor creaked and at one point he felt his head brush close to the ceiling.

It was the personal touches that got to him the most. The ornaments, most of them broken and then glued together again. The home-made curtains screening open shelves. Stuff that should have been in a junkshop, but instead it was here. Two weeks of this had been the best that the family had been able to afford.

They hadn't even made it to the end of the first.

It had been a night-time accident. One of a family of heavy sleepers the boy had always been an exception, but this had never caused them any serious problem before. He'd get up and wander around a little, play with his toys, and they'd find him the next morning lying wherever sleep had caught up with him. Because he was too small to reach the light switches, this had usually been on the floor in front of the open refrigerator with its interior light burning and the milk slowly going sour. He'd be there with a jigsaw, his toy trucks, a storybook. But the refrigerator here was a tiny benchtop unit tucked well-back alongside the sink, so Aldridge could only assume that the boy had been forced to look further afield for some night-time entertainment.

They were still arguing over who'd left the caravan's door unlocked. Both parents suspected each other and blamed themselves. The truth of it would probably never be established, not for certain, but when the one-time welder had risen in the morning it had been to find the door wide open to the day and the boy missing. Also missing had been an inflatable crocodile that belonged to the caravan and which they'd stowed, fully-inflated, in the space underneath rather than face the effort of pumping it up afresh for every lakeside play session. The crocodile, being bright green and buoyant enough to sit high in the water, had been spotted within the first half-hour of the search. The child, floating low in his sodden pyjamas and looking more like a log in the undertow, had been found much later in the day.

Aldridge moved to the door, the entire van trembling at his every step. There was nothing for him here. He took one last look back, and then opened the door to fresh air and daylight. Now he could tell the owners that he'd checked out their property and that everything was in order; he could finish his report and then file it and move on. As he stood on the wooden steps outside and locked up after him, he couldn't help noting that the door was a poor fit. The catch barely held it. One sharp tug, and maybe . . .

He tugged.

The lock held. But only just.

But enough to keep in a five-year-old, he thought, and he turned and descended the steps. He walked down the dirt access track to the main paved avenue of the site, and when he reached the administration block he dropped the keys through the mail flap rather than talk to the site owner again. He could sense that the man was watching him as he crossed over to his car, but he didn't look back.

The lake was calm. Many of the vans overlooked it and the site had its own beach, of a kind; several tons of sand that had been trucked in and dumped at the water's edge. This for the kids, a Country and Western club for the parents. It was modest and inexpensive and probably a five-year-old's idea of paradise. What had happened here was wrong, in a sense that had stirred Aldridge deeply; almost as if Death had slipped in and stolen the child and then led it on a dance, over the hills and far away like some shadowy, irresistible piper. He couldn't help thinking back to the stillborn form that they'd let him hold, all cleaned-up and wrapped in a shawl, in a room next to the hospital's chapel for all of half an hour; half an hour of fatherhood, spent with a daughter who would never know of his love. Whatever jealous force took children in this way, whatever face it wore – disease, accident, ill-intent – he knew that there was only one somewhat old-fashioned word to describe it, and that word was *evil*. True evil. He'd looked into the faces of regular murderers and seen only the commonplace; but in the death of children, he saw ultimate darkness.

He started the car. He had a thousand and one things to do, and not one of them seemed terrifically important to him right at this moment. Two days before he'd been giving his evidence in the Coroner's Court and his eyes had briefly met those of old Doctor McEnery up on the bench, and something had flickered between the two of them . . . nothing unprofessional that could have been seen by anyone else in the courtroom, but almost a recognition that they were occupying the same places and going through the same routines rather too often for comfort. The details changed, the form remained the same. The Hammond boy and his girlfriend. Walter Hardy, drowned in his own bathtub. The drunk who'd fallen overboard at a yacht party and whose disappearance hadn't even been noticed until the next day. The dinghy accident.

The others.

The verdicts of *accidental death* had come in, one after another, and nobody had known better than Aldridge how unavoidable these conclusions were. He'd checked out the scenes, he'd talked to the people. And yet . . .

Death by drowning, or something like it, again and again. Inevitable when you considered how much of the territory was taken up by a lake that was virtually an inland sea, but disturbing in its frequency. Maybe there *was* such a thing as luck, and its bad-luck counterpart; he'd noticed it with air disasters and rail disasters, how they seemed to hit the news in clusters, and he wondered if something similar might be an influence here. If it was, it made him uneasy. Such things were fine for the pages of downmarket photo magazines, tucked in between the horoscopes and the sob stories, but the thought of something so hard-edged and yet unknown entering his life was something else.

Coincidence, he told himself as he drove out through the site gates and rejoined the main road. Traffic wasn't too bad and, as ever, they all touched their brakes and slowed at the sight of the car.

Coincidence.

What else could it possibly be?

TWENTY-NINE

Pavel checked the needle on the gauge. He was down to a quarter of a tank, and almost into the red-lined sector. The car had never let him down yet but, by God, it used up the juice.

But then this was hardly surprising, given that he was now spending about eight to twelve hours of every day on the move. The times that he didn't spend in the car, he seemed to spend in public phone booths feeding the slots from endless bags of change. Now his cash was getting low again. Not crisis-low, but low enough to nudge him into action; he knew that rock-bottom was the hardest place to get up from, and he didn't want to be there again. He'd only let it happen to him once since the very beginning, and he'd pulled himself out of that by shoplifting books which he'd then messed-up a little and sold as secondhand. He hadn't liked it, but he'd done it.

He shifted in the seat. A lot of the time he got sore, and his back got stiff.

But he could ignore that.

There was a gang of about half a dozen on the corner ahead. No good, but he slowed and took a closer look at them anyway. They all stared back; all of them black kids in their late teens, one or two of them with their hair in those long knitted caps that looked like overstuffed cushions. One of them broke away, and started to walk towards the car. It was a notorious part of town, and this was unlikely to be the local glee club. That didn't matter, but the numbers were too high; Pavel picked up speed and moved on.

Of course, this *had* been a police car . . . and although it had no markings, there was probably something about the make and the year and the neutral colour and the lack of any personalisation that gave off a definite signal like a lowlife's version of a pheromone. But surely, he was thinking, the effect had to be a diminishing one. As the car was roughened-up more and more, its driver became rougher still. Nobody now could take a close look at the two of them together and leap to the conclusion that here was a Mister Clean in his Clean Machine. Depending on where he cruised, they'd more likely offer him sex or drugs or perhaps even the services of an

underage boy . . . at which point they'd get a big surprise, and
Pavel would wipe out however much of the night's earnings they
carried.

He didn't pretend that it was any kind of justice, but it did feel
better than plain thieving. Although it didn't always work as well as
it might; two teeth on one side were still feeling loose after a kicking
he'd received behind a small-town nightclub a couple of weeks
before, and the bruises had taken most of that time to fade. But it was
worth the occasional risk because the approach had the advantage of
causing no official complaints, so that he continued to sail onward
and stay invisible. Methods and the local territory might have
changed, but there was so much here that he could recognise from
his other life.

The car turned another corner. He seemed to see nothing but
failed businesses and boarded-up shops, with occasional empty lots
as if an entire structure had been sucked into the ground and the
hole quickly screened-in with sheets of ply. The plywood had been
fly-posted with ads for rock groups and poll tax protest meetings,
and the posters had been oversprayed with layers of graffiti.

But wait.

There ahead of him, a little way on from a defunct carpet warehouse and a place that sold tiles in job lots, a young man was bending
over a car that had pulled in by the side of the road. Its engine was
running, and its brake lights were on. The side-window was open
and the young man was talking to the driver. As Pavel moved to
draw in behind he saw the young man abruptly straighten and look
his way, waving the driver on with a slight but definite gesture as he
watched this new approaching vehicle with suspicion.

As he came level, Pavel dropped the electric window halfway.
The boy stooped and peered in through the opening, still on his
guard.

"How're you doing?" he said. His breath was like dogfood.

"I'm doing fine," Pavel said. "Are you in business?"

"Just hanging around."

"I need to clear my head," Pavel said. "Is there anything you
could suggest?"

"Let's stop fucking about," the boy said wearily. "It's twenty a
packet, take it or leave it but make it quick."

Pavel pulled out a twenty. It was his last. He glanced around
before he held it out, but the rest of the street was empty.

The boy reached for the money. Pavel hit the button by his seat
and the electric window rolled up, trapping the boy's hand at the
wrist. The hand was filthy, with rims of dirt under the nails. The boy

165

tried to pull back, but his wristbones were clamped tight and there was no give in the window. He screamed.

"Not so loud," Pavel said. "Now come with me."

And he let out the clutch.

The boy staggered and stumbled backward, drawn with the car as Pavel rolled along in low gear. At the next corner he turned, and pulled the boy along with him into an alleyway between two rows of buildings. The boy was cursing and trying to break the window, but he couldn't do it one-handed and off-balance. Under the grime, the fingers of his trapped hand had turned white.

Pavel stopped the car, and clambered across the seats to get out on the passenger side. The boy was calling him names now, many of which he'd never heard before.

Broken glass crunched underfoot on the stone cobbles. The alley was about three, no more than four metres across, and as sleazy a piece of territory as he'd ever seen. To either side were the rear yards of buildings. Some of them had been roofed-over and converted into garages, although with some the walls had simply been pulled down to make a small parking area. All of the yard doors looked as if they'd seen long, hard service in some other place before ending up here; they were various styles and painted in various colours, all of them blasted and peeling. On some of them, street numbers had been daubed in a giant hand.

Pavel winced as he picked his way around the car. An open box of rubbish had been dumped out behind one of the buildings, and the alley was strewn with soiled disposable nappies. This was no self-respecting way to make a living. The boy tried to claw at him with his free hand, and Pavel hit him once in the middle to double him over and disable him.

The boy's pockets were empty. His drugs and his money were all in his underpants. He was gasping and trying to speak, but he couldn't take a breath.

"Take it slowly," Pavel suggested. "Don't struggle for it so much, just relax."

He took the cash. He left the drugs. He opened the driver's door, and the boy swung back with it; but then Pavel reached in and lowered the window, and the boy fell back heavily to sit on the ground.

He nursed his deadened hand.

"Rub it," Pavel suggested. "When the circulation comes back, it's going to hurt quite a lot."

The boy was still trying to speak. Pavel paused before he got in behind the wheel; it seemed only courteous to give him a hearing.

Gasping like a fish, the boy finally managed to get out a few words.
"You're *dead*," the boy spat.
Pavel looked down at him for a moment.
"I know it," he said.
And then he got back into the car, reversed out of the alley, and drove away.

THIRTY

It was about a week later when Diane dropped in at the yard; she'd been putting it off for as long as she could, but she couldn't put it off any longer. Ever since the day that she'd taken Ross Aldridge out to look at the six dead deer, she'd been troubled by a persistent squeaking from somewhere at the back of the Toyota. What Diane knew about motor vehicles could be tattooed on a gnat's left buttock and still leave space for *Mother*; it might need a penny's worth of grease, it might be halfway to losing a wheel. But she knew when she needed qualified advice, and she needed it now.

The two dogs bounded out to meet her, looking happy and stupid. One of them lost interest almost immediately and went snuffling away along the ground, the other followed her in. There was a radio playing in the car workshop and a Mercedes on the hoist, but nobody around. She called out, "Hello?" and then she went through to take a look in the marine section.

She stood in the yard, but still could see nobody.

"Hey," a voice called from somewhere above her. "Hey, how's it going?"

It was Pete McCarthy. He was up on the deck of one of the landlocked craft, looking down over the rail. Then he disappeared for half a minute before coming around to her from the other side, this time at ground level. He looked rough and dusty and hardworking, and he was wiping his hands on a paint-stained rag.

"Ignore the mess," he said, balling the rag and then tossing it with some brushed-together debris in the shadow of the hull. "What is this, business or social?"

"Call it both," she said, and explained about her worry.

"Sounds like a brake shoe," Pete said, and they went out to where she'd parked so that he could take a look.

There wasn't much that he could tell with a superficial inspection; he crouched down and took hold of the wheel and tried to rock it on the axle, but there was no undue play. She said, "Look, if it's going to be a problem, I can do some phoning around. I know how busy you are."

"It's no problem," Pete told her. "Ted's back in action, and the marina's back on its feet now we've got the Wilson boys in. If you can leave it with us, I'll fit it in as soon as I can."

"How soon is that likely to be?"

"Maybe tonight. Shouldn't be any later than in the next couple of days."

"Fine," Diane said uncertainly. And then she said, "Listen, you wouldn't have anything I could borrow until it's fixed, would you?"

She was thinking of the only two estate vehicles that she had to fall back on; Dizzy's huge and expensive limo, and the lumbering, wire-meshed Land Rover that the gamekeeper had been using until his ignominious departure. There was a little Morgan sports job that she'd discovered in one of the stables, but after thirty years' use as a byre it was somewhat in need of restoration.

"Depends how proud you are," Pete said, and he reached into his pocket and handed her a set of keys.

"What are these for?" she said.

"James Bond's Aston Martin," he said, and nodded toward a car behind her. She turned, and found herself facing his black Zodiac.

He said, "I know it's the ugliest thing on four wheels, but it runs. I can use the breakdown wagon to get around in, if I need to."

She looked at it, flaking paint, taped headlight, and all. If it hadn't been for Jed, she wouldn't have been in a corner. School holidays meant that she couldn't even fall back on the school bus, and she had to get him to Mrs Neary's somehow; the alternative was to drag him around with her like a piece of luggage as she worked. The job would suffer, Jed would suffer without protest, and Diane would feel guilty for a week.

But even so . . . *this* car?

"Well, if you're sure," she said, smiling what she hoped was a bright smile.

"I'm sure," Pete said.

"Thanks."

When she was behind the wheel, he showed her how to close the door so that it would stay closed. When the engine started, she found herself sitting in the middle of a racket that put her modest little squeak into a complete new perspective.

She tried to wind down the window. Nothing happened for a moment and then the glass dropped, all at once. Pete smiled encouragingly.

"Looks good on you," he said.

"You're kidding me," she said. "I feel like something out of *Wacky Races*. How do you keep it on the road?"

"Most people don't ask how, they ask why."

"Why?"

"It depends on me in its twilight years. If I didn't look after it, who would?"

She blipped the accelerator and then, after a moment, the engine responded.

And although she hadn't meant to raise the subject at all, she heard herself saying, "It's been some time since I saw you last. How's everything?"

His face turned serious.

She was immediately sorry that she'd spoken, but it was already too late. Something seemed to go out of him, like a man who'd managed to forget a grief for a while only to find it reclaiming him in some unexpected and unguarded moment.

And he said, "I don't know."

"You don't know?"

"Yeah. Makes no sense at all, does it?"

"Has something else happened?"

"No, nothing. Alina's moving out. She says. I don't know where she's going to go or when, but she's doing it."

"So what's wrong with that?" she said. "Isn't it what you wanted?"

He nodded, slowly. But then he seemed to make an effort, and to shake the feeling off.

"Hey," he said. "You want to hear something funny?" And he told her about Alina's proposal for getting the two of them together.

Diane's jaw dropped. "They're actually saying that?" she said. "They're saying I was a battered wife?"

Pete was obviously trying to show an adult kind of concern. But he couldn't quite hide his curiosity, as well.

"Were you?" he said.

"No!" Diane said. "I'd have killed him."

"Not with a shotgun, you wouldn't," Pete said.

She was shaking her head. "I can't believe it," she said. "I can't *believe* people around here."

"So then, you're not going to believe all that stuff that some of them were saying about me?"

There was one of those moments of perfect balance.

And then she said, "Right," and she wondered why she felt as if she'd walked into the most carefully-engineered of traps, even though she knew that it hadn't been planned.

At least, she *thought* she knew.

"Pay no attention to me," Pete said. "There's something about her that worries me, that's all, and I don't know what it is. And it

170

won't matter anyway, because pretty soon she's going to stop being my problem."

"And become somebody else's?"

He smiled faintly, as if in concession. "Who knows?"

She thanked him again for the loan of the car.

And then, feeling pretty buoyant, she drove away.

She went down the track, around the turn, and past the trees before the iron bridge. The air-blower didn't seem to work but she wound the window the rest of the way down to get the breeze, and after she'd left the village behind she turned on the radio. It was strange, but on the way out she didn't seem to have noticed how downright pleasant the day really was. She tried all of the radio's preset buttons, but the only signal coming through with any clarity was that of the local station down on the coast. It was the wrap-up for the eleven o'clock news.

It wasn't this, but the message that came in on the tail-end of the bulletin that almost caused her to swerve and bang up the Zodiac's other headlight as she was turning into the narrow dirt road leading to the Hall.

She parked messily, and ran inside to her office. Wednesday was the day that the rugs were taken out and the hall tiles washed down in the morning, and she almost skidded on the wet marble and arrived in the former library in a heap. Luckily, Jed wasn't here to see her breaking almost all of the rules that she'd laid down for him. She pulled open the desk drawer where she vaguely remembered that she'd put the auto-marine's business card, and then when she'd found it she picked up the phone to call Pete.

But she couldn't, because there was already someone on the line.

She recognised the voice immediately. No one else that she'd ever known had spoken with an accent quite like it.

"*All right*," the Peterson woman was saying. "*But you come along and you tell nobody where you're going. I wouldn't want this to get out . . .*"

And then her voice tailed away, as if she'd become aware that someone was listening.

As silently as she could, Diane replaced the receiver. She winced as it clicked down the last quarter-inch. And then she sat back from her desk and waited.

It had to have been Dizzy on the other end; this line was shared with an extension up in his private suite, and nobody else could use it. When Bob Ivie or Tony Marinello wanted to make a call, they had to come down and borrow Diane's. The household staff had a pay phone in what had once been the pantry. Dizzy's Women sometimes called out, but there were none of them around and hadn't been for several weeks now; so Dizzy himself it was.

Dizzy and the Peterson woman, arranging a private meeting? Diane had known about the two of them going up to his private apartments on the night of the party, but then she'd seen Dizzy coming down alone only a few minutes later. Whatever he'd been planning, it clearly hadn't happened. But it was equally clear now that this hadn't been the end of it.

Her door was open, and she could hear Dizzy as he came down the stairs. She was expecting him to come in, either to explain or to make a complaint about her cutting in on the call, but he did neither; instead he went down the hallway and on out of the main door, and when Diane went over to look out of one of the windows she saw his limousine, the big black monster with the tinted glass, swinging around to head out of the estate.

Slowly, she walked back to her desk. She stood there, thinking for a few moments. And then she sat down, picked up the phone, and began to dial.

Her first impulse had been to call Pete at the yard. The item that she'd heard on the Zodiac's scratchy radio had a direct relevance to him, after all, and if she hadn't been so close to home she'd probably have swung right around and gone back to tell him about it.

But something about the situation troubled her.

There's something about her that worries me, he'd said, *and I don't know what it is.*

Me, too, Diane was thinking.

She finished dialling, not the auto-marine's code but a number that was still running through her mind in the mnemonic of the radio station's jingle.

And when she finally got through, she said, "I'm ringing about the emergency message that you broadcast at the end of the news . . ."

THIRTY-ONE

Dizzy Liston tended not to do much of his own driving; this had seemed like a good idea ever since a Marylebone magistrate had taken his licence away, some eleven months before. Caution wasn't uppermost in his mind now, however, as he turned the big shadow-silent car out onto the valley road. His mind was on the directions that he was now repeating, over and over, fixing them in his memory with continuous rehearsal. Even though he was technically the major landowner at this end of the valley, he knew his way around no better than the average visitor; most of his life so far had been spent at Winchester school, a minor Oxford college, and a series of Mayfair addresses all taken on short leasehold. It was said that the Liston males had stopped taking much of an interest in their home territory around the time that the custom of *droit de seigneur* had fallen out of use. Most of the land was now in hock, anyway, and the house was halfway to a ruin; Dizzy's plan had been to kick around here for a few months obeying doctor's orders and getting his topspin back, and then head once more for the bright lights, leaving Diane in command for good. She'd be charged with the duty of keeping the estate staff in mortal terror and liaising with the forestry people so that Dizzy's cash float would be regularly renewed.

That had been the idea; but the waitress had changed everything.

He saw a gated track just before the village, marked by a boulder painted white at the edge of the road; he took the limo up as far as he could go, and then he left it to walk the rest of the way. What if he was in the wrong place? What if he was in the right place, and she didn't come?

The first question was settled when he came to a slate-built stile, which was exactly as she'd described it to him. The second remained unanswered, because when he scrambled over and walked out into the wooded clearing on the other side of the wall, she wasn't there.

It was part of an estate forest – one of his own, he supposed. The gate and the KEEP OUT notices that he'd left behind ought to be enough to ensure privacy, even so close to the village and at this time of the year. But he didn't want solitude, he wanted to see

Alina. She'd promised, so where was she? What was he supposed to do, go down to her tatty little café like one of the herd and try to bid for a minute of her distracted attention?

Never, he thought.

But underneath the thought, he knew that if it proved to be the only way, he'd probably do it.

"Well?" she said.

He spun around, spooked like a rabbit. She was standing by the stile, one hand still on the topstone, and she was looking at him; he hadn't heard anything of her approach, anything at all.

He said, "I thought you wouldn't come."

"Why would I lie to you?"

"That's not what I meant. But you've strung me out for so long, I was starting to believe that it would never happen." He was also starting to sound the way he knew that he'd sounded on the phone, but he couldn't help it.

"I'm not so hard to get hold of," she said.

"You want to bet?"

"I'm a working girl, Mister Liston, I can't come running every time you call. Why is it so important to you, anyway?"

This was it; and he knew, without need of omens or evidence, that he was somehow going to mess up the next couple of minutes.

He said, "I don't know what you did to me."

"Me?" Alina Peterson moved away from the stile and into the clearing, not toward him but in a wide circle around him. It was as if she were deliberately staying out of his reach – half taunt, half provocation. She made no sound on the bark and fallen leaves. She said, "I've done nothing."

"That night," he insisted, "at the party. I thought that you'd stay, but you didn't. I tried to call you, and you kept putting me off. What do I have to *do*?"

"Try explaining what you mean."

He wasn't sure that he could. He said, "I can't stop thinking about you. It's way out of control. I can't relax, I can't sleep. I sit around all the time just wondering how you are, and what you're doing."

She stopped, and fixed him with a hard look. "Are you trying to say that you're in love with me?"

"No," he said bleakly. "I might understand it if I was, but how can I be? We went upstairs, we talked for ten minutes, you disappeared. Nothing works that fast. I'm thirty-five years old, and I've made a fool of myself often enough to know the real thing when I get it. This is something else."

"So now you're asking me for an explanation, and I can't give it to you."

"Do you affect anyone else like this?"

"I don't know. I'm not the one to ask."

She looked away from him now, and moved toward a fallen trunk to sit. The trunk was hollowed-out and scorched, lightning-burned. As she took a perch, Liston said, "It's tearing me up, and every day I don't see you it gets worse. If I don't get help, I'm going to crack up."

But she wasn't exactly taking all of his soul-baring with the sympathy that he'd hoped for.

"So see a doctor," she said.

"I don't need a doctor, I need you."

"How?"

"Come and stay with me. I've heard about the place where you're living now, and I can give you better than that. All I'm asking for in return is the chance to get you out of my system."

She looked at him for a long moment, her hands clasped around her knees and something in her expression that might have been amusement. Over on the far side of the wall behind her a stream could be heard, a constant sluicing like rain on the darkest of nights. A breeze sighed, and lightly shook the branches overhead.

"My, my," she said. "How you sweep a girl off her feet with your romantic talk. You may have made it through thirty-five years, Mister Liston, but you don't seem to have learned much about other people. If you can stop looking on the rest of humanity as minor characters in your biography, then perhaps we can start to discuss this. Until then, I don't think there's anything more to be said."

And with that, she got up from the burned log and walked back toward the stile over which she'd arrived. "Alina, *please*," Liston began as she passed him, not reaching out to stop her even though she was close enough for him to be able to; and she half-glanced back, as if in approval.

"That's a start," she said. "Keep trying."

"Can I call you?"

"No." She reached for the topstone again. "I have to make a few changes in my life around here. When I've made a final decision on what I want to do, then you'll hear from me. Until then you wait, and you say nothing to anyone about this."

He was about to speak, but he quickly changed his mind. Unless he was mistaken, she'd just offered him some hope. He had a profound sense of being like a fish on a line; she was playing him and it was painful, and with every move the hook was biting deeper.

175

It was maddening, frustrating; he was used to women that he could pick up and use, blow off his infatuation like so much steam before letting them go. Alina seemed to know it, and she wasn't going to play it his way; instead, he was going to have to follow the rules that she'd laid down for the occasion.

He didn't understand it.

But he didn't have any choice, either.

She paused at the top of the stile, as if she'd just thought of something; and she said, "Who cut in on the call?"

Liston shrugged. He'd heard the click of the extension, but that happened all the time and everyone in the Hall knew better than to stick around and eavesdrop.

"I don't know," he said.

Alina seemed to think for a moment; and then she lightly swung herself from the stile, and landed without a sound on the other side.

By the time that Dizzy Liston had reached it, she was gone.

THIRTY-TWO

From the moment that he walked into the rendezvous, Pavel sensed trouble.

It wasn't a place that he'd have chosen, but perhaps the woman had thought that she'd be safer if she were to meet him somewhere public like this. She knew nothing of him, after all, and the sight of him now would probably do little to reassure her. He looked across the bar to the reservations counter, and saw two of the staff in a hurried conference.

He crossed to an alcove, and sat down.

It was a three-masted restaurant ship moored in the harbour by the town's market square, and the message had specified for him to be there at seven. He was early, and the bar was empty. It was also an upmarket-looking kind of a place, all wood panelling and buttoned velvet padding, and Pavel was aware that he was no longer an upmarket-looking kind of a person. He didn't even like to look in a mirror any more; his eyes were so dark-ringed and sunken that it was a shock to stare into them. He knew that he had the appearance of someone who was either close to exhaustion, or long-gone on drugs.

He leaned out, and checked the clock over the bar. One of the staff glanced his way and, on meeting his eyes, hurriedly looked away again.

He wondered how close to the road's end he really was.

A teenaged girl came over and offered him a menu. He said, "Thank you, but I'm only here to meet someone. It was her idea to come here, not mine. As soon as I've had the chance to speak to her, I'll leave. Perhaps just some coffee?" He could afford coffee. Just about.

She backed off uncertainly. He didn't get to see exactly how they took his reassurances behind the scenes, but after a few minutes he noted that they seemed to be leaving him alone for now.

He stretched out a little, and leaned back.

If she didn't get here soon, he'd probably fall asleep where he was sitting. He didn't seem to be sleeping much at all, these days, almost as if he'd trained himself out of the need; but what sleep he did get was mostly in odd moments like this, and then he'd either be roused by somebody or have to remember to rouse himself and move on. It was affecting him, he knew. Sometimes the effect could be a little weird; sometimes it could feel as if the world around him was utterly unreal.

He took a cardboard coaster from the table, and started idly to pick it apart. He hadn't expected to be so calm. Perhaps something in him knew that this was finally going to be it, leaving him no room for anxiety.

Well, he could hope.

"Are you the one I'm here to see?" she said.

"The radio message," he said. "Yes, I'm the one." And he half-smiled then, and could feel the ghost of a warm human being looking out from inside the automaton. Perhaps she sensed it, too, because she seemed to relax slightly.

They sat down.

"You're another Russian," she said.

"You know all about that?"

"Not from her, but I know about it. The one I don't know about is you."

"So, what can I tell you?"

"Exactly who you are. And why you're so desperate to find her."

The coffee tray arrived, set out for two. Pavel waited until the teenaged girl had withdrawn before saying, "Who I am is easy. I'm the policeman who was sent out to bring her back from the border, the first time she got caught. I was one of those who guarded her while she sat in a cell, waiting for them to decide what they were going to do with her. And after she'd been helped to escape from the prison hospital, I was the one that she went to for shelter."

"Why?"

"Because I'd all but begged her to. Like a dog. If I could have got her out of there myself, I'd have done it. Once she'd been freed, I risked everything to keep her. I helped to search for her by day, I went home to her at night. One evening when I went back to my apartment, I found her with a dead man in my bathtub. The dead man was a doctor named Belov – she'd once told him about me and he'd tracked down my address and she'd panicked. Later it came out that he was the one who'd forged her release papers. I took him out at two in the morning and dropped him into the river. I tried to make it look like a botched robbery. I didn't succeed."

The woman stared.

178

"My God," she said.

"I know," Pavel said. "I know."

"What will you do when you get to her?"

"I don't know. So much depends. Is she happy?"

"She seems to be getting along. You're not doing all this because it's your job. Are you doing it because you're in love with her?"

He looked down, smiled, and rubbed at his forehead with the back of his hand. "Love," he said. "I don't even know what it means, any more. Being so miserable you'd be happy to die rather than go on living with loss, is that love? Because then I suppose you could say that I am."

"This man who died. This doctor. Something went wrong for her, didn't it? I mean, how responsible was she?"

"She murdered him," Pavel said.

"But was it because he was threatening to take her back to prison, or what?"

Pavel looked at her. She was intent, very serious, and he felt like a man who'd travelled far and seen desperate sights that he could never quite communicate to those who'd stayed at home. Whatever he told her, he could recount only a small part of his vision.

He said, "Do you know what a *rusalka* is?"

The woman shook her head.

"You'd call it . . . you'd say it was something from a fairytale. A female spirit of the water. Very beautiful, and very deadly. They carry people away to live with them under the sea or in a lake or in a river. It's an old, old story."

"I grew out of fairytales a long time ago."

Pavel looked straight into her eyes.

"Alina never did," he said.

He told her what he knew about Alina as a child; about the unwitnessed death of the simpleton named Viktor and the explanation she'd constructed to defend herself of blame – a story that she'd clung to even harder the more they'd tried to prise her from it – and how, years later, it had been tied in with the incident at the school that had led to the loss of her job, then her apartment, and finally to her first, unsuccessful attempt to cross the border. She'd always said that the reason for her dismissal was a mystery but Pavel knew that it was due to a parents' petition over the suitability of *Death by Drowning* as an essay subject – not once, but more than five times in the course of a school year. The children were having nightmares, and Alina's long fall from grace had begun.

"I still believe she'd have been all right had it not been for the hospital," he said. "The hospitals then were used for punishment, not for a cure. I believe that she was sane when they took her in. There was a line, and she wasn't yet on the wrong side of it. That changed."

"Are you trying to tell me she's dangerous?"

"Belov was like a door that she opened. There was no going back. When we were together, she used to put bread outside the window; one time, I found her trying to drown a cat that she'd lured in. She was ashamed and wouldn't talk about it. But I don't know that it stopped her. Have there been deaths?"

He saw her ready to make a denial.

But he also saw her hesitation.

"*Have* there?" he said.

He followed her up onto the deck, to the obvious relief of the staff in the bar below. They hadn't touched the coffee, but he'd picked up all of the *Sweet'n' Low* sachets from the sugar bowl.

Pavel knew that he hadn't entirely managed to get the woman onto his side. He wanted to grab her and face her again, to explain that she was making a big mistake; he wanted somehow to make her realise that he was worthy of her trust, to make her see that inside his raggedy-man exterior there was hope and pain and sorrow that deserved her understanding.

At the head of the gangplank to the shore, she stopped and turned to him. It was almost dark now, just a couple of lustrous grey streaks leaving a trace of the day in the evening sky, and strings of fairylights in the overhead rigging had been switched on. A faint breeze blew across the deck.

"I don't know what I'm going to do about this," she said.

"You mean you don't believe me."

"Maybe I should go and tell her what you told me. See what she says about it."

"She'll run," he said. "And it'll start again somewhere else."

"Nothing's started," she said. "Now I'm starting to be sorry that I even told you all that stuff."

And it was clear to Pavel that neither of them believed it.

He glanced around, at the cobbled quay and the darkness of the harbour below. The harbour esplanade was still early-evening quiet, just a few strollers browsing along the more expensive shops and about half a dozen teenaged kids sitting over at the non-functional fountain.

"She'll be somewhere close to water," he said. "Is she here? In this town?"

"I'm going now," the woman said.

180

He followed her down, descending with a steadying hand on the rope balustrade.

"Please, is she here?" he said again.

"I need time to think," she said. "Give me until tomorrow night. I want to talk to Pete before I do anything else. I'll leave you a message at the same number."

He stopped, knowing that if he pushed too hard then he'd lose her for good. She was his lifeline, he couldn't take the risk of that happening.

"Please," he said. "Be sure to call."

Without realising it, she'd given him a name. And now, she was walking back to a black car. It had been reports of a black car that they'd been following on the first night, all those weeks ago. Could it be? Could it all be coming together for him at last?

She'd parked at the end of the row on the harbour esplanade, no more than half a dozen spaces along from his own car; but of course, she'd have no way of knowing that. He could see that the interior light was on and that there was a child inside, sitting in the back and apparently reading. The boy looked up as the woman unlocked the driver's door.

She glanced back once at Pavel, as he stood by the foot of the gangplank. She probably felt safer, now she was at a distance from him. She didn't smile, or wave, or anything. Her face was troubled.

Somebody called Pete. The car. The area.

Even if she gave him nothing more, he was getting closer.

THIRTY-THREE

Pete was working late that night; he'd stayed on at the yard to clear up a few small jobs, which included taking a look at Diane's Toyota after Frank Lowry had gone home. Alina wasn't working, but was up at the house; after their last serious conversation Pete felt a certain awkwardness when he was around her, and so it had been no tough decision to keep going. Instead of heading for the Step, he'd run the pickup onto the hoist and reached for the air-spanner.

Ted joined him after a while. He came in through the side door, and he was carrying something that Pete recognised after a moment's lag; it was Wayne's radio-cassette player, Pete's own present to him of two Christmases back.

"I came to give you a hand," Ted said. "It's too damn quiet over in the house." And he placed the ghettoblaster on the workbench, pulled out the FM aerial, and switched it on. It put out a lot of sound for such a small unit.

"Yeah," Pete said, wincing. "That ought to cure it."

Ted lowered the volume. He hitched up onto the bench beside the radio and watched for a while and then said, "Any problem?"

"Not for a mere expert."

Ted watched for a while longer. Then he said, "I've heard of enthusiasm, but this is ridiculous."

"Just a little after-hours special," Pete said, tossing the offending brake shoe onto the bench beside Ted. "I assumed you wouldn't mind."

"Mind?" Ted said. "Why should I mind? That's Diane Jackson's car, isn't it?"

"The man has brains as well as eyes."

"This has got to be the weirdest courtship in the history of sexual relations."

"Oh, no," Pete said. "Don't start that. I'm thinking of jacking it all in and becoming a monk."

"Why?"

"Diane won't come anywhere near me while Alina's around, but then every time Alina talks about leaving I get this strange feeling

182

that I won't know what I'll do if she goes. Now, what would you call that?"

"A mess," Ted said.

"Exactly. So I'm going to be a monk. I'm going to wear a sack, and I'm going to shave one of those little domes on the top of my head."

"Yeah," Ted said, leaning over to peer at the crown of Pete's hair. "I can see you've made a start."

He picked up the damaged pad and inspected it, turning it over like a valuer with some not-so-rare antique. The radio thumped away in the background.

And then he looked up and said, "Beer would help."

"Back in the seat, please, Jed," his mother told him as she indicated to pull off the road onto the forecourt of the last late-opening petrol station before civilisation ran out and darkness began, and Jed did as he'd been ordered. He'd been standing up and hanging himself forward over the backrest of the passenger seat, swinging his arms like a monkey. This was great. Bedtime was sliding past, and no one had said a word about it. He was on strange roads, at night, in the safety of an unfamiliar car; the world seemed to have lots of exciting new edges to it, and he was in no hurry to get home.

He looked out of the window. The forecourt was like a piece of a neon city, bright as day and utterly deserted. He could see the late-night cashier in his booth, in the last lighted corner of one of those shops where they sold a few dozen things that had to do with cars and a few hundred that didn't. Sometimes his mother would let him go with her and browse around while she was waiting to get her credit card back. She never let him buy anything, but it was always interesting to look. There was no point in him even asking tonight; at this time the shop was all closed, the cashier sealed-in behind a teller's window and a cheap intercom system. He was reading a magazine.

"Stay here," his mother said.

She got out and went over to unhook the pump nozzle. It looked like a weird kind of gun and she carried it two-handed, it was so heavy. Then she hunted around for the Zodiac's filler cap, located it, and a few seconds later the car started to hum with the transmitted vibration of the pump. Jed looked up at her through the rear window, but she was staring off into space across the roof of the car. Armed now with the knowledge that she wasn't watching, he squeezed forward between the seat backs and clambered into the forbidden passenger seat.

She'd now said exactly eight words to him since she'd returned from the big boat. Jed would have liked to have gone onto the big boat as well, but she'd told him that it was like a bar, no children allowed. They could always go on a different boat, another time.

No children allowed. The number of things they promised you, and always for when you got older.

Something was worrying her, which meant that Jed was uneasy as well. But at least she knew what she was worrying *about*, whereas for Jed it was just like some vague feeling that was in the air that he breathed and could do nothing to resolve. He could watch her for reassurance, and that was all. From the back of the car he'd been able to see her eyes in the mirror whenever she'd checked the road behind them; but she'd seemed to be looking directly at him, as if catching him out in his concern, and so he'd glanced away.

He liked the big Hi-Lux, especially on those rare occasions when his mother let him ride around the back in the open pickup area, but the Zodiac was even better because it was black and it looked mean. With that tape and stuff around the front, it was like a battle wagon straight out of *Mad Max*. Maybe he could have a crack at driving it, one day, somewhere around the estate roads where it wouldn't matter that he didn't have a licence.

One day.

When he got older.

He heard the *klunk* of the nozzle being withdrawn. His mother hung it back on the pump and headed off to pay; from here it looked as if she had about an acre of empty, oil-stained concrete to cross, stepping up and over one of the other raised islands when she was about halfway.

Jed turned around and looked back toward the road. There was another car entering the forecourt. It was newer than the Zodiac, but it didn't look in much better shape; it was so dusty that even from here you could see the Smiley faces that someone had drawn onto one of its doors, while vision through the windscreen must have been restricted to a couple of overlapping arcs where the washers and wipers had cleared it. He was expecting the vehicle to carry on across to one of the other islands, but it didn't; it made a sudden, tighter turn, and came in alongside so close to the Zodiac that there was less than an arm's length between them.

It stopped level.

Quickly, Jed hit the door locking button. It was something that his mother had drilled into him so often that he barely thought about it, the response was so automatic. He could see the face of the other car's driver. He was a strange-looking character, but he was smiling.

He raised his hand and made a finger-twirling gesture, and Jed supposed that the stranger meant for him to open his window.

Conflicting impulses fought within Jed. There was *Don't talk to any strangers*, but then there was *Always be polite*. He glanced back across the forecourt; his mother was at the cashier's window, her back toward him, seeing none of this. No help from there.

But where was the harm? He was safe in the car.

He turned the handle to wind down the window. Nothing happened, and then the glass dropped halfway all at once.

The other car's driver was still smiling.

"A fine set of wheels," he said.

He sounded strange. Jed supposed he was a foreigner. He didn't know what he ought to say in reply.

Getting no answer the man said, "That's Pete's car, isn't it?"

This changed everything. The man was no stranger after all.

Jed said, "Yes, it is. We're borrowing it."

"From Peter Shakespeare, yes?"

"No," Jed said, puzzled, "Peter McCarthy."

"My mistake," the man said. "Sorry," and his car revved and suddenly he was gone. He didn't stop for petrol or anything, just swung off into the night and disappeared.

Nonplussed, Jed started to wind up the window again. He wondered if he'd said something wrong.

He looked across the forecourt, toward the pay window. His mother was just starting to turn around. Knowing her, she'd probably demand to hear the conversation word-for-word and then rebuke him for being unable to remember most of it.

Better not to say anything, he thought.

And so, when she came back, he didn't.

THIRTY-FOUR

As Pavel had been hoping, the woman had led him straight to the place where he most needed to be. He'd never have told her so much or taken so great a risk if he hadn't believed that she'd react this way; but he'd managed to alarm her, and in Alina's case there was nothing more alarming than the truth.

The woman wasn't entirely naive – she'd made at least one definite attempt to establish whether or not she was being followed, pulling off the road and waiting for no obvious reason – but then she wasn't exactly adept in the ways of subterfuge, either. Pavel had simply driven on by, backed into a blind opening that concealed him from the road, and then picked her up again when she passed. This time he followed without lights, and at more of a distance.

She made the turnoff about twenty minutes later.

He almost missed it; he'd seen her tail-lights go but the entrance to the track was so hard to spot, he had to overshoot and back up. Further in, the track climbed and narrowed. There was space here for one car's-width only.

The track was rough, but Pavel was floating.

The exhaustion and the adrenalin were a potent combination. The car hit a rut and bounced; Pavel lifted his hands from the wheel and the car went on, steering itself as if directed by the power of his mind alone. Tonight was a night on which he could do anything. He'd already achieved the impossible in finding her; after this he felt as if he could walk on water and raise the dead.

The car started to head off the track. He grabbed the wheel, and steered it back in.

A couple of gateposts, the overgrown remnants of what had once been a wall; at the sight of these and the hint of some kind of a destination, he ran the car off the road and into the bushes and continued on foot. Roots tripped him and branches clawed at him; he'd have to move carefully in order not to give himself away. After a dozen yards or so, he glanced back. The car was just about visible, but only if you knew where to look for it.

He climbed onward.

He could see the house through the trees. There were lights showing, and the black car was out in front. He could see the woman standing on the covered porch before the door. She was knocking.

But nobody was answering.

He stopped and watched her for a while, but nothing much seemed to be happening. He saw her glance toward the still-running car, where the boy's pale face was watching her through the glass. She looked back at the house, again at the car; she was torn.

And then the boy yawned, and that clinched it.

She stayed for long enough to write some kind of a note and stick it in the narrow gap between the house's main door and its frame, and then she got back in the car and swung it around for the descent. Pavel ducked before the headlights swept across him, and then he listened to her engine note as it faded away. Then, pushing the leaves aside, he stepped out into the open.

Slowly, wondering if somebody might be watching, he walked toward the house. He could see why somewhere like this would appeal to her; wooden, rambling, overgrown, it was almost like something out of her own past. He climbed the steps to the porch; if she was anywhere around, surely she'd be able to hear him.

He tugged the note free from where she'd left it, and opened out the paper. *Peter*, it said. *Call me or come and see me. It's urgent.* And then the woman's name.

Peter was the one that Alina was with. So any final doubts were now overcome. Unlike the woman, he tried the door without bothering to knock.

It opened.

"Anybody here?" he called, but there was no reply.

He stepped inside, into the silence.

When he pushed open the nearest door, it revealed an empty room. "Alina?" he called, and then he switched to words that only she would be able to recognise. "It's Pavel, I'm here alone. Please, Alina!"

The next room was a bathroom; but in the one after that, he found final confirmation.

It was her scrapbook, immediately recognisable even though it was propped over beyond the far side of the bed. This was *her* room, he knew; he could sense her presence, almost as if she'd walked out of it only seconds before and left some trace – her scent, her body heat, her aura – that had yet to disperse. He was the one who bought the scrapbook for her, to replace the box in which she'd kept all of her old photographs and clippings; they'd been her only link with the life that she'd been forced to leave behind when she'd finally moved into his apartment. That was when he'd felt that Beauty had fallen into the arms of the Beast and that the Beast, for a while, had prevented her from falling any further.

How could she have ended it as she did? He'd genuinely come to believe that she had some affection for him. He couldn't hope for love, that would be asking for too much, but surely he'd deserved better than such an abrupt desertion. Pavel would have run with her, if she'd wanted him to. He'd have done anything for her, and she'd known it. He'd been there all through her nightmares, sometimes reporting for work and going out on the road with no more than a couple of hours' sleep behind him. He'd concealed her, protected her, supported her. He'd understood her, as far as it was possible.

But she'd taken her book, and she'd left him.

He'd bought it for her because she'd almost worn out the box with use by constantly going through its contents, taking out each item and staring at it, sometimes for an hour or more. It was as if, with everything else lost or otherwise taken away, this was the only means by which she could hold onto her old sense of self. Now it seemed that she'd almost worn out the album, as well; he could see that she'd taken some of the pages that had come loose, and she'd arranged them around the dressing-table in a kind of display.

And then he heard a noise.

It was almost nothing, but he knew immediately that someone was leaving the house. He turned and raced back out of the room toward the entranceway, but he was too late. He stood on the porch in a circle of light that spread some distance before the house, leaving the trees beyond in darkness.

"Please, Alina," he called out to the darkness. "At least talk to me. You know I'm not here to hurt you, I couldn't."

Nothing but silence, and a sense of being watched.

So he went back inside. A couple of minutes later he came out again, carrying her album and a lit candle stuck onto a plate by a pool of its own melted wax. He'd found it in the kitchen, on a shelf above the stove. He set it on the square post at the end of the porch rail.

"Don't make me do this," he said, and he waited.

But nothing happened.

So then he took one of the loose pages, held it up high for her to see, and then brought it down and touched its corner to the flame.

An inhuman sound echoed through the forest. It might have been an animal in deep pain and some distance away, but Pavel doubted it. He dropped the burning paper and it hit the ground before the porch, turning over a couple of times and shedding sparks and ash.

The sound died, and nothing else happened; so he prepared to burn a second page.

And that, at last, brought her out.

"No!" she said, and she stepped into the light.

He almost couldn't believe that the moment had finally come. He'd thrown away everything, stripped his life right down to nothing, and all of it had been for this. She'd all but destroyed him and he knew it, just as he knew that if he could have returned to the beginning he'd have made all the same choices over again. That, he'd long ago come to understand, was the penalty of loving the *Rusalka*; it was to embrace your own destruction, and embrace it willingly.

And now, here it stood.

Pavel was so relieved that he almost wanted to weep. He stared at her, drank her in; but he didn't dare to move towards her in case she should turn and leave him again.

"Why did you follow me?" she said.

"You know why," he said. "I never had a choice."

"Are you alone?"

"Since the summer began. They sent me over to find you, but I ran away. They never knew about us."

Alina moved to the steps now, but she didn't climb them to him.

"Oh, Pavel," she said, sadly.

He could read her. The signs that would have been invisible to others were plain to the eyes of one who knew her so well.

He said, "She's stronger, isn't she?"

"She's stronger. There's no difference between us any more. I thought that if I left the land, I could break the spell. But it didn't work. Wherever I am, becomes the land again. Pavel, why did you come? You were *safe* from me back there."

"Because there's no life for me without you," Pavel said, and it was no less than the truth. She looked up at him for a while and he fed upon that look, on its affection and its apprehension and its regret.

And then, without meeting his eyes any more, Alina climbed the steps and took the scrapbook from his hands.

"Come with me," she said, and she placed the book safely in the shelter of the porch. "There's something I want you to see."

Pavel was on edge, sensing the moment that was coming even though its details had yet to become clear.

He said, "Is it far?"

"It's no distance at all," Alina said, and she took his arm to guide him down.

"Wake up, Jed," Diane whispered gently. After parking the Zodiac on the gravel by the side-entrance to Liston Hall, she'd said, *Home at last* in what she'd hoped was a confident, untroubled voice, and she'd turned around to find him with his eyes closed and his mouth open and his comics still held close to his chest. His eyes fluttered now as she spoke. She knew that she could probably walk him up to his bedroom and undress him and put him into bed, and he wouldn't remember anything about it in the morning. He'd say that he did, but he wouldn't.

"Come on," she said as she slipped her hand behind his head, and she supported him as he groped and fumbled his way out onto the gravel. There he winced, and peered around, but already his eyelids were drooping again. One of his comics fell, and she picked it up as she began to guide him towards the house.

The stranger had followed her for some of the way, of that much she was certain. There had been far-off headlights in her rearview mirror for some considerable distance. She'd cut the Zodiac's own lights and pulled into an off-the-road layby which consisted of a picnic area and a screen of trees with a *No Camping* sign, and she was pretty sure that she'd managed to lose him; she heard him pass and saw his lights as a flicker through the bushes, and then she'd waited another ten minutes in case he came back. He hadn't. She'd inadvertently led him towards the valley and the lake (*She'll be somewhere close to water*, he'd said) but at least she would take him no further.

Jed thought it was all some kind of big adventure. Tomorrow, he'd probably think it had been some kind of a dream. She'd let him go on thinking so. She wondered if Pete would see her note and call her tonight, or if his interpretation of the word *urgent* meant that sometime in the morning would do. Would that matter? Surely nothing was going to happen before morning.

Jed came first. Always. Every time. That was the principle she believed in, anyway, even if she sometimes found her behaviour drifting away from the ideal.

First thing tomorrow, if he hadn't been in touch, she'd go down to the yard and tell Pete about everything that had happened. He could decide how much of it to believe, if anything.

A few hours couldn't make any difference.

So now, with her hand gently cradling the back of his head, she steered Jed onward in the direction of his room.

190

Alina has stayed a few paces before him on the descent to the shore. Pavel has been stumbling in the darkness and having trouble keeping up; she seems to move with hardly any effort, and she never puts a foot wrong.

Finally, they reach the water's edge. There hasn't been any rainfall in a while and the level has dropped, making a narrow strip of shoreline which ends at the high-water point like a bite taken out of the turf. This small, temporary beach is covered in twigs and straw debris that has dried out in the heat of the days and which now crunches underfoot like the bones of mice. Alina draws him across, and turns him to face the valley; the vestigial light of the long day is enough to block in the shape of its immense sides, even now.

She says, "This is it. What do you see?"

"Water," he says. "Mountains. Stars."

"Does it remind you of anywhere?"

"Home," he says, even though it doesn't. The mountains are too high and the stars are all wrong, but he knows that this will be what she's expecting to hear. She sees it differently, and he hasn't sought her out to argue.

"It is my home now," she says. "Stand at the edge. Don't turn around."

Nervously, he does as he's been told.

From behind him, she says, "Do you know what you're asking?"

"I think I do."

"Watch, then. Watch the water. But I have to warn you, it's already too late for me to let you go."

So he watches the lake as it catches whatever faint lights are available to it; close inshore, it seems to be stirring as the unseen rocks just below its surface warp and change the patterns with their mass. It flexes and shines like enchanted oil, a magic mirror onto a world of madness.

Exhaustion, *he tells himself.* Exhilaration. *That's all it is.*

She says, "Who sent you to me?"

"Nobody. I followed a woman who said she knew you."

"How did you meet?"

"What?" He hasn't fully understood the question, simple though it is; he's being distracted by shapes and shadows that seem to be forming under the water.

"Can you see anything in the lake?"

"No. Just reflections."

"Try for a little longer. And then I'll tell you what I can see. How did you come to be talking about me?"

"I put out a message for you, on the radio. She heard it and called in."

"What did she look like?"

"Taller than you, dark . . ."

His voice trails away.

"You've seen something?"

"No."

"Then close your eyes, and just listen. I'll describe it for you."

He closes his eyes, and she begins to tell him; she begins to show him her world through the eyes of the Rusalka.

She describes how the first of the figures rises from the water and stands a little way offshore, starlit and cadaverous and with water sluicing from it. The second rises as a dark female form beside this. Both are like thin shells of hard matter around an infinity of darkness and stars; there's no glint or glow to suggest whether they have eyes, or pearls for eyes, or anything at all.

Pavel's eyes flicker open for a moment. He sees only the surface of the water, undisturbed.

"Did she drive a big car?" Alina says. "A car like a truck?"

"No . . . I don't . . ."

He screws his eyes shut again. Against all reason he wishes that he could see what she's describing, because to see would be to enter her world completely.

Others rising from the water; an old man, three young, straight wraiths, a couple of children, a carpenter . . . and then from out beyond them come a number of stags, a few cats and dogs, birds popping up and trying to unfold their sodden wings without success and without any kind of sound at all. They face inward in a half-circle, an audience of the dead summoned for a performance of the living.

And of all this, Pavel sees nothing.

"You've made such a long journey," she says. "Now there's only one last step to take. Can you manage it alone?"

He opens his eyes, then, and looks down at her. The face that he knows so well is now just angles and planes in darkness, all expression lost; there's little to tell between the girl on the shore and the creatures that she imagines to be in the lake. He tries to read sympathy there, he tries to read encouragement; but these are hopes rather than solid certainties, where the only real certainty is that she's probably much too far-gone in her madness for him ever to be able to carry her home.

He'd hoped that he might somehow be able to take her back. Or at the very least, for the two of them to find some corner where they could build a kind of happiness. But he knows now that this can never be.

She pushes him, taking him by surprise, and he stumbles and loses his footing on the bank. When he hits the water he almost falls, but then he manages to get his balance on the lakebed. The water is surprisingly cold, soaking into his clothes and making them heavy. He takes a deep, shuddering breath, and turns back to face Alina; she hasn't moved.

"What was that for?" he says.

"You want to be with me," she says. "I'm showing you the way."

He takes a step toward the shore, but something catches at him under the waterline and he falls, plunging face-first into the water. For a moment he's completely submerged, and as the water closes over his head the cold penetrates the rest of his clothes with a shock that feels as if it will stop his heart.

There are weeds down here, and he's tangled in amongst them. They waft at him, they stroke him, they hold him in a grip like a dead man's hands. Now he's afraid. He pulls at the weeds and feels some of them tearing, but others are tightening in the same move.

Already, the breath is beginning to leave him.

It's strange; he finds that he's starting to experience flash-memories and scenes from his childhood as he tries to fight his way back to the surface. It's only inches away, but even inches can be fatal. The dizziness and the agony in his lungs begin to recede as the memories become more and more clear, until he's being hoisted up onto his father's shoulder as they walk along the sands . . .

Which coincides with him coming up out of the water, ripping free and gasping for air.

Alina is still waiting on the shore.

He'd hoped they could be together. But he's lost her finally now, and he knows it. He'd even have entered her insanity, if he could have done it and there had been no other way . . . but even this has been barred to him.

"Help him, children," Alina says.

And suddenly there are hands on him, instantly plunging him back under so that the next breath that he takes is no breath at all.

THIRTY-FIVE

"It's done," Ted Hammond said, "but don't look at me. I only passed the spanners and fiddled with the radio." He was looking red-eyed and somewhat hung-over, but even so this was the best shape that Diane had seen him in for a while. She'd always liked Ted, from Day One; and if she'd been unconsciously avoiding him of late . . . well, it was only that she hardly knew where to begin.

She glanced back at the Toyota, which was standing on the verge outside the workshop, and said, "Thanks, but I really need to see Pete, first."

"Pete's out on a job," Ted said. "Somebody ran a car into the lake last night. He's gone to winch it out. If you want to drop by later on . . ."

"It could be urgent," she said. "Can you tell me where I'll find him?"

So Ted shrugged, and told her. All she needed to do would be to drive south on the lakeside road until she came to a wagon train of emergency vehicles, about five miles down. The police were there, the forestry people were there, possibly a TV crew as well; although why there should be so much interest in a routine wreck, Ted couldn't say.

Ted got the Toyota's keys and walked out to the vehicle with her. Chuck and Bob, who'd come bounding up to say hello when she'd arrived, had wandered off and were now mooching around the verge looking for something to piss on.

Ted said, "I'm glad you called by. Gives me a chance to say thanks."

"For what?"

"For coming to the funeral. It was appreciated, even though I wasn't in much of a state to say so at the time."

"Nobody's been expecting thanks. But if it isn't a stupid question, how've you been feeling?"

"I'm getting by," he said. "That's about as much as you can hope for, really."

194

She got into the car, and closed the door. The side-window was already open. Even after only one day in the Zodiac, the switch back to the high cab made her feel momentarily strange.

She said, "Thanks, Ted."

"Pleasure," Hammond said. "And, look, I'm sorry I've taken so long to get anything done about the Princess. I've got no excuses for it. If you still want me to handle the sale, I'm happy to go ahead."

"Excuses?" Diane said. "Ted, I've never even thought about it that way. I juggled the books, moved some money around between the accounts. It wasn't any problem."

"So Dizzy keeps his boat?"

"Until next year. It'll stay in the boat house and it won't see daylight, and next year I'll go through all the same arguments again."

"Well, the police gave me back the boat-house key. Want me to dig it out now?"

"There's no hurry."

"Get it from Pete, then," he said. "He can hand it over the next time he sees you."

The road was the one on which she'd returned from town the previous evening; daylight turned it into a completely different journey, almost as if she was coming down out of primitive country and into civilisation. The mountains to either side were just as remote and the forested valley sides were just as sheer, but down here the lower slopes had been tamed and the pale faces of houses and hotels looked out like small children from the bushes. For the moment they were few and well-spaced, but they were only the outposts of the big resort that lay ahead.

The emergency-vehicle setup, when she finally found it, was rather different to the scene that Ted Hammond had suggested.

To begin with, she'd been expecting something like a carnival train of vehicles at the side of the road itself; but when she stopped and asked a couple of forestry workers for help, they directed her back to a spot where the lake and the road parted company for half a mile or more with woodland between. Ten minutes later she was following a dirt trail, and less than five minutes after that she was getting out of the pickup alongside what looked like a grey, under-equipped ambulance.

It was only one of half a dozen vehicles, which included a couple of ordinary cars and the yard's breakdown wagon. She saw Pete almost immediately; he was standing on the outskirts of the circle of interest, unoccupied for the moment but seemingly too fascinated to drag himself away.

At the centre of the circle stood the car in question. Except that it hadn't made it as far as the lake; instead, it had burned.

It looked as if it had been rolling or was being driven towards the water, but had become stuck on the jagged rocks between the dirt track and the edge of the lake. How it had come to burn, it was difficult to say; the front end was just a blackened mess, the paint scorched away, the tyres gone and leaving two tangled heaps of fine wire that were already beginning to rust, the windshield melted to a fringe. The rest of the glass was dark and discoloured, the ground about the car a wasted area scattered with carbonised ash. However it had started, the car had burned fiercely and fast.

Ross Aldridge, in uniform, was standing by what had been the driver's door. He was in serious conversation with two men who were wearing grey overalls and heavy rubber gloves, and didn't notice her as she made her way around to Pete. There was an atmosphere here, and Diane couldn't exactly define what it was.

Pete seemed surprised to see her.

"Hey," he said with a look of concern. "You shouldn't be here."

"What happened?" she said, looking toward the wreck; one of the two overalled men (both of whom, incongruously, appeared to be wearing neat shirts and ties under their greys) was about to apply a prybar to the buckled driver's door.

"Nobody knows," Pete said, "but I wouldn't watch this part, if I were you."

The door popped open with a binding, crunching sound.

Diane turned to look, her reactions running out of step with her conscious mind that was now, belatedly, absorbing the implications and telling her *No!* The overalled men moved in and blocked her view of the car's interior, but not before she'd had a moment to register the thin, charred stick-figure whose meatless head was bowed over what remained of the steering wheel.

She felt faint, as if she'd been hit hard by a big wave that had left her floating without even a rudimentary sense of up or down. She felt Pete's hand on her arm, turning her and guiding her away as Ross Aldridge beckoned for a well-used steel coffin to be brought over to the wreck.

"Did you see that?" she said as they moved around behind Aldridge's white Metro. Her voice sounded hollow in her own ears, as if her head was in a glass bowl.

"I saw it earlier," Pete said. "Once was enough."

"But, the *car* . . ."

"They can't tell how it happened. He must have been deliberately trying to drive it into the lake. But then it all went wrong on him, somehow."

"When did it happen?"

"Last night, late. After midnight, anyway. But no one realised there was a body until we came to shift it this morning." Pete shook his head. There's no explaining it, he seemed to be saying.

But Diane was thinking about the Smiley faces that had been drawn in the dust on the undamaged rear end of the car, and which still showed clearly through the soot that now lay over them.

Jed had been talking about Smiley faces, as she'd guided him into his pyjamas.

"Pete," she said. "Did you see Alina last night?"

He was looking at her warily; not a question he'd have expected, considering the circumstances. "I got home late, and she'd gone out. Nothing unusual."

"And you didn't get my note?"

"What note?"

She shook her head. "We have to talk."

"Sure."

"But not here."

He checked the scene behind them. Diane didn't turn. He said, "Well, I may be tied up for a while yet. Aldridge wants it photographed and checked over by some of his people, and then I've to take it to some laboratory out of town. I'm still wondering how I'm going to hook it up to the hoist. Could be an all-day thing."

Diane said, "Then I'll meet you at the yard when you're done. Just promise me that you won't go home."

"What?"

"It's important, Pete. Don't go home until we've had a chance to talk."

He studied her for a moment, and saw how serious she was.

"Okay," he said.

Routine estate work seemed to be out of the question for the day, but she felt no stirrings of conscience over this; didn't even give it a thought, in fact. Before heading for home she went on into town and called at the library, where she spent an hour looking through back issues of the local newspaper and getting photocopies of every accident, every fatality, every missing-persons report that had appeared over the past few months. She made notes of the dates. Then, as a kind of afterthought, she asked if there was any reference entry for *Rusalka*, and the librarian said, "I think that's an opera, isn't it? You could try the music library."

But she didn't.

Back in her office at the Hall, she was cutting the fatality items out of the xeroxed sheets and had become so absorbed that she wasn't even aware of Dizzy Liston's arrival until he was standing in front of her.

"Hi," he said.

She managed a smile. "I thought you were hibernating."

"No, just . . . keeping out of the way. How's everything?"

"Everything's fine," Diane said. Which wasn't the most truthful statement that she'd ever made.

It was good enough for Dizzy, though. He nodded and then drifted away, almost shambling. His yellow colour had gone, but he seemed wasted. He'd been staying in his suite for most of the time and he hardly ever came out; no guests arrived at the weekends, and no visitors came during the week. Dizzy's Women were becoming one of the endangered species.

Diane thought of him, waiting endlessly in the same chair as he stared at the same patch of wall. And she remembered the voice on the telephone.

Then she went out into the gardens to look for Bob Ivie.

Ivie was out on a sun lounger on the lawn, his shirt unbuttoned as he lay with a magazine. It was probably true to say that the last few weeks had been the most boring of his life so far, with the same to be said of Tony Marinello. It had been one of Ivie's boasts that he hadn't opened the covers of a book since the day he'd left school; already this year he'd read four, and was wondering if there wasn't somewhere he could apply for a medal. Marinello spent most of the afternoons in his room, smoking dope and watching daytime TV.

Diane said, "Bob, I've got a big favour to ask," and Ivie looked up at her with an interest that was almost gratitude.

"Name it," he said, putting the magazine aside.

"I want Jed to go to his grandparents' place for a few days, get him away from the Bay for a while. Will you drive him down for me?"

"When?"

"This afternoon. I'll pack him a bag, and you can pick him up from Mrs Neary's."

"Consider it done," Ivie said. "Where do they live?"

"Richmond," Diane said, and saw Ivie's interested smile fade a little.

198

"Oh," he said hollowly, but it was too late; she had him.

"Thanks, Bob, you're a love," she said. "I'd take him myself . . . but suddenly I've a zillion things to do."

VI: SEEK AND DESTROY

No one gets out of here alive
Jim Morrison

THIRTY-SIX

It was late in the afternoon when Ross Aldridge left his Metro in the square by the Lakeside Restaurant and climbed the pavilion steps to come inside; Angelica Venetz saw him through the window as she passed through on her way to the kitchen and her first, anxious thought was for Alina.

And then Aldridge, after taking off his uniform cap, asked if they could speak privately somewhere, and so she led him through into the tiny office where, twice a week, she placed their orders and brought the accounts up to date. Aldridge's eyes were hard, his manner almost grim.

But the waitress wasn't the reason for his visit, after all.

He began by telling Angelica about his day's work so far; about the unknown, untraceable stranger who'd somehow managed to incinerate himself in his similarly untraceable car. When he started to tell her about how the body had come apart as the morgue men had begun to remove it from the vehicle, she got him a chair and persuaded him to sit.

"I don't see how you can ever get used to anything like that," she told him.

"You can't," he said bleakly.

"Have a brandy."

"I'm all right." He looked up at her. "You can do something for me, though."

"What's that?"

"Tell me what you know about Tom Amis."

This was unexpected; it was as if the conversational ground had suddenly shifted, and it took Angelica a moment to regain her balance.

"He's a carpenter," she said. "He hung a couple of doors for me at the start of the season."

"You know where he's from?"

"Down south, somewhere. He says he travels around in his van, going wherever the work is. Why?"

"I'd just like to get a look at him. Is he still in the area?"

"I wouldn't know. He was working up at that new ski centre, but I haven't seen him in a while. What *is* it, Ross?"

Aldridge hesitated for a moment, as if this was one of those newly-shaped thoughts that had never before been put into words. Then he said, "Probably nothing. It's just that there have been too many coincidences around here of late, and I'm not happy. This is the fifth 'accident' in the past three months, even if you don't count Ted Hammond's boy and his girlfriend. We average maybe one serious incident a year around here, and the season isn't halfway over yet. Back on my desk I've got seven missing-persons reports, just general sheets from other regions on kids who set out hitching and were *maybe* heading this way. That's apart from dead stags and dead dogs and who knows what. It's too many."

"What are you saying?" Angelica asked, and Aldridge made a *who knows?* gesture as if he'd already said more than he'd planned.

"Nothing," he said. "I don't know. But there's a classic picture for a situation like this, and I'm looking for someone who fits it. Someone who lives on his own, so nobody knows too much about him. Friendly on the surface, but he mainly likes his own company. And he didn't get here until sometime after the beginning of the year."

Next door in the kitchen, the warning signal on the water-heater began to sound. Someone switched it off.

"Oh, no, Ross," Angelica said, disbelievingly. "Not Tom."

But Aldridge was already getting to his feet, and he held up a calming hand.

"Look," he said, "nothing about this to anybody. It's just a stupid idea of mine, and *I* want to be the one to knock it on the head before it goes any further. There's no theory or anything, it's just . . . too many accidents."

So, feeling strangely like some kind of a Judas even though she knew that Tom Amis couldn't have been involved, she told him how to find the old hunting lodge up on the treeline that, after a few false starts in the past three or four years, was undergoing final conversion to become the new High Rigg ski centre. It wasn't a place that Aldridge had known much about, although this was bound to change when the next winter season arrived. This is simply a matter of elimination, Angelica told herself; a helping hand toward proof of innocence, rather than a betrayal.

"Thanks," Aldridge told her as he made for the door. "I've got a few calls to make about the wreck, and then I'll go up and see him. Not a word to anyone."

And then he left.

Angelica stood at the main door, watching through the lace-curtained glass as his car made a turn in the square. Now she was thinking, what did she *really* know about Tom Amis anyway? And she was so intrigued by this new light on an untested idea that she didn't even notice Alina's emergence from the kitchen until the waitress was standing alongside her.

"Miss Venetz?" she said.

Angelica looked at her, a little dazed as if she'd just been jogged out of a waking dream.

Alina went on, "I wonder if I can take the afternoon off. I'm not feeling so well."

"Of course," Angelica said. "Sonia can cover." She looked out again through the glass.

"And may I borrow the van to get me home," Alina added, "if you weren't planning to use it? I can bring it back in the morning. I wouldn't ask, but I don't quite feel up to the walk."

"I'll drive you," Angelica said, beginning to tear herself away, but Alina didn't seem to want to cause so much disruption.

"I can drive," she said. "Please, I'd rather."

It didn't even occur to Angelica, at least not straight away, that an illegal immigrant with no valid licence probably wasn't the best insurance risk in the event of any accident; almost absently she went back to the office and opened a drawer to let Alina have the van keys, and then she returned to one of the windows overlooking the square. It was almost as if the life going on outside had taken on an entirely new and fascinating aspect for her.

Tom Amis? she was thinking, almost entranced.

And she was still thinking it a few minutes later when their small Renault van went by, with Alina at the wheel.

THIRTY-SEVEN

Pete had been back at the yard for little more than half an hour and was making himself useful by restocking the Coke machine on the marina wharf when he saw Diane again; he quickly threw the cans in wherever they'd fit, Coke in the Fanta line and Fanta in the Seven-Up, and then he closed up the front of the machine and went to meet her.

"Busy day?" she said, looking him over. Getting the burned-out car up onto the hoist in a way that satisfied the police lab officials had been a messy, complicated job. He'd tidied himself up on his return but there hadn't been time for him to run home and change; he'd considered it, but he hadn't wanted to risk missing her.

"Busy enough," he said. "How about you?"

"You're going to hear all about it," she said. "Can we go somewhere and talk?"

Pete glanced across the yard. "How about in the house? Ted won't mind."

"That could be a problem. I don't want Ted or anybody else to hear this."

So Pete looked around; a big Birchwood and a smaller Chris Craft stood empty at a couple of the nearer jetties, but they were sales stock and it wouldn't look good if the yard staff were to be seen using them like a rest area.

"Let's take one of the cars, then," he said.

And Diane quickly said, "Let's make it mine."

They walked through the main part of the yard, Pete leaving the Coke machine keys with one of the Wilson boys and looking in to say a quick goodbye to Ted and to Frank Lowry on the way out. But Lowry had already gone home and Ted was on the phone in his office, having trouble getting himself out of a none-too-fascinating business conversation with somebody called Ellis. With the phone still to his ear Ted leaned out to look past Pete and then, having seen Diane just outside the doorway, he caught Pete's eye again and pointed to an envelope that was just out of reach in his OUT tray. Pete saw that it had Diane's name on it, and he took it outside to her.

She opened it as they walked toward the Toyota. It contained the key to the boat house, and nothing else.

"I didn't know what to say about this," she said, looking at it bleakly.

"It's only a key," Pete said.

Diane looked at it a moment longer.

"Is it?" she said, and then she slipped it, envelope and all, into one of the pockets of her jacket.

"You can get right in, the car isn't locked," she said.

Ross Aldridge was going to be home late again.

He could avoid it by leaving this conversation with Tom Amis for another day, and he was tempted to do exactly that . . . but the professional side of his nature told him that he ought to know better and, besides, for some time now Loren had been in the kind of mood where nothing seemed to suit her no matter what he did. Whether he came home early, or came home late; whether they went out, or stayed in and sat around. The company of a total stranger would have been better than this; a stranger would feel an obligation to be civil, at least. Loren was rarely straight-out rude, but she no longer seemed to be able to answer a simple question without throwing in a dash of attitude. He didn't know what he could do about it. He wasn't a saint, he couldn't go on like this forever; for the first two years after the stillbirth he'd felt as if he was carrying her across a tightrope while she bit and clawed at him every step of the way. They'd come through that, but not to return to the relationship they'd once had. Everything was different. *She* was different. Sometimes he felt as if she didn't want a husband any more, just a guilty witness to the hard time that she always reckoned she was having.

The sun was getting low in the sky as he turned his Metro towards the old sawmill track that would lead to the ski centre. The owners had been upgrading the road but it was only half-finished, a bed of crushed stone that had already fallen into ruts from forestry traffic. As the car laboured upward he passed the raw fresh scars of trees recently tended, and great white splashes of sawdust on the forest floor. At a place where another track crossed, several large stumps had been wrapped in chains and were now waiting to be hooked onto tractors and dragged elsewhere. The car bounced hard a couple of times, jarring all the equipment in the back; he knew that he wasn't concentrating as much as he should, and he tried to focus himself on the job in hand.

They never talked about the child they'd never had. Not even to give her a name; beforehand they'd bought one of those books of names and their meanings and they'd each made their own lists, but it had all come to nothing.

So Aldridge had given her a name of his own, although he'd never said as much out loud.

The lodge announced itself with a blinding reflection from the main windows, flooding his car with the sun's late rays and forcing him to slow down and shade his eyes until he'd driven around into the shadow side of the reception block. The ride suddenly turned smooth on him. The tarmac here looked pretty new, when his eyes got over the dazzle enough for him to make it out. He stopped and sat for a minute or more, waiting for the fireworks to subside before he got out.

And what exactly was he expecting to find, here?

Nothing, he hoped.

Which was exactly what he found.

There were signs of Amis everywhere, but no Amis. There was a varnishing job in the foyer that was only half-done, the brushes wrapped in polythene bags to keep them soft while the varnish itself had set hard. His old Bedford van stood out around the back, bonnet half-open, keys in, battery dead. Aldridge stood in the carpenter's makeshift bedroom, looking down at the man's neat stack of second-hand paperbacks and wondering where he could be. He'd already checked on the generator in its open cage in the utility shed; switched-on but stalled, the generator had been cold.

He found the bathroom that Amis had been using, a small private suite next to what would eventually be the manager's office. It had a toilet, a shower stall, a mirror, and a washbasin. On a glass shelf above the basin were a battered leather travelling-case with shaving kit laid out alongside it.

This bothered him. He stood looking at the setup for a while, half-aware of his own reflection in the mirror. Damn it, he ought to be able to concentrate better than this. He kept thinking of the two of them, himself and Loren, as if they were chained together and drowning. She'd tried, he couldn't pretend that she hadn't. For a few months in the winter she'd joined a housewives' guitar group, where they all wore long dresses and sang John Denver songs to deaf old people. It hadn't lasted.

There was a vehicle approaching, somewhere outside. He turned and walked through the manager's office and out into the foyer, and there he stopped. The Venetz sisters' Renault van was turning onto the forecourt, its windscreen flaring in a momentary double-reflection from the window behind which he now stood. He knew

208

the van, he'd walked past it barely half an hour before; it had the name of the business and their telephone number on its panelled sides. What did the sisters want here? Were they looking for him?

But no, neither of the sisters was driving. It was one of the waitresses, the one that always seemed to fade into the background whenever he called by. What was her name, again?

He couldn't remember. He'd heard it somewhere, perhaps that evening at the Hall; he was sure that it would come back to him. She'd stopped now, and began to reverse the van towards the cafeteria block. She seemed to be in a hurry.

Perhaps she'd overheard him. It wouldn't have been impossible.

Aldridge was now having no problems with his concentration at all.

He saw her get out of the Renault. She was small and graceful, and she was moving with purpose; no looking around to see who might be there, no calling out, no waiting to see if anyone emerged to meet her. She took a couple of grey plastic trash bags out of the Renault, and went straight in through the unsecured doors of the cafeteria block. As they swung shut behind her, the last fierce rays of the sunset began to die in the distant mountains.

Aldridge moved across the foyer. The cafeteria block was the one part of the site that he hadn't yet checked. His own car was around the side and out of sight, so the waitress wouldn't yet know that he was here; and for the next few minutes, at least, that was how he wanted it to stay.

This entire situation was probably innocent.

But he was going to make sure of it, his own way.

Here's a dream that Pete McCarthy's been having, on and off, for the past five or six weeks:

Alina is leading him through the lobby of an expensive-looking hotel. He's acutely aware of the fact that he looks out of place in his work clothes, but the people who pass them on either side don't seem to notice; they're programmed, unseeing, mere walk-ons in the dreamscape.

Alina looks back over her shoulder at him.

You'll have to see this in the end, she tells him. So, let's get it over with now.

They come to an unmarked door. She tries it, and it opens. They go on through.

Everything changes on the other side of the door. They move from the plush of the lobby to the bare cast-concrete of a service passageway, one side of it stacked waist-high with unopened boxes of cleaning materials. The lighting is patchy; only two of the bulbs are working, one just inside the door and the other about halfway along to the fire door at the far end. The pools they cast are pale and sharp-edged, leaving a good part of the area in near-darkness.

Pete closes the door behind him, shutting out the lobby muzak and all the set-dressing that lies no more than an inch deep over the low-rent reality that surrounds them now. Alina has stopped. She's a silhouette in the darkness, no more than a step beyond the light.

I can't deceive you any longer, she says. And she raises her hand.

It comes into the light.

But it isn't her hand, not as he remembers it; this one is fishbelly-white, delicately veined in moss green. It's slim and elegant like Alina's . . . but it's clawed.

I warned you, she says. I told you to stay away from me.

The hand turns. She holds it relaxed, palm-upward. Pete is transfixed. When she flexes her fingers in a lazy kind of gesture, he hears a faint clicking like that of well-oiled gears.

She takes a step forward, and comes fully into the light. She seems to stand a little taller, her eyes blazing with the green of the deep, her skin washed with the pallor of the drowned. Her hair is coiled, wet, dark, glistening like weed.

Pete tries to look into her eyes, but can see nothing deeper than their glittering surface.

And then he wakes, remembering nothing.

The waitress was having a problem.

She'd gone through the empty cafeteria block and into the kitchens at the back; watching at a window, Aldridge had witnessed the bizarre setup inside. A deep chest-freezer, its power line trailing and unconnected, had been dragged out from its place against the wall so that it was now over by the double-drainer basins. The freezer's lid had been roped down with several turns of a nylon line that went around and under the body of the appliance to leave it securely, if messily, trussed.

But the oddest feature of the setup was the short length of hose that ran from one of the basin taps. At a guess, the freezer had been dragged out so that the hose would be able to reach; it disappeared under the freezer lid like some weird drip-feed. Aldridge could see that the tap had to be running, because the sides of the appliance streamed with water and the floor was awash. It must have been running unchecked for hours.

Days, even.

The waitress had untied the knots and then withdrawn the nylon line, throwing it aside; then she'd raised the lid and bent over to reach in. Aldridge couldn't see what she was reaching for, but he saw the water which cascaded out over the sides. Whatever she was trying to drag out from under, it wouldn't come. She soaked herself in the effort.

But this was something that she hardly seemed to notice as she stepped back, considering. The light wasn't so good now that the sun was going down, but Aldridge could see the quiet concentration in her stance. After a moment she picked up the nylon line from the floor and made a big noose with it, and with this in her hand she climbed over the side and into the appliance to get a better angle on whatever lay within. Yet more water poured out onto the tiles, spilling over with a noise that he could hear through the glass. Whatever it was, it was lying so awkwardly that even this approach didn't seem to be working. By the time that she gave up she'd immersed herself completely several times, so that when she finally climbed out again her hair and her dress were plastered to her and dripping.

Aldridge now had his first indication of the freezer's contents. A hand, stiff and bloodless, reached vainly for heaven; she'd hauled it up and there it stayed, the ivory-white hand of a showman of death making a call for eternal silence.

She was wet, but she didn't even shake herself. She stepped back and considered again, as someone might consider an arrangement of wedding gifts on a table.

Amis, he thought.

How much more wrong could he have been?

The waitress was going about this business as if it was just a minor, routine part of her day; no big challenge, nothing to get too excited about, simply take a dead man out of one hiding place and put him somewhere else. And if it was a task out of proportion to her stature, she didn't seem to feel it – the strength that she now showed as she pulled out the running hose and hauled the freezer across the floor was greater than Aldridge would have expected from her. After swinging it around, she got behind the appliance and started to push it towards the big two-way doors that stood floor-to-ceiling in the far wall. She moved like a compact, powerful engine, the freezer rolling like a block of stone on its way to the pyramid. When she came level with the doors, she left it for a moment in order to open them.

They were delivery doors, opening to the outside. Beyond them was a loading platform, and beyond that a dead-ended spur of road with a turnaround for vehicles. A hook and winch hung in silhouette above like gallows tackle; the waitress got behind the freezer again, and carefully manoeuvred it to stand directly underneath.

If she was planning to use the winch, she'd need power. With the generator stopped, every power point on the site would be dead. She turned and started across the kitchen, and for a moment Aldridge thought that she was heading straight for him; but she was walking towards the door at his side, and he backed off and into the growing shadows as she emerged and passed by.

She didn't even glance his way. He waited as she crossed the forecourt and disappeared around the back of the reception block, intending to go into the kitchen the moment that she was out of sight. But he almost couldn't bring himself to move; something had slipped through his senses and his intellect and found the coldest spot on his soul . . . and now, having been touched, the cold spot was spreading.

And before he could begin to fight it, every damned light in the place came on.

He'd assumed that she'd be restarting the generator, but he hadn't been expecting this; all of the switches must have been down when the generator had failed. He could take her now; he'd seen enough.

But he slipped around the corner, where she wouldn't be able to see him and where he could watch her from another window.

Her returning footsteps were as even and confident as before; and although he was placed so that he couldn't see her, he could see her long shadow thrown out in three overlapping versions by the floodlights. She seemed to be carrying something, but he couldn't tell what. He heard the cafeteria door open, and then bang shut again.

Aldridge eased himself level with the window and paused to take another look, more carefully this time because he knew that there was more of a chance that he might be seen. The kitchen now blazed white under row after row of unshaded fluorescent tubes, the spilled water on the grey-tiled floor making a long, mirror-like trail from the gap to the loading bay. Where previously the open doorway had been a square of light, it was now a square of darkness.

The waitress was back at the freezer. Now he could see what she'd been carrying.

It was a ski stick. A pretty obvious thing to find lying around, considering the nature of the place. It was the fibreglass type, about three feet long, with a slim metal spike at one end and a wrist loop at the other. She'd climbed onto the top of the appliance again,

212

holding the stick in her left hand; in her right was the wooden mallet from the carpenter's own toolkit.

She positioned the spike carefully in the open freezer below her. Then she raised the mallet, and gave the top of the stick a single, hard blow to get it sited. There was a lot of spring in the shaft and the job wasn't easy, but the stick seemed to go in about an inch. When she paused to change her grip, the stick stood up on its own.

It was hard going. Aldridge watched, unable to drag himself away, as the ski stick was hammered fraction by fraction into the body at the bottom of the freezer. Halfway through she had to change position, alter her angle a little; she gripped the stick with both hands and stirred it around, as if seeking the route of least resistance through bones and sinew.

Aldridge was sickened. *Go in and stop her*, he was thinking.

But he was also fascinated.

Twenty minutes or more must have gone by, twenty minutes of calm, patient work as the carpenter's corpse was efficiently spitted. Finally the waitress hopped down, went around to the other side, and thrust her arm in deep as if feeling for something; and then, apparently satisfied, she went over to the control box beside the door and pressed the button to lower the winch.

She used the nylon rope again, attaching one end to the wrist loop on the stick and the other to the winch's hook. Then, returning to the control box, she started the raising.

Slowly, Amis sat up.

His face was almost black. The ski stick had entered his chest just below the breastbone, and had taken a lot of his shirt through with it. There was no blood. He sat like a doll, newly-baptised, water running from his hair; the fibreglass shaft was bent almost double, trembling with the strain of holding him up, and it seemed likely to break if the body should be raised any further.

But the waitress appeared to have planned for this. Stopping the winch before he could rise any more, she moved around behind the body with a second loop of the nylon line. Although he couldn't see exactly what she was doing, Aldridge could make a guess; he reckoned that she was throwing the loop over the protruding spike of the stick to centre his weight under the hook. This done, she returned to the winch control and continued the operation.

No rigor, it would seem. Amis came out hunched into the shape of the freezer's interior, but then he slowly began to unfold as if the dead matter was too dull and stupid to give anything better than a delayed reaction to the change in circumstance. He looked as if he'd been that way for some time. He was shoeless.

The waitress walked around him, sizing him up as he swung slightly in the breeze outside the open doors. The water still ran from his sodden clothes and skin, splashing down into the freezer from his dangling form.

A neat arrangement. The waitress seemed to be taking time out to appreciate her own work.

Which finally gave Aldridge the break that he needed to pull himself away. How long had he wasted, transfixed by the scene? Too long. He stepped back from the window and, walking as quietly as he could, headed for his car. He could make the arrest any time now, no problem; Aldridge stood about five-eleven, weighed around a hundred and seventy pounds, worked out with weights on rare occasions, could still swim a mile, and had once run a decent half-marathon. The waitress was considerably smaller, and probably little more than half his weight. But he'd made his decision; he was going to wait and watch some more, and use the waiting time to get a head start on calling in some backup.

Because if she took the body down to the lake, and started to fake up yet another of those "accidents" . . . well, he wouldn't just be grabbing her for Amis.

He'd be taking her for all of them.

The Venetz sisters' Renault stood before him, waiting for its gruesome load. He made a wide circle around it, and glanced back to be sure that he wasn't being followed.

Help would take something close to an hour to get to him. There would have to be CID, forensic, scenes of crime, press officers, the works. The valley would be like one big circus for a while, and the aftermath would probably never be forgotten.

He unlatched the door of the Metro.

"I owe you an apology," the waitress said.

THIRTY-EIGHT

He spun around. She was behind him, still a few yards away, but she must have been moving so silently that she could have been on him before he'd known it.

She said, "I think I made a mess of your radio."

He didn't need to look. The car hadn't been locked, and the radio was easy enough to reach. She must have done it all that time before, and she must have known that he was there and watching as she'd staked Amis and hung him up to dry. Waiting for him to betray himself, waiting for him to make a move. He couldn't even imagine how anyone could be so cool.

"Why?" he said. "Why have you done this?"

But she only shrugged. "We were a long way from the lake," she said, as if that would explain everything. "I'd planned to move him later, but . . . you got here ahead of me."

He was looking her over. She'd probably claw and scratch and struggle like a wild thing, but his size and strength would count for more as long as he was prepared to use them ruthlessly. Amis might have done the same, but he couldn't have been prepared.

"Miss Peterson, isn't it?" he said, trying to reassure her as he looked for a way to come in at his best angle, but she didn't reply. "It's all over, all right? Now let me help you."

She smiled in a way that he didn't understand.

"I've had your kind of help before," she said.

"Come on," he said, putting a cautious hand out to take her arm. "Get in the car with me. It's the best thing you can do."

She looked into his eyes.

It was as if a screen of humanity had dropped away behind her own, a screen that had been no more than paper-thin. Aldridge was looking into twin pits that bored all the way down into Hades itself. The river of fear ran through him, and it ran cold. There was no question any more about what had happened or how, no bewilderment to be felt because now he *saw*. Nothing about her had changed, and everything was different. A hole had been punched in the fabric of reality, and a demon had stepped through.

A demon that wore a young woman's skin; but no less of a demon for that.

"You don't know who I am," she said. "You've no conception of *what* I am."

"We'll find out," he said, taking her arm.

But her arm wasn't there.

Something hit him hard from behind, and he started to go down. His mind was out of step, unable to register what was happening. Something blurred before him and his head snapped around to the side, and then he hit the ground. He struggled to rise. She grabbed the back of his shirt in two handfuls and shook him like a rug, beating the breath out of him in two great shockwaves.

He lay there, numbed and dazed and dizzy and dismayed, and realised that she'd done all of this in a matter of maybe a couple of seconds. It was as if he'd been hit by a car.

She was lifting his feet.

She was dragging him toward the cafeteria.

He scrabbled for purchase with his hands on the new tarmac, and felt his fingernails tear. She had a grip like a blacksmith. He tried to raise himself and kick his legs free; she flicked him like a rope, and his head cracked hard against the floor.

He saw lights. They were like popping flashbulbs.

And he let himself go limp.

He wouldn't underestimate her twice. She was whip-fast and totally ruthless, like the maddest of mad dogs. Size wasn't the issue here and neither was strength, although she had plenty of that. He had some unofficial mace in the car, a little handbag-sized spray that he'd picked up somewhere and never had a use for. He wished that it was in his hand right now. He could zap her and then, while she was blinded and struggling, maybe he could get one wrist cuffed to an ankle.

They were almost at the cafeteria again. She dropped his legs, and walked over to open the doors.

He waited until he could hear the sound of the hinge, playing dead right up until that moment.

And then, without looking back, he launched himself up and he ran.

She was faster. She caught at the loose part of his shirt but he spun around and managed to pull free, sending her off-balance for a moment. He didn't stay to watch her recovery, but lit out at top speed for the only place of safety that he could think of; not the woods, where she'd move with ease, and not any of the buildings either.

He aimed for the generator shed, just a few yards away and around the corner.

The unmuted beat of the generator told him that the door would be open even before he could see it. He dived through and into the cage, slamming the cage door shut behind him and scrabbling for the key that he hoped to hell would still be in the lock. It was, but on the awkward side; he'd barely got it turned and out when Alina flew through the door and, without even attempting to stop, hit the bars hard. Her arm shot forward like a piston, grabbing for Aldridge as he dodged back.

She caught him, but only just. She missed his throat and took a pinch of the flesh under his chin; even then she might have been able to draw him closer, but the sweat of fear and exertion had made him slippery and difficult to hold. She held him for a second, but then he fell back against the thumping generator and left her clutching the air.

He was on fire. He felt as if he'd been nipped by red-hot pincers, titanium crabs' claws with a brutal strength behind them. Alina slowly withdrew her arm, and held the bars with both hands.

She was smiling again.

She said, raising her voice to make herself heard, "I know someone whose wife loves him more than anything, but he's no longer sure that he loves her back. She lost his baby and he tries not to blame her, but he does. Isn't guilt a strange thing, Mister Aldridge?"

It almost worked; he was only a heartbeat away from throwing himself against the bars to reach her. If he did, it would be over. It took everything that he had to resist her. The cage wasn't big, but it was big enough; and as long as he stayed in the middle, he'd be safe.

"I could wait for you to come out," she said.

"Don't stay around on my account."

But she inclined her head slightly, as if conceding a point. "There's too much to be done," she said. "I suppose I'll have to find you later." And then, with her smile still in place, she moved to leave. The shutters had been restored.

"Give it up," he called after her. "You're finished."

She looked back at him.

"You mean, my secret's out?" she said. "You won't live that long."

He couldn't believe that it was going to be so easy; and he was right. She was busy outside for a time. Then he heard her on the roof. She was pouring something around and suddenly the hut was filled with the stink of petrol. It was the spare can from the back of

217

his own car, at a guess. Quietly, alert to her every move, he turned the key in the cage lock and let the door swing open; and when he knew for sure that she was climbing down on the opposite side, he eased open the door of the hut itself and made a silent dash for cover.

A while after that, he heard the Renault leaving. Parts of the hut were already in flames by then.

Had he still been in the cage when the generator's tanks went up, he'd have been barbecue meat.

"Oh, Jesus," Pete said. "Oh, God Almighty."

"I know," Diane said. "I know."

"How can you really be sure it was the man who followed you?"

"You know I can't, he was too burned-up. But I know it was his car because of the pictures in the dust . . ."

"Pictures in the dust? Come on."

". . . and because I got more than half of his number as he went by me after I'd stopped on the road. Same car, same man, Pete. He says that Alina's dangerous and the question we've got to face now is, do we believe him and what do we do about it?"

"I don't know," Pete said.

By the Toyota's interior light, he looked again at the cuttings that Diane had handed to him. They were out by the lake, having pulled off the road onto an unmade strip of soft shoulder that overlooked the water. It was a pleasant spot with a view, but at best there was space for no more than half a dozen cars. No one ever stopped here for long, and most went by and never stopped here at all. Some people had pulled in ahead of them, and had walked the few yards down to the shore with a big golden dog that was now splashing around after a ball. The long shadows of the mountains lay across the water, deepening by the minute.

On top of all the accident and incident reports that were in the familiar layout of the area's local newspaper, there were three or four sheets of facsimile paper with the header line of a London-based cuttings library. Two of the faxed items were marked as coming from the *Herald-Tribune*. The others were from something that he'd once heard of but had never before seen, the English-language edition of *Pravda*.

Diane said, "Petrovna? Peterson? That's got to be her, hasn't it?"

And Pete nodded.

Diane went on, "I had to pay money to get all this, but it was worth it. She's mentioned by name in the index of some archive, as well. We could probably get a copy, but it's somewhere in Munich."

218

"Radio Liberty," Pete said absently, leafing through some of the other cuttings without actually reading any.

"She told you?"

"I think she mentioned it one time."

"She talked about all that to you? About being Russian and being in hospital, and everything? Then you know it's all true."

He closed the book. "I know that the first part is true. The *first* part. But she never told me she'd killed anybody."

"Oh, sure. She wouldn't want to hold back on something like that, would she? I mean, if it was me, I'd work it into the conversation every chance I got."

Pete said quietly, not meeting her eyes, "You can stop trying to sell this to me. You don't have to."

He was thinking; *It's like there's two of me. One who knows what she wants, and the other who tells her what she can have.*

He was thinking; *Rusalka, you'd say heartbreaker. I have it on the best authority.*

He was thinking of how the woodland seemed to know, falling silent when she stepped out; here walks madness, let it pass.

And even now in his heart he could sense the lure of the *Rusalka*, her siren call to the hungry and the incomplete.

"I can believe it," he said. "I think I just . . . I just don't want it to be."

There was silence in the cab for a while. On the banking below them, the big golden dog emerged from the water and shook off a spray like a hail of diamonds.

Diane said, "What do you want to do?"

"I think we ought to talk to her," Pete said.

THIRTY-NINE

He watched the fire for a while. It was spreading to the main building now, running in tongues along the gutters. There was a big fire hose on a standpipe across the yard, but on its own it could be of little use. Sparks were lifting and floating toward the trees, dying like fireflies before the journey was completed; it would only need one to reach the tinder of the undergrowth, and he'd have the beginnings of a major woodland blaze on his hands.

But right at this moment, that was the least of his concerns.

The sight of destruction was almost hypnotic, but Aldridge tore himself away and made for his car. The keys were gone and his radio, as she'd promised, had been taken out, stamped upon, and neatly put back into its place. He had no less than three personal radios that were intended for issue to volunteer Special Constables and which could be clipped to a lapel or carried in a pocket, but all of these were at the house on their plug-in charger.

He looked around. On foot, it would take him anything up to an hour to make it to the lights of home. He had to get a message through somehow. He wondered if there was a working phone in the ski centre itself.

The air inside was already hazy with smoke and, of course, the lights had failed; he made his way by the fireglow from the windows and found the phone in the place where the carpenter had been sleeping. He picked it up, and heard a tone. He dialled quickly, not knowing how long it would be before the line came down. The smoke was getting perceptibly thicker. Any minute now, the walls or the roof would burn through and he didn't want to be inside when that happened.

He closed his eyes and gave a brief, teeth-baring groan of frustration when he heard the ringing tone stop and the line switch to the distinctive hiss of the answering machine. His own voice came on a moment later and he drummed his fingers, looking around; the message seemed endless. He wondered if Loren was home, or not. Sometimes she just ignored the phone and let the machine take care of business; she'd stand by and listen, but she wouldn't pick it up.

"Loren?" he said. "It's me. It's Ross. If you're there, lock the doors and windows. Or better still, get out of the house. Don't leave a message or anything to say where you've gone, I'll phone around and find you. Don't be scared. I'll explain when I get back."

An intense, reddish light under one of the doors told him that it was time to get out of there, and fast.

He hung up, and he ran. He was coughing when he got outside. The building was lit from within now, like a shadow-theatre, and it was almost as if he could see figures dancing across the big foyer windows.

But he turned his back, and started away.

He'd only one regret.

And this was that he'd told her, *Don't be scared.*

It was dark when he finally got there, but the outside light was on. Maybe Loren had only just arrived back from wherever she'd been. The side door to the house was on the latch but there was a window open alongside it. Village life had tended to make them lazy about home security. He went in and called her name.

There was no response. The house gave back nothing but an ambience of emptiness.

She'd heard the message, and had gone around to a neighbour. What else could she have done? But she should have secured the place behind her, at least. He went through into the small police office to check on whether the answering machine had been reset.

It hadn't.

It had been unplugged. Both cassettes had been removed, the one for the incoming messages and the looped cassette that carried his own voice. They were nowhere around. He looked at his desk. There was no definite sign, but he knew almost immediately that it had been searched and then set right again. It was still something of a mess, but it wasn't quite *his* mess any more. He turned around and went out, intending to call Loren's name to the empty house once more.

He found her on the stairs.

She was lying just above the middle landing, around the corner where she couldn't be seen from the hallway. She was head-down, feet pointing back the way she'd apparently fallen. One shoe had come off and was sitting on the third step from the top. To his eye it looked too neat, too much as if it had been placed there for an effect rather than simply lying where it had landed.

Aldridge sat down heavily on the lower stairway, and put his head in his hands.

He didn't make a sound. He didn't do anything. His mind raced, but to no purpose whatsoever. He seemed to stand apart from his own thoughts, watching them go by like an out-of-control carousel too fast to be boarded. And all that he could say was a low, "Ohhh, *shit*," again and again.

After a while, he sighed and straightened.

She was still warm. And she was damned heavy.

There had been a time when he could lift her like nothing. These last few years, he hadn't ever lifted her at all. They'd outgrown those kinds of games. Seemed to have outgrown everything, in fact, and nothing had come along to fill up the spaces. Their time in the Bay and the valley hadn't been their best.

But, still . . .

He managed to pull her to the top of the stairs and then, with a little more dignity, to lift her up and carry her through to the bed. He laid her on top of the covers and then went back for the lost shoe. But then he couldn't get it onto her foot, and so he took off the other one and set the pair on the floor next to her. He avoided looking at her face. Her face was a stranger's now, too relaxed, and with its lines wiped like a tape. He ought to cover it with something, really, but somehow he couldn't bring himself to do it. Too much of an admission of the end. Too final.

He straightened her clothes. He crossed her hands and they fell into place quite naturally; by her hands, she might almost be sleeping. He kissed her once, on the forehead. Her body was warm, but the skin on her face was cool. The curtains were half-open. He drew them shut.

From the doorway, he looked back. The way he'd laid her out, she looked like a Pope or something. A sudden rage turned in him like a beast in the deep, but within a second he'd fought it down. The surface remained calm. He went along the upper landing to the linen cupboard, and got out a folded bedsheet. It wasn't one of those they'd bought for the nursery; that had all been cot-sized stuff. He wasn't exactly sure at which point she'd got rid of it; like everything else it had just gone, with no mention from either of them.

Like everything else.

This time, he looked at her face. All hurts forgotten.

And then he covered her.

*   *   *

He walked down the stairs like a man of twice the weight. He felt sick and impossibly, impossibly weary. His mind took in the details but made very little of them. Nothing stolen, nothing interfered with; to the unsuspicious observer, it might well have looked like yet another accident. No drowning element this time, though. She was widening her scope. One death by fire, another by falling.

For how long did the woman think she could go on like this?

Forever, in her own mind, perhaps; because Aldridge could see no end to it. He thought of the others. He thought of the children. And now this.

How was he going to tell anyone? You couldn't explain her. Not without looking into those eyes, and glimpsing what concealed itself behind them. Whatever it was, it was sharp and it was very, very clever. Whether it was really only a part of her, he couldn't say; expensive doctors argued over that kind of thing in courtrooms for days.

Mad dog, he thought.

According to procedure, he ought now to be calling his area sergeant. But he went back into the police office.

And there, without anger and without any obvious trace of passion, he got out the keys to his gun cupboard.

Ted Hammond's dream.

He's walking through the boatyard, while a mist is rising out over the lake. In the dream he comes across the dripping figures of Wayne and Sandy; they're down by one of the docks, the old dry-dock that he's been cleaning out and restoring. Now that the boards are completely off, it's a square, dark pit that in certain light can look like an open grave. Although he's drained it now, in his dream it's still half-filled by water and weeds. The two of them are stepping up out of the darkness of the pit.

His appearance is a surprise to them.

He says, "Wayne? Is that you?"

And Wayne says, "Go back, Dad. You're not supposed to see us."

"But why, Wayne?" he says – the one, all-encompassing question that he's been asking over and over since the day of their discovery. "Why?"

"She wouldn't like it," Wayne says.

"Come home," Ted pleads. "I'm sorry I got angry about your exams."

"No, Dad," Wayne says, and he turns to look out over the water.

There might be something in his expression, but Ted can't actually make out his face.

Sandy is beside him, saying nothing.

"I've told you," Wayne says, "we can't come home. We're with her, now."

FORTY

It was getting late into the evening. Pete and Diane went to the restaurant, to see if Alina would be there. She wasn't, but Angelica explained how she'd borrowed the van and gone home. Diane glanced at Pete, and Pete said nothing. He hadn't seen Alina looking ill or unhealthy for some time, now; not since the evening of the big party. Then, she'd seemed to be struggling to hold herself together. After that night, it had never been an issue again.

And then, pressing them to complete secrecy – as she'd already pressed five other people so far in the evening – Angelica told them about Ross Aldridge's sensational new theory about the serial killer who had set up covert operations in the valley. Set up around the same time that Tom Amis had put in an appearance, she hinted heavily, and added that Aldridge had gone to interview him.

Again, Diane glanced at Pete.

Again, Pete said nothing.

Their next stop was at the yard for Pete to pick up his car; at this hour there shouldn't have been much of anything going on, just boat owners drifting in and out along the lakeside boardwalk or maybe using the laundromat or the vending machines. But the workshop lights were on, and Frank Lowry's car was still outside; for Lowry to stick around so late was pretty well unprecedented, and so Pete asked Diane to wait for a couple of minutes while he looked in to see if there was any problem.

"Ted's over at the marina," Lowry told him. "But don't expect him to make a lot of sense."

"What do you mean?"

"Don't ask me. I've given up trying to make him out. You're his friend, you take over. Something's wrong with him, and I'm sick of asking him what."

Pete went out between the workshop and the showroom, through an enclosed space that was crowded with big cruisers being stored out of the water. They'd been raised up on Valvoline drums and made secure with planks and wedges. They were crammed close together with a dozen well-used car batteries in the shelter under each of them, and the big hulls dwarfed anybody who walked through. He couldn't help feeling a little spooked. In daylight, he'd never given it a second thought.

Or in darkness, before tonight.

He could see Ted's lights out on the rough ground behind the house. They were the old incandescent gas-powered lamps with big reflectors that were hardly ever used, except in the winter time when they were handy for heating up the workshop. This part of the yard had always been something of a dumping-ground for the relics of the trade – spare hulls and old skiffs, stacks of timber, cracked and useless celluloid windscreens, duckboarding . . . even an entire wooden building complete with windows, dismantled into sections and stacked for so long that they'd gone mossy and rotten. The lights were almost at the end of the property, where a row of fence posts and wire marched out into deep water to mark the boundary between the yard and the adjacent woodland.

The old dry-dock, Pete realised as he drew nearer. The reflectors on the lights were angled into it.

All that Pete could see was the top of a ladder as he picked his way over the uncertain ground, but when he called Ted's name he saw the ladder move after a moment's delay. Ted appeared a few seconds later, clambering out of the dock as Pete approached. He stood looking flushed, slightly breathless, and – was Pete imagining this? – just a little wild.

"Ted," he said. "You've got Frank so worried, he won't go home. What's going on?"

"Nothing. I've told him as much."

Pete was going to take a look over into the dock, but Ted was somehow blocking his way. It didn't look deliberate.

Pete said, "So, what are you doing?"

"Cleaning it out, trying to free up the gear. There's thirty years of seepage and slime in there, but it's basically sound."

"Yeah, but at this hour . . ."

"When else?" Ted said. "What am I going to do, sit in the house and think? No thanks. It's difficult enough. Tell Frank to stop being such an old woman and get himself home. And you do the same."

"Are you sure you're all right?"

"I'm all right. So get on with your life. Go."

So Pete went. He glanced back once, in time to see Ted disappearing down the ladder into his pit. Ted didn't wave, or even look at Pete.

Back in the workshop, he reported the drift of the brief conversation to Frank Lowry. "He looks a bit tired," Pete said. "But nothing weird."

"He was down in that old dock, right?"

"Yeah."

"Except that he isn't working on it. He's taken an old chair down and set it on a flat piece of board to stop the legs sinking in. He just sits there, like he's waiting for something to happen."

"Like what?"

"Try asking him," Lowry said darkly, "and see what you get."

There seemed to be nothing more that he could do at the yard. So Pete drove home in his own car, and Diane followed in the pickup. He could see in the mirror that it was a bumpy climb for her. The Zodiac had put down ruts over the months, and the Toyota didn't fit them. They both had to brake hard when a rabbit dashed out into the lights and froze, something that Pete had found to be a regular hazard when night-driving along this stretch. He felt as if his life had begun to spin so fast that it was in danger of tearing itself apart. He felt as if he'd become accountable for responsibilities that he wasn't even aware of. He felt as if he was beginning a long slide into one of his own nightmares.

And when they finally reached the old wooden cottage, they found it closed-down and dark.

"She's not home," Pete said.

"She could be sleeping."

"I don't think so. The van would be here. We'll have to wait for her. Can you do that with me?"

"Of course," Diane said.

They got out of the pickup. The porch steps creaked as they climbed them.

She said, "Let's be careful anyway."

"She once said that she wouldn't ever want to hurt me. This could be her chance to prove it."

He went inside, and switched on the hall light. Within moments there were a couple of craneflies and a moth dancing around the shade, lured in from the darkness outside. Pete led the way down to Alina's room. Her door was slightly ajar, no light inside. He gave the door a push, so that it swung inward.

A single, metallic click.

"If you were shorter and better-looking," a man's voice said, "I'd have blown your head off."

FORTY-ONE

Alina's bedside reading lamp came on, revealing Ross Aldridge in the act of reaching across for the switch. He was in a chair that had been positioned so that it faced the door square-on, and the lamp was beside him. His free hand held a rock-steady shotgun that was pointing directly at Pete.

Pete said, "Is this how the police say welcome home?"

Aldridge didn't smile. He didn't show any inclination to lower the shotgun, either; it was as if he considered himself to be in a strange land where there are no certain allies.

He said, "Where is she?"

"Gone, by the look of it."

"Until when?"

A good question, and one that Pete wouldn't have minded the answer to; but then he found it in a single glance around.

"Quite possibly for good." He pointed toward the empty dressing-table. Aldridge didn't even move his eyes to follow. "Her scrapbook of home, it isn't there. It's the dearest thing she owns. It's just about the *only* thing she owns. She wouldn't be without it."

Diane moved into the room behind him now, as Aldridge said, "So the next question is, why?"

"I think the next question ought to be what do you think you're doing, sitting here in my house with a loaded gun ready to blast anyone who walks in. Or is that the latest trend in rural policing?"

"I can think of one reason," Diane said quietly from behind Pete. "That it's all true, and he's seen what she can do."

Nothing moved for a while. There was no sound, other than that of the death-dance of the craneflies in the hall behind them.

But finally, Aldridge lowered the shotgun.

"I think we're going to have to trade some information, here," he said.

When the sun came over the Step the next morning, it found the three of them still talking. In all that time Alina didn't come home, as Pete had guessed that she wouldn't.

Aldridge told them about what he'd seen up at the ski lodge, and what had happened to him there. He said nothing about anything else. Diane showed her cuttings and repeated Pavel's story, and Pete finally found a release in pouring out everything that had been troubling him about Alina since those first days when he'd brought her to the valley. He'd been afraid that some of it might sound stupid and trivial. But nobody seemed to think so. Their accounts all meshed together with a kind of quiet perfection . . . and it all traced a line back to that one moment in the motorway services, when he'd looked up into those grey eyes and made a choice instead of an excuse.

She'd even warned him, in her way.

But he hadn't listened.

Aldridge was the one that he couldn't quite make out. He'd no car, and apparently he'd scrambled all the way up to the house the previous night, stalking its windows like a raider until he'd realised that there was no one around. Then he'd broken in.

"Any ideas on where she might have gone?" Aldridge said, standing at the window and watching the dawn light as it filled out the sky beyond the ridge.

"I don't know," Pete said. "But I don't think she'll have left the area completely." This made the most sense to him. He'd watched Alina's growing love-affair with the valley, one that had become deeper and darker with every midnight tryst, and he didn't think that she'd ever be able to tear herself away.

And what was a *rusalka*, after all, without a lake to call its home?

"Did she make any friends?" Aldridge said. "I mean, anyone she might run to who'd hide her?"

"I can think of someone," Diane said.

Aldridge said that he wanted to pick up some equipment before they went up to the Hall, and so they stopped off in the village. He didn't seem to want them to go with him into the house; seemed to make a point of it, in fact. So they waited with the vehicles at the end of the close. Pete was frowning as he watched Aldridge walk away. "What's wrong?" Diane said, but he made as if to brush the worry aside.

"Nothing," he said. "Unless you count the obvious."

"Well, the obvious ought to be enough."

"I know. But I'm not so sure about him, Diane."

"What do you mean?"

"I mean that we spent all last night hammering out what we knew about Alina, and what's he doing now? He's planning for the three of us to go looking for her. That's not my idea of a police response. He ought to be calling someone."

"He could be calling someone now."

Pete said, "Come on. This is hardly going by the book. He broke into my place with a shotgun. You know what he said to me last night, one time when you weren't around? He said he'd looked into her eyes and he didn't think she was human."

Diane looked toward the house. Pete had noted that even though it was daylight, the upper-storey curtains were still drawn. Apart from that, Aldridge's world seemed like a pretty regular one.

"Just a way of putting it," she said uncertainly.

"That's what I thought at the time. Now I'm not so certain."

Aldridge was coming out again with an armload of stuff. He turned and carefully locked the door behind him.

And then it seemed to Pete that he stopped for a moment, and for no obvious reason; he stood with his free hand gripping the door handle and his head bowed slightly, like a programmed thing that had hit some momentary gap in the instructions that it was receiving.

For a moment, it was as if the birds didn't sing.

And then Aldridge straightened, and started back toward them.

Dizzy's black limousine was on the forecourt when Diane arrived, and she parked alongside it. She glanced around as she got out, remembering Aldridge's warnings. But this was daylight and familiar ground, and she sensed no danger.

On her way around to the side-entrance she came across Bob Ivie, stretched out as before on his sunlounger. This time he wasn't even pretending to be interested in a magazine; he was simply staring off into space and looking about as forlorn as it was possible to get.

Diane couldn't help feeling sorry for him; and for Tony Marinello, whom she'd overheard in his room singing along with *Button Moon* one afternoon the previous week. Dizzy's minders were almost useless when lifted out of their city environment; but they'd have to stand it, because both of them knew that they were otherwise unemployable. They were probably yearning for the end of summer and their return to town, for the late nights and the bad debts and the fights quietly defused before they'd started, and for the legwork involved when Dizzy got tied up with some of the bizarre business ventures of his friends and which would sometimes actually make them all a spot of money. Life out here had been standing still too long for them, and like anything else in the same situation it was beginning to go sour.

"Bob?" she said, and he looked up, startled. "Sorry, Bob. Were you napping?"

"No," he said, "just thinking. It's getting to be a bad habit."

"Has Dizzy got anyone with him, do you know?"

Ivie slowly started to get to his feet, moving as if he'd gone soft from lying too long. "I don't think so," he said. "Was there anyone in particular you had in mind?" But she sensed more of an evasion than an answer, and Ivie shot a dark glance toward the parapet and Dizzy's apartments above. At that moment, loud rock music suddenly fell onto them like an airburst.

The level dropped straight away, but it stayed fairly loud; it was the effect of someone having switched on a sound system without realising quite how high they'd set the volume, and it was coming from the suite upstairs. For it to be so loud, Dizzy's verandah windows had to be open.

Diane looked at Bob Ivie, and saw that he was as tense as a wire.

She said, "Is something wrong?"

Ivie forced his attention back down to her. "No," he said, and then he seemed to make a conscious effort to relax. As they went in through the old kitchen, he said, "Spoken to Jed, yet?"

"I'll ring him tonight," she said, glancing around the kitchen for any hint of a visitor. "Thanks again for the transport."

"Anytime. Although I *was* relieved when I found out you meant Richmond, Yorkshire and not Richmond, Surrey. We had a good drive, stopped a couple of times."

"Did the old folks feed you?"

"Like a pig. I couldn't get away."

By now they were through into the hall, Ivie stepping aside to let Diane precede him through the doorway. The music wasn't as loud in here, blocked by interior walls and closed doors.

It certainly wasn't loud enough to cover one shrill, terrified scream.

"You carry on," Ivie said sharply to Diane as he started to move. "I'll handle this."

He ran for the stairs, with Diane no more than a couple of paces behind him. His previous unease and his present speed of reaction seemed to suggest that he'd been half-expecting something of the kind.

Diane said, "Is it her? Is it the waitress?" But Ivie didn't answer. He took the stairs in twos and threes, all of his apparent softness gone as he raced to deal with something that he could at last understand.

The door to Liston's suite was locked, but Ivie fumbled out a

231

passkey. "Diane," he said. "Do me a favour. Just go. I'll take care of everything."

He managed to get the door unlocked. It gave half an inch, and then stuck solid against something that appeared to have been jammed up under the handles on the other side.

"Dizzy?" he shouted urgently. "Boss?"

But there was no reply.

Diane reached into her jacket as Ivie tried the door again, again without getting anywhere. She saw the expression of surprise on his face as he turned to speak to her again and saw the compact police radio that she was switching on in the way that Ross Aldridge had shown her.

"Ross?" she said. "Pete? She's here, all right. In the house, upstairs."

FORTY-TWO

They swung in through the narrow gateway with only inches to spare. The dirt-road dash to the house was short, fast, and over in seconds.

Pete didn't worry about neatness, but left the car standing at the end of its slewed turn into the forecourt, blocking the end of the driveway and leaving deep, fresh scars in the gravel. As he ran for the house Aldridge was behind him, slowed a little by the shotgun. Their first sight as they charged into the hallway through the open doors was of Tony Marinello, faintly stoned and looking as if he'd walked into a long-running play and discovered that he'd learned the wrong script.

"Up here!" Diane called from the gallery, and they headed for the stairs.

Bob Ivie was still trying to insist that everything was under control, but nobody was listening and he wasn't trying too hard. He got out of the way when he saw that Pete was aiming to hit the door, whether he moved or not. The first attempt at breaking through bruised Pete's shoulder and had little effect; the second, with the policeman's added weight, sent the door flying inward with a crash of splintering wood. They fell into the suite through the remains of the antique chair that had been keeping them out. Loud music hit them like an incoming wave.

Aldridge already had the shotgun levelled at the kneeling figure out in the middle of the polished wooden floor.

But it wasn't her.

It wasn't Liston, either; she didn't look much more than a child, and by her on-the-road uniform of T-shirt, faded jeans and training shoes Pete would have guessed her to be one of the region's hitch-hikers. Her head was bowed, dark braids hanging, and she was holding her throat and trying to be sick. She heaved in silence, because the sound system was drowning her out.

There was nobody else.

Pete crossed the room, and switched off the stereo. The pause that followed was like a dead silence for the moment that it took them all to readjust, but then real sound started to return; their hollow footsteps on the boards, the faint breeze that was lifting the net curtains at the windows, the choking of the young girl. Diane crouched by her with a hand on the child's back, looking to find out what was wrong.

Aldridge said, "Other rooms?"

"Through there," Ivie said, and he pointed.

"Show me."

Pete followed them. Aldridge checked the rooms to the left, giving a quick glance into each and moving on when he saw nobody there, and Pete covered the rest of the wing. He was beginning to wonder if there would be any way of telling whether Alina had been here at all; but then, in the master bedroom, he saw something that confirmed it for him beyond a doubt.

Diane looked up as the three of them went back into the main room. Tony Marinello was with her now, and the child had stopped retching and was sitting upright. Her eyes were wide, and her skin was an awesomely pale tint of blue.

Diane said, "Any sign of Dizzy?"

"He's hiding in the bedroom and he won't come out," Aldridge told her. "We looked over the door, and he's alone. But the exit to the back stairs is still locked from the inside, and there's no other exit."

"There's the windows and the terrace," Pete said. "She was definitely here." And he showed them his find: her scrapbook of home, which he'd found with her other stuff on the chair by the unmade bed. He'd looked at the rumpled sheets and the king-sized mattress, and he'd wondered.

Pete laid the book on the table before them, and fanned the pages. They all looked as the photographs went by in a blur; the display was totally personal, and pretty well meaningless to anyone other than the book's owner.

"That's him!" Diane said, reaching out and stopping the book at one of the pages. The paper's cheap binding was so worn that even this light pressure was enough to detach it, and it came away in her hand. "This is the man I met!"

Aldridge took a look, half-interested. "Keep it somewhere safe," he said.

"For evidence?" Diane said.

"Something like that," Aldridge said, moving off towards the french windows as if the legal niceties couldn't be further from his mind right now.

They went out to take a look at the terrace. There was no way down other than to drop from the parapet, but the ground beneath was soft. There might have been some mark of where she'd landed, but it was impossible to be certain from here.

Aldridge said nothing for a moment. But he seemed to be running through his options, rather than hesitating.

"Right," he said when he'd reached a decision. "We're going to have to move." He turned to the girl, who was standing in the window behind them. "Are you all right?"

"I just want to go," the girl said in a small voice.

"You know you're a witness."

"I didn't even want to come here. My dad'll kill me if he ever finds out. Can't I just leave?"

Aldridge glanced out across the overgrown gardens. Pete could see no movement out there.

"I'll tell you what to do," Aldridge said to the girl. "Get your stuff and walk out of the gates and don't look back. Don't tell anybody what you saw here today, and no one'll come looking for you. That's the deal."

"You're on," she said, and hurried to get her pack.

They went down to check the ground under the terrace, leaving Ivie and Marinello in a hurried whispered conference. The empty sun lounger stood out on the lawn, a faint breeze riffling the pages of Ivie's abandoned magazine. On the ground by the wall there was no convincing sign, but after a minute Ivie appeared at the parapet above them and called down, "The limo's gone."

"Gone where?" Aldridge said.

"How should I know? It was there ten minutes ago, it ain't there now."

The five of them met up again in Diane's office, where Diane unlocked her grey metal gun cupboard. Laid out on the desk, the four shotguns – Aldridge's own included – made a formidable-looking arsenal. Ivie and Marinello were both contemplating it with the same dazed look; but Pete's dismay was mainly felt when he looked at Ross Aldridge.

He was beginning to feel railroaded, hustled along the young policeman's path before he'd had time to consider the game that he was entering. This entire affair was beginning to take on an ugly aspect, almost like the organisation of a lynch mob. Aldridge wasn't pursuing his professional duty; this seemed to be turning more into some kind of a vendetta, with Aldridge merely using his profession to legitimise it.

The four guns, and the schoolteacher's scrapbook. There was the situation, in one simple picture. Aldridge was asking each of them about their firearms experience.

235

"Don't look at me," Pete said. "Most I ever handled was a bent air rifle in a fairground."

Tony Marinello said more or less the same. Ivie had hit a few birds in his time. Diane had hit very little in hers, but she was still included as one of the experienced shots.

"Now," Aldridge said. "This is the situation. We know she's taken the limo. Pete's car's still blocking the way out, so she could only have gone into the Estate. How many tracks are there?"

Ivie and Marinello looked blank. Diane rubbed her forehead as she thought for a moment.

"Three main ones," she said. "Lakeside, woodland, and across the top. There are little dirt roads as well, but that car's too wide."

"So that's three possibilities, but we've only got two cars – Diane's pickup, and Pete's wreck."

"Thanks," Pete said drily, but Aldridge didn't seem to hear; and besides, Bob Ivie was chipping in with a suggestion.

"Three," he said. "There's the Land Rover in the stables."

"Okay. Three possibilities, three cars. We want a gun and a radio in each. Those with no weapons experience handle the driving. If you find her, raise the alarm and don't let her get near. Use the gun if you have to. I mean, a warning shot first if it'll do any good, but then I'm saying *use* it. I've seen her in action and I'm telling you, don't even hesitate. Any questions?"

"Yeah," Tony Marinello said. "What the fuck's going on?"

"Later," Aldridge told him. "Just hope you don't find out the hard way."

Pete was watching Aldridge as he handed out the weapons and counted shells.

Forget it, buster, he was thinking. *Let's just forget the whole thing.*

FORTY-THREE

Ivie had been having bad feelings about the situation ever since Dizzy had called him up to the doorway of his suite to explain that he'd been joined by "a lady friend" during the night, and that her presence at the Hall was going to have to be the best-kept secret since Winston Churchill's sex change. It hadn't taken much for Ivie to guess that the lady friend in question would be the little waitress from the village that Dizzy had been pining over for so long.

It had felt like trouble to Ivie even then, and when he'd seen them going out together in the limo and then returning after half an hour with an obviously under-aged kid that they'd taken up to the suite with them, the mental alarm bells had really started to ring. He'd watched them unseen from a doorway as they'd ascended, and he'd felt his skin creep into gooseflesh as he'd heard the waitress whispering to the child in a way that was somehow empty of words but filled with promises. When the door had closed behind them and the lock had clicked shut, Ivie had begun to feel sick. It was then that he'd gone to the key board in the housekeeper's closet and helped himself to her passkey; but, until the loud music and the scream, he hadn't been able to raise the nerve to use it.

Now he and Marinello were in the estate's Land Rover, the one with the wire-protected windows that was like a mobile jail, bumping along the middle track through the centre of the estate. McCarthy and Diane had taken the lower road along the very edge of the lake while Ross Aldridge, alone and in Diane's pickup truck, was way up on the high ground where the woodland ended and the shooting moor began.

Ivie was at the wheel. Marinello rode shotgun. In spite of Aldridge's insistence that there was a possibility of real danger, he might have felt happier if it could have been the other way around.

"What do you think?" Marinello asked suddenly, as if his thoughts had been slowly heating up and now had to boil over.

"I don't know," Ivie said, scanning the woodland out of the meshed window as they rolled forward at no more than ten miles an hour. "Doesn't make any sense to me. You'd think the copper would know what he was talking about."

"Unless there's more to it, and nobody's saying."

"What do you mean?"

"I was in the village, first thing. The news is all over. They're saying the copper's wife walked out on him last night. What if this ties in?"

Ivie thought it over.

It made a certain kind of sense, even though he couldn't see all of the connections; and Tony's information in such matters was usually good, thanks to the network of local contacts that he'd kept up since his all-comers dance marathon on the night of the party. If the girl was supposed to be so dangerous – and there was nothing about the way that she looked to suggest that she was – then, why was Aldridge throwing together a rag-tag vigilante force instead of calling on his own people? Perhaps his own people were on their way, but Ivie had seen nothing to suggest it.

He was about to say as much, when the small police radio crackled into life and gave them both a start. It was Aldridge, calling on both of his parties to check in.

Ivie reached for the radio, which he'd hung up by its carrying-strap from the Rover's rearview mirror. Pressing the transmission button, he said, "Bob Ivie. Nothing so far."

"Where are you?"

"About a mile out, still moving."

A couple of seconds later, they heard Diane reporting on the same channel. She said that she and McCarthy hadn't seen anything yet, either.

Marinello said, "I don't like it. I don't know what's going on, but I haven't seen anything to warrant any of this." The whole car dropped with a jolt as they hit a bad pothole, and the engine complained as Ivie changed down a gear to get them out of it. The Rover was an ex-army model, unbelievably old and not fit for much more than carrying small parties up to the shooting butts. Marinello added, as Ivie was changing back up again, "I think we're being set up, here."

"For what?"

"I don't know. But say they've got a situation, the four of them, and now everything's gone wrong and nobody's thinking straight. Can't you just see it?"

"I suppose it's possible."

"What do they think we are? Stupid?"

Ivie couldn't say that he was as fully convinced as Marinello seemed to be, but he didn't have any evidence that he could offer for his doubts.

But he'd heard that whispering, on the stairs. And he'd seen the way that the waitress had been looking at the child.

Aldridge said that he'd seen her in action, and perhaps this was the same kind of thing. If you hadn't been there, it was impossible to explain.

Ivie suddenly hit the brakes, and then started to reverse.

"I saw something," he said.

What he'd seen proved to be the glint of a hubcap, lying in the grass beyond a gatepost a few yards back. The post itself was leaning, the wood splintered and showing fresh . . . as if somebody inexperienced in a big, unfamiliar car had taken the entrance too fast.

"I'll call," Ivie said, reaching for the radio.

"No," Marinello said abruptly. "Let's be sure we get to her before anyone else does."

And so instead of calling, he hauled on the wheel to turn the heavy vehicle into the driveway.

Ivie recognised the track. It led out to the old trap shooting range where Diane had sometimes come to practise. It was all overgrown now, but another car had been here ahead of them and it had passed by fairly recently.

They came to the limousine about a hundred yards further on, around the bend and out of sight of the main track. Ahead of it was the clearing for the range with its group of small, weathered-silver wooden huts. The limo's side had been damaged and its rear bumper had been torn halfway loose; the driver's door was wide open and at a strange angle.

There was nobody inside it, or anywhere around.

They stopped the Rover, and got out. The woodland was strangely quiet – no birdsong, even. Marinello didn't seem worried, but he took the shotgun anyway. He'd told Ivie that he was keeping the safety on, almost as if in concession to their shared doubts.

"What's her name?" Marinello said. "Can you remember?"

"Anna, I think."

"Not Anna," Marinello said. "More unusual. Anya. No . . . Alina." And then he turned and cupped his hands and called through them to the entire forest. "Hey, Alina," he called. "You can come out, we're not going to hurt you. We know you haven't done anything." He waited for a while, and then carried on, "It's either us, or the others. You know what it means if they find you?"

More silence.

"She could be well away by now," Ivie suggested, half-hoping.

"Last chance!" Marinello called, almost shouting himself hoarse this time.

And just as it was starting to seem that Ivie was right, she stepped out of cover.

She'd been around behind one of the huts, not so far away; she was shoeless, looking lost and scared, and she was shivering in her lightweight cotton dress even though it wasn't particularly cold. Tony Marinello started toward her immediately. Glancing back over his shoulder, he said, "God, look at the state of her. Get that car rug out of the back, Bob."

He was already striding out toward her. She looked every bit as bleak and as lost as that child back there in the Hall; Ivie was now thinking that his fears and his suspicions were showing themselves to be formless, finding no reflection in this reality at all.

Marinello had reached Alina and put his arm around her shoulders. The shotgun was over his other forearm. He'd broken it open for extra safety, and the empty barrel was pointing at the ground. They were walking back toward the Rover.

Ivie gave himself a shake. What could he have been thinking of? He turned away and reached into the back of the Rover for the checkered wool travelling-blanket that lay folded on one of the vinyl benches. It would be musty, but it would do for now. As he was bringing it out, he glanced at the radio that was hanging from the mirror bracket.

"No, I don't think so," Ivie muttered, and turned back to meet the others.

Marinello was in trouble.

He'd fallen to his knees after covering only half of the return distance, and now it was Alina who was showing concern for *him*. The shotgun lay on the ground where he'd dropped it, a few strides back. Ivie started to run forward. As he did Marinello looked up, purpling, eyes literally starting to bulge in a manner so unnatural that it was almost fascinating; he started to raise his hand in a gesture of appeal, asking for Ivie's help in something that he simply couldn't understand.

Alina looked up, too.

Ivie saw the green fire in her eyes, and a new and frightening intensity in her attitude; he knew then that everything had been a sham, that his first instincts had been the only correct ones, and that Aldridge had been telling the truth even though he hadn't been telling it all. Ivie realised all of this in the time that it took for Alina to cover the distance between them.

She struck at him, her hand as hard and flat as a blade, but the rug that he was holding took the main force of the blow. He threw it at her and ran for the Rover, flat-out and feeling his age. He'd wondered for maybe a half-second about reaching the gun, but knew that he had no chance. Why couldn't he have bagged it way back at the very beginning? Fortunately the door was still open, and he dived straight for the radio and snatched it down with a force that snapped the bracket and brought the mirror along as well.

He fumbled for the transmission switch. He tried to say *She's here, we've got her* . . .

But instead it came out as, "She's got us!"

A hand suddenly grabbed his collar, and in a show of immense strength he was hauled out of the Rover backwards. His head clipped the top of the door arch, hard.

This was all that he knew.

FORTY-FOUR

Pete's heart started to sink when he heard the garbled call. He'd deliberately done his best to bag the lakeside part of the search, citing the Zodiac's condition as his reason but really believing that it would give him his best chance of finding Alina before Aldridge could. Now he realised that he was not only wrong, but he was also trapped; he had the lake on one side and a new wire fence on the other, and there wasn't enough road for him to make a turn.

"Keep going," Diane suggested. "According to the estate plan, there's supposed to be a track somewhere ahead. It'll take us up to meet the forest road."

"I just hope it isn't too rough," Pete said. "She weighs half a ton and she steers like a tank, but there the resemblance ends." And he put on as much speed as he was able, which wasn't much with the edge of the banking only inches away.

After half a minute, Diane said, "Coming up. See it?"

"Gotcha," Pete said, and made the turn.

The track hadn't been used in years. It soon narrowed and became overgrown, with long grass in a Mohican strip up the centre where tyres had never worn it down. It whipped at the underside of the car as Pete changed all the way down into first gear and still had trouble making the slope.

After a while, he didn't have to worry about it. Because the track dead-ended at a gate which had been secured with a rusty lock and chain, and the ground beyond it was fit for nothing less rugged than a farm vehicle.

"It looked great on the map," Diane said hollowly. And Pete thought of Aldridge, tasting blood and driving hard to get there first.

"Watch the back while I reverse," he said to Diane, "and cross your fingers."

She had to climb around on her seat to see well enough to direct him as they went. Pete let off the brake and they started to freewheel backward, gathering speed and jolting hard.

Too hard. He returned some pressure to the brake, but it was too late. They were sliding too fast and out of control, and as the wheels

242

locked Pete found that the grass underneath gave his tyres almost no traction at all. They hit one bump, and then another which almost threw Diane up against the roof; and it was at this point that Pete felt a queasy slackness in the wheel which told him immediately that the Zodiac's steering rack had gone. The brakes weren't holding, the wheel was a useless ornament.

They left the track, and ploughed into the undergrowth at its side. Diane took a dive over the seat and disappeared completely; for one awful moment Pete thought that she'd gone through the rear screen, but he turned and saw that she was safe in the back.

The Zodiac plunged on backward, well out of control.

There wasn't much that he could do until a fifteen-yard depth of bushes slowed and stopped them, and the engine stalled. There was silence. Pete levered himself upright. Greenery pressed up against the windows on three sides of the car. Diane was trying to sort herself out in the rear seat.

"You okay?" he said.

"No," she said. "I caught my leg between the seats as I went over. I think it's my ankle."

He opened one of the doors and forced the brush far enough back for them to squeeze through, and then he helped her out. She tried to stand on her own. She couldn't.

"Damn," she said, wincing. "How's the car?"

"Shot. We're on foot from here. I'll check with Ross."

She kept her balance with one hand against the car as he reached in and passed the gun out to her, and then reached for their radio. Diane upended the stock, and leaned on the shotgun for support.

She said, "Will we be safe if we're not in the car?"

"I don't know," Pete said. "If she's up there and we're down here, we ought to be okay for a while. I'll see if I can get Ross to pick us up."

Awkwardly, Diane tested her ankle as Pete tried to raise Aldridge. It didn't seem promising. The slightest weight, and Pete could see how her face screwed up in pain. As for Pete himself, he was getting a response on the radio but it was made indistinct by a lot of howling and noise. Holding the receiver close and speaking as clearly as he could, he explained the situation and hoped that Aldridge would be able to hear.

There was something from Aldridge that might have been *Okay*.

Pete said, "Come down for us before you do anything else, all right? Don't try to go it alone."

Another reply, this one completely unintelligible.

Diane said, "You think he got that?"

"Yeah," Pete said, knowing that he didn't sound entirely convinced, and then he looked all around. "Come on, he'll have no chance of finding us up here. I'll have to get you back down to the road."

And with one last affectionate slap on the Zodiac's roof – scrap value only after a bang like this – he put his arm around Diane to support her, and they started to make slow progress downhill towards the lakeside track.

FORTY-FIVE

Pete was wrong in at least one detail.

Aldridge wasn't heading down to collect them, nor was he tearing through the woodland to get to Alina. Instead he'd stopped the Toyota up on the edge of the olive-green moor, and he was holding his radio out of the open window to get a fix on the signal that was messing up the frequency. Ivie's radio was still transmitting. That Ivie himself was dead, or at least close to it, was a matter on which Aldridge had little doubt.

It was a rough method, but at least it gave him a direction. When he turned the volume all the way up as far as it would go, he thought that he could hear somebody breathing. It was impossible to be sure.

He raised his window before he set off again. He'd been out of her reach in the generator cage and now he was out of her reach in the cab, and as far as Aldridge was concerned this was the best way to be. In an ideal world he'd be able to take her alive, but if he couldn't then he was fully prepared to run her down. He had four-wheel-drive, he had no witnesses. She might be full of surprises, but she surely couldn't argue with an oncoming truck.

He followed the signal.

Ten minutes later, he was at the scene.

He came in slowly, watching all around. He could see the battered limousine, and the silent Rover with its far door open. He drove the Toyota all the way around almost in a complete circle, but there were no signs of life at all.

He stopped level with the Rover. He could see inside from here. No bodies, just a tartan blanket half in the cab and half on the ground. It was a weird, deserted scene, looking like some aftermath of germ warfare – property abandoned, actions uncompleted – and the appeal of opening his door and stepping out would rank about the same in both cases.

Something thumped on the Toyota behind him.

He glimpsed a movement in his mirror, then it was gone. But then he turned in his seat, and he could see her; she was throwing back the snap-cover and climbing into the pickup's load area, and it was too late for him to do anything about it. She was hauling herself up already, and she had what looked like a firm grip on one of the four diagonal bars protecting the cab's rear windshield.

She gave him an evil-looking, sharp-toothed grin.

"I said I'd come back for you," she said through the glass.

"You won't get me this time, either," Aldridge said, wondering how he could best throw her off and run her down with minimal risk. "I'm all locked in."

"You're forgetting the obvious," she said, and Aldridge found himself looking out into the dark *O* of Bob Ivie's shotgun. That would have been the thump that he'd heard, the sound of the gun being slung in ahead of her; and he could only sit and gape at his own lack of foresight as he contemplated the more prominent one on the Winchester.

Alina squeezed the trigger.

Nothing happened.

The safety was on; Aldridge realised it with a heartsurge of glee. Alina was turning the gun in puzzlement, unsure of what to do next.

He had a chance.

He hit the accelerator and let out the clutch, and as the Toyota spurted forward he turned the wheel hard in an attempt to catch her off-balance and pitch her out. But then he glanced in the mirror and saw her hand, again grabbing the strut as the pickup spun around. He gunned the engine again, wrenched the wheel over the other way . . .

And, watching his mirror more than the ground ahead, slammed sideways into the Land Rover. The Rover shook, but it barely moved.

Aldridge was thrown sideways across the passenger seat. His head bounced on the door padding. The pickup was out of gear with its engine still running, and Aldridge was almost on the floor; he scrambled up again, and looked into the back. He couldn't see her . . . and he thought, Have I done it? Was that enough, the woman dead and not even a shot fired?

A hand came up, and its fingers curled around one of the bars. She hauled herself up after, inches away on the other side of the laminated glass. She was still grinning.

Aldridge slammed the pickup into gear again.

The engine raced, but the pickup didn't move.

He'd killed the rear transmission. He was going nowhere.

He wondered if there wasn't some way; there was *always* a way, wasn't there? Could he perhaps switch the drive to the two front wheels and drag himself out of there like an injured dog? But even as he glanced again in the mirror he knew that his time had run out, saw that the shotgun was being levelled again, understood that nothing he could do was going to alter anything now.

He saw the windshield craze before he heard the blast.

Rachel, he thought miserably.

But then he never got to hear the blast at all.

FORTY-SIX

"He should have reached us by now," Diane said. "The bastard, he isn't coming."

"I've got to get up there," Pete said.

The implication of this was obvious. With Diane more or less hopping along and Pete having to support her, they'd been making only minimal progress. They were barely a quarter of a mile from where they'd started, and they were getting slower and slower. They'd nearly reached the boat house, which marked no more than a fraction of the distance they'd have to cover. Pete had tried the radio again a couple of times, but neither Aldridge nor anybody else had replied.

"On your own?" Diane said. "Come on, she'll be getting desperate now."

"I know her better than anybody."

"You thought you knew her yesterday, Pete, but then look what you learned. You don't know her at all."

"She owes me, and she knows it. She said she'd never hurt me."

"She killed her lover and burned him in his own car. The lady isn't noted for her scruples."

There was silence for a while as they limped on, a three-legged twosome getting wearier by the minute. It was a stubborn silence, and there was only one way that it could come to an end.

"Go on, then," Diane said with a sudden flareup of anger, getting free and pushing him away, and she almost lost her balance in the process. "Go to her. Go running to her, if she's the one you really want. See if she treats you any better than the others."

Pete stopped, and looked at her. Diane's cheeks were bright and streaked with tears, and she made an ineffectual attempt to rub them away with the sleeve of her jacket. Her eyes were blazing and steady.

"I've never touched her," Pete said.

"No, but she's the one you dream about. Isn't she?"

There was an opening, a hint of uncertainty in her look now, and he went for it.

"No, I never have," he said.

248

She watched him, and perhaps they both knew that there was some part of the truth, some part of a lie in what he was saying, and that whatever was to happen between them from now on would depend on what she chose to believe.

She said, "Then, why do this?"

"Because I brought her here. She hurt the people closest to me and I'm responsible. I can feel sorry for her. But I know she's got to be stopped."

Diane looked down.

"At least take the gun," she said.

He put his arm out to support her again, and she let him slide it around her.

"I wouldn't know how to handle it," he said. "Do you still have the key to the boat house?"

He passed close behind the Hall on his way upslope, climbing over gates and wire fences to take the most direct line that he could. Aldridge wasn't going to meet him, halfway or any other way, so there was no point in watching for his car. By going across country he could pick up the middle track a lot faster, and follow it along until he found some trace of the others. At one point he tried the radio again, once more turning the volume up all of the way and once more getting the strange effect that he hadn't wanted Diane to hear.

It was the sound of breathing. Or something very like it.

He was climbing through coniferous woodland now, so dense that there was permanent twilight underneath with bare ground where nothing was growing. Daylight and the rest of the world could be dimly glimpsed as a distant filigree pattern of branches, leaves and silver sky in the middle distance. He had to duck frequently because many of the lower branches were at head-height; some trunks were streaked with birdlime, and one or two that he saw had been rubbed bare of bark by animals. Deer, at a guess, although he couldn't be sure.

He pressed on. Smaller trees had stunted and died and then fallen. Even the healthy ones looked as if they'd been painted with light green moss on the windward side, moss the colour of Nile water. All around him was slow growth, and slow decay.

While ahead of him lay . . . what?

Within minutes he was emerging, breathless and somewhat scratched, onto the roadway not too far from the broken gate where the limo's hubcap still lay like a marker. He followed the tyremarks to the small auto graveyard that stood in the clearing, and there he made a careful circuit of all the vehicles so that he could look without actually touching any of them.

Nothing moved. Nothing made a sound, apart from the wind in the leaves.

He saw the two aligned holes in the front and rear screens of the Toyota, and he saw the widening spray of blood and glass fragments across the bonnet; but he saw no bodies, and he saw no signs of where they might have been taken.

He did find his heavy breather, though. In one of the trees over on the edge of the clearing he spotted a radio – Ivie's, presumably – hanging by its carrying strap from one of the lower branches. The breeze was moving it gently, and probably making a fair imitation of a human sound. He walked over to it and took it down, noting the way that the transmission button had been taped with a piece of yellow insulation plastic that was probably out of the Rover's toolkit.

What he couldn't see, was its purpose in being there.

But of course! he realised after a moment. Bait . . . and as the word came up into his mind, something very hard and moving very fast made a good, solid contact with the back of his head.

Definitely bait, he acknowledged as he folded like a sack.

FORTY-SEVEN

Diane hated this. She hated being left, she hated the thought of Pete going off alone, she hated her own body for letting her down. Surely they'd reached the point where the only way ahead was to go back to the Hall, pick up the phone, and call in the cavalry? The fact of it was that Pete McCarthy had been the first of them to encounter Alina Petrovna, and he was the last to understand, *really* understand, that of which she was capable. He hadn't seen the graphic aftermath of her work that Ross Aldridge said he'd witnessed, and he hadn't been through Diane's experience of a sincere if rambling first-hand account from a man named Pavel, followed by the sight of his charcoaled body only a few hours later. No, he had to go running up there like a man with his hand out to a mad dog, convinced of his safety because he'd never yet encountered a dog that hadn't liked him.

Unfortunately, Diane couldn't help noticing how Alina seemed to deal out the same kind of treatment to her friends as to her enemies.

The best that she could hope for was that Alina would already be gone when he got there, using whatever time she might have bought for herself to get up and away from the scene. If she could get off the estate, maybe follow one of the walkers' routes over one of the mountain passes, then she could make it into another part of the region and perhaps even get away altogether. Find some other ride on some other road, find a new place to settle, start the process all over again while the police hunt ran itself dry with nothing to go on. Otherwise, what would Pete be facing? A radical revision of his illusions, at best.

She didn't even want to think about the worst.

She'd submitted to being left in the boat house like so much luggage for one reason, and one reason only. Pete had thought that he was dropping her off in the only available place of safety; and from where she was standing it seemed safe enough, with its heavy landward door and solid walls and its thick and grimy skylight of reinforced glass that barely let in the light, let alone anything more.

But she hadn't come here to hide, whatever Pete might have been thinking.

She'd come in here because down below, in the dock, stood an unsold Princess.

And in the Princess, there was a multichannel VHF radio telephone.

The boat-house lights weren't working, and hadn't been since the night of the party. But there were deck lights and cabin lights on the Princess, and the Princess was only one short flight of stairs away.

But short flight or not, this was going to be one of the toughest journeys that Diane had ever undertaken. Her ankle was giving her hell. She was sure that it was broken; she hadn't felt any snap as she'd gone over, but she was halfway convinced that she could feel the splintered ends of the bone as they ground together with each faltering step. She was still using the shotgun – unloaded, of course – as a makeshift crutch, but progress was slow and getting slower as the pain and the pressure increased. All the same, she couldn't help thinking that it was the most effective use she'd ever made of a twelve-bore since she'd first begun to shoot.

Maybe there was something in the first-aid kit that she could use. Painkillers, maybe even an emergency splint.

But before anything else, the call.

She checked that the boat-house door was securely locked, and took out the key. She wasn't likely to forget that Wayne Hammond and his girlfriend had died in here. For that, if for no other reason, she'd have been happier if the light in here had been just a little better.

Childish fears, she told herself.

And, only halfway believing it, she began her slow shuffle towards the boat-house stairs.

Pete was in the back of the Rover when he came around.

He didn't realise it straight away; for a time he hovered, half-awake, while in his mind he followed his vision of an altered Alina through the dark spaces under that strange hotel. She led him along, her marbled and beautifully-clawed hand beckoning him every now and again, until they reached a door at the corridor's end; and then, with a regretful smile and a sad shake of her head, she stepped through the door and closed it on him. Only then did he begin to see the kick-scuffed grey metal before his eyes, and to feel the coarse woollen blanket that had been placed under his head as a pillow.

It was the first time that he'd ever been knocked out and he decided, everything considered, that he wouldn't care to try it again.

He didn't much want to move, either, but he knew that he'd have to.

He'd been lying on the floor of the Rover's rear passenger-carrying section, cramped into the space in a near-foetal curl. He felt dusty and gritty, and he had a five-aspirin headache. Alina was on the outside; she raised her head from whatever she'd been doing to look in through one of the rear-door windows.

Her face, seen through the wire, seemed to show a genuine concern. Pete struggled up to sit on one of the Rover's inward-facing bench seats.

"Are you all right?" she said.

"Considering." Pete made to touch the back of his head, and decided midway that it wouldn't be a good idea.

Alina said, "Don't bother trying to get out. You can't."

"Why are you doing this?"

"To make you safe."

"From you?"

She hesitated for a moment; and then she nodded once, making an admission that was obviously difficult for her. "You're safe as long as you don't try to follow," she said. "I won't be coming back. By the time someone finds you, I'll be gone."

"And the others will be dead."

"They don't die," she said. "I can't help what I do, Peter. I tried for a long time, and in the end it got me nowhere. I'm sorry."

"What do you mean, they don't die?"

"They join me," she said, her grey eyes open and empty of secrets. "They become my children of the lake." And then she turned her face away. "I *am* sorry, Peter. I wish there was some other way."

He stared at her through the glass, at that delicate, downturned head, as graceful and as heartless as a stone angel, and he knew then that he'd been wrong to think that he was anything other than lost. This was no fitful madness, no staged insanity; the depth and sincerity of her belief in her developed state were awesome. She *was* the *Rusalka*, in a faith that could be neither challenged nor shaken. In her own mind, she lived as the beast . . . and perhaps in the end, she could only be met and recognised as the beast.

"You're breaking your promise," he reminded her.

"A little," she said, looking at him again and smiling wanly. "As you broke yours, a little. I can leave you and you can't hurt me, no one will believe what you say. But I can't leave others to support you."

"What will happen to Diane?"

"Could she be in love with you?"

"I don't know. It's too early to say."

"If she is, then she'll call to you. And in the night, she may even come to you. And then perhaps you'll come down to the water's edge, and you'll beg me to take you."

"And will you?"

"Yes. Because then I'll be beyond promises." She took a step back from the wired window. "Goodbye, Peter," she said, and she turned to go.

She was going for Diane, to clear out the last of the cell, and Pete realised now that he'd engineered the entire setup himself when he'd broadcast his intentions to Ross Aldridge and to anybody else who might have been listening.

"You can't get to her," he shouted after Alina, and Alina, already halfway across the clearing, turned and looked back.

"I only wish that could be true," she said, and then she walked on.

FORTY-EIGHT

He tried the rear doors but Alina had sealed them somehow, probably by tying the two handles together. Whatever she'd used, he couldn't force them open; after a few seconds he gave up trying, and looked around for another way out. Every window had a wire mesh cover on the outside, a way to protect the glass on badly-kept and underused trails; there was a clear cutout section before the driver's position, but it would be too small to crawl through.

Pete scrambled over from the back and into the forward part of the cab, to take a look at the other doors.

Trying the driver's door would have been an obvious waste of time, not only because it had been crushed inward by the collision but also because it still had most of the Toyota holding it shut. Something like a tyre iron had been used to jam the passenger door handle on the outside; dismantling the lock from in here would make no difference, even if he'd had the tools to attempt it.

He lifted out the loose seat sections and started to throw them into the back. The usual locker space under the passenger seat was occupied by a second fuel tank but there was another, smaller locker in the middle that contained a pump and an X-shaped wheel brace. Each arm of the X was for a different bolt size.

Think. Ignore this aching head, and concentrate on finding a way out. Alina was already on her way down to the shore. He'd serviced this Rover at least once before; it was ex-army and pretty ancient. He could think of a dozen ways out, but none of them was fast.

Except, perhaps, one.

He tore back the rubber mats on the floor, and then the dusty felt from underneath. The floor here was a single square panel held in place by bolts. He had a start; some of the bolts were already missing.

It was worth a try. He turned the wheelbrace around to see if anything came close to a fit.

Diane had thought that descending the stairway had been a tough job, until it came to getting aboard; there was no gangplank, just a wide step from the dockside across to a gap in the Princess's rail, and then to get around into the cabin she had to make an awkward shuffle and a high step up to the after deck. There were grab rails on the flying bridge above her, and she made full use of them.

God, this was a marathon. She all but collapsed onto the after deck, her ankle raging hot and feeling as if it had swollen to about five times its usual size. She was in near-darkness here, the only illumination a kind of pale, dancing underlight from the water that flickered around the walls and through gaps in the boarded quayside. She knew that it was daylight from the lake, getting in under the water doors and being refracted upward, but it gave the place an atmosphere like some forgotten chamber in drowned Atlantis. The deck and flybridge of the Princess stood as an almost solid mass of darkness before her now. She didn't know her way around particularly well, but she did know that a set of keys was hidden under the cover of one of the deck filler points for fuel and water.

A couple of minutes later, she was letting herself in through the sliding glass door and descending the three steps into the after deck saloon.

She tried to remember the layout. How many times had she been on board? Not many. She could remember a chart table to her left, a dinette area ahead of it, the helm and all the instruments forward and to her right. She hopped forward, dragging her heavy boot of molten iron, and with every hop she felt a stab of pain as she jarred the injury. Halfway across the cabin she stumbled and fell. The carpet was intended for hard wear, and wasn't as soft as it might have been. The temptation to give up and lie still was there, but it wasn't quite overpowering. So she dragged herself up, and went on.

At the end of the cabin, she dropped into the padded helmsman's chair.

The control position came alive as she turned the key. Lever controls, twin-scale echo sounder, high-speed compass, engine hour meter, rudder position indicator . . . she found a cabin light switch and turned it on, and the layout immediately became a little less intimidating.

She found the radio telephone. She was hoping that it would work from here inside the boat house because, if it didn't, she'd gone about as far as she could get and for nothing. She had about as much hope of being able to open the lake doors and take the Princess out as she did of dancing *Giselle*.

She picked up the handset and set one of the frequencies. She didn't know which would be the best, but she could try them all.

"Hello," she said, swivelling the helmsman's chair a little so that she could stretch out her bad leg. "Hello, Mayday. Is anyone receiving me? Mayday."

She turned up the receiver volume, and listened.

Nothing.

She worked her way through every frequency on the set, with no variation in the results. Just the audio snowstorm, the same white noise across all of the channels. She could only suppose that her signal wasn't getting out beyond the walls, or that if it was it was too poor to carry for any useful distance. The valley was notorious for its radio reception at the best of times, and this was hardly one of those.

She tried again, taking frequencies at random.

"Mayday. Mayday. This is Diane Jackson. Can anybody hear me? Mayday."

And then –

"Diane? Is that you? Are you serious?"

It was Ted Hammond. The signal wasn't good, but it was definitely Ted Hammond.

"Never more serious in my life, Ted," she said. "Where are you?"

"I'm on the lake with some customers. We just left the marina. What's the problem?"

And so, in as concise and unsensational a manner as she could manage, she told him.

There was silence. "Ted?" she said anxiously, thinking that the signal must have faded as she was speaking and wondering if he'd heard enough to realise the seriousness of the situation, but then he came back on.

"I'm on my way," he said.

"Get a message out. Call the police and make sure they know what they're heading for. She's been fooling people for too long."

"Will do," Ted said, but already his voice was beginning to break up.

There was nothing after that.

Now she didn't have time to mess around looking for the first-aid kit. She shut down the radio, but she left on the lights. Now she had to travel all the way back along the quay and up the stairway and across the upper level to the door, and it would probably take her at least as long to do this as it would take Ted Hammond to cover the distance across the water. She didn't know what kind of craft he'd been showing to his customers, but she hoped that it was something fast.

The temptation to stay and relax in the helmsman's chair, just for one minute, was immense. But she knew that one minute would turn into two, and then four, and in the end she'd have as tough a time prising herself out as she did getting Jed out of bed for school on a dark winter's morning. There was urgency, here.

There was urgency . . .

She snapped out of it, and started to move.

She'd once heard that one of the main requirements for any kind of success was the kind of doggedness that led one to persist way beyond the point where anyone else would have thrown in the towel and turned to other pursuits. She had a (probable) broken ankle, she had distance to cover. Maybe she was adding to the damage this way, it was impossible to tell – it was hard to imagine it hurting any more than it already did.

But she would persist, and she would succeed.

Because let's face it, she was thinking, her range of other choices was more or less nil.

With the lights of the cabin behind her, she prepared to make the transfer back from the Princess to the quay. She couldn't be sure, perhaps it was just a trick of the lights, but it seemed as if the boat had shifted in its mooring a little and the gap had widened. Holding onto the stanchioned safety wires that took the place of rails along this section, Diane lowered herself to sit on the narrow walkway with the angled cabin wall against her back almost seeming to be pushing her out toward the drop. With her good leg, she got a tentative foothold on the quay. There was an unused mooring ring about a yard further along; if she could reach over and get a hold on that, she'd be more than halfway there. She'd have to face an unnerving point of balance as she moved her weight from ship to shore over the drop, but as long as she held tight to the iron ring she was unlikely to fall.

She reached out. It was a stretch, but she caught it. She was now at that point of balance, her bad leg hanging uselessly as her body bridged the gap. She couldn't help but look down into the flickering semi-darkness of the water.

Where a hand came shooting up in a cloud of erupting spray, and grasped her leg around the ankle.

FORTY-NINE

Shock and pain ran through Diane's nervous system like two trains running head-to-head on the same line; she was being pulled downward as they hit, and their explosion doused her in white heat and fire. A body was coming half-up out of the water, raising itself on the nailed grip that it was exerting on Diane's tortured flesh.

She hung on to the ring. It was all that she could think to do. Her good leg slipped from the quay, and swung down.

Her foot connected with something solid.

The grip was released.

Spray drenched her as she saw Alina make a messy, uncontrolled backward landing in the dock. The water seemed to part and enfold her, and then was gone. Diane swung herself up onto the quay, and started to run. She'd actually made it almost to the stairway when her body remembered that it was already hurt, and seemed to pull the plugs on her; she went sprawling, and landed hard on the planks.

She rolled over and looked back. Alina was rising from the dock, dripping, gleaming in the underlight. Behind her was the dark Princess, cabin lights ablaze, a sinister-looking beacon that cast her long shadow across the quay. Her hair lay sleek and wet and her thin cotton dress had plastered itself to her body. She was pure hostility, looking to do harm.

Diane started to push herself back. With the upper-level door locked from the inside, she was safe from nothing other than rescue. She had to get to it, but all that she could do now was to crawl. She kept on pushing herself back before this slight, dangerous figure that was advancing on her from the zone where the nightmares played.

The stairs were at her back. She could go no further.

"What did they do with my book?" Alina said quietly.

"I don't . . . I don't know what you mean," Diane heard herself say.

"My pictures. Did they move them? Did they hide them? I really have to know."

The photographs? Was she kidding? Diane's mind raced, looking for an angle, any angle, that she could exploit. She'd had two shotgun shells in her pocket; but she seemed to have lost even these in the scramble and, besides, the shotgun itself was still on the far side of the quay.

She'd have to improvise.

"I think they burned it," she said.

Alina stopped.

"You're lying," she said.

"Why should I lie? All that's left is this." Propping herself on one elbow, Diane reached inside her jacket. She pulled out a single sheet of stiff coloured paper, made awkward by the photographs that had been glued onto either side. It was the loose page with the photograph of Pavel that Aldridge, hardly concentrating, had told her to keep as evidence. The way that he'd said it, Diane had been able to tell that precise details of procedure weren't uppermost in his mind. She'd had to fold it to put it away, and it had taken more creases since. As a last surviving remnant, it looked pretty convincing.

"Please," Alina said. She was staring at the page like a junkie in the presence of the world's last fix.

"Why do you need this?"

"It's my last dream of home," Alina said bleakly.

Diane wondered how she saw herself. Did she hold up her own hand and see scales, claws? Did she see the souls of her victims as she released them to stand in that dark country beyond death itself? Diane wondered how profound a belief had to be before others were drawn in and persuaded by it. An easy trap to fall into; Diane had already begun to think of Alina and the *Rusalka* as two separate entities, each intertwining with the other like a body and its disease.

But which was she talking to now?

"Give me the photographs," Alina said carefully, as if each word was a test, "and I'll let you leave."

"Can you really promise that?"

There was a struggle for a while.

And then Alina admitted. "No, I don't have that much control."

"Over what you do?"

"Over what I've turned into."

"Looks like we've got a stalemate, then," Diane said, and she wished that she could make herself sound more convinced; because it was a pretty unequal balance with only one crumpled sheet of paper on her side against the *Rusalka*'s track record on the other. All that she could do would be to start tearing the photographs up, and it wouldn't take much to stop her from doing even this. Alina was holding back, but she was under patient assault from within. It couldn't last.

Even she seemed to know it, and after a tense silence she was the first one to speak.

"I'll do what I can," she said. "Go up the stairs, let yourself out of the door. Leave the photographs inside, and lock yourself out. I'll try to hold back. But do one thing for me, please."

"What?"

"Whatever happens, try to remember me as I was. Don't hate me for what I became."

And then, as Diane hesitated in her uncertainty as to whether or not this was a ruse, she added, "*Go!*" with such urgency that Diane struggled to stand and turned to face the stairway, the page clutched tightly in her hand.

There was at least one moment when the *Rusalka* could have flown at her unseen.

But she didn't.

It was a long haul, one step at a time. She had to hold the folded page in her teeth in order to free both hands for the climb. Having her back toward Alina was the hardest part, but nothing happened. Except that, from behind and below her, there came a sound like that of quiet, frustrated weeping.

Diane's shadow was long across the ceiling as she hobbled toward the door, reaching for her pocket as she went.

"Why have you stopped?" Alina shouted to her a few moments later. There was a new harshness in her voice that set Diane on her guard, but she had no choice but to reply.

"I must have lost the key when I fell," she said, hearing her own voice as if it was coming from somebody else. "Will you throw it to me?" And please, she thought, don't let it have fallen into the dock or else the whole thing ends right here.

No weeping noises now, but a sound like a nest of snakes coiling around one another. The pattern of water-reflected shadows on the high roof changed as Alina moved, unseen beyond the edge of the platform. Was she doing as Diane had asked?

Or was she coming for her?

The tension buzzed in Diane's ears.

The key came spinning through the air, and it landed on the boards close to the top of the stairs. Diane crouched awkwardly and, still holding the paper that had bought her some safety, she reached for it.

As her hand made contact, there was a low, rattling rasp . . . she looked over the topmost stair, and saw the *Rusalka* almost flying towards her with its eyes blazing like green lasers.

Diane threw the paper into the air. It flipped open like a kite, slowed, and began to flutter downward. Alina switched direction and followed it like a leaping fish, away from the stairs and out over the dock; it seemed an impossibility but she caught the page in midair, grabbing it to her as she fell in a headfirst dive toward the open water. One of the photographs had come loose, and it followed her down like a spiralling leaf.

She hit the surface just as the world exploded.

A big motor cruiser came rearing in through the bursting doors on a high bow wave, its nose barely damaged by an impact that had torn through slatted wood like so much paper. The huge white dart of the GRP hull came running in like a spear, ramming the Princess off-centre and causing her mass to ride up in the dock as she was slammed back into the wharf timbers. Diane had a brief glimpse of Alina being swept up and tumbled under as the cruiser's bow fell, but then there was so much heaving water and so much spray that she couldn't see any more as she screwed her eyes up against the welcome daylight.

Down below, the newly-arrived boat's engines were still idling. She saw Pete scrambling out of the deck cabin and onto the coachroof.

FIFTY

Pete had come down through the woodland like Death's own carriage running late to a hanging; as he'd fought his way through bracken to the shoreline he'd seen Ted Hammond on the flybridge of one of the Birchwoods, bringing the craft in for a mooring at the boat house's narrow extended jetty. He didn't stop to wonder how or why or even to give thanks; he simply kept on running, his legs beginning to feel drained and unsteady and his breath like knives in his chest, until he'd hit the jetty and covered the last dozen yards. One of Ted's clients, an obvious weekender in a bright green lifejacket, was already ashore with a line; Pete said, "Thanks," and took it from him and threw it back aboard before clambering after.

"I think I just lost you a sale," Pete said as he gunned the still-idling engines and backed the craft away from the jetty. The weekender was standing there, as stunned-looking as a Jesuit being welcomed at the gates of Hell.

"Get away," Ted said drily from beside him on the flybridge. "Now what?"

"Duck," Pete suggested, and with the Birchwood's nose aimed at the boat-house doors he slammed open the throttles.

The Birchwood was in one piece but the Princess had taken serious damage, and he could guess why; any one of those badly-protected girders underpinning the wharf would have been enough to rip the hull. The Princess was taking on water, and starting to list already.

"Diane!" Pete called over the noise of the engines. "Are you all right?" And to his relief, she answered him from somewhere above.

"I'm fine," Diane shouted, "but she's here!"

"Where?"

"She's in the water!"

The deck fell suddenly, ripping free of the joist on which the hull had been snagged. Pete grabbed the rail as they hit, spray thrown up all around and drenching him. By now Ted had boarded the Princess as well, but Pete couldn't see what he was doing. Pete shouted, and Ted shouted something unintelligible back.

And then, as the spray fell, Pete saw Alina.

She was down by the side of the boat, almost under the collapsed part of the wharf. She was holding onto one of the cross-braces but seemed unable to climb any further; her knuckles were showing white, and her head was only just out of the water.

Pete jumped the gap. The wharf shifted as he hit it, a telling sign of deep structural damage. Down below, the water still heaved as if boiling. Ted was out of the Princess and crossing the wharf behind him now; Pete threw himself flat on the decking and reached down over the edge. The boards were sprung and uneven.

He stretched his hand out as far as he could. His fingers brushed Alina's wrist, and she looked up.

She appeared to be in some pain; he wondered if she might be trapped somehow beneath the surface. "Give me your hand," he said, although over the violent swell and the roar of marine engines in the confined space it wasn't easy to make himself heard.

Someone was calling his name. He didn't respond, but concentrated on trying to reach just a little further.

Alina's hand closed around his own in a life-grip. He held on to hers just as tightly.

"You followed me," she said wonderingly, as if such a thing simply couldn't be. Pete was locked to her eyes, seeing her fear as she stood at the edge and looked into the darkness beyond. Her face was as pale as a stone from a riverbed, her hair darker than in reality because it was so wet; but he thought that he could recognise the true Alina, the Alina that only he knew, the frightened girl that he'd reassured on the eve of the Liston Hall party.

But he was wrong.

He knew that he was wrong because suddenly he wasn't pulling her up; she was drawing him down. And now he could see that there was a strange light in those eyes, a hint of something almost feral in its intensity.

He grabbed at the edge and held on. But he could feel the long board starting to give, its nails already prised half-out and his pressure increasing the strain on them. He began to panic, and looked around for some kind of help. They were still calling to him, and didn't seem to realise that he could no longer move to respond.

There they were . . . Ted had carried Diane across to the Birchwood, and they were yelling to him to follow. They were yelling because there was fire in the Princess. How, he didn't know . . . but they were lit by a hell-light and shrouded in smoke, and before them the windows of the Princess glowed like holes punched in a nightshade.

There was fuel aboard both cruisers, there were gas tanks in the galleys. Suddenly the boat house was not a good place to be.

And still Alina was drawing him down toward the water. Its heaving surface was greasy with spilled marine fuel. He'd braced himself as hard as he could, but already his shoulders were over the edge and his feet were beginning to slide.

He looked back to her.

"You can be with me now," she said in a tense whisper, a voice meant for only him to hear. In her own mind she seemed to be detached from her surroundings, and from her desperate situation. "You can be with me forever. Isn't that what you always wanted from the beginning? Isn't it really?"

"Just let me help you," Pete said, hanging on grimly and wondering for how much longer. "That's all I want to do."

Something changed in her expression. At first, he wasn't sure what. Her grip didn't slacken, but there was a difference in her grey eyes. A moment ago, he hadn't known her.

And now he did.

"So many people have said that to me. And you were the only one who ever really meant it. I'm sorry, Peter. I'm sorry it didn't work out."

"Me too," he said. "Come on, try to pull yourself up."

Diane was still calling his name. Desperately, now.

Alina glanced over his shoulder. Wet hair fell across her face and she shook it free with a single, violent flip.

"I told you she'd be right for you," she said. "I told you I could help the two of you to get together. I wasn't wrong, was I?"

"No, you weren't wrong," Pete managed to say. "Now climb, damn it!" His arm, now lifting her, was starting to shake with the upkeep of the pressure.

She responded by raising herself a little, so that their faces were closer together. The strain on Pete's arm grew fiercer. His entire body was braced and trembling. In spite of everything that was going on around them, she could now lower her voice almost to a breath and still be heard.

"Remember when you first brought me to the valley?" she said. "We made a deal. You had to promise never to fall in love with me. And I said I'd try never to hurt you. I suppose you thought that was a strange thing to say."

"Grab the edge!" he said, "You can do it!"

But unexpectedly, she opened her hand. He was left holding on alone. Already he could feel her wet skin beginning to slide.

"Now perhaps you can understand," she said.

Her hand slipped through his own like smoke, leaving him not knowing whether he let her or whether he lost her, just staring at the oily surface of the water where she'd been not an instant before.

The Birchwood was reversing out again with Ted at the helm, releasing more daylight to pierce the smoke as it withdrew. The nose was crumpled, but the hull was in one piece. The Princess was listing badly and its interior furnishings were beginning to blaze. Something inside her fireballed with a soft thump.

The gap was widening; Pete took it at a run, and almost didn't make it.

The explosion that followed blew the roof off the boat house, scared the birds out of the trees for miles around, and echoed off into heaven like a distant thunder.

EPILOGUE:
AFTER THE DROWNING (II)

It was two years later to the day – or rather, to the night – that Ted Hammond took a plastic office chair out to the end of an empty jetty so that he could sit and watch the lake and the valley's few lights. It was a warm evening, but he had some cool beers that were going to stay cool because he'd put them in a net bag and lowered the bag into the water. He also had Wayne's radio-cassette player and a couple of his tapes, and he set this out beside him on the jetty and turned the volume up good and loud. Chuck and Bob lay on the boards, waiting for the empty cans to crunch.

He sat back, breathed the air. He'd done this a few times before, but tonight seemed special; almost an anniversary.

Wayne didn't talk to him any more. He missed it, but he was also relieved because it meant that his mind wasn't going after all. His doctor had told him that such a thing wasn't common but it wasn't exactly abnormal either, and after a period of attendance in an out-patients' clinic and a course of antidepressants they considered that he'd been "stabilised" – which mostly meant that he'd ceased in his reporting of symptoms that they couldn't explain.

And the doctors hadn't even heard the worst of it.

Out across the bay, he saw the lights in the restaurant go out at the end of the evening's business. Further lights on the north shore were so dim that they were like dying stars. Ted fished up the net, took out his second can, and dropped the others back over the side.

It was about half an hour later when a van door slammed and the two dogs came suddenly alert. He calmed them with a word, but they stayed watchful.

Then, after a minute or so, Angelica Venetz walked out along the jetty toward them.

She'd picked up a chair for herself along the way. Ted didn't stand, or look surprised; this, again, was nothing new, but neither was it yet a routine so familiar that the formalities of it could be skipped.

Ted said, "Is it the noise? I didn't think it would reach you from here."

269

"It doesn't," Angelica said. "I just came to join you for a while. Assuming that's all right."

" 'Course it is," Ted told her, and gestured for her to set her chair next to his own.

They'd had three or four of these informal late-night get-togethers since Adele's second, more major stroke back in February. Ted had been the one who'd stepped in when the usually competent Angelica had been caught wrong-footed, when without being asked and without needing to be invited he hired them a relief chef and kept their business ticking over until Angelica had been able to give it some attention once again. Shouldering someone else's worries had been an unexpected recreation for him; at least, it had been a break from his own.

"Will you have a drink?" he said. "Unfortunately there's only beer, beer and beer, but at least it's cool."

"I believe I will," she said, and so he hauled up the net and took out a can and then, after unzipping the ringpull, passed it over to her. The dogs' eyes followed every move.

"No glasses, either," he apologised. "Looks like I'm not too well set up for visitors."

"No glasses, nothing to wash up. I'm thinking of trying the same arrangement over there." Then she took a sip, and made a face.

"No good?"

"I wouldn't know. I'm not used to it."

"I'll lay on something else for next time."

"This is fine for now."

They sat in easy silence for a while, watching the night and listening to the music.

No, he hadn't told the doctor everything.

I'm not at peace, Dad, Wayne had said to him from the dank shadows in the bottom of the dock. None of us are. She's going to keep us like this forever. Please don't let her do it. And then, when a puzzled Frank Lowry had shone a light in because he was wondering why the bell had been ringing and ringing with no one to answer it, the Wayne-thing had simply broken up. Ceased to be.

The truth, of course, was that it had never been there at all.

One kind of truth, anyway.

But it was the other truth that he'd been observing when he'd taken an axe to one of the bulkheads in the sinking Princess in order to puncture a fuel tank and feed his fire. By rolling the gas cylinders into the flames before abandoning ship, he'd killed the woman who'd killed his boy. No quiet hospital for her, he'd thought at first, even

270

a hospital with bars; but then, as the rest of the story had come out, he'd realised that he'd probably done her a kindness.

But by then, it hadn't mattered.

"Peter and Diane came in tonight," Angelica said. "Little Jed was with them." And she made a slightly wry face as she said his name, as if she still couldn't quite come to terms with it. "He said something very strange. He said that when somebody drowns in the lake, they don't die, but their spirit becomes a part of it. Where do you suppose he heard that?"

"Probably at school," Ted said. "Some old fairy story."

"You don't think there's anything in it."

"Nah," he said, and he reached down to turn the player slightly so that it faced the water.

The next track, he knew, would be one of Wayne's favourites.

Be at peace now, he thought. *And God bless.*

Meanwhile, in the cottage on the Step, Pete McCarthy stood at the window of his bedroom. He was leaning on the frame and looking out, with the sash half-raised to let in the night air and the night-time sounds. He still got bouts of insomnia and occasional headaches, even after all this time. They'd told him that both were due to the double-concussion that he'd received, once when Alina had hit him from behind and again from his closeness to the boat-house explosion. They no longer talked about charging him with the shelter of an illegal alien. The situation was complicated enough, and the story would probably never be known in all its details.

In the bed behind him, Diane stirred slightly . . . but she slept on. No complications there.

But for soundness of sleep, Jed took the prize; road drills wouldn't wake him. He was in Alina's old room now, with his Hulk posters and his Spidey lampshade and the printed cover that turned the bed into the likeness of a racing car. He said that he liked it here, better than any of the other places that they'd stayed. He said that it felt more like home.

Home.

Leaving had once seemed like the best idea but, in all of their wanderings, each of them had known that they'd eventually come back to this place. Even Ted Hammond had known it, keeping it empty for them and spinning his sister some line so that he wouldn't have to rent it out. Jed had been the first one to put it into words; and after that, it had seemed kind of inevitable.

Pete returned his attention to the view – the foliage, the rise, the valley beyond like another country just over the hill that could

271

never be reached. He was thinking about what Jed had said at the restaurant earlier, and wondering what might have caused him to say it. Could he have overheard them talking and if so, when? Or had he perhaps seen or heard something in his wanderings on the Step, something down by the lakeside that perhaps rose from the water and spoke to him, slipping through those doors in his mind that hadn't yet become closed to visits from the outlands of reality?

If she's in love with you, she'll call to you. And in the night, she may even come to you. And then perhaps you'll come down to the water's edge, and you'll beg me to take you.

He'd stood like this many times around this hour, sometimes with Diane unknowing beside him and sometimes alone, watching the ridgeline against the moonlight, against the stars, against a darkened sky with only memory to assure him that there was anything there at all; and nothing, and nobody, had come, which meant that no, the feeling wasn't love.

But that didn't help him to know what it was that drew him here night after night. He'd never mentioned it to Diane and she'd never asked, although he sometimes suspected that she might have guessed. He wondered if it would fade, but wasn't even sure that he wanted it to.

Diane stirred again. It was time for him to return.

And he would – after just a little while longer.